P9-CQI-703

Praise for the Novels of the Darkyn

Dark Need

"Thrilling. . . . What makes the Darkyn novels so compelling is the dichotomy of good and evil. *Dark Need* has a gritty realism and some frightening and creepy characters that will keep you awake late at night. Balancing the darkness is the searing heat and eroticism that is generated between Samantha and Lucan." —Vampire Genre

Private Demon

"Lynn Viehl's vampire saga began spectacularly in *If Angels Burn*, and this second novel in the Darkyn series justifies the great beginning. Indeed, it is as splendid if not more than the first one."
—Curled Up with a Good Book (www.curledup.com)

"Strong . . . a tense multifaceted thriller. . . . Fans of Lori Handeland's 'Moon' novels will want to read Lynn Viehl's delightful tale." —*Midwest Book Review*

If Angels Burn

"Erotic, darker than sin, and better than good chocolate."
—Holly Lisle

"This exciting vampire romance is action-packed. . . . The story line contains terrific characters that make the Darkyn seem like a real species. . . . Lynn Viehl writes a fascinating paranormal tale that readers will appreciate with each bite and look forward to sequels." —The Best Reviews

OTHER NOVELS OF THE DARKYN

Dark Need

Private Demon

If Angels Burn

NIGHT LOST

LOST

A NOVEL OF THE DARKYN

Lynn Viehl

A SIGNET ECLIPSE BOOK

SIGNET ECLIPSE
Published by New American Library, a division of
Penguin Group (USA) Inc., 375 Hudson Street,
New York, New York 10014, USA
Penguin Group (Canada), 90 Eglinton Avenue East, Suite 700, Toronto,
Ontario M4P 2Y3, Canada (a division of Pearson Penguin Canada Inc.)
Penguin Books Ltd., 80 Strand, London WC2R 0RL, England
Penguin Ireland, 25 St. Stephen's Green, Dublin 2,
Ireland (a division of Penguin Books Ltd.)
Penguin Group (Australia), 250 Camberwell Road, Camberwell, Victoria 3124,
Australia (a division of Pearson Australia Group Pty. Ltd.)
Penguin Books India Pvt. Ltd., 11 Community Centre, Panchsheel Park,
New Delhi - 110 017, India
Penguin Group (NZ), 67 Apollo Drive, Mairangi Bay,
Auckland 1311, New Zealand (a division of Pearson New Zealand Ltd.)
Penguin Books (South Africa) (Pty.) Ltd., 24 Sturdee Avenue,
Rosebank, Johannesburg 2196, South Africa

Penguin Books Ltd., Registered Offices:
80 Strand, London WC2R 0RL, England

First published by Signet Eclipse, an imprint of New American Library,
a division of Penguin Group (USA) Inc.

First Printing, May 2007
10 9 8 7 6 5 4 3 2 1

PUBLISHER'S NOTE
This is a work of fiction. Names, characters, places, and incidents either are the product of
the author's imagination or are used fictitiously, and any resemblance to actual persons,
living or dead, business establishments, events, or locales is entirely coincidental.
　　The publisher does not have any control over and does not assume any responsibility for
author or third-party Web sites or their content.

To Chad Kroeger, Ryan Peake,
Mike Kroeger, and Daniel Adair,
with respect, appreciation, and
endless gratitude.
Your music wrote this book
as much as I did.

When the white flame in us is gone,
And we that lost the world's delight
Stiffen in darkness, left alone
To crumble in our separate night;

When your swift hair is quiet in death,
And through the lips corruption thrust
Has stilled the labour of my breath—
When we are dust, when we are dust!—

Not dead, not undesirous yet,
Still sentient, still unsatisfied,
We'll ride the air, and shine and flit,
Around the places where we died,

And dance as dust before the sun,
And light of foot, and unconfined,
Hurry from road to road, and run
About the errands of the wind.

—Rupert Brooke, *Dust*

Chapter 1

P^{*ass through.*}
        Curled up on the inn's narrow, lumpy bed, Nicola
Jefferson slept, her closed eyelids moving slightly. A black
Shoei motorcycle helmet with a smoke-colored full-face
visor hung by a strap from one of the bed frame's tarnished
brass knobs, appearing in the shadows like some decapitated alien head.

On a small table in the corner of the room, her laptop
sat blank-screened, humming as it performed its daily scan
for viruses. A scarred, pitted wooden baseball bat stood
propped against the side of the mattress, a few inches from
Nick's right hand.

When Nick slept, the bat was never out of her reach.

A very long time ago, when the world had been an easier place in which to live, Nick had stolen her stepfather's
wood-burning tool and used it to etch her name into the bat
shaft. She couldn't bear to give up the last connection she
had to her past, those long summer evenings after dinner
when Malcolm would give up his television programs to
help her with her swing. After Nick left England, she had
sanded the shaft every night until the childish, looping letters melted into fine sandy dust.

A pity Nick couldn't do that to her memories.

Nick never enjoyed sleeping, or coveted it. Like other
necessities, she skipped it as often as she dared. Sleep was
a pit stop, one her body desperately needed, but it wasted

too much of her time. Three or four hours a day were all she could spare for it.

Always see.

She had places to go, attention to dodge, and searches to run. She'd hacked into some regional police databases and snagged a couple of decent leads to check out. Every minute she wasn't on the road was one that might bring the knock on the door, the polite demand for her passport, and the cold steel of cuffs. If they took her computer, they'd hack in and find out who she was and what she'd been doing. They'd toss her in jail, and the hunt would be over.

She couldn't stop now. She was so close to finding the Golden Madonna. She could feel it.

Never remember.

Nick knew she was dreaming, but felt no fear. She could wake up at any moment she chose, no matter how deeply she slept or how frightening her dreams became. Even the worst of them couldn't compete with the real nightmares out there in the cold, unforgiving sunlight: cops, thugs, freaks, monsters, and that cold-blooded maniac who daily terrified thousands: the European taxi driver.

Not that Nick could really call this one she'd been having a nightmare. Not until the end.

The dream started the same way it always had: Nick, alone, walking through a forest toward something. What, she didn't know. Why, also a question mark. Whatever it was, though, it drew her like the scent of Chantilly cream wrapped in paper-thin, buttery pastry.

Nick made her way through the wood, detoured now and then by massive tree trunks, soft pine needles brushing against her bare arms and legs. Her footsteps disturbed the carpet of old leaves and new moss, causing countless tiny blue butterflies hiding there to take to the air and flutter away.

Setting sunbeams played a lousy game of hide-and-seek with Nick under the treetop-framed purple sky. She avoided a spiderweb the size of a dinner plate, and paused for a moment to admire its black-and-yellow-striped maker. The spinner raised two legs and curled them, beckoning her or waving to her, Nick wasn't sure which.

She liked nature. Walks in the woods were okay by her. Thanks to her stepdad, who had treated her like the son that he and her mother would never have, Nick didn't get girlie about bugs. And, weird as he was, the guy she knew she would meet on the way to whatever was depending on her. For what, she didn't know, but it felt nice to be that important to someone.

Pass through.

The pine and fir trees thinned, and then parted to show her the same meadow she'd seen a hundred times, but only in her dreams. She smiled and stepped out of the trees, happy to have reached it. It was a good place, this meadow, his place. Wildflowers, soft green grass, and birdsong enveloped her. Dandelion fluff drifted past her face, floating on a mild breeze, carrying the wishes of other dreamers. She caught a bit in her fingers, held it for a moment, and then released it.

Ma bien-aimée.

Nick's heart skipped a beat as she looked up. *There you are.*

On the other side of the clearing the Green Man appeared, in the exact same place he did every time, a narrow gap between two ancient oak trees whose massive limbs over time had grown entwined. As tanned as she was fair, the man dressed in only a pair of loose brown leather trousers.

Always see.

Whoever he was, he was tall and built like a long-distance runner, with a deep chest and powerful thighs that tapered into elegantly lean legs. The strap of a quiver hung from his left shoulder, but Nick knew from previous dreams that the cylindrical, cured-hide case on his back was empty, and he never carried a bow. Part of her knew that although he looked like a hunter, he couldn't or wouldn't let himself kill anything.

Never harm.

A perfectly normal, definitely handsome guy, her dream man, if you ignored the long pine needles hanging around his face and spilling over his shoulders, and the dark emerald color of his skin.

"The princess should have kissed you harder," Nick murmured to herself as she watched him.

He stretched out his arms and braced his hands against the scaly brown-black bark, as if trying to push the trees apart. There was too much distance between them for Nick to tell what color his eyes were, but they never left her.

A handful of large green and brown moths flew around her head as a voice spoke inside it. *Why do you come back,* ma bien-aimée? *Have you lost your way again?*

"Just dreaming." She took a cautious step forward. She knew the Green Man was the one talking to her, although he never moved his lips. She also knew that if she went too fast the dream would change, and she'd lose her chance to speak to him before she had to move on. "How about you?"

I am forever lost.

As tragically poetic as ever. It should have been silly, but he meant it, and she felt an echo of the same despair in her own hidden, hollow loneliness. "Forever's a long time. Can't you ask for directions?"

No one can hear me but you.

Pretty as they were, Nick rarely understood the Green Man's cryptic remarks. This time she wondered if he meant lost literally: that he was somewhere waiting to be found. "I'm in a lousy student hostel outside Paris. Where are you?"

I do not know. He wrenched his arms away from the trees and stepped into the meadow. The moment his foot touched the cool, sweet grass, it pulled away from him, rolling toward Nick in a disappearing wave, leaving behind a tangle of weeds and brush and piles of broken stone. The forest behind the Green Man sank down behind crumbling brick walls, crooked turrets, and hollow, web-covered windows. *They left me here. Do you know this place?*

Hundreds of marigolds popped up out of the grass on Nick's side of the meadow. She stared up as she moved forward, studying the ruins behind him. She'd seen other places like this, but none so neglected. "No, sorry. Why would someone bring you here? It looks abandoned."

She saw him tense and halted in her tracks. She felt the same inexplicable frustration that came with every dream of the Green Man. On some level she knew that time was their enemy, but for different reasons, and that this man could do nothing to help her find the Madonna. On another she was pretty sure this was all some subconscious mind game she was playing with herself, making up the Green Man as a surreal imaginary lover.

At least he's not made of gold.

"I could look around," she offered. "If I find it, this place, this building, do I find you, too?"

He looked away from her. *I am lost.*

"Yeah, you told me." She sat down on the edge of a broken stone the size of an armchair. The marble felt cold and smooth under her palms. Beneath it, she knew, someone had buried an old man and woman killed during some forgotten war. *Maybe the feelings go both ways.* "Do you know where I am? Can you come to me?"

Only here, in the nightlands. He held out his hand to her but stepped back into the shadows, only the glow of his eyes visible. *Come to me,* ma bien-aimée. *Come to me now.*

Butterflies and moths erupted around Nick as she rose from the stone. The dream shifted, its colors darkening and melting away into a void of black, with nothing to guide her through the emptiness. She moved through it, uncaring, seeking the warmth that was the Green Man, until she felt long-fingered hands catch her shoulders and strong arms enfold her.

Safe.

I am here. You are here. We are not alone. We dream. We live. We will find each other someday.

She pressed against him, so overwhelmed by the contact that she was unable to speak, unable to do anything but stand in his embrace. Being like this with him made her forget everything. It was ridiculous; the only thing they shared was a dream. She knew *he* was only a dream.

Pass through.

Nick held on to him anyway, her cheek against his heart, his hand stroking her curly hair.

The Green Man pushed her away as hot light filled her eyes, and the ground between them collapsed. Nick fell back, cringing as the earth vanished into two deep, rough trenches. Beetles and roaches began crawling out of the largest hole, swamping the ground until it seemed to writhe.

Always see.

The Green Man stared at Nick's hands. *What have you done?*

A rat with a short white stick clamped between its long yellow teeth scampered toward her. Like a puppy, it laid the stick at Nick's feet. She reached down for it, her hand black now with soil and blood, her fingernails jagged and broken. She stopped only when she saw the plain band of gold gleaming just above the gnawed end.

Never remember.

Nick woke up, as she always did, weeping.

"Too weak to escape," a voice said in the darkness, "and too strong to die."

Awakened to his new room in hell, the prisoner did not move. Reaction, like emotion, had become meaningless as well as useless. He no longer bothered to brace himself or cringe; waiting for what would be done required all of his self-control.

Much had been done to Gabriel Seran.

More would be done, yet he would endure. Skills acquired during seven centuries of existence had permitted him to survive what might have killed him a thousand times over during his brief human life. It had also helped him through these last two years as a captive of the Brethren. His talent had kept his body from weakening, but the soul his captors did not believe he possessed had done the rest.

As for his mind, he did not know. He had traded emotion for what he used to survive, and rarely did he feel anything beyond pain anymore. He had become a glacier encased in tortured flesh.

Perhaps he owed his life to a phantom. As he thought of her, that invention of his own desperate loneliness, her image came to him: a pale, fair-haired maiden, alone in the forest, searching. What she sought, Gabriel did not know; nor had he ever seen her beyond his dreams. But as imaginary as she was, having her come to him these last months had kept him from surrendering himself to the eternal comforts of oblivion. Thanks to her, he could live with knowing that no one else in the world cared for him or thought of him anymore.

"If you will not come to the light, I must bring it to you." A tiny scrape and a hiss of burning sulfur brought a small flare of flame into the airless, lightless chamber. The human holding the struck match touched it to the blackened wick of the kerosene lamp the old priest had left behind, and the circle of light spread. He lifted the lamp so that it shed its yellow glow over his face and Gabriel. "You see, vampire? Unlike you, I am no monster."

Someone out of sight grunted. A sack dropped with a weighty thud.

The human wore the garb of a monster: a black cassock with three crosses embroidered in bloodred silk over his left breast. One, Gabriel knew, for every Darkyn the human had personally killed. The Brethren wore them as modern soldiers would medals.

Gabriel wondered if he would earn the human a fourth, and why he did not care if he did.

"We haven't been properly introduced yet, have we?" Blunt, small teeth gleamed between ruddy lips. "I am Father Benait."

Benait posed as a Catholic priest, as did all the other members of the secret order of *Les Frères de la Lumière*, the Brethren of the Light. This human and his fellow zealots possessed the blind dedication of true fanatics, which fueled their belief that Gabriel and others like him were a curse upon humanity.

The Brethren did not care that Gabriel and his kind, the Darkyn, had learned to temper their need for human blood, their only nourishment, and no longer killed humans for it. During his first year in captivity Gabriel had drawn on all his powers of persuasion to negotiate peace with his captors, but nothing moved them. They cared only for the preservation of their own twisted faith, and the perversions it allowed them to practice. Such as capturing *vrykolakas* like Gabriel and torturing them until they betrayed other Kyn.

Gabriel no longer bothered with useless diplomacy. Whatever the Brethren did to him in this place, he would endure it. It was his duty to do so. Even if he had wished to die, his body's ability to heal spontaneously ensured that he would survive almost anything. The numbing void created by using his talent kept out everything else.

That was the Kyn's true curse: to live beyond the desire for life.

Am I dead inside, and my body does not yet know it? Gabriel could not say.

Wheels nearby squealed as they turned; another, heavier load was dumped outside the room, sending vibrations through the wall. Benait smiled as he removed a cell phone from his cassock and dialed a number. Unconsciously he moved away from Gabriel as he spoke in rapid Italian.

Gabriel took advantage of the light to study the unfamiliar place he occupied. No windows, no exits or entrances, save the one open doorway through which the human had obviously entered. The room offered no clues as to exactly where he had been brought; all he had seen above in the moonlight when they had removed him from the truck were the overgrown grounds of some vast property and the outlines of a ruined, ancient structure. The trip from Paris to this place had taken many hours, yet he was fairly certain that he was still in France.

Why am I still in France?

That the Brethren hadn't moved him out of the country puzzled him. In Paris, he had overheard the interrogators discussing a ring of thieves who had been targeting and looting Brethren strongholds for icons and religious treasures. Evidently while burglarizing such places, they had been lured to several imprisoned Kyn and had released them. When the Brethren had taken Gabriel from the city, he assumed it was to keep the thieves from liberating him.

Freedom might never be his again. Gabriel had accepted this possibility a long time ago. But he had not yet run out of hope that he might reveal to the Kyn what he had learned as a prisoner of the Brethren. That knowledge, too, became as if another curse upon his head.

Unfortunately Benait spoke correctly: Gabriel was presently too weak from blood loss and injury to free himself. His only hope remained a slim chance to use his talent again, or perhaps lure one of the local humans in this new place to him—or the girl from his dreams. Surely if he kept dreaming of her, it meant that she was real.

Surely he was not mad.

The Brethren assumed that Gabriel had long ago gone insane, in the same way Thierry Durand had in Ireland, and often left him unguarded now. It was a pity the last interrogation had reduced him to such pitiful condition, or he might free himself. Neither his old nor new wounds would close, however, until his talent or a human provided him with enough blood to heal them.

Finding the desire to heal . . .

Dark and ugly reality gripped him, a merciless gauntlet of iron, smashing the wavering image of the pale-haired maiden of the forest. Such dreams meant nothing. Those Gabriel had loved were dead; his entire family had been butchered by the Brethren. His loyalty and silence had been for nothing; no Kyn had come to fight for him or release him. After two years he could think only that he had been forgotten, given up for dead, or purposely discarded. Even with the burden of what he had learned about the Brethren, the prospect of prolonging his existence, of serving only as a toy for his sadistic captors, no longer appealed to him.

In the end, even the most noble persistence became pointless, as futile as the Brethren's interrogations.

Benait was speaking to him again. "Do you never wonder why they left your face untouched, vampire?"

Gabriel had stopped wondering about most things done to him after his first year in captivity. He would have said as much, but he had stopped speaking to his captors at approximately that same time. Originally he had kept his silence as the only form of defiance left to him. Now it had become his only retreat, his final sanctuary. A fortress of ice made no sound.

He couldn't speak if he wished to; they had gagged him in Paris by welding together the ends of a thin band of copper over his mouth. That, too, gave him valuable information about his present state. They had brought him someplace where they could not afford for him to make noise.

Benait stepped closer. "My Irish brothers were under orders not to mar your visage. I suppose they took photographs of you and sent them to your king. Their proof that you were being well treated, at least, from the neck up."

Gabriel heard more sounds of activity on the other side of the wall. Stones hitting stones, water, the scrape of metal against brick. He stared at the glass bowl of the lamp, partly filled with liquid. They had repeatedly burned him with heated rods and irons as well as countless copper implements, but never with kerosene or oil. How long would it take his nearly desiccated body to burn? Hours? Days?

Why didn't he care? Had they drained the last of the terror—of remnant feeling—out of him in Paris?

"Your king never met their demands for your release." Benait's ruddy lips compressed. "Instead he sent his assassin to Dublin just after we brought you to Paris."

Lucan.

"He slaughtered every living thing there," Benait continued. "Brethren and *maledicti* alike. The security cameras captured it all on videotape."

A woman screamed inside Gabriel's memory, drowning out the human's voice. In Dublin, she had cried out repeatedly from a chamber near Gabriel's. He had never caught a glimpse of her, but her shrieks had been in an old tongue, the one the priests could not speak. She had screamed that they were skinning her alive. He had spent the better part of a year replaying the hours of her screams in his head, over and over. He still did not know if she had been a stranger, or his younger sister, Angelica, who had also been captured with him and the Durands.

Had she been Angelica? Had Lucan found her, broken and flayed, unable to heal from the horrors done to her? Had he killed her out of mercy?

Not knowing those answers added to Gabriel's bleak inner winter hourly, one acid snowflake at a time.

"We know from their reports that they were never able to break you in Dublin, or convince your king to meet their demands," his captor was saying. "Despite the dedicated efforts of my brothers in Paris over the last year, you resisted them as well." Benait set the lamp down on the rickety table near the fireplace and stretched his arms out, groaning with pleasure as a joint popped. "You have proven to be virtually useless to us."

Virtually useless. A condemnation. A compliment. As meaningful as maintaining his honor.

No, Gabriel thought. *For if I had been broken, I would have betrayed Kyn, and others would have suffered my fate. I was right to resist.*

Would the girl from his forest dreams understand, if she were real? Would she forgive him for being unable to go to her?

"No need to be afraid, vampire." Benait turned down the wick so that the light became a softer glow. "You are comfortably situated at your final destination, and I bear the responsibility of performing these last small rites."

Relief and shame set fire to the last of Gabriel's rigid self-discipline and indifference. His head demanded he fight, endure, and survive, but the human's words enveloped his frozen heart. No more endless interrogations, no more pointless torture. No more agony at being abandoned by his own kind, and left alone and wretched in the silent shadows. No more sorrow for outliving every soul he had ever loved. No more surrendering more and more of himself to his talent. No more succumbing to the icy hell inside him only to stay alive. Now this human would mutter his prayers, take out a sword, and cut off Gabriel's head, and this level of hell would be his last.

Done, I am done, it is over.

Everything he had drawn upon in order to keep his silence had been gathering for this moment. So long as he did not beg for his life, it was finished. He had lost, but he had won. They had not broken him. Not once. That much victory he could claim.

She would understand this, his pale maiden. She would let him go into the dark alone and unafraid. There . . . there he would wait for her.

Beyond the room a bucket clanged, and someone muttered curses in another language.

"It might have gone differently for you if you had co-operated with us," Benait said, nodding as if in agreement with Gabriel's thoughts as he moved closer. "We would have brought you into the light with us, to fight for God. Eventually you might have redeemed your filthy soul."

The Brethren always felt compelled to make such speeches before they inflicted some monstrous ordeal upon him. Not for his benefit, Gabriel felt, but more to bestow some sort of absolution on themselves prior to committing their atrocities. It did not always work; one of the brutes in Dublin had begun to go mad, and whispered of his hallucinations to Gabriel.

Benait took out a Bible, opening it to the last chapter before he began to read a passage. "'. . . the angel of the bottomless pit, whose name in the Hebrew tongue is Abaddon . . .'"

They tried to use the Holy Scriptures as another, subtler form of torment, but Gabriel, named by his father for God's celestial messenger, had long ago made his peace with his fate. He was no angel, but he no longer believed the Kyn were cursed. He had seen too many atrocities in his human and Kyn lifetimes; crimes against humanity far more obscene and brutal than any of his own pitiful sins. The God he had served throughout his human life would not single out a handful of misguided warrior priests for divine retribution while permitting the butchers of millions to grow decrepit and die in beds of gold.

Metal scraped against brick with a softer, more liquid sound.

Benait finished reading the passage from Revelations, closed his Bible, and kissed the cover before setting it aside.

"You never made confession of your sins, vampire, and so there can be no absolution." He removed a small glass vial of reddish liquid from his sleeve and opened it. "But we still have one more use for your angelic face. Perhaps when this is finished, D'Orio will take your head and have it mounted on the wall of his study."

Gabriel's eyes shifted as an old, liver-spotted hand

reached into the open entrance to his chamber and spread a layer of mortar onto the floor space between the sides of the frame. The trawl disappeared, and the same hand began laying bricks carefully in the wet mortar. He realized what was being done on the other side of the wall, a horror that swept away all that had been done before this moment. They were sealing the room. Sealing him in it.

He turned his face away and jerked against his chains.

"You would not see the light, vampire." Benait reached up and seized a handful of filthy hair, making Gabriel look at the bricks being stacked and mortared across the threshold of the chamber before he brought the vial toward his face. "Now all that you will know is darkness."

Chapter 2

A thousand kilometers from France, within the silent walls of a remote, well-guarded fortress in Ireland, another prisoner struggled against her imprisonment. This one did not accept her fate; nor did she retreat into silence. As she had every day since she had been brought to Dundellan Castle, Dr. Alexandra Keller fought and shouted.

"I don't want to go in there. I told you, it's not mine. Will you let *go* of me, you jackass?"

Richard Tremayne, high lord of the Darkyn, did not set aside the reports he had been studying, but finished reading details of the latest Brethren activity in the south of France. As Alexandra's protests grew closer and louder, he briefly considered the merits of soundproofing and one-sided locking mechanisms. Neither would solve the problem of his latest, troublesome acquisition, but they might restore a semblance of peace to his early evenings.

Or the illusion of it, Richard thought as the sound of knocking startled his favorite tabby out of his lap. "Enter."

A footman appeared.

"Dr. Alexandra Keller, seigneur," the servant announced as Richard's seneschal and a guard dragged a small, writhing figure into the library.

"I was just out walking," she protested as they hauled her to stand in the pool of light before Richard's desk. "What, I'm not allowed to have fresh air?" She puffed out some air and blew some chestnut curls out of her face.

Black soil powdered her nose, cheek, and chin. "I'm supposed to be a guest, aren't I?"

The tabby cautiously approached the American and sniffed delicately at the bare toes of her dirty right foot. An unlaced, too-large trainer covered her left.

Few things annoyed the high lord of the Darkyn more than having his routine disrupted, but his unwilling houseguest likely thought it her right. Now dealing with her attempts to escape Dundellan had become almost a daily chore.

"Where did you find her this time?" he asked Korvel, his seneschal.

"By the bailey wall, my lord." Korvel, who also served as the captain of the guard, kept a firm grip on the doctor.

"It's a nice night for once, so I stepped outside," Alexandra insisted. Like his men, she did not look directly at him. "For a little walk. To get away from the endless sunshine and happiness of this place for a few minutes, okay? That's all."

Richard eyed her garments and remaining shoe, which he recognized as belonging to a junior porter. "Dressed as one of my household?"

"You took *my* clothes, and I'm tired of those stupid ball gowns." She lifted her chin. "You try wearing something that comes with five crinolines and a built-in corset; see how you like it."

"Indeed. And what is young Jamison wearing at this moment? Little more than torn strips of your bed linens knotted about his limbs, I daresay." When she scowled, he instructed the footman to go and search her rooms.

"We also found this"—Stefan, the guard, displayed an iron poker bent into the shape of a hook, to which a coil of rope had been tied—"hanging from the battlement behind her."

"I told you, it's not mine," the doctor insisted. "I have no idea how it got there. Maybe someone else left it behind when they climbed the wall. Shouldn't you be out looking for one of the other hostages?"

Korvel and Stefan exchanged a long-suffering look over the petite American's head.

Richard held out one gloved, distorted hand and took the hand-fashioned grappling device to inspect it. He was impressed; the thick iron had been bent as easily as if it were a thin reed. "I had not thought her this strong."

"She broke Martin's arm in two places after he apprehended her trying to jump from the rooftop last week, my lord," Korvel reminded him.

"I set Martin's arm after I broke it," Alexandra pointed out. "I also said I was very sorry and would try not to fracture anyone else's bones. Quit talking around me. I'm not one of your zombies."

Zombies. No one, not even Kyn, had ever dared refer to the humans Richard obtained and enraptured in such scathing terms. They were politely ignored, just as Richard's condition was. He went to her and bent close to her ear.

"I should cut out your tongue," he said softly, exercising a small amount of his talent. He knew just to what degree his powerful voice drilled into her head, causing her considerable if momentary pain.

Alexandra paled but stood her ground. "With that ice-pick voice of yours, why bother? You can tell me to shut up and I will. Or kill me. There are doctors all over the place; you can kidnap as many as you want." She stared into his eyes, and her scent washed over him. "Don't hold back on my account."

The idiot female *wanted* to provoke him into anger.

"Shall we take her to the lower level, my lord?" Stefan asked, a bit too eagerly. "Gunther has readied a cell. You have but to say." His gaze shifted to the top of Alexandra's head, and his free hand twitched, as if he meant to touch her hair.

Stefan and his dour dungeon master, like most of Richard's men, wanted nothing more than to have Dr. Keller at their mercy, to do as they pleased with her. That was the other problem with the American: Her presence had driven almost every male Kyn who served him into a constant state of appalled, confused lust.

"You're not throwing me in some dungeon," Alexandra said as she kicked Stefan and wrenched free of his hold. "Just let me out of here, Tremayne, or I'll—"

"Be quiet, Dr. Keller, and sit down." Richard watched his troublesome houseguest obey him, and then told the men, "Leave her with me now."

As his guards withdrew, Richard regarded the woman sitting cross-legged on the carpet in front of his desk. She should have sat in one of his chairs, not on the floor. But his particular talent, a voice so powerful that a mere whisper of his could pleasure, control, maim, or even kill another being, did not always affect Alexandra in the usual manner. She should have obeyed him to the letter, but more often now she managed some small defiance of it.

Was she, as he suspected, neither human nor Darkyn, but something else? Something new?

Richard studied his prisoner. Alexandra did not meet any of his standards for beauty, but he could yet appreciate her particular attractions. Her unremarkable features and petite stature did not dim the exotic creaminess of her mixed-race skin, the brilliance of her clever brown eyes, or the subdued fire of her long chestnut curls.

Bitch though she was, Alexandra Keller radiated warmth and life like the beacon of a lighthouse in the midst of the winter storm.

Even her voice, edged as it generally was with sarcasm or contempt, proved very pleasant to the ear. Perhaps she had been gifted with more than a single talent. Talent that, according to her own research, affected Kyn as well as humans.

As tempted as he was, as dangerous as she might prove to be, he would not destroy such a woman. Not while she might be the only one capable of bringing the Kyn back from extinction, and giving him the means to at last prevail over the Brethren.

"These escape attempts become as vexing as they are useless," he said to her. "My men will not permit you to leave Dundellan unless I wish it. Do you not understand this, Dr. Keller?"

"I understand that you're a maniac," she said, all politeness. The tabby had crawled onto her lap, and she was stroking it absently. "You can't keep me here forever. Michael is coming for me. Anything else?"

Richard rose before his uncertain temper did, and limped over to the curtained window overlooking his garden maze. Perfectly clipped hedges of hawthorn formed the living, eight-foot-high walls of the labyrinth, designed by a former lord of the castle who had been fond of chasing stable lads and spit boys through them. Although the sun had set an hour ago, the sky to the west remained a brilliant shade of deep porcelain blue.

Michael would come; that much Richard knew. The American's escape attempts made that only too clear. Cyprien would negotiate with him, however. He could not mount a siege against Dundellan, and he would not dare start a Kyn civil war over a woman.

Abducting Dr. Keller from America and bringing her to Ireland had not been perhaps the wisest decision Richard had made in recent months. She had not long been Kyn, and she seemed to resent everything about them. She certainly did not acknowledge his privilege of rule over her. Yet he needed an answer to his dilemma, and the present options left to him were not enough.

This female was a modern woman, trained in the medical and surgical arts. One of only three humans to survive the change from human to Darkyn in six centuries, even though her transition had been highly irregular. The fact remained that she was one of his kind now, and, whether she liked it or not, she owed to him complete and abiding fealty. Ultimately her talent belonged to him, as she did, blood, body, and immortal soul.

Michael had to accept that. So did Alexandra.

"I am your king," Richard told her. "You are my subject, and you will obey my commands."

"I'm an American. We don't have kings. We elect presidents. I didn't vote for you." Alexandra ran her fingernails down along the purring feline's spine. "Your cat's a doll, though. What's his name?"

"I don't name animals." He had not thought about the cultural differences. "Americans should have a talent for subservience. You are nothing but the descendents of indentured servants and African slaves."

"Don't forget the religious malcontents." She lifted the cat and rubbed noses with it. "We're also the biggest shoppers in the world, we own more plutonium than anyone else, and if you piss us off enough, we'll bomb your country." She gave him a bright smile.

Richard took the cat from her. "I will not release you; nor will I allow you to escape," he said. "Accept this, do as you intended, and find a cure for the changelings."

The cat yowled before jumping out of his arms and slinking away.

Alexandra feigned a yawn. "Sorry, me being an inferior American and all, I'm not licensed to practice medicine in this country. Use your own docs."

He did not appreciate the reminder of his loss of control. Under his cloak, his changed muscles tightened and knotted. "They are all dead."

"What?"

"I lost my temper and killed them."

That, at least, silenced her.

"I destroyed their laboratory and their research before I regained control of myself." He turned, removing one of his gloves as he did so, and displayed his distorted hand, allowing his claws to emerge and extend to their full length. "What is left of my humanity will go rather quickly now, too, I think. What will happen, Doctor, when I next lose my temper?"

She stared at the black talons for a moment before turning her head away. "I won't help you."

"I think you will." Richard called in his men and instructed Stefan to lock her in one of the safe rooms. "Korvel, remain." He waited until the guard had escorted Alexandra out of the library before he said, "She likely bespelled Jamison; none of the human staff will be safe now. Station a Kyn guard by her door at all times."

"As you command, my lord." His seneschal looked as if he meant to add more, but fell silent.

"Try as I will, I cannot read your thoughts, Captain."

"Words do not come easily to me, my lord. Not when I bear such news as this." Korvel shifted his weight. "None of Cyprien's suzerains have replied to your summons or will speak to me. I am handed excuses right and left by their human servants."

"Michael has always inspired loyalty among his men," Richard said. "It is why I chose him to be the American seigneur."

"His tax agents have frozen our American accounts and properties," Korvel continued. "All of our usual means and avenues of transportation to the United States have been temporarily shut down. He has, in effect, closed his borders to us."

Richard chuckled. "I taught him well."

"His *sygkenis* causes almost as much trouble," Korvel stated flatly. "I fear she will be more dangerous than her master."

"How so?"

"She has no modesty, no regard for proper behavior. Her insolence toward you is open and appalling. She is also very resourceful." His seneschal gestured toward the grappling hook Alexandra had fashioned. "Yet she is utterly charming. She makes the men laugh with her antics, and seduces them with her smiles. You saw Stefan. Twice I have had to discourage him from handling her more than is necessary."

Richard refused to believe this half-human, half-Kyn leech could wield so much power over his men. "It is being parted from Cyprien, nothing more."

"That is the other danger. Her scent is persuasive, and she sheds more of it by the hour. How long her control will last, I cannot say, but the men are growing more restless by the day." Korvel nodded toward the garrison's quarters. "Soon I will not be able to keep them from her, or her from them."

Giving Alexandra to Korvel might tire her out—his seneschal regularly plowed through human and Kyn females with methodical indifference—but Richard had not brought her to Dundellan to subjugate her, or to provide physical relief for his household. He had enraptured humans for that. Also, in a few weeks it would make no difference. "What may be done about her?"

"I cannot advise you, my lord." The captain rested a hand on his sword hilt. "The only solution I know is slightly too permanent."

Richard considered sealing her in her room, but that would not motivate her to begin testing. "I will think on it."

"Cannot Korvel seduce her before she has the entire garrison under her spell?" a fair and coolly beautiful woman asked as she stepped inside.

"My lady." Korvel sketched a respectful bow. To Richard, he said, "My lord, I must see to the prisoner." Without another word he departed the room.

"How easily your captain takes offense," Elizabeth said as she swept her full silk skirts back in a superb curtsy. "My maid told me of the leech attempting to again escape. She seems most determined to leave us."

All of Richard's cats silently fled the room.

"She has yet to adjust to her new situation here," Richard said, tugging the glove back over his hand. "When she does, she will serve me."

"Undoubtedly." Lady Elizabeth rarely frowned or smiled, preferring to maintain the serene facade of high-born indifference. Now, however, a definite line appeared between her fair brows. "But must you wait upon her leisure, my husband? Given this increasing lack of self-control, can you yet afford to?"

Richard had not married Elizabeth for her arctic beauty and winsome form, breathtaking as they were. She had been born to an ancient, noble house, and taught how to scheme and plot in the manner of royals nearly from the moment she had been weaned. Seven centuries after taking her to wife and making her Kyn, Richard regarded her talent for design and manipulation as one of the chief assets in his arsenal.

"Tell me how I may not," he said simply.

"Many ways occur to me." Elizabeth shrugged modestly before arranging herself on a love seat near his desk. "This leech seems an overly emotional creature. She loves with the abandonment of a child, does she not? I did not expect that such a learned female would be as reckless and disrespectful as one, either. But then, she is veritably driven by such crude affections."

Richard inclined his head.

"It is in the spirit of her defiance that you may find a weapon." Elizabeth fussed with a fold of her skirt before coyly glancing up at him through her lashes. "You will agree that she might go to great lengths to protect those she loves. If one of them could be brought here to Dundellan as your particular guest, that should make the leech more amenable to do your bidding."

"We cannot take anyone from America," Richard said. "Michael has seen to it."

"There is still one of Cyprien's lords who remains loyal to you, and he is most resourceful. You have only to ask it of him." His wife picked up the telephone on his desk. "Shall I arrange it now?"

"You are looking for something in particular, *garçon*?" the bookstore clerk asked in crisp, annoyed English.

Nick replaced the book on medieval castles and scanned the rest of the shelf. She didn't mind that the clerk had mistaken her for a boy; she had cut her hair short and dyed it dark brown specifically to give that impression. He must have guessed she was English from watching her comb through the section of *livres en anglais.*

She got most of her research off the Internet, but now and then she raided a bookshop. Reading was one of the few pleasures she indulged herself with regularly. She couldn't carry books around with her on the road, though, so after she read them she left them behind or sold them to another bookshop.

"I need a picture book of old French estate homes," she told him. Over his shoulder she saw that the clerk had drawn the curtains at the front display window, and was now rather pointedly glancing at his wristwatch. The sun had sunk below the horizon; obviously he wanted to close the shop and go home. "Anything from a manor to a mansion."

"Ah." The clerk, a middle-aged man with thick graying brown hair and reading glasses hanging from the neat collar of his pressed shirt, reached for a book above her head. "Perhaps this will suit you?"

Nick skimmed through the pages of the coffee-table book, most of which had at least two or three color plates of different buildings on them. It would take her a couple of hours to go through it and mark her map with a route, but at least it was a starting place.

"Exactly what I needed, thank you." She removed her wallet from her back pocket and followed the clerk up to the counter.

As the book was used, the clerk charged her fifty percent off the original price, and then wrapped it up carefully in tissue paper. "Are you a student of medieval architecture, *garçon*?"

"I just like looking around old places," Nick lied. She tugged on the strap of her camera case. "I take photos of them. Keep the change," she added as he offered her a small handful of coins.

As the clerk handed her the book, his gaze shifted from the short, dark curls of her hair to her smooth cheeks. "You do not look old enough to be a professional photographer."

"It's a hobby." Nick saw something and reached into a recess between the register and the counter. She pulled out an identification card wedged there, which she handed to the clerk. "This yours?"

"Oui." The man frowned as he examined the dusty card. "I lost it a month ago. I have not had time to replace it." He sighed as he tucked it into his pocket. "You have saved me hours of standing in a queue. *Merci beaucoup, garçon.*"

"You're welcome. Have you ever seen a really old house, one where the walls are caving in? It's abandoned, and there are a million marigolds all over the front lawns." She almost bit her tongue after she realized what she was asking. She wasn't interested in that place; it didn't exist.

"Pardonne-moi, je t'en prie. I have not."

"Okay, well, thanks—"

"Tourists are kept from such places, as they are not safe." The clerk tapped the side of his nose with a finger as he thought. "But you may wish to speak of this to Sarmoin, the baker across the street."

She lifted her eyebrows. "The baker?"

"His wife paints." The clerk made this sound like a form of infidelity. "He takes her into the country every Sunday, when his ovens are shut down to cool. There is a painting in the bakery of a place much as you describe."

Nick thanked him and exited the shop quickly. The bakery facing the bookstore had green shutters and SARMOIN'S painted in scrolled white lettering on the window. She could see two housewives inside, their market baskets hanging from their arms as they inspected trays of thin, crusty baguettes.

She stepped across the uneven pavement until she reached the door, and there hesitated again. What was she trying to prove? She should be on her bike and headed back to the hostel to pack up her stuff. She couldn't risk staying in the city another night.

What if the place does exist? What if it's all part of this?

Nick opened the door, breathing in deeply of the wondrous scents of dough and yeast and butter as she stepped inside. Two housewives stood fiercely debating the number and type of baguettes to buy for their weekend meals; Frenchwomen took their bread very seriously. The young girl waiting on them gave Nick a look of amused resignation.

A glance at the wall behind the counter made Nick's throat tighten before she could ask for the baker. She stared at the small, unframed painting hung beside a photograph of the pope.

The girl behind the counter gave up on the housewives and smiled at Nick. "May I assist you, monsieur?"

"Is that for sale?" she asked in French, pointing to it.

"I cannot say, monsieur. My mother . . . One moment, please." The girl disappeared into the back of the shop, and emerged with a thick-bodied man dressed in thin shorts and a flour-spattered T-shirt. "The monsieur wishes to buy Mama's painting, Papa."

The baker stiffened and gave Nick a thorough inspection. "Why?"

"It's beautiful." She stuck to the lie she'd told the bookshop clerk and showed him her camera bag. "I like to photograph places like that."

"It is not for sale," he advised her. "You would not be permitted to photograph the chapel at St. Valereye. The groundskeeper made my wife leave a few minutes after she arrived there. And she had set up her easel on the side of the road, not on the property, you understand."

Nick nodded, ignoring the nervous excitement tightened inside her chest. It was like the things she had found and stashed away—part of them, part of the trail leading to the Golden Madonna. She had to go to St. Valereye and see this chapel. Now. "I'd still like to know where it is."

The baker sighed. "Thirty-two kilometers to the south."
He gave her terse directions on which of the back roads to
take, and after glancing at her worn jeans and ancient
brown leather jacket, added, "There is a village inn at the
bottom of the hill there. Give them my name, and they will
not treat you like a German."

Nick grinned. "I will. Thank you, monsieur."

To demonstrate her appreciation, and to get a few more
minutes to check out the interior of the bakery and see the
best way to break in, she bought a bag of mini fruit pas-
tries. She'd come back later, after midnight, and get the
painting.

As she walked out of the bakery Sarmoin came from
around the back of the shop.

"Boy." Sarmoin looked one way and then the other before he thrust the small painting at her. "Here, take it."

So much for going back and stealing it. An odd guilt
swamped her. "How much do you want for it, monsieur?"

"Nothing. I never want to see it again." He pushed it
into her hands, and then grimaced. "I am wrong to tell you
dis," he said in thick, broken English. "Do not go château.
Someding wrong—*très mal*—dere."

"What do you mean?"

"That chapel . . ." The baker's English failed him, and
he switched to rapid, whispered French. "My wife was
there for only a few minutes, and she woke up screaming
every night after we returned from seeing it. She burned all
but one of the paintings she made of it, and I had to take
the last one away. She still has the nightmares."

Nick stared down at the pretty painting with its delicate
details. "What frightened her so much?"

"Something in the chapel," Sarmoin said. "What, I do
not know. But in her dreams, it hides inside. It watches her;
it wants something terrible."

"What does it want?"

He looked miserable. "She says it wants to eat her."

Chapter 3

"We've done Disney, Universal, and Sea World for you guys," a balding, middle-aged man with a sunburned face said as he led four sullen-looking boys into the main entrance of Knight's Realm. "This is something educational. You could write school reports about this place."

"This is going to be dumb." The oldest boy glanced back at the woman wearily following behind them. "Mom, do we have to?"

"It's all about medieval times," she said, and forced a smile. "We'll get to watch knights in shining armor jousting on horses after we eat dinner. Won't that be exciting?"

In the complex's security room, Michael Cyprien watched the family via closed-circuit camera as they paid the admission fees. Many such tourists weary of cartoon and fairy-tale castles flocked to the Middle Ages–themed attraction. In the castle's main guardroom, dining guests feasted on roasted turkey legs and drank ale from pewter tankards while being entertained by court jesters, harp-strumming bards, and the ever-present lady of the castle and her maidens, demurely garbed in silk gowns and dazzling white wimples.

After dining, guests could adjourn to the tourney grounds, where live performances of jousts, duels, and melees provided archaic thrills. College students in faux armor brandished blunted aluminum swords, impressing hordes of schoolgirls as they waged carefully choreographed duels or rode in gleaming splendor atop farm nags outfitted to resemble warhorses. No one had any idea that the silent men overseeing the four main evening shows had actually once lived during the Middle Ages.

Not every visitor appreciated the authenticity or the history surrounding them, however.

"Dad, there's no video arcade," one of the boys wailed as he looked around. "And I left my Game Boy back at the hotel!"

The youngest's gaze bounced from a standing suit of armor to the lances displayed on the stone walls. "Do those things shoot laser beams, Mom?"

"No, stupid," the oldest boy answered for her in a gloomy tone. "They're just long sticks. They ride horses and poke each other with them."

The fourth boy scowled. "So it's going to be *really* dumb."

Cyprien switched off the sound from the security monitor and watched the children trudge through the turnstile one at a time. It reminded him of when he was a boy, and how he had felt whenever his father had insisted on dragging him and his cousins to a tourney.

You will learn to wield a sword instead of a brush, Michael.

So he had, and now would again.

One of Byrne's guards stepped into the room. "They are ready for you, seigneur."

Michael followed the guard through a private hall and down into the vast underground complex that had been built beneath Knight's Realm. Members of Byrne's *jardin* occupied many of the combat rooms as they trained and fought practice bouts. Michael went to the master's chamber, where Byrne and the others had gathered.

"Master." Michael's seneschal, Phillipe, was also waiting for him. "Suzerain Jaus has arrived."

"See to his needs." Michael stripped out of his jacket and shirt and removed his footwear. With each movement he made, the scent of dark roses around him grew stronger. After he took two swords from the weapons rack, he advanced across the sparring room's tile floor to the centered, twelve-foot-wide circle of polished, interlocking stones. He paid no attention to the three watchers standing against opposite walls, or the troubled look his seneschal gave to his opponent before Phillipe bowed and withdrew.

Suzerain Locksley, who also held short swords in both hands, faced him. Like Michael, he stood barefoot and wore only a pair of black trousers. The light but insistent fragrance of bergamot radiated from his skin. "We may engage later, seigneur, if you would see Jaus now."

"Valentin can wait." Michael slowed, shifting to the right as he focused on Locksley's motionless blades.

"As you say, my lord." The suzerain of Atlanta maintained his casual stance, not reacting as Michael approached him.

Metal screamed as, at the last possible moment, Locksley brought up his blades to keep one of Michael's from splitting his face in two. The cold, swelling rage inside Cyprien, eager for satiation, rammed against the fortress wall of his will. He drew on it, channeling its ferocity into his swords.

Air parted with high-pitched whispers around razor-edged steel.

"Perhaps I should mention my loyalty to you is consummate," the suzerain murmured as he avoided Michael's sweeping thrusts with deft movements and rapid, flashing parries.

Michael did not relent, but fought Locksley back, making advantage where there was none. "So you will not fight me?"

"I will not kill you." Locksley abruptly turned and tried to shift around him, but ended up cornered. "The high lord may not feel such restraint."

"He took her," Michael heard himself mutter. "He bespelled us all with his cursed tongue, and took her from me, before my very eyes. I could do nothing to stop him."

"Richard is desperate." Locksley's black hair slipped from its queue, making a slash of jet above the amethyst glitter of his eyes. "Or perhaps he seeks to force his will on you through her." He grimaced as the edge of Michael's right sword grazed his shoulder. The wound bled for only an instant before closing and vanishing. "He has done so before, my lord."

He didn't like being reminded of how he had been made to betray Alexandra by secretly passing her medical data to Richard. "He vowed he would not harm her."

"I doubt that he has." Locksley sounded exasperated. "Truly, Michael, what can you hope to accomplish? The Irish built Dundellan so well that not even Cromwell could take the bloody thing. Even if you should breach Tremayne's defenses, it is hopeless. Not even Lucan could kill the high lord."

Lucan, who might have spared Michael this if he had carried out his orders to assassinate their king.

"Richard is not invincible." Michael brought down his left blade, knocking the sword from Locksley's right. "I am not Lucan."

"Richard has long been our liege lord—"

"No one takes what is mine." He drove the suzerain to his knees and held him there by holding one razor-sharp sword tip at his throat, and the other under his nose. "No one."

Turquoise eyes burned into violet. Blood brightened the blade, and the smell of bergamot grew heavy.

"Easy, lad." A big man stepped out of the shadows, from where he had been observing the bout. A definite note of heather mingled with the bergamot and roses in the air, and had a curious but immediate calming effect. "Rob, if you're fond of that beak of yours, shut your mouth and drop your weapon."

The other sword in Locksley's hand clattered as it hit

the stone floor. Byrne's talent and the sound combined dispelled enough of Michael's killing rage for him to step back and allow the suzerain to rise and retreat from the sparring circle. He blinked the haze from his eyes and saw the red stain on his blade, and a thin ribbon of the same streaming down the front of Locksley's wide, pale chest.

"I beg your pardon." He handed his blades to Byrne. "I have not been myself."

"A Kyn lord separated from his *sygkenis* rarely is." The Scotsman inspected him. "If this is what I can expect from taking a life companion, I think I will keep to my bachelor life."

"Aye, so shall I," Scarlet, Locksley's seneschal, muttered. "And perhaps borrow some of Lord Byrne's armor when next you spar."

"You worry like an old woman, Will. Bring us some wine, will you?" As his seneschal left, Locksley gingerly touched the rapidly healing wound under his chin before glancing at Byrne's tattooed face. "I could use the armor, I daresay."

"Stay out of the circle, Rob; you'll live longer. Seigneur." Byrne turned to Michael. "I would feel better about this siege of Dundellan if you would have me to serve as your second. 'Twould not be the first time I took back a castle from a bloody Englishman."

Michael rubbed his eyes. "This is not Bothwell, and I do not have fourteen months."

"Or seven thousand men," Locksley added.

As the three blending fragrances radiating from the male Kyn receded, Jayr, Byrne's seneschal, came from the other side of the room to join them. She moved without sound, and handed a red towel to Locksley without comment. Her unusual scent, like that of tansy flowers, always reminded Michael of the spiced cider he had often enjoyed during his human life. It seemed odd that the remote, reserved girl invoked such happy memories. She was the least friendly Kyn he had ever encountered.

"I appreciate your loyalty, but I need you both here,"

Michael said as he watched Rob wipe the blood and sweat from his chest. "If I do not return, Jaus will be my successor."

"Bollocks," Byrne said.

"What my large friend means is, you won't return," Rob said. "Valentin is worthy, but he cannot rule as seigneur in your place for long. This John Keller can do nothing but become another weapon in Richard's hands. The high lord can destroy his mind with a single whisper. Byrne's seneschal has seen it done."

Jayr glanced briefly at Locksley and her master but said nothing. Michael had noticed over these last days of preparation that she would not speak unless addressed directly, and only then with a bare minimum of words. Many of the Kyn preferred females to be seen and not heard, but Michael had not known Byrne was one of them.

"The high lord will not harm anyone but me," Michael said, "and he will not use his voice to do so."

"Richard does as he pleases." Byrne studied his face for a moment, and his stoic expression darkened. "Mother of God, I see it now. You cannot mean to challenge him over a woman, lad."

"He took what is mine," Michael said simply. "It is my right."

His statement made the two suzerain fall silent. Jayr stepped into the circle, picked up Locksley's blades, wiped them clean, and returned them to the wall rack.

Rob cleared his throat. "Even so, I would not take the human to Dundellan. The high lord issued orders for his head. Whatever the outcome of your challenge, it is unlikely that the human will leave the castle alive. Leave him here and we will look after him."

Michael thought of John Keller's determination, and his own promise to let Alexandra's brother help him take her back. He needed a human to do what the Kyn could not, and he doubted he could have persuaded Keller to remain behind unless he had clapped him in irons. "I vowed I would take him, and if I did not he would go anyway. With us, he has a chance."

"A chance to displease the most powerful Kyn in existence," Byrne said, his disgust plain. "Who, if you have forgotten, has never been challenged. If you will not use me, seigneur, at least summon Lucan."

Michael had already considered it. Richard could kill anything living with his voice, but Lucan could do the same with a touch.

Lucan had been poorly used by Richard and the Kyn over the years, until the killing had driven him to abandon his position as the high lord's chief assassin. Michael had offered Lucan a *jardin* only to keep him from creating havoc in America.

But his old enemy had changed. Now Lucan no longer walked alone, but had taken Samantha Brown, a human female changed by Alexandra's blood into Kyn, as his *sygkenis*. With his life companion's help, he had begun to thrive as suzerain.

Doubtless Michael could use Lucan's reluctant gratitude to persuade him to act as his second, but he no longer wished to kill. Michael knew if he was not successful at Dundellan, Lucan might be the only Kyn left with talent powerful enough to stop Richard.

"I will not ask this of him," Michael said. "Lucan has earned the right to live in peace." *Unless I fail.*

Jayr stiffened and drew a dagger, turning toward the door. A heartbeat later it opened, but not to Will bringing in wine.

"As you say, suzerain." A tall, black-haired woman came in, the full skirt of her dark gray silk gown embroidered with arcane symbols in heavy silver thread. She did not bow or curtsy, but regarded Michael with unblinking dark eyes. "It seems that some of us have yet to earn such a gift."

Byrne's seneschal sheathed her dagger.

"Cella." Michael went to her and took her hands in his as he kissed her cheeks. "I did not think you would come."

"You have never summoned me until now." Marcella Evareaux looked past him at Jayr for several moments before she produced an empty smile. "Your *sygkenis* has repaired my brother's wounds many times. She offered me friendship, although I would not take it. The Evareaux are in her debt. I will serve."

Michael knew Alexandra had treated Marcella's brother, Arnaud, for shotgun wounds on more than one occasion. "You know that she would not ask this of you."

"She did not summon me. You did." Her smile tightened. "I will serve, my lord, if you will hold me in reserve until the last." She looked at Jayr again, nodded to the other Kyn, and left the room, taking with her the elegant scent of wisteria.

"Evareaux's sister is lovelier than I remember," Rob murmured. "I have not laid eyes on her since King George's redcoats ran tail between their legs back to the homeland. Why does she not walk among the Kyn?"

"I cannot say." Michael dragged a hand through his hair. "Cella keeps to herself."

"She does it well; I had thought her long dead." Byrne eyed his seneschal, who stared at the door. "What is it, Jayr?"

The girl didn't answer immediately. "Nothing, my lord."

"It is decided." Michael shrugged into his shirt. "Thierry and Jamys will remain here with Jaus to protect our interests. Marcella serves as my second. We leave for London within the hour."

"Aye," Byrne muttered. "God help us all."

Gabriel's dream maiden would not come to him, and he had no desire to remain in the thin, pain-racked darkness without her. He brought himself out of the strange state that provided rest for the Darkyn but only mimicked human sleep, and forced his sluggish senses to do the same. Benait may have locked him in an eternal night, but a familiar lethargy in Gabriel's muscles told him that the sun still burned in the sky.

Will I ever see it again?

Gabriel remembered how in the dreams she had often turned her face up, as if to bathe it in sunlight. Unlike him, she was human, a creature of the day. Were she real, she would be awake now, working and thinking and being with those for whom she cared. Doubtless she took delight in such things.

He envied her that, the ability to thrive in the true light of the world. Of all the simple pleasures of mortal life, he missed those waking hours, riding across the fields, walking through his mother's gardens, following the track of deer through the dappled green mansion of the forest.

The night played thief, stealing all the color from the world, until it became a haunted house of strange shapes and frightening shadows.

Think of her, in the sunlight. Where she walks in splendor.

Gabriel might have blamed his wistful regrets for her recurring presence in his dreams, but his pale maiden seemed too real to be an invention of his guilt and sadness. Nor could he recall a time when he had met a female like her. Her appearance sometimes changed—the curls of her hair, like wisps of moonlight, would stream down past her shoulders one night, then cluster around her ears the next—but the contours of her face and eyes remained constant.

She felt more real than he did.

Other things tugged at his reason. At times she seemed very young, with the wayward curiosity of a child, but she held herself with an alertness that belied her surface appearance and actions. Gabriel sensed that if she were real, she had not strayed innocently into the nightlands. Some purpose had caused their paths to cross, one that had nothing to do with him or finding him. She never came into the dreams seeking him; that much he had sensed from the beginning. Yet after the first encounters she had begun greeting him with obvious pleasure and affection. She might be the only comfort left in his dark world, but he might be nothing more to her than a pleasant fantasy.

He had tried to speak of it to her. *Have you lost your way again?*

Just dreaming.

A strange sound roused Gabriel from thoughts of her. He lifted his head and listened. He knew it was likely to be only Claudio, the elderly human male whom he had occasionally smelled. Gabriel knew his name only because Benait had spoken it before he had departed. Claudio had been left behind to serve as a sentry, perhaps, to keep other humans away and assure that Gabriel would not escape this, the last of their prisons. The old man never came into the basement level or near the narrow stairwell leading to it.

He never will.

Gabriel's open wounds had ceased bleeding, but blood starvation now sapped his strength. What little he could do about it dwindled by the hour. Soon his talent would fail him, and then his body would begin to feed upon itself.

There were stories among his kind of Kyn trapped in prisons or other places from which they could not escape. They were much stronger than humans, so it often took a year or more for them to die. When the end finally came, they left behind skeletons so desiccated that a touch caused them to disintegrate.

No one spoke of the agony of withering away to dust, but some part of Gabriel knew it would surpass everything the Brethren had inflicted upon him.

I am not dust yet.

The sound came again, distant and muffled—a high-pitched, mechanical sound—and then it slowed and stopped.

A small vehicle, Gabriel guessed. Not a car; the engine was too small. He looped the memory of the sound in his mind until he identified it: that of a motorcycle. No vehicle had driven near the property since Benait had left, and Claudio traveled about on foot, so Gabriel had guessed that the roads around the château were seldom used.

A tourist, stopping by the road to picnic? Or to explore?

Minutes ticked away in silence. The engine did not start again. When Gabriel heard the soft weight of footsteps crossing the ground, he almost did not believe his ears. But no, the newcomer walked with purpose, almost hurrying toward him.

Gabriel wondered if his mind was inventing the footsteps as some new form of self-torture, until ancient wood creaked, and the temperature of the air seeping into his chamber changed minutely. The sound of hard-soled shoes on the stone above his head confirmed the reality of the visitor.

Someone had entered the chapel. Not the old man; the steps sounded too quick, too light. Someone else.

Benait had intended the chamber to be airtight, but long months and other things had eaten away at the mortar between the bricks. Gabriel breathed in, filling his lungs with as much air as possible, identifying every change in it until he tasted . . .

Woman.

Gabriel had once been the best hunter and tracker among the Kyn, and nothing the Brethren had done had damaged his senses. The scent of the human, like that of any animal's, told him many things. She was young, healthy, and clean. She wore leather and cotton, and had recently walked through damp moss and rich soil. Perfume did not mask the natural fragrance of her body, which came into his head like cool, pure water from a stream. Her body was not cold, however. Her passage colored the air with radiant human warmth.

Gabriel's *dents acérées*, which had not extruded into his

mouth since his capture, slowly emerged from the shriveled spaces in his palate, tearing through the thin layer of
flesh that had grown over them. As they extended, his
hands curled against the need that came with them, the
need to take her, his teeth in her flesh, her veins pulsing,
her heart beating steadily as she gave him life.

I will have her.

He ignored the slavering hunger surging inside him and
turned his focus within. He could not use his talent to bring
her to him; unless she were bespelled his appearance
would terrify her. He could not control her mind at all unless she came close enough to smell him.

When she did, she would do whatever he wished—or so
he hoped.

Before Gabriel had been imprisoned, using *l'attrait* to
attract humans to him had been effortless and usually involuntary. Starvation had at first made his scent stronger,
but years of deprivation had made it as weak as his limbs.
In his condition, he would have to draw on his last reserve
of strength and force his body to produce enough scent to
permeate the closed chamber and perhaps lure her to him.
Before he did, he had to wait to see if she would venture
down the stairs.

He would not waste this, perhaps his only chance to
escape.

She did not move down the center of the chapel, as Benait and Claudio had. She skirted the edges of it, as if keeping close to the walls. His sensitive ears heard her touching
things here and there, the brush of her palms light but lingering. He could taste the heat of sunlight; she was not
feeling her way through darkness. No, the woman sought
something—something in the very walls themselves—
with slow, careful fingers.

If only her quest would lead her to him.

Gabriel tracked the sounds of her movements as she made
a complete circuit of the chapel. The sounds not only told
him of her location but gave him the first approximation of

the area of the chapel itself. Small and narrow, it must have been built to serve a noble family of modest means.

Throughout the ages, great families had made a show of their devotion to God by building enormous chapels and churches on their property. The government of modern France had spent billions buying, restoring, and turning such places into visitor attractions. Wherever they had brought him, it would not be a site that commanded historic restoration. That, combined with the direction and distance the truck had traveled from Paris, meant that the Brethren had brought him south, perhaps only a short distance east of his estate in Toulouse.

Temerleone, Gabriel thought, recalling remote properties that had been left to rot in the Bordelais region. *Or St. Valereye*. Given the respective populations around both of the châteaux, it was more likely that the latter served as his prison. *She will tell me. She will tell me everything I must know, and then her flesh will yield to mine, and I will know all of her tastes.*

Denial made his perpetual hunger swell, causing his *dents acérées* to throb and his exhausted limbs to tighten. At the same time his heart shriveled. Since learning to control his appetite for human blood, Gabriel had never fallen into thrall, or caused a human to die by draining her body of blood while within the corresponding state of rapture.

That did not mean he had forgotten what it felt like, and it felt like this. The woman searching the chapel now might be his savior, but the moment she released him, he would be her killer.

The beast inside him that demanded feeding did not care. *It is her life, or mine.* So did that part of his soul, rendered unfeeling by his talent. *She will not be made to suffer, as I have been—*

No.

Gabriel had once been human, like the woman. He remembered the vows he had taken during that life, and the God he had worshiped. He had been a warrior, and had fought for the Holy Land, but he had never thirsted for blood. He had obeyed his Templar master, and guarded well the secrets of their order, but he had never put his own needs before those of others.

He no longer walked the earth as a human, but he had not forgotten how it felt to brave the world in a fragile form, undaunted, unafraid.

I cannot take her life to save my own.

Even as that knowledge scalded him, the old man's voice wrenched him out of his snarled thoughts. "What are you doing here, boy?"

Boy? Gabriel inhaled again. The old man's sweat, acrid with his fear, added a sour top note to the air, but it did not disguise or alter the taste of the female.

"I wanted to take photos." She spoke in low, somewhat stilted French, but it was the timbre of her voice that shocked Gabriel. "This place is very old. Are you fixing it up for someone?"

It cannot be her.

"It is too old to be fixed, boy. No one is allowed here." Claudio's voice moved to the center of the chapel. "You see that beam? It came down only yesterday. The rest of the roof could fall in at any moment. Go back to the village. Take your pictures of the church there."

"I'll only be a minute—"

"Get out, idiot, or I call the police."

No sound came except the rasp of the old man's breath, and then the light, soft footsteps that crossed the chapel floor and outside onto the grounds.

She was leaving.

The chains binding Gabriel rattled as his muscles went lax. The sound of the motorcycle engine barely registered. That he had come so close to escape did not dismay him as much as the woman's voice did.

It was not madness or delusion.

He now knew the shape of her mouth, the blond-white gleam of the tousled hair that framed her soft cheeks, the depth of the tiny dent in the center of her chin. That if she stood before him, the top of her bright head would barely reach the top of his shoulder. He saw without seeing her spare, boyish frame, the hollows of her throat, the scars across the knuckles of her roughened, blunt-nailed hands. He did not have to look into her eyes to know they were bluer than a midsummer sky, or that her eyelashes and eyebrows were four shades darker than her hair.

He knew all of these things because he knew her, had known her these many months, had taken solace from the curve of her lips, the brightness of her eyes, the sound of that voice. The same voice that had called to him too many times for him to be mistaken about this.

His maiden was not a dream.

Chapter 4

As Gabriel encountered the reality of his dreams, another outcast endured what was becoming his personal nightmare.

The one person John Keller loved most in the world, his sister, Alexandra, was in terrible danger. To save her, he had to trust creatures he had been told were soulless demons intent on destroying humanity. The soulless demons, who had until a short time ago considered him one of their enemies, had reluctantly allowed him into the ranks. In a few hours they were all jumping on a plane together and going to Ireland to fight the Demon King and rescue his sister.

As plans went, this one had total disaster written all over it.

John knew the Kyn felt suspicious of him, but he saw no sign of it. Since coming to Orlando, he had been treated courteously, even indulgently. He had also been kept out of discussions about his sister and the plans being made to retrieve her from the Darkyn's high lord. Being treated as an uninvited, unwanted guest didn't bother him, but not knowing what was happening to his sister was quietly driving him out of his mind.

"You are Alexandra's brother."

The scent of camellias, not the voice, alerted John to the fact that he was no longer alone. He turned away from the charming Monet he had been studying and faced the short, slim, fair-haired man standing behind him.

"John Keller." He hadn't heard the man come into the room, but as silently as the Kyn could move, he never would. This one looked and sounded familiar, although it took him a moment to place him. "We met in Chicago, didn't we?"

"We did. I am Suzerain Valentin Jaus." The vampire did not offer to shake hands as a human would, but when he removed his coat John saw that he had trouble using his right arm. "I was very sorry to hear about Alexandra's abduction. Has there been any word of her?"

"Not that I've been told." Not that anyone intended to tell him anything. He recalled that Alex had liked this particular vampire—she and Michael had stayed in his enormous mansion as guests—and Alex had surgically reattached his arm after it had been severed during a duel. While the Kyn healed spontaneously, it appeared even they had limits. "Are you going to Ireland with us?"

"I would be of little use." Jaus touched his stiff right arm. "I am to stay behind and protect the seigneur's interests until he returns. You should consider doing the same."

That would make Cyprien happy, but John wasn't interested in placating Alexandra's boyfriend. "She's my sister. I'm going."

"You are human. You cannot physically prevail over even one of us, and hundreds of Kyn guard Richard's castle. You do not strike me as suicidal." Jaus removed his sunglasses and tossed his coat over the back of a chair before he approached him.

"I don't have to be immortal to be useful." He hoped.

"Your motives puzzle me as well. What can you hope to accomplish with this . . . how do you think of it?" Jaus cocked his head. "A gesture of brotherly concern, perhaps?"

John turned his back on the man and looked at the painting again. "It's none of your business."

"I hold your sister in high regard, as well as friendship, so I must disagree." The suzerain came to stand beside him. "You are a Catholic priest, a member of the Brethren. You showed little interest in Alexandra's welfare when she asked for your help in Chicago. Now, inexplicably, you are here and you wish to die for her. Yet you are the same man. Explain this to me, please."

He was the same fool the Brethren had used to get to her. "I'm not a priest anymore, and I never belonged to the order. They used me only to get to Alexandra and Cyprien."

"As you say." The vampire's striking, pale blue eyes shifted. "Monet was a genius at depicting water and light, I think. I have one of his paintings of the Seine in my home." Jaus reached out suddenly and put a hand on the back of John's neck, and the scent of camellias became heavy. "Now you will tell me the truth, priest. Why do you wish to go to Ireland with the seigneur?"

"To save her." John didn't want to say that, but something forced the words out of him. "To explain everything that I didn't. To stop the killing."

Jaus's voice became silky. "What will you do on behalf of the Brethren while you are there?"

"Nothing. They're bigger monsters than the Kyn." That the vampire was using the strange power of the Kyn to force him to speak the truth didn't bother John, only that he felt he had to do so. "I won't let them use me anymore."

"Will you betray Cyprien to save yourself?"

"No one can save me." John jerked out of Jaus's reach and stared at him. "Just ask next time. I don't lie."

"You must not be human, then." Jaus studied John's face as the door to the study opened and Cyprien came in. "He has not deceived you, Michael. He does care deeply for Alexandra, more so than perhaps even she knows. If he is acquiring a tolerance to *l'attrait*, he may provide some reasonable assistance to you."

"Thank you, Valentin. Byrne has acquired a new breeding stallion for his mares and wishes someone to admire his gift for choosing superb animals. Perhaps you would care to indulge his ego?" Cyprien waited until Jaus had left the study before speaking to John. "Humans cannot lie to Jaus. I had to be sure of you."

Anger that Cyprien doubted him, and shame that he had every reason to, warred inside John. "I know what you're thinking."

Cyprien's eyebrow arched. "I genuinely doubt that."

"I should have taken better care of my sister, but that's the past and I can't change it." No matter how much he wanted to. "I'm not going to walk away from her now. So if you want me out, you'll have to lock me up or kill me."

"These things I could do. Or I could exercise my own talent, and make you forget that you ever had a sister." Cyprien lit a cigarette and watched him through the smoke. "Many times I have been tempted to erase her from your mind, and you from hers."

"I can't stop you." John spread his hands. "If you're that much afraid of me, go ahead. Do it."

"However much I wish you were not," Cyprien said, "you are most definitely her brother." His mouth became a bitter line. "I have made promises as well, Father Keller."

"I'm not a priest anymore. It's John." He dropped his hands. "I didn't come here to fight with you, or to be humored. I don't have any psychic tricks or immortal attitude. I just want to get my sister home safely."

"It will not be that simple." The vampire went to his desk and removed a file. "As Val said, Dundellan is a fortress. Richard has spent decades securing it and hand-picking the Kyn who make up his garrison. They were all chosen for the strength of their talents as well as their battle experience."

"We could ask him to give her back," John said. "Negotiate with him."

"He has everything he wants." Cyprien rubbed the back of his neck with an irritable gesture. "Richard will never surrender Alexandra, not now that she is under his complete control. She is too valuable to him."

"Because he thinks she can cure him?" That got Cyprien's attention. "I do speak French, and I've overheard enough bits and pieces of your conversations to get that much. He didn't have to kidnap her. You know as well as I do that Alexandra would have helped him for nothing."

"Richard needs more Kyn to battle the Brethren, but had no hope of such until Alexandra became involved with me. Yes, she may cure his own condition, but it is not what she can do as much as what she is. He now knows that her blood changed Lucan's woman from human to Kyn." He met John's gaze. "Alexandra is the key to our future, to our very survival as a species. I believe the high lord will do anything to keep her."

"That's why you'll do whatever it takes to get her out of there." Cyprien nodded, and John relaxed a little. "I can help. You'll need a human to do some things for you, especially during the day. I don't know how else I can help, but I can and I will. Anything you say. Use me."

The two words hung between them for a moment before Cyprien checked his watch. "I must go and make the final arrangements." He picked up the file and held it out to him. "These are the floor plans for Dundellan Castle. Study them while we are on the plane; you will need to know the layout."

Before John could reply, a Kyn dressed as a teenage boy came into the room. Jamys Durand glanced at Cyprien but came to John. His expression and the hand he held out were only too familiar to John. Jamys could communicate only by using his Kyn talent to speak through humans, so John had been acting as his unofficial interpreter.

"Jamys has something to tell you before we leave." John braced himself for the mute vampire's touch, and the eerie sensation of hearing him inside his mind.

Before you leave for Ireland, I must tell the seigneur about the cell in Dublin. Although he couldn't make a sound, Jamys's telepathic voice resonated with depth and feeling inside John. *I think the high lord had an informant among the interrogators. One of them left the cell only an hour or so before Lucan came and freed us.*

Sweat trickled down John's face as he repeated the message to Michael. Although Jamys's telepathic voice didn't cause pain, it usually rendered the humans in contact with it unconscious after only a few minutes.

"You'd better make this quick," John told the youthful-looking vampire. "I already feel light-headed."

Through John, Jamys told Cyprien about a Brethren interrogator named Orson Leary, who had been acting strangely just before Richard's former chief assassin had arrived to free the Durands.

"If Leary is the high lord's informant, he may have access to Dundellan that we don't," John said. "Jamys thinks we should talk to him, learn what his connection to Richard is and how much he knows." His vision doubled, and he stepped out of reach, abruptly breaking contact. To Jamys, he said, "Sorry. I'm ready to pass out."

Cyprien turned to his computer and went to work. After a minute, he nodded. "Orson Leary is in London. We can collect him before we go to Ireland."

"Collect?" John knew better. "You mean abduct."

"I do not play games with humans," Cyprien told him. "If this man can help us gain access to Dundellan, we will take him to Ireland with us."

"I doubt he'll be willing." John resented the easy way the Kyn took and used human beings for their own purposes. Their smug indifference to anything but their own interests might become as destructive as the Brethren's zealous, irrational persecution. "But that doesn't matter, does it?"

"Nothing matters to me but Alexandra." Cyprien stood. "Leary is a trained interrogator; he will recognize Kyn. I will need you to make the initial contact and bring him to me." When he saw John's expression, his eyes narrowed. "You said that you wished to help, and that you would do anything for your sister. Have you changed your mind again?"

He could change his mind; that was what Cyprien was saying without saying. For a moment John was tempted. He had seen, firsthand, how the Kyn fought their enemies. Heads would, literally, roll. Leary's might be the first.

John knew how the Kyn had suffered at the hands of the Brethren, and how much Leary likely deserved an unpleasant, painful death. But he believed, just as Alexandra did, that violence wasn't the answer.

The killing had to stop, and these two old enemies had to find some measure of peace. With a Kyn sister and a Brethren mentor, John might be the only one who could make that happen.

"As long as you promise not to hurt Leary," John said slowly, extending his hand, "I'll do it."

"I vow I will not hurt the priest." Michael shook hands with him. "Go up to the garage and wait there; Phillipe will bring the car around shortly." He turned to Jamys. "I must speak with your father before we depart. Come."

John left the study and climbed the stairs to the upper public level of Knight's Realm, where the last show had finished. He merged into the crowd of weary but happy tourists heading for the parking garage.

As he entered the first level of the garage, he smelled peppermint. It grew stronger as a red-haired girl in a party dress bumped into him and hurried past. She slowed from a run to a walk, glanced back, and gave him a contrite smile. "Excuse me, mister."

John rubbed his hand—her sharp little nails had stabbed into the back of it—but he smiled back. "It's okay." Night made the garage seem darker than he remembered, and he squinted, trying to spot Cyprien's limo.

Beneath his feet, the ground tilted slightly.

A white sedan came to an abrupt stop in front of John, and a tall, thick-bodied man in a dark suit climbed out. He walked toward John. "Are you feeling all right, Father?" he asked, some sort of accent blurring the words.

"No." John saw a miniature of himself reflected in the

man's mirrored sunglasses, and stopped between two cars. As the thick scent of cloves filled his head and the ground began to roll in concrete waves, he reached out blindly and braced himself. Something dripped from the end of his nose—sweat?—and his lungs burned. The man had called him "Father," but John was wearing street clothes. "How did you . . . ?"

The girl joined her father and grinned up at John. A trickle of blood stained the tip of her index finger, which looked like it ended in a silver claw. The scent of peppermint became smothering. "Hey, daddykins. Want to go for a ride?"

Nick pulled on her helmet and jerked the chinstrap tight. Dark yellow flecks of petals from the marigolds taking over the front lawns of Château St. Valereye speckled the toes of her boot. She didn't stop to look back at the jagged walls of the manor house, or the corner occupied by the chapel, which seemed to have escaped the ravages of time and neglect.

She could feel the old man watching her from the filmy windows of the caretaker's cottage. He was making sure she was leaving, and if she came back, she had no doubt he would make good on his threat and call the police.

Why did he lie to me?

Whoever he was, he acted as if he owned the place. He might just be that, the last of an old French family, living out his golden years watching the old château slowly decay into a pile of rubble. It was already halfway there, and definitely uninhabitable.

But the chapel was a different story.

Nick had gotten the chance to do a quick if not too thorough survey of the interior. Unlike the main house, the chapel had been built almost entirely from brick and stone. Whatever had long ago burned the wooden structures of the château had only dusted the inside of the church with a careless, blackened brush.

The altar had been dismantled, and no one had bothered to take out the pews and chop them up for firewood. They faced the empty space behind the railing at the front of the chapel, as if filled with a ghost parish worshiping a God who had deserted them.

Nick didn't believe in ghosts, and that wasn't the vibe she was getting from the place anyway.

The chapel had not served its purpose in decades, maybe centuries, but the structure was solid. Only one of the roof's ornamental rafters had come down, and that had been pulled down deliberately, as if to make it appear that the roof was unsound.

As authentic as it looked, Nick knew a setup job when she saw one.

She put her bike into gear and rode six bumpy miles over dirt before hitting the paved road that led back to the village. As she went, she scanned the pastoral hills surrounding the château. Two farmhouses, both appearing as if they'd been abandoned at the turn of the century. No animals, no squatters, not so much as a single squab hunter or farmer with his pig rooting around the tree trunks for truffles. The château's only neighbors were trees, thickets of woody brush, and the fields and pastures they were slowly reclaiming.

No one came out here, either. The dirt road had been wind-worn smooth of ruts. She didn't pass a single car, bike, or truck until she had crossed the outer boundary of the village, and melded into the light traffic of delivery boys on Vespas, lorry drivers hauling produce and meat in from the south, and the occasional wandering tourist in a rental car.

The old man had lied to her to get her off the property, and to scare her enough to keep her off, but why? Why guard a decrepit pile of worthless rock like St. Valereye so jealously if no one ever went there, and there was nothing worth stealing?

She knew something was there. She could feel it again,

the same way she did every time just before she found something old that had been lost. Was that who he was, the Green Man in her dreams? Was he waiting, as the Golden Madonna waited, for Nick to find him?

So I dreamed of the place. It doesn't make him real. He's just wishful thinking.

Nick didn't have time to overanalyze the situation. She had to know what was going on at the château, and she'd found nothing about it on the Internet. That meant gathering some information from the locals. She decided to start at the inn where she had taken a room for the week.

Jean Laguerre, a taciturn man in his mid-thirties, spent the day stationed behind a bar that had been converted to serve as his reception desk. When Nick approached the innkeeper, she saw that he was sorting through receipts and adding up figures.

Nick was grateful he spoke flawless English. She usually embarrassed herself trying to speak French to the natives. "Excuse me, M. Laguerre, but may I ask you something?"

"Of course." He scanned a yellow delivery slip while his fingers tapped the keys of an old adding machine.

"Is your wife here?" Nick kept her tone casual. "I'd like to ask her about one of the old houses around town."

"Adélie is in the kitchen." He nodded toward the back of the inn. "If you go in there, she will ask you to sample her fish stock. It tastes like dishwater and smells worse."

"Whoa."

He leveled a stern eye on her. "If you sample it, you will tell her it is ambrosia, or she will fret and burn my dinner for the next two weeks."

Nick cleared her throat, mostly to stop a rising chuckle. "I'm allergic to fish."

"I wish that I were." He flipped over the receipt and began adding in figures from another.

Nick went back to the kitchen, where she found Adélie Laguerre at the sturdy old wooden table, up to her elbows in chopped vegetables and mushrooms. Table grapes, two fresh, braided *natte aux pivots* loaves, and a small bunch of garlic bulbs sat waiting their turn in the double-sided willow basket she took when she went to the village market.

French kitchens were a lot like Brit kitchens, Nick had noticed. Well, the French always had a bottle of wine standing around to be added to whatever was simmering in the pot for dinner, and they were a bit obsessive-compulsive about having fresh bread every day of the week. But the British were just as much a pain with their pots of tea and after-dinner puddings.

The dark-haired woman smiled as Nick came in, but like her husband did not stop working. "I just made up your room, mademoiselle. You are very tidy for an American."

Accustomed to the French way of delivering back-handed compliments, Nick grinned. "I travel light. Madame, the petrol station owner told me that you've lived in St. Valereye all your life. Is he right?"

"He is." With a flick of her chopping knife the innkeeper's wife decapitated a stalk of broccoli and began expertly reducing it to a pile of small florets. "My grandparents came here from Périgueux with my father when he was a boy, to escape the war. I wanted to go to Paris when I was young, but Papa would not allow it. So I married Jean, which was almost as good—he is from Marseilles," she added. "Why do you ask?"

"I was wondering if you knew anything about that old château up on the hillside?" Nick gestured in the general direction.

Adélie put down the knife in her hand and turned to stare at her. "I know of it. You have gone there today, mademoiselle?"

"I was riding around and saw it from the road," Nick lied. "I tried to take a walk around the place, but an old man chased me off."

"The crazy Basque." Adélie made a sound of contempt

that only women born in France could produce and went
back to chopping. "He does this to everyone, not just visitors. Jean and I tried to speak to him about it after Mass
one Sunday. Some of the Germans like to hike and have
picnics, and there is a pretty stream there. He told us to
keep our guests away or he would have them arrested—
and he is supposed to be a priest."

So he used the same threat even with the locals. *Interesting.* "Does he give services at the church?"

"He only comes to Mass. But I heard the men who came
here with him call him Father Claudio."

He might be a retired priest, or he might be something
else. "Does he own the property?"

"Him? Oh, no." She shook her head as she began heap-
ing the vegetables into a wire *potée* basket already stocked
with lamb and onions. "The château belongs to the
church."

Nick glanced through the kitchen windows at the
charming little sanctuary where most of the villagers at-
tended Mass.

Adélie followed the direction of her gaze. "Not our
church, mademoiselle. The Holy Father's church in Rome.
They own many such properties in France. Some believe
the ghost who haunts it may have been a priest, murdered
during the revolution."

Nick straightened. "There's a ghost haunting it?"

"So they say." The older woman wiped her hands on her
apron. "Every old house has a ghost or two, *non*?"

Nick moved closer. "Tell me more about this ghost."

Adélie sighed. "I first heard of it after the crazy Basque
came to town to complain about my brother's son, Misha.
Misha and his friends are boys who like to play harmless
tricks, you know? They had been going out to the château
and trying to scare the old man."

"Making noises like a ghost," Nick guessed.

The innkeeper's wife nodded. "My brother scolded
Misha, and told him to stay away, but my nephew would

not listen. He and two of his school friends went out to *le château* one night to, how do you say, get even with the crazy one?"

"What happened?"

Adélie looked uneasy. "Misha went into the chapel to hide, but never came out. His friends looked through the windows but did not see him. They ran all the way back to the village to tell my brother. He drove out there to look for Misha, and found my nephew walking on the road. Misha would not say anything for hours, until we tried to take him to the hospital. Then he wept in terror, and told us that the ghost had tried to steal his soul."

"It's not a place for kids even during the day," Nick said. "I can only imagine how scary it looks at night."

"It was not that, mademoiselle. I know the tricks a young imagination can play. When I was a girl, I became convinced that a troll lived under my bed," the older woman said. "I heard it breathing and moving under there. After many nights I worked up the courage to look, and something reached out and scratched me. I screamed the house down until Papa came and moved my bed to show me there was nothing beneath it but my cat, Lupi."

"Your nephew probably encountered something similar," Nick told her.

"No, mademoiselle. He saw nothing. He only heard the ghost rattling his chains, and calling his name—calling him Michel—and a terrible hammering sound." Her eyes went to her hands. "I would not have believed him myself, but he was paralyzed by fear. I cannot believe it was all a lie."

Nick recalled the grimy condition of the chapel's interior. "He might have imagined that, too."

"We can only hope." She picked up the *potée* basket, lowering it into the pottery dish and pouring a generous measure of wine over it before covering it with a lid for cooking. "I will tell you this. After what happened to Misha, there is not a man in this village who will go near the château. Not even my Jean."

Nick had heard a hundred stories of hauntings and ghosts, and knew most had occurred only in the mind of the storyteller. Had the details been slightly different, she would have believed that Misha had done the same. A boy in trouble might say anything to appease an angry parent.

There was only one problem, and it was not the name-calling or the chain dragging. Anyone who had read Dickens enough times would attribute the same sounds to any unhappy spirit.

The hammering sound didn't fit.

No one was making any repairs to the old chapel, the old man had said, and no one would work in there at night. She had not seen any tools, nor any indication anything was being used to fix the old place.

So who had been hammering up there, and why?

Chapter 5

"Dr. Keller, I would speak with you."

Éliane Selvais, Richard Tremayne's *tresora*, came into the room where the guards had locked Alex. The tall, slim blonde in the pastel blue suit usually radiated a composed, wintry persona, but one glance told Alex that Éliane's calm had more cracks in it than the ceiling of the Sistine Chapel.

"These ridiculous attempts of yours to escape the castle are causing a great deal of—" Éliane stopped speaking as soon as she saw the window Alex was working on. "*Mon Dieu.* What are you doing?"

"Escaping the castle." Alex worked another piece of the window frame loose and tore it off, tossing it over her shoulder. Prying up the wooden frame had been easy; she hadn't yet figured out how to knock out the iron bars. "You don't happen to have a hammer and chisel on you that I can borrow, do you?"

The Frenchwoman quickly closed the door and locked it. "You go too far, Doctor. The high lord is already seriously displeased with you."

"I haven't gone far enough, and fuck the high lord." Peering through the bars over the window, Alex tried to estimate the drop. For a human it would be a lethal one, but she might manage it without breaking her legs. Or maybe she'd throw Éliane out first, use her as a drop cushion. "Are we four stories up here, or five?"

"Alexandra, please."

Now there were two words Alex had never thought she'd hear out of Éliane's perfect, disapproving lips.

She let go of the edge of the sill. "I'm sorry; refresh my memory here. Exactly *when* did you and I become old pals?"

"I know we are not friends." The other woman sighed. "But we can be civil to each other."

"Not without drugs, which no longer work on me," Alex told her. "So, go back to kissing Richard's ass or whatever it is you do for him, *tresora*, and leave me alone."

The skin around the base of Éliane's nose whitened. "I am the only friend you have here."

"Then I'm in serious trouble." Alex plucked a splinter of wood out from under her fingernail. "How do you think my chances are with that big guard with the neck tat?"

The Frenchwoman's lips thinned. "Stop joking."

"Who's joking? We're not friends." Alex knew needling Éliane wouldn't help get her out of Dundellan, but she couldn't seem to help herself. "Or have you conveniently forgotten that you once tried to feed me to Cyprien?"

"Once," the *tresora* admitted. "I also saved your life when the Brethren tried to take you in New Orleans."

True enough, although the Frenchwoman's motives had hardly been driven-snow pure. "Okay. So we're friends. Now be a pal, run back to your lord and master, and tell him that this song and dance didn't work, either."

"He does not know that I am here." She looked around the room before continuing in a lower voice. "I came to say that I will do whatever I can to reunite you with Cyprien, if you will help my lord."

Alex made a rude sound.

"Richard truly is losing the battle with his body, Alexandra." Éliane bent and began picking up the pieces of broken frame from the floor. "Each day his mind slips further into the madness. Each night I fear he will lose control again. The last time he did, he destroyed the medical lab and slaughtered twenty men. They were good men, devoted and loyal to him."

The only questionable behavior Alex had observed in the high lord was a bit of irritability, but she'd caused that herself.

"Richard's homicidal rages are not my problem," she pointed out. "I didn't ask to be kidnapped. I don't have a cure. I don't think I'm going to develop one, or Stockholm syndrome, either. Why isn't anyone getting this?"

"You have made the disgust you feel for my lord all too plain." Éliane brought the broken frame pieces to the window and opened it, tossing them out through the iron bars. "If you hope to shame him, you should know that your tantrums do not move him in the slightest. Very little will now, I believe."

"You don't want me here. I'm not going to do anything to help him. So why not give me a hand and get me out?" Alex asked. "Richard will never know. I won't tell Michael it was you." She raised three fingers. "Girl Scout's honor."

"I am not a Girl Scout." Smooth blond hair caught the light as Éliane straightened her shoulders. "But you can help Richard. You restored Michael's face. You have the knowledge. It would be nothing for you."

"You've been watching too many reruns of *ER*." When the other woman frowned, she added, "Richard is mutating into something I've never even considered possible, much less treated in a human or Kyn. I can't intubate him, seduce an intern, and save the day before the closing credits roll. I'm a reconstructive surgeon, not George Clooney."

"You have not even examined him."

The snotty bitch was right, of course. Richard's thugs had dragged her down to the laboratory in the dungeon several times, but Alex had refused to touch so much as a petri dish. When Richard himself had used his voice to compel her to work, she had been able to resist him just enough to fumble and drop things until he had ordered the guards to take her out of the lab. She hoped that resistance would get stronger, because if she didn't get out of here soon . . .

"I can't do this right now. Go away." She began pacing.

"You are the only doctor who understands the Kyn," the other woman argued. "You must do this. It is your calling."

"Humans were my work, not vampires." Alex kicked a piece of wood out of her way. "I rebuild wrecked bodies, not mutated DNA. Yeah, I was able to operate on Michael and fix physical damage. But this isn't a bad injury, Blondie. I don't have the knowledge or the training necessary. Richard needs to be evaluated by—minimum—a microbiologist, a geneticist, and an epidemiologist." She cleared her throat. "Bottom line: Even if I wanted to, I couldn't help him."

"What is wrong?"

"Nothing." Alex's annoyance changed into bands of heat inching up her arms and a cold, clenching hunger tightening under her sternum. The roof of her mouth burned, which meant her *dents acérées* wanted to pop out and go to work. So far she'd been able to control her temper and suppress the disgusting desire to bite someone, but the urges were growing stronger—especially when she was around humans. "You need to leave now, before I lose my temper."

"Ah," the Frenchwoman said, drawing out the single syllable. "You are feeling the separation."

"Just get out." She put some distance between her and the blonde.

"I have seen it happen to others kept apart from their lords. The longer the separation, the worse it will become." The Frenchwoman made a sideways gesture with one hand. "He endures the same need."

That reminded Alex of how she and Michael had gone at it in Florida. Skimping on sex had turned the two of them into minks; what would this do? "We won't be apart much longer."

"I have no doubt that Michael will come to Ireland, but

my lord will not permit him near Dundellan." Éliane nodded toward the outer bailey, where the guards had their quarters. "You have seen the size of the garrison. They are all Kyn, Doctor, and completely loyal. They will die before they allow Cyprien to enter the castle or touch Richard."

Alex didn't want to believe her, but she had seen how Richard's men behaved. He was their king, and men of their time died happily for the crown. She had to vacate the premises before that happened, but she wasn't going to be able to do it on her own. Michael was taking too long, or maybe he couldn't get to her. Whatever the case, Alex needed the Frenchwoman's help as much as she needed hers.

She had to get out of here.

"Let's make a deal," Alex said. "I'll take a look at Richard's blood sample and tell you what I think can be done. In return, you get me out of here." When the other woman would have spoken, she held up her hand. "Take it or leave it."

"You cannot tell from studying his blood alone," Éliane argued. "You must give him a physical examination. If you do so, he is more likely to believe that you have had a change of heart."

The thought of seeing Richard's mutated body made Alex's stomach roll, but if it would convince him that she was playing nice . . . "All right. I need to set up some things in the new lab first. Can you get Atlas and Igor to let me out of here?"

Éliane nodded. "Give me an hour." When the door to the room opened, she didn't flinch, but turned smoothly to face the Kyn who entered. "Captain Korvel, Dr. Keller has agreed to cooperate."

The captain of the castle guard, whose bicep bulges were larger than Alex's head, regarded the *tresora* with an impassive expression. "I shall not release her until the master bids me do so."

"I will go and relate this change of heart to him." Éliane

gave Alex a pointed look before she inclined her head. "Dr. Keller."

Korvel did not leave with the Frenchwoman, and when they were alone he eyed the damage Alex had done to the window frame. "Is this a sample of your newfound cooperation?"

"I got bored." She didn't like the captain or the way he talked over her head, as if she were too small and insignificant for him to bother looking down. He probably thought the ring of thorns around his neck made him look like a tough guy instead of one with poor taste in tattoo artists. The only good thing about him was that, unlike every other Kyn in the castle, he didn't smother her with the scent of *l'attrait*. "I do need to go down to the lab and prepare to do a physical on Tremayne."

"When the high lord issues the order, I shall escort you," Korvel said. "Until then, you will stay here."

More waiting games. "So what do you want? Richard send you to slap me around?"

"I came only to check on you." His eyes shifted. "Who is Atlas?"

"The statue of the guy with the world on his shoulders. Aside from the lousy neck tattoo, you're a dead ringer for him." Alex almost laughed when he did a double take. "Don't you guys ever go to a museum or read a book around here?"

Korvel shook his head.

"Your loss. Your double looks really cute in a loincloth." One day the Kyn were going to develop a sense of humor, Alex thought. Probably around the same time that hell hosted the Winter Olympics. Something occurred to her. "Your immune system should have erased that tattoo of yours. What kind of ink did they use?"

"None." The seneschal touched his neck. "After my lord and I rose from our graves, we were pursued by the sheriff. I was captured and hung from a gallows with copper-spiked rope. I have had the mark ever since."

"You and Richard died together?" Alex walked up to him and pushed his hand aside to have a better look. "How?"

"My lord came back from the Holy Land and fell ill with plague," Korvel told her. "I was his steward, and succumbed to the same illness while tending to him. We were buried within a day of each other."

"So he comes home and infects you. Nice boss." The crappy tattoo was actually a series of flat keloids with a strange green tint to them. Each was so thick she couldn't make a dent in them with her fingernail when she prodded them. "How long did that sheriff leave you hanging?"

"I cannot say. Weeks. Perhaps months." He stared down at her. "What is it? Do you wish to study me as well?"

Alex jerked away from him. She did not want to take a skin sample from him. She didn't care what had happened to his neck. She wanted Michael, this minute, so badly she thought she might scream. "Just bored. You can go back to patrolling the castle now."

"I wished to speak with you."

If he didn't quit being so goddamn polite, she *would* scream. "We're speaking."

He hesitated, as if searching for words. "You rouse the men too much."

She'd certainly kept them busy chasing after her. "Look, pal, I didn't ask to be brought here."

"As you have made plain to the entire household," he assured her. "I do not refer to your attempts to escape."

Alex frowned. "Then what?"

"Your presence disturbs the men. You have made them very restless. They become more curious about you each day." Korvel moved to the window and closed it before looking at a spot on the wall behind her. "I have made my lord aware of this."

"Gee, thanks." Alex still wasn't sure what he was trying to tell her. "Are you saying I'm getting on everyone's nerves? I do that with people I like."

"No. You are too vulnerable, too open." Now he looked down at her. "If you wish to remain safe, you must begin to conduct yourself properly, as do the other women in the castle."

The other women in the castle kept their mouths shut, looked at the floor a lot, and curtsied to Richard every five seconds. "Not going to happen, Captain. Your men will just have to put up with me."

"They wish to do more." A muscle under Korvel's right eye twitched. "Stefan and the dungeon master already plan how they will share you between them when Richard gives them permission to use you."

Share her? "Very funny."

He shook his head slowly. "Soon I think even my lord's permission will not matter to them. I cannot watch you and protect my master every hour of the day and night."

He wasn't kidding. Alex wasn't blind; she'd noticed how every Kyn male in the castle with the exception of Korvel and Richard had been looking at her. After a year of living with Michael, she also understood that most of the Kyn didn't behave like modern men. In their time, women had no rights, no value, and generally were treated worse than farm animals.

Which was how, apparently, Stefan and the dungeon troll wanted to treat her.

It should have made her furious, and probably would when she thought about it, but Korvel was doing her a favor by warning her like this.

"I'm not deliberately leading them on," she assured him. "I wouldn't; I'm not stupid."

"This I know." His voice lost some of its edge. "You must take care not to be alone with any of the men."

"Right." She pressed her fingers against her temples, which were pounding. "What makes it stop?"

"Keep your emotions in check. Freeze the anger you feel. The more emotional you become, the more scent you shed. Do not think about Cyprien." He crouched down to put himself on her eye level. "I shall do what I can, but you must discipline yourself."

She was shedding scent now; the whole room smelled of lavender. For the first time she caught his scent, too. It was something like pound cake fresh out of the oven. Vanilla pound cake.

Kyn bodies gave off an appealing sweet scent that acted like a superpheromone; it enabled them to hunt and mesmerize humans long enough to feed on them. Alex didn't realize the scent affected Kyn as well, but then thought of how often the scent of roses—Michael's scent—had aroused her. Other Kyn scent didn't have the same effect. Phillipe's made her feel warm and secure. Valentin Jaus's had brought a familiar, comfortable sensation, like a hug from a friend.

As tasty as it was, Korvel's scent only made her want to punch him.

Someday Alex would study Kyn pheromones and figure it all out. For now, she had to find out how much trouble she was facing here. "Éliane said what I'm feeling—this *sygkenis* separation anxiety—would get worse. Can I control that?"

"To test the bond between master and *sygkenis* invites torment," Korvel said. "To deny it drives those who suffer to madness and violence."

"What?" She was appalled that Michael had never told her about this. What else didn't she know? "How soon does it happen? How will I know?"

He stood up and suddenly wouldn't look at her. "You are different. My master says, more human than we are. It may not be the same for you."

"Give me a ballpark, then." When he didn't answer, she added, "Korvel, I didn't know anything about this, and I can't fix what I don't understand. Talk to me."

"You cannot fix this. You will lose all control." He faced her. "It will either destroy your bond with Cyprien or your sanity."

The only time she had lost control was with Michael, and that had been strictly sexual. "I just don't see that happening."

"As I said, you are different." Korvel shrugged.

Alex felt like slapping him, but only because what he had said made sense. She was running on nerves, not thinking clearly—and anger had been her best friend lately. Then there was Thierry Durand, and the insanity he had suffered after believing that his Kyn wife had been tortured to death. "If I do this—become violent—will Richard give me back to Michael?"

"He may, if you do as he asks," Korvel said as he went to the door.

"And if I don't? What then?"

"If you lose your bond to Cyprien, likely nothing. But if you lose your mind . . ." He glanced back at her. "He will have me take your head."

What Adélie had told Nick sent her out of the inn to make some rounds of the village shops. She bought a few overpriced trinkets in order to coax more stories out of the shopkeepers and clerks, but it wasn't all that difficult to get them to talk. No one liked the château any more than they did its surly caretaker.

"Two Gypsy families came through town a month ago," the grocer told her. "They camp by water, and found a place near *le château* where the Basque did not see them."

Nick spotted an impact wrench kit sitting next to a refrigerated meat case and picked it up. "This for sale?"

"No. I do not sell such things." He frowned at the kit. "Someone must have left it here." He looked at Nick. "The Gypsies always stay here for the summer, but they left a day after they arrived. The woman came here for supplies before they went north. She told me that the water turned red under the moonlight, and that their dog never stopped barking until dawn."

Nick gathered some other interesting gossip about Father Claudio and the château. The village priest had been repeatedly called upon by the parish to visit Father Claudio and bless the ruin, but he flatly refused to go within a mile of the old man or the château, and repeatedly warned his congregation to stay away.

A wayward cow from a valley dairy had strayed onto the château's property, and never gave milk again. The butcher's wife, a robust and cheerful woman who had never been ill a day in her life, had become ill with a mysterious rash that seemed to drain away her vitality more each day until her husband took her to the hospital. The doctors claimed it was a bad case of anemia, but the villagers knew better.

"That wretched place is cursed," the flower seller confided to Nick. "I for one will sleep better when it is demolished."

The scents of the flowers made Nick's stomach roll— she hated flowers—and she gritted her teeth. "Are there any plans to do that?"

"No," the old woman admitted. "Only talk of diverting the stream away from *le château.*"

"Why?"

She grimaced. "The farmers say it collects in stagnant pools there, where mosquitoes and flies breed."

Nick's last stop was the village garage, where she talked the owner into selling her the hand tools she needed. Once she told him that she would use them to work on her bike, he warmed to her and related his own story about the château.

"The crazy Basque come to the village with three men in a big truck, stop here to buy petrol and cigarettes," he said as he loaded the hand tools into a sturdy box. "One of them ask where he find a brickyard. I say to him, 'Hey, you need that work done for you, you hire me and my sons.' We fix wall, build new one, whatever he want. We build half the houses in the village."

"But they didn't hire you," Nick guessed.

The garage owner spit on the ground. "He say it for *le château*. I tell him there are no enough brick in France, fix that. The crazy Basque, he start telling me shut up, you know? And him a priest! So I forget where the brickyard is. And when the truck come back, such a pity, but I have no more petrol to sell them."

"Excellent payback." Nick looked past him at the beautifully organized rack of tools hanging behind his counter and saw a telling space. "You lose an electric impact wrench kit?"

The shops had closed by the time Nick returned to the inn, and only the small café at the corner seemed to be doing any business. Young and old couples sat outside, watching the sky darken as they gossiped and enjoyed their wine and crudités. Nick decided to check out the patrons at the café, and took the tools up to her room. She then walked down to the café and found an empty corner table where she could sit and observe.

The sound of hammering, Nick thought. The butcher's wife and her mysterious rash. Looking for a brickyard.

Someone had installed an old Wurlitzer jukebox at the back of the cafe, which played a polyglot of old French love songs and bopping tunes from the fifties. As Bill Haley and the Comets rocked around the clock, Nick noticed she had attracted some attention. An older teenager at the bar had turned around and was staring at her from behind a half-empty bottle of beer.

"His name is Bernard," the waitress told her as she brought the glass of wine Nick had ordered. "He likes foreign women."

She studied the bold smile the boy gave her. "Glad to hear it." She dug a couple of bills out of her pocket, but the young woman shook her head.

"The wine is from him," the waitress said, and giggled. "I think he likes you." She went to wait on the next table.

Bernard climbed down from the bar stool and sauntered over to Nick's table. "Hey. American, right?"

"Right." Nick watched him as he turned the chair across from hers around and sat down. "Thanks for the drink."

He acknowledged her gratitude by scooting closer and lowering his voice to a seductive murmur. "Anything for you, baby."

Get away from me and forget you ever saw me. Nick smiled through her weary irritation. "You live around here?"

"Here and in our country house," Bernard advised her. "My father is mayor of the village."

That changed things. Nick noted the lack of razor stubble and the Silent Poets T-shirt. The mayor's son might be coming on to her like Valentino, but he was probably just a kid. "How old are you?"

"Twenty-two. Older than you, *chérie.*" He waggled his eyebrows. "Old enough, eh?"

Nick felt a thousand years old. Old and tired of boys on the make, tired of a world that most often looked through lust-blind eyes. She hadn't slept in forty-eight hours. She was planning to do something that was at worst going to get her shot and at best killed. Bernard hitting on her, she didn't need.

I have to find the Madonna. Use him.

"Old enough," she agreed. His eyes zeroed in on her fingers as she toyed with the stem of the wineglass. "You ever heard any stories about the Golden Madonna?"

"Lettice, the butcher's wife, she is wild for the Madonna. Statues in the shop, in the garden, in her windows . . ." He shrugged as if to say she was crazy but it couldn't be helped. "Me, not so much. Why go to church when I can be getting down with the real ladies, you know?"

Nick doubted he'd gotten down much farther than first base yet, but she nodded agreeably. "I like to take pictures of the Madonna. Do you know where Lettice lives?"

"In the flat above the butcher shop," Bernard said. He caught the lapel of her jacket between his fingers and gave it a slow, suggestive stroke. "But, hey, you're not going anywhere but here, right, baby?"

"Yeah, right." Nick caught his hand and curled her fingers around it. "You ever see Lettice out walking anywhere outside town?"

"Sure. She goes into the woods all the time." Bernard licked his lips and shifted his legs, trying to disguise the erection straining at the crotch of his shorts. "She picks *les cèpes*, the wild mushrooms to sell in the shop. You want to go back to your room, baby? I show you a good time."

For a moment Nick imagined it. The beer on his breath didn't mask the smell of his skin, and his penis was standing up and begging for her like a friendly puppy. He'd be rough and clumsy, or quick and clumsy, but that didn't matter. Boys like him were fast learners. Young and strong as he was, he'd last until dawn. She could show him a few tricks along the way.

His hand slid over hers where it rested on the table. "Come on," he urged. "Let's go make the magic."

His touch made the faint shimmer of desire in her belly flare. Why shouldn't she? Nick didn't have sex that often, and she missed it, missed the skin-to-skin intimacy and the welcome burst of the release. He'd love it, and he'd be safer with her than with some skanky backpacker busy screwing her way through Europe and spreading STDs. *He's as old as I was when—*

"Not tonight." Disgusted with herself, Nick drained her wineglass and tucked some bills under the base. "Thanks, Bernard." She stood, and then bent and picked up the wallet on the floor next to his chair, and put it in his hand. "You should go home now. Rest up, you know, for the ladies." Without looking back at him she strode out of the café.

Chapter 6

Incense and peppermint, crimson and cloves . . . rings on her fingers and bells on her toes . . . she will have sunlight wherever she goes . . .

John Keller rolled over into soft cloth and coughed, his throat sore and his nose throbbing. The foul taste in his mouth told him that he'd been sick, but his stomach seemed all right now that he was . . .

Where?

He pushed himself up on his elbows to check the room. He didn't recognize the bed or the furnishings, but they weren't hotel quality. This was someone's room, someone's house.

He had been stripped of his clothes and dressed in some sort of oversize white shirt that hung to his knees. He reached up to rub the last of the sleep from his eyes and saw a deep scratch on the back of his hand.

Hey, daddykins. Want to go for a ride?

The red-haired girl who had bumped into him in the garage; somehow she'd managed to drug him. The man in the pale blue suit must have been a part of it. John remembered the strong smells of peppermint and cloves, and assumed the two had been Kyn. But why defy Michael Cyprien and risk exposing themselves to abduct a washed-out human priest?

A heavy, cloying scent wafted around him. "Good evening, John Patrick."

He flipped over to face a petite blond woman dressed in

what appeared to be a ball gown made of apricot-colored lace. She stood at the foot of the bed, her hands folded demurely in front of her full skirt. Thin coils of golden braid made gleaming circlets around a face that Botticelli might have loved painting.

"Who are you?"

"You may call me 'my lady.' " She walked around to the side of the bed, drawing the coverlet up over his bare legs. "Your clothes are being cleaned—apparently you became very ill on the plane—but soon they will be returned to you."

The floral scent came from her, and it was growing stronger. John tried to focus on what she'd said. "You had me kidnapped and brought here? Why?"

"My lady," she prompted.

"Why, my lady?" John heard himself say.

"We often entertain special guests here." She reached out to touch his face, and pursed her lips when he scrambled out of reach. "There's no reason to avoid my touch, John Patrick. I look forward to the two of us becoming very close during your stay."

Her words sounded sweet, but they felt tinny inside John's ears. Her perfect teeth glittered, small and sharp and white. Staring at them reminded him of the damp, decaying cloy of rotting wood . . . old fruit crates in an alley, behind a produce warehouse where he had slept as a kid . . . and the rats that came out of the crates at night, looking for meat. . . .

Her smile widened. "Sweet boy, don't be afraid. I'll look after you."

"No." Panic forced John backward again, until he half fell off the side of the bed. The cold floor under his feet cleared some of the terror out of his head. This wasn't Chicago. He wasn't eight years old anymore. He picked up a table lamp and pulled the cord free. "Is this the castle? Do you have my sister?"

"All of your questions will be answered in good time." The lady turned back the coverlet, giving the bed an inviting pat with her hand. "You should rest now. Or are you hungry? I can arrange to have a tray brought up to you."

Hungry. The way the rats had been. And she knew that, knew somehow that he had lived in fear of the street scavengers biting him or baby Alex. She knew, and he could see in her eyes that it gave her some sort of twisted pleasure to know his fear.

John knew fear better than most people. This woman was deliberately making him relive memories that brought out the worst of his emotions. *To control me and make me do what she wants.*

"You're Kyn." He backed away from the bed and eyed the single window in the room. It was closed, and there were copper bars securing it on the outside. "Tell whoever's in charge that I need to speak to him."

"Don't run away just yet, John Patrick," the lady said, her words curling into voracious squeals in his ears. "We have so much to discuss."

The stink of dead flowers seemed to be burning away all the oxygen in the room. The lady didn't move, but something about her changed, and John remembered how still the rats would go, only their whiskers twitching, just before they jumped on a leg and bit down into a child's soft, vulnerable flesh—

"Help me." He stumbled to the door and tried to open it at the same time someone pushed it in from the other side.

"Sorry, lad." A huge hand clamped on John's shoulder and guided him back as a shaggy blond head ducked under the low threshold. "You're not to go wandering."

John knew it was all a Kyn mind trick, but he still couldn't bring himself to look back at the lady. If he did he would scream.

"Please," he whispered, sweat chilling on his flushed skin. "Please don't leave me in here alone with her."

The giant man looked over John's shoulder and breathed in. "It's all right, lad. There's no one in here but you and me."

"She's standing right there, on the other side of the bed." John made himself turn and face her, only she wasn't there anymore. There was only the bed and the window. "She was in here. I swear—when I woke up she was waiting for me. I think she's making me hallucinate."

The man steered John back to the bed. "The drugs they gave you, they play tricks on the mind. I'll bring you a bite to eat; that should settle your belly."

He had been hallucinating? John sat down, confusion numbing away the terror. "She seemed so real." He looked up. "Where am I? Why was I brought here?"

The guard only shook his head and left.

Nick had passed the butcher's shop on her information junket around the village, but this time she went down a narrow side street and came around the back of the shop. Light shone through one of the windows on the ground floor, and she peered in to see what was happening inside. The butcher stood with his back to her as he worked portioning and packaging various cuts of meat.

On the sill of the window was a small blue-and-white ceramic statue of the blessed Virgin Mary, her hands extended, her smile as modest as her downcast eyes.

Nick looked up the length of the building. No fire escape, but a drainpipe went up past the open window on the second floor. She could pull herself up by grabbing the strips of metal anchoring it to the building. An electrical panel and a good-sized exhaust fan unit beneath the upper window would provide some footholds.

Nick pulled off her boots and set them out of sight behind a stack of empty wooden crates before she tested the drainpipe with a hard tug. It didn't part company with the building, so she climbed atop the crates and swung over onto the pipe. After waiting another few seconds to be sure it would hold her weight, she reached up for the edge of the exhaust fan unit.

She was halfway to the upper window when a delivery

bell jingled, and the back door of the shop opened. The butcher stepped outside, two full trash bags in his hands. Nick went still, hoping the shadow of the building concealed her. The butcher dropped the bags into a can and came back to the door, then paused.

Don't look up don't look up don't—

The man below sat down on the edge of one of the crates, took out a cigarette, and lit it.

Nick didn't dare breathe. She felt her weight dragging at the drainpipe, and measured the space between her and the window. Four feet might as well have been forty; even if she moved fast he'd hear her and look up before she could crawl into the window.

It took the butcher ten minutes to finish his smoke before he went back inside. Nick gradually unlocked her stiff limbs and hauled herself up to the window. Another, larger statue of the Madonna stood in one corner of the window; this one had been draped with a gold-and-white-beaded crucifix. The full moon illuminated the bedroom beautifully, and Nick made sure the woman inside was sleeping soundly before she climbed over the windowsill.

White scrolled furniture picked up the moon's glow, filtered as it was through the fine lace curtains. Nick eyed the heavily ruffled bed skirt and feather-stuffed satin comforter neatly rolled up at the foot of the bed, also pure white. Milk-glass lamps with fussy lace shades and a creamy-looking carpet made her feel as if she'd stepped into a bowl of vanilla ice cream.

Statues of the Madonna in various sizes had been placed on virtually every flat surface in the room. Lettice favored the standing Mary, but here and there were small reproductions of Pietàs and the Annunciation. A benevolent portrait of the Blessed Mother beamed down from elaborate frames hung in the center of each wall. Some of the frames were antiques, but not one of the Madonnas was golden.

Lettice's light snores sounded regular, and as Nick

moved to the side of the bed she was surprised to see that the woman's pretty face was covered with what looked like a bad case of the measles under some opaque, dried skin lotion. She wore a plain cotton slip for sleeping, and had pushed the sheet covering her down to her waist. The same type of rash as on her face also marked her arms, neck, and chest. Under more of the skin lotion, the tiny red blisters formed a vee just below her collarbone, marking her in the same way that a sunburn might if she had been wearing a blouse with an open collar.

Nick silently searched the room, but found nothing. She then leaned over the woman, inspecting her welts. With the amount of lotion she had applied, it was hard to tell, but Nick saw no signs of puncture wounds, gashes, or tears. On a patch of skin Lettice had missed while applying her topical medication, Nick noted that the rash was not made up of pustules, but rather something more like insect bites.

She's stung, not bitten. Nick felt perplexed. *If they're not tapping the locals, then how are they feeding it?*

Unless they weren't feeding it.

The sound of a dead bolt being turned below her feet made Nick hurry. She bent as close as she dared to the woman and sniffed her skin. All she could smell was soap, dried herbs—likely from a sachet in the drawer where the slip had been kept—and the chalky scent of the rash lotion. Not a hint of flowers.

Something's not right.

Footsteps thumped; the butcher was coming upstairs. Nick looked out the window before climbing out and onto the drainpipe. It shimmied a little this time, so she slid down as fast as she dared, hopping off and grabbing her boots. She didn't pause to put them on, but carried them tucked under her arm as she hurried around the corner. Only when she was out of sight of the butcher shop did she halt and push her feet into them.

She'd get back on the computer and pull every incident report she could find on this village and the surrounding area. With all the "bad luck" being blamed on the château, there had to be something.

"You left me alone," a young, slurred voice said in French from behind her. "American women are whores. My father says so."

Shit. Nick turned to see Bernard coming at her, his gait uneven, a fresh bottle of beer in his hand. He didn't look like he wanted to go back to her room now.

"Yep, we're all whores." It was better than arguing with him. "Now go home, kid."

"Kid? Who you calling the kid?" He took a swig from his beer before smashing the bottle against the brick wall of the alley. Beer splashed his legs and foamed around his feet. "I was nice to you. I bought you the wine. Then you try to steal my money."

"I *found* your wallet on the floor and gave it to you," she pointed out.

"The men at the café, they saw. You made me look like a fool. They laughed at me." He tried to take a drink from the broken bottle, stared at it as if not sure what it was, and then held it up. "See what you made me do, American whore?"

"No charge. Bye." Nick turned and started walking fast.

He caught up to her, whirled her around, and held the broken end of the bottle under her nose. "You pay for this."

Bernard meant business, and was just sober enough to inflict some real damage. She'd left her baseball bat back at the inn. There were no police in the village; she'd made sure of that.

"Don't hurt me," Nick said, putting a whimper behind the words as she dropped down on her knees.

Bernard smiled at her as he yanked down his zipper. "Maybe I won't; maybe I will. . . ." His voice dwindled to a strained wheeze as he looked down.

Grabbing a man by the testicles always shut him up in a hurry, Nick observed as she increased the pressure. She could have ended this confrontation another way—an easier, simpler way—but the village had no police, and Bernard might try this again with another tourist. There were too many young women knocking around Europe who didn't know how to protect themselves against mayors' sons on the make.

"Drop the bottle now," she said pleasantly, giving his balls a small, neat twist, "or I'll make you into a Bernice."

He threw the bottle away.

Slowly Nick stood without relaxing her grip. As she did, his body did the exact opposite, hunching over, comically paying tribute to the strength of her hold.

Now for the Q&A. "Have you ever raped a woman, Bernard?"

He shook his head, still unable to speak.

"Good. Because if you had, I might separate you from these." Nick put her mouth close to his ear. " 'I'll never hurt or threaten to hurt a woman again.' Say it."

He managed to squeak out the words.

"Very good, Bernard. Now you're going straight home and get some ice for this. The swelling will go down in a day or two." She lowered her voice to a whisper. "Every time you get angry at a woman, I want you to remember this pain."

He nodded frantically, almost doubled over.

"I'll be in France for a while, and I'll be checking on this village." Time for the big finish. With her free hand she took the stiletto out of her jacket pocket and popped the blade, touching his cheek with the flat of it. "I hear some girl gets hurt, you know who I'm going to come back and castrate."

He didn't move, but liquid spattered on the road between them, and the scent of urine grew thick.

"I see you do." Nick took her hand out of his pants and kept the stiletto between them. "I don't want to ever see your face again, Bernard. Make sure that happens."

She watched as he clutched at his crotch with a shaking hand and went down on his knees. She didn't hang around to watch him vomit, but headed back to the inn.

Once up in her room, she stripped off her jacket and ignored her laptop as she dropped onto the bed. The run-in with Bernard had left a bad taste in her mouth. He'd deserved the pain, but she had gotten too angry. If she'd really let loose on him . . .

I didn't cripple him, and I didn't hurt him permanently. I taught him a lesson. Lesson learned. Let it go.

She decided against working on the computer. If there had been anything real going on in this place, she would have found it by now. It was all smoke and superstition—a product of living isolated lives in a small, out-of-the-way village. Lettice was just another European woman obsessed with the Virgin Mary.

The Golden Madonna was not here in St. Valereye.

As for the dreams, they could only be a coincidence. The hammering sounds, sick locals, and water that turned the color of blood would have to be someone else's problem. Whatever was going on with Father Claudio and his broken-down château would have to resolve itself without her.

She'd get twelve hours of sleep and then leave the village tomorrow and head north. She'd passed through the village of St. Estéphe on the way here from Paris; doubtless there were some old churches and chapels around the Gironde River estuary, or tucked away behind the endless acres of vineyards with their clusters of dark purple grapes.

Despite her resolve, Nick didn't sleep, not for hours. Finally near dawn she drifted off, and in her dreams went home.

She knew she was back home on the farm, although she couldn't see anything. She could hear the cows, smell the bread baking in the kitchen, and felt the familiar dampness of the country air. She didn't recognize where she was at first, until she smelled herbs. Her mother had grown them, bundled them, and hung them to dry.

Someone had locked her in the cold pantry.

"Nicky?" Her mother was there, too, a disembodied voice, hovering somewhere just over her head.

"Mom?" Nick turned around, looking up, trying to see through the blackness.

"Nicky, I won't tolerate another minute of this," Annette Jefferson said, her sweet voice furious. "Come out. Come out of there this instant!"

A door appeared, although not the weathered wooden one at the farm. This one was made of pure gold, and shaped like a peaceful woman's face. It shook from the pounding someone on the other side was giving it.

"Wait." Nick reached for the face/knob, but it scowled at her and began moving up and sideways and down on the door, always just an inch or two out of her reach. "I can't get out, Mom. I don't know how."

"Open the door, Nicola." The deeper, kinder voice belonged to Malcolm, her stepdad. "Let us in and we'll help you. Come on, girl. We'll put on the kettle. I'll make that Irish tea you like so much."

Despite her stepdad's soothing words, Nick was abruptly afraid to let them in. Her parents had the keys; she knew that. They had put her in here, locked her in, hadn't they? So why did they want her to open the door?

The knob grinned at her. "They saw you watching, Nicola. They knew. Before they died, they knew."

She backed into a tall, hard cabinet, and turned to see its doors opening. Books packed the four shelves at the top, as well as the three long drawers someone had left open on the bottom. There was more light now, although from where it was coming, Nick couldn't tell. She read the titles on the book spines—*Le Voyage d'Hiver, Quand Je Dors, Amour Immortel*—and wondered why her mother had been hiding French books.

Annette couldn't read French; neither could Malcolm. That was why he'd sent for the translation of the old book he'd found. The one with the legends of the Golden Madonna. To be sure what he had dug up from the cellar was real.

"*. . . aurem tuam ad preces nostras,*" Malcolm was

reciting on the other side of the closet door, *"quibus mis-
ericordiam tuam supplices deprecamur, ut animam famuli
tui Abbadon . . ."*

The cabinet fell forward onto her. Nick had time only to
fling her arms over her head before she was dragged into
the cabinet and through a mirror that didn't shatter. On the
other side stood the dark figure of a man, his hands tied together, his eyes covered by a black shadow, like a blindfold. He stood bent over, bowed by the weight of the cape
on his shoulders. A green cape, edged in pine needles.

You cannot leave me.

Nick went to him, ripping the rope from his hands.
Where are you?

I do not know. Find me. His freed hands framed her
face. *And I will save us.* Blood trickled out from under the
black shadow over his eyes and ran down his cheeks. He
was weeping blood.

She couldn't bear to see him like this. *How can I find
you? Tell me, please, and I'll leave right away. I'll come to
you as soon as I wake up.*

You were there. Come back to me.

Nick found herself back in the cold pantry, alone, and
terribly afraid. Something had gnawed through the base of
the wood. The sight of it made her shudder; she hated rats.

The hole began to grow.

In a panic she backed away, her shoulders colliding
with the golden door. The knob opened its mouth, baring
jagged teeth, and tried to bite her. The hole stretched up
and out until it became large enough for her to walk
through it.

Nick couldn't see what was on the other side. Light
poured out of the hole and onto her face, and the moment
it touched her all the fear and worry inside her melted
away.

Like the sun . . . Because she traveled mostly at night,
she hardly got outside during the day. *Feels so warm . . .*

Gold and red and lovely, the light caressed her with the

touch of a reverent hand. The way his hands had felt on her face.

So nice. Nobody had ever touched her the way he did. She wanted to close her eyes and wallow in the sensation.

The light drew her, pulling her toward the hole, and although she couldn't see now, there was nothing she wanted to do more than to step through it to the other side.

What does he want? He couldn't want her; she was nothing, no one. She could feel his presence growing stronger. *What do you want from me?*

True ben wall.

His voice, low and soft, barely a whisper, speaking in the language she knew but could no longer understand. So much sadness, so much need, as if he were in terrible pain. She had to go to him, but . . .

Mah be yen ah me a day wall.

The light grew brighter and hotter, and it didn't feel so good anymore.

May a pell dee sang ah voh tray sang mah be yen ah me.

His light was going to suck her in and burn her up, like the fires of hell, and it was filling the closet and her head until she was sure it would scorch the eyes out of her sockets.

Non.

Nick stumbled back, away from the light, and screamed.

"Mademoiselle." Tight hands shook her. "Wake up, please; you must."

Nick woke up. She was sitting huddled in the corner of her room, her arms cradling her head. Sweat soaked her jeans and T-shirt, and she was shaking so hard that her teeth chattered.

"Are you hurt? You were shouting." Adélie crouched down and touched Nick's shoulder, making her jerk with reaction. "Was someone in here?" She looked around the room quickly.

"No. It was only a bad dream." Nick felt as if she might

throw up or start screaming, or both, but then the innkeeper's wife might call for an ambulance. "Sorry. I didn't mean to wake you."

Adélie drew back. "You could not help it." She reached down and helped her to her feet. "Go back to bed. I will bring you some warm milk. That will help you sleep."

That *would* make her puke. "No, I think I'll be all right. Thank you for waking me up."

"If you are sure." The older woman waited until Nick stood straight, and then retreated to the door. She hesitated and looked back. "You miss your family, mademoiselle? It is still early in America, if you wish to use the telephone—"

"Thanks, but I'm okay." Nick sat down on the edge of the bed. She couldn't call anyone, because there was no one left to call. The neighbors still believed that her parents had gone over to America to start a farm there, leaving Nick behind to live on their English property. No one suspected that Annette and Malcolm Jefferson had been dead for years. Dead and in unmarked graves in the middle of Annette's rose garden.

Nick knew because she had buried them there.

Chapter 7

Gabriel spent the long, empty hours in the darkness thinking about the woman Claudio had chased off, and working on his right wrist. The reality of her stayed with him, feeding his hope as nothing else could. Her memory remained so vivid and warm that he could almost still taste her in every breath he took.

What is her name? In his imagination, she was his maiden from the dreams, slim and strong, pale curls dancing around her young face. In reality, she might be plump and dark or flame-haired and angular. It didn't matter. He guessed from the dreams that she would be quiet, perhaps shy. *Does she dream of me?*

Frustration over the little he did know about her made him renew his efforts to prepare for her return. He could not call out to her, and his bonds prevented any real movement. Yet while attempting to move, he discovered that the wound in one of his wrists had stopped festering and had partially healed. Gabriel found that he could clench his fist and extend his fingers and, by doing so, widen the wound in his wrist. After he did so several times, it bled slowly, sluggishly.

Thanks to his weakness, it did not heal.

After a day of his working at it, his wound widened. He discovered that if he flexed his arm a certain way, the give in the wound allowed enough movement for him to rattle the chains binding him.

He didn't waste his energy making noise for old Claudio to hear, but concentrated on keeping the wound from healing again. Losing more blood was dangerous, but if she returned—when she returned—he stood a better chance of attracting her attention and bringing her within range of his scent—and under his command.

She would return, of course. She had to return.

To keep from worrying and wasting scent, Gabriel rehearsed everything in his head. He would lure her down to the basement. Once she came within hearing range, he could make enough noise for her to find his cell. His scent would do the rest. This was assuming that she was not resistant to *l'attrait*. Some humans were.

No, fate would not play such a joke on him.

The human female would have to break through the wall and free him before old Claudio discovered her presence. Gabriel didn't think the old man would harm her, but he couldn't leave that to chance. She didn't deserve to be injured or killed for helping him.

He would have to use his talent to keep the old man busy and out of the basement.

As he planned it out in his mind, a part of him emerged from his thoughts, the part that he most needed to protect the woman and ensure the success of his plan. It was a cold, unfeeling copy of himself, eager to return to the brimming void of the many that his talent stirred. It had no emotions left, save the desire to survive and to join with the many.

It wanted to use the woman in another way. *She will feed you well, make you strong enough to escape alone.*

Gabriel had always resisted the obvious, oblivious hunger—he knew too well how it could devour the soul—but over time the coldness had grown stronger and more persuasive.

As soon as she comes, summon the many, and take her.

Gabriel knew he would have to take some of her blood in order to regain his strength and heal enough to make his escape. Like all the other Kyn, he had always healed spontaneously when he fed well. His one worry was his control.

Since capturing him, the Brethren had never fed him.

One of the interrogators had told Gabriel how surprised they were that he did not waste away as quickly as other Kyn they had captured. They never realized what he resorted to in order to obtain his nourishment, or how often he had taken small amounts from the various interrogators who had tortured him during his captivity. They believed the many were visited upon him by their vengeful God, as part curse and part endorsement of their brutality.

Gabriel had never enjoyed feeding from humans. His dependency on blood was an unpleasant part of his immortal existence; he barely tolerated it. His distaste and self-discipline were such that he had never once fallen into bloodlust, or suffered from thrall, the dream state induced by draining all of the blood from a human. Even when he had emerged from his grave, something had held him back from freely attacking humans. He wanted to believe it was compassion, but perhaps it was fear for whatever was left of his soul.

We will need all of her blood to leave this place.

Gabriel's disgust faded as his hunger and his coldness engulfed him. There was logic to it, and he would not have to hurt her. The many would take her, and by doing so would prevent any blood thrall from immobilizing him. They would see to it that she would not suffer. He had lived in daily torment for years; if she came to him he had the right to take her. As for the old man, he need not protect his life, either. The many would deal with him as well—

No.

Gabriel sagged in his bonds. Whatever came of this, he would not kill the woman, nor the old man. He would keep them both safe. Especially the woman; he would have to take certain measures to keep her from becoming yet another victim of the Brethren.

If she returned. *When* she returned.

Gabriel worked at his wrist until the wound burned and the need to sleep dragged at him with brutal weight. It came like this more often now, as if his exhausted body utterly rebelled against him. He needed to rest, to conserve himself, but if she came while he was sleeping . . . And that was his last thought as he drifted past the dark borders of the nightlands.

The forest gave way to rolling green pastures and the gentle creatures who roamed them. Gabriel walked through crisp, deliciously cool grass, breathing in the earthy scents that he had almost forgotten. His kinship with the land had always been a comfort, although he did not recognize this place. The rich, black soil here did not smell of home.

Go back, a part of him whispered. *This is no place for you.*

There was nothing to fear that Gabriel could see but a charming, whitewashed farmhouse. It was a humble structure, hardly more than an overbuilt cottage, but those who lived there had planted gardens and kept the grounds neat. Peonies and larkspur created splashes of color as they lined a little flagstone path leading to the back of the house.

Go back. She said the words now, and her voice held a note of fear. *You shouldn't be here. Please.*

He ignored the warning and hurried forward into an enormous flower garden. Roses and carnations bunched around a copper fountain with a marble statue of the Virgin Mary as its centerpiece. The marble glowed with a strange, fiery color, as if the statue had been carved from hot metal that had never cooled.

How can I find you? her voice called out to him from the shadows of the garden.

Gabriel had no name for where he had left his body. *You were there. Come back to me.*

Black-feathered chickens, hunting through the grass and pecking at bugs, swarmed around his bare feet. He paused to admire the dark rainbow sheen of their glossy plumage; even the dozen little chicks racing to follow their mother hen had down of pure ebony. A dark rooster snatched at the edge of his tunic, making Gabriel glance down.

He wore the cassock of a Brethren, the breast embroidered with five red crosses. It took a moment for him to connect the number with what had happened to him: one for every Kyn who had been taken with him.

Thierry, Jamys, Marcel, Liliette. The names burned into his heart. *Angelica.*

You shouldn't have come here.

She came out of the rose garden, his pale maiden, but something terrible had been done to her. Her body had been bloodied and bruised, her cotton slip soiled with earth. In her hands she held a short tree branch with tight green leaves and clusters of silver-blue berries.

He reached out to touch her cheek and froze as she recoiled. *I mean you no harm.*

The harm's been done. She pushed the branch into his hands as if she couldn't bear to hold it a moment longer. *Do you love me?*

He loved the presence of her, the way she soothed him, the sadness in her eyes that sang to the torment in his heart. He loved that she came to him and spoke to him even though he was not part of her quest. He loved the interludes she shared with him on her journey through the nightlands.

Real or imagined, he loved her.

But she did not know the horror of what he had become, and he would not inflict himself upon her. *I am not like other men. I cannot—*

She threw herself at him, her hands grabbing his shoulders as her body stiffened against him. When he looked down, he saw that she had impaled herself on the juniper branch.

Her eyes met his. *When I come to you, I want you to kill me.*

Ma bien-aimée. She could not wish to die. He stared

down at the wound in her belly, and saw the juniper branch disappear into it. He put his hand against it, trying to stanch the flow of silver-blue blood gushing from her. *Never.*

You have to be the one. Tears cleaned a path to her jaw. *I can't do it. I don't know how. I can't find the way.*

The flock of chickens crowded around them, pecking at the blood pooling around their feet. Gabriel swept her up into his arms and carried her into the rose garden, looking for something to dress her wound. Then his arms emptied, and he stood among the roses, at the edge of a deep, rectangular pit. He looked down and saw her body, limp and lifeless. The sides of the grave began falling in on her, burying her. He tried to jump in, to lift her out, but his body would not move. Tears of rage and frustration blinded him.

Don't cry. Her eyes opened just before the earth covered her face. *I can't love you either.*

"Their name is Legion," Father Orson Leary murmured, lighting a candle with a shaking hand, "for they are many."

He had been kneeling before the statue of Saint Paul and beseeching him all morning, but his patron saint offered no consolation. No matter how many prayers he offered, the stern, beloved face, rendered so aptly in the slate gray marble, stared down at him with silent disapproval. If Saint Paul could speak, Leary knew how he would chastise him.

Do you not know that you are the temple of God and that the spirit of God dwells in you? If anyone defiles the temple of God, God will destroy him. For the temple of God is holy, which temple you are* . . . you were . . .

Saint Paul had deserted Orson Leary, as had the Father. It was no better than he deserved. Michaelmas loomed ahead, a black date on the calendar when he would once again be obliged to fulfill the bargain he had made with the demons. Leary had tried to resist in the past; spending days

---

*1 Corinthians 3:16–17, NKJV

in prayer, bathing in blessed water, partaking of the host, and purifying himself in every manner he knew before the day of obligation arrived. None of it had rid him of the evil he suffered. The only time he had not obliged them, he had been made to bleed from Christ's wounds for a fortnight.

The Mother had known. Her spirit had flown through the night and found him huddled and weeping in the silence of the church.

What do you here, my son?

Leary would not think of her, or her laughter, or the ways she used him. She polluted the purity of his body and mind. She had made him violate the sanctity of his oath. Surely Saint Paul could see that it was she who had defiled his carnal temple.

Prayer would not save him, however, any more than the demons would.

He had struck a bargain with their Demon King. Richard had promised to save his sanity—a reward for the evil Leary did on his behalf—but the demon himself was now going insane.

Leary feared Richard. His demonic form and insidious voice marked him as a creature of hell. But when Richard had offered the bargain, Leary had been desperate enough to cling to it, the only earthly hope of winning back his soul. Leary had believed Richard could save him, until he had learned that Richard had slaughtered his own servants on Midsummer Eve. Not as a sacrifice to the Evil One, but on a mere whim, as a cat let loose in a rats' nest kept killing even after its belly was full.

Perhaps the Mother had done this to the Demon King to prevent Leary from escaping her. He would not put it past her. Her evil affected all men.

Leary tried to see his dilemma as blessed suffering, the sort of evil to which the Apostle himself had been subjected. Had not Saint Paul been beaten with rods, thrust in stocks, stoned, and pursued by the wicked? Delivered by the wicked unto wild beasts, thrown from a wall, defamed, bound, and beaten, Saint Paul had withstood everything in the name of God—and perhaps guilt over his own crimes before Jesus Christ had saved him.

*For you have heard of my former conduct in Judaism, how I persecuted the church of God beyond measure and tried to destroy it.**

The Apostle had gone to Rome even when he had known it would mean his death. Courageous Saint Paul had to stand before the mightiest of men—the Emperor Nero himself—not to be judged, but to show that he could not be judged. It was why the emperor had put him to death. The greatest of the Apostles, the hand of God on earth, had shamed him.

Perhaps that was what Leary had to do: stand before the Demon King, and allow him to consume him with his madness.

"Begging your pardon, Father." Tim Bright, the cleaning woman's son who came in to help her sweep up and dust on Fridays, approached him in a timid fashion. "My mum sent me to say that there's an international call for you. He wouldn't give a name, but Mum said he speaks English, and sounds like a Yank."

Leary knew who it was. "Thank you, Timothy." He rose, ignoring his stiff knees and numbed legs, and walked toward the little office beside the vestry.

The modern phone he had had installed upon taking over the church had some particular features known only to Leary. After closing and locking the office door, he pressed a button under the console that prevented anyone from listening in on the line.

His head pounded as he lifted the receiver to his ear. "Father Leary."

"Orson," the Brooklyn-accented voice on the other end of the line said. "I'm impressed. Not many brothers could spend all morning on their knees, staring at Saint Paul's hangnails."

*Galatians 1:13, NKJV

"I was in prayer, Your Grace." How Cardinal D'Orio always knew what he had been doing in the church wasn't a mystery; every church under Brethren control had hidden security cameras installed. Most Brethren never knew they were being watched; Leary had discovered the cameras by accident. "To what do I owe the pleasure of speaking with you?"

"Your general incompetence," Cardinal D'Orio said pleasantly. "Time to pack your bags again. I'm moving you to Ireland."

Leary's mind blanked. "Ireland?"

"That country to the north you Englishmen have never been able to keep in line," the cardinal said. "You'd be buried there, if you hadn't run out on your brothers in Dublin."

Dublin. Where it had all begun. Where it had to end.

"I had no warning." How easily and smoothly he lied now, as if the evil inside him took control of his tongue and spoke for him. "Had I known that the *maledicti* meant to attack, I would have stayed and died fighting with my brothers."

"You?" D'Orio made a contemptuous sound. "You'd have squealed and tried to run away like a little girl. But that doesn't matter anymore. You survived; they didn't. Now the monsters are coming for you."

Leary knew his transfer to the church in London had been only temporary, and that his days as a member of the order had been numbered. After Cardinal Stoss, the leader of the Brethren, had been murdered in America, the confusion within their ranks had been close to sheer chaos. Electing Cardinal D'Orio to serve as the new Lightkeeper had been a canny move by the Lightmaster; D'Orio was well-known for his dogged pursuit and elimination of traitors within the order.

But for all of D'Orio's zeal, the cardinal still did not know that Richard kept his stronghold in Ireland. If he had, the Lightkeeper would have moved heaven and earth to destroy it.

D'Orio was speaking to him again, Leary realized. "I'm

sorry, Your Grace, but our connection is poor. What did you say?"

"Get your head out of Saint Paul's ass and listen to me, Orson," the cardinal said. "Your prisoners are free. That bitch surgeon may have put their pieces back together, but they remember what you did to them. They're going to want revenge."

"They will find me." Of that he was sure.

"That's why you're going to make excellent bait. Get a paper and pen and write this down." D'Orio gave him contact names and numbers for Brethren in Ireland. "You're taking over the parish in Bardow. Pack and go up by train. A rental will be waiting for you in Galway. Don't travel under your own name."

Bardow was the name of a village not twenty miles from Dundellan Castle. "Wouldn't it be better if I stayed in the city? I could—"

"No." D'Orio's voice changed. "You'll go where you're told, and you'll watch for them. Don't screw this up, Orson. It's your last chance to prove your loyalty to me."

The line clicked abruptly.

Leary's fears bloomed inside him. He could not go to Bardow. He was too frightened now. Through fear he would be made clumsy, and he would betray himself to both the Brethren and the *maledicti*. Richard would never believe that he had been assigned to Bardow for any reason other than to expose him to the order. If Leary could escape the Demon King's wrath, the order would provide no haven to him. D'Orio would never forgive him for what he had done, or what he had concealed from them.

Leary walked out into the church. He could not pray for an answer; God had turned His face from him. He could pray for death, but in his disgust Saint Paul would likely make him immortal, so that he could suffer on until the end of time. The scent of flowers closed around him, and he glanced at the altar, but the vases were filled with lilies, not roses and wisteria.

"Are you Father Orson Leary?"

He turned to face a tall gentleman in an exquisitely tailored suit. White hair framed the man's chiseled features and streaked the dark mane that he had pulled back into a neat queue. Behind him, a beautiful black-haired woman and a scarred-faced man stood waiting by the altar.

D'Orio would not send a Frenchman to him. "I am."

"I would speak with you."

Leary looked past the man at the others. The dark-haired woman was not merely beautiful; she was stunning. Certainly far too lovely for the oversize brute standing at her side. He would have thought them tourists, but for the quality of their garments and the sweet, flowery fragrance coming from all three of them.

"You are Legion," he whispered.

The scarred-faced one stepped forward, his eyes intent.

"We are from America," the Frenchman was saying.

"I know what you are, and from where you come." Leary backed away. "Demons. Demons from the abyss." He looked around wildly. "This is holy ground. You cannot come here." His voice rose to a shout. "You trespass in the house of God!"

"Be calm, Father," the Frenchman said. "We will not harm you or your church."

Leary turned to run and found the scarred-faced giant in front of him. Someone screamed in horror and fear before shouting in Latin—was that his own voice?—and then a heavy hand landed on Leary's neck, and the air grew thick with honeysuckle. He tried again to run, but his body had turned to stone.

The scarred-faced man's cool amber eyes moved to look past him. "I have him, master."

Hell-eyed demon. She sent him. Leary began to shake.

The Frenchman came closer. "There is nothing to fear." He placed his hand against Leary's throat.

Heat poured through the priest's body, burning away

the honeysuckle that gripped him and the sourness of his own sweat.

Minutes, hours, an eternity later, the hands lifted, taking with them many things. All that had been muddled now had been made clear. The Mother, the Demon King, D'Orio, the order. The solution was so simple that Leary almost wept with relief.

Kill the women. All *the women.*

He smiled at his savior, the Frenchman. "How can I help you, my lord?"

Nick knew it was ridiculous letting one bad dream get to her, but no matter how hard she tried she couldn't forget what he'd said.

You were there. Come back to me.

He was at the château. Or in the village. Or maybe back in Paris. Wherever he was, she'd been there. He knew it. She knew it. She'd felt it.

Or it was wishful thinking, she knew nothing, and the dreams were finally getting to her in the worst way.

Nick made a bargain with herself: She'd go out to the château one more time and see what, if anything, the old guy was hiding. If it was nothing, she'd laugh it off and be on her way. If her dream guy was there, being held prisoner, she'd set him free.

Either way she'd blow this village like a bad taco stand tomorrow.

Nick felt certain that after the little lesson she'd taught Bernard, he wouldn't come after her, but she spent the day in her room updating her computer anyway. A few years back she'd scanned and transferred her map onto the system, and now marked off the places she'd been with a software program designed for bikers who enjoyed riding off the beaten path. The flags told her it was time to move on to Provence. After that, she'd probably head back to England and lie low for the winter.

She glanced at the little painting the baker in Paris had

given her. *Unless I find him, and he turns out to be one of them. Then what do I do?*

Nick switched off the laptop and for a moment pressed the heels of her hands against her dry eyes. "Quit thinking about it and get busy."

As she packed up the tools she thought she might need, she mentally reviewed the first and only trip she'd made out to the château. According to the villagers, Father Claudio was living in the cottage at the south corner of the property near the road; she'd do better to come in from the north. That meant riding at least ten miles out of the way, but she could park the bike out of sight in the woods and hike her way in.

Once she was inside the chapel, she'd check out the door behind the altar. It didn't lead into the collapsed side of the house, and the chapel's outer wall on that end was large enough to accommodate only a six-by-six-foot section. Based on her knowledge of old architecture, Nick was betting the door led to either a closet or a stairwell to a basement level.

She watched the sunset from her window before dressing in her newest black T-shirt, jeans, and leather jacket. She carried the tools she'd stowed in her gym bag in one hand and her helmet in the other, and made her way down the back stairs, watching to see that the way was clear before she slipped out through the inn's back door.

She'd left her bike behind the innkeeper's garden shed, where she could get to it easily but where it wouldn't be seen by the locals. As motorcycles went, hers was a mongrel: a twenty-five-year-old stock BMW GS out of which over the years she had torn the rotors, the transmission, and most of the electrical system. Removing all the decals and detailing, and spray-painting black the aluminum panniers in which she carried her gear, made the bike less flashy and therefore less memorable.

Nick would have preferred invisible, but no one had come up with stealth tech for motorcycles yet.

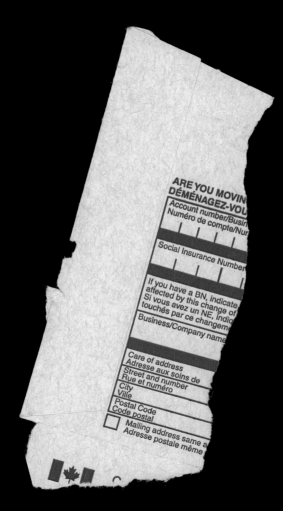

ARE YOU MOVIN
DÉMÉNAGEZ-VOU

Account number/Busin
Numéro de compte/Nur

Social Insurance Number

If you have a BN, indicate
affected by this change or
Si vous avez un NE, indic
touchés par ce changem

Business/Company name

Care of address
Adresse aux soins de

Street and number
Rue et numéro

City
Ville

Postal Code
Code postal

☐ Mailing address same a
Adresse postale même

NOTE:

IF YOU ARE MOVING OR IF THE
ADDRESS INFORMATION THAT
HAVE IS INCORRECT, COMPLE
THE BACK OF THIS ENVELOP
AND MAIL IT TO YOUR TAX
CENTRE. THE ADDRESS OF
TAX CENTRE CAN BE FOUN
THE FRONT OF YOUR NOT

BMW bike suppliers were sometimes hard to come by, especially in the backwater parts of Europe, so she kept a small stock of replacement parts in one of the rear boxes. The other she used for her clothes and tools; whatever else she carried with her had to fit in her panniers, tank bag, backpack, or in her pockets.

It was a mutt of a bike, too ugly to appeal to thieves, and one that would have made her stepdad, Malcolm, proud. He had been tearing down and rebuilding old motorcycles since his teens; once he had discovered how much Nick loved messing around with tools he had made her his apprentice.

We'll make a proper grease monkey out of you yet, girl.

She unlocked one of the panniers and took out the wallet tucked inside. She carried a dummy wallet she'd stuffed with a handful of euros, some expired credit cards, and a condom. For some reason, the condom always convinced thieves and muggers that it was real.

Her real wallet, concealed in the false bottom of the pannier, contained a roll of traveler's checks, the keys to her caches of money and passports in safety-deposit boxes all over Europe, a card with a list of phone numbers to reliable fences, another ten fake IDs, and a photo of her mom and Malcolm, smiling and happy on their wedding day.

Whenever things got very bad, Nick always reached for the photo first.

After strapping her gym bag to the back of her seat with a stretch cord, she climbed on, started the motor, and listened to it idle. The bike had been running smoothly since she'd left Paris, but the thought of breaking down on the side of a road no one ever used didn't appeal to her. Satisfied by the engine's even chugging, she kicked up the center stand and drove up onto the road behind the inn.

Anyone seeing her leave the village would think she was headed out to ride through the vineyards, not cut through the farm roads to sneak up on the local haunted château.

The stars glittered in the clear black sky by the time Nick reached the north edge of St. Valereye. Gnats and mosquitoes rose out of the grass as she wheeled the bike into some woody shrubs, so she kept her gloves on and her helmet visor down.

The only light Nick could see was a faint glow coming from the old man's cottage windows. It was not constant, but flickered, as if it came from fire or candlelight. She resisted the temptation to go over and peek through the windows to see if Father Claudio was up and about; she'd make a racket walking through the grass and weeds. She secured the bike to a tree—habit more than fear of thieves—and carried her bag out to the edge of the tree line. From there she'd have to cross several hundred yards of overgrown weeds to get to the chapel.

Don't run, Nick thought as she trekked across the neglected lawn. Tiny black crickets scattered with every step she took, but their chirps masked some of the crackle and shush of her passage through the grass. *Almost there.*

The outside doors to the chapel had been chained and padlocked, something they hadn't been the last time she'd come here. She set down her bag to take out her bolt cutters, and neatly clipped one link in the center of the chain, where she could later use a tie wrap to hold it together without it looking obvious. After she glanced back at the cottage and listened for a moment, she slipped the chain off, picked up her bag, and stepped inside.

A dark cloud swallowed her.

It took Nick a minute to register that she was standing in a swarm of flies, not bees or wasps. Thankful for her helmet visor, she closed the door behind her and placed the chain and lock on a pew where she would see it on the way out.

The chapel appeared to be as infested as Father Claudio had claimed, but as Nick moved forward toward the altar area, the flies seemed to disperse. Another, shiny new padlock had been installed on the door at the back, the one she was sure led to a hidden space. Apparently her visit had rattled the old man enough to make him want to lock up the place.

If he'd wanted to keep out tourists, why not install locks in the first place? Why this sudden urge to secure an abandoned ruin that scared everyone within fifty miles of the place?

The sensation of knowing something hidden lay nearby, waiting to be found, became overwhelming. *Maybe he's not keeping things out, but keeping them in.*

After checking on the flies, which were still swarmed by the entry door, Nick took off her helmet. The odor of dust, mold, and rotting wood made her wrinkle her nose briefly, until she caught a trace of something else. If she hadn't been standing in the middle of the chapel, she'd have sworn she was back out in the trees.

Whatever it was, the sharp, resinous, pungent scent—almost like green wood after it had been cut—seemed to grow stronger as she walked up to the altar space. She breathed in deeply, and snapshots from childhood flashed through her mind. Swags her mother had bundled, decorated, and hung over every door. The big tree Malcolm had hauled home in the Rover every December to set up next to the fireplace.

Evergreen.

Nick employed her bolt cutters again and cut off the padlock. She pocketed the ruined lock and eased open the door. It creaked so loudly that she winced, but then a blast of dusty air came out at her at a strange angle. She took out her flashlight and switched it on.

The world's ricketiest-looking wooden stairs curved down and disappeared into a well of blackness.

Nick listened carefully, but there was no sound coming from below, not so much as a cricket chirp. She angled the flashlight to illuminate the dusty, cobwebbed stone walls before stepping inside.

The scent of Christmas morning drifted up to greet her.

Chapter 8

Dark, silent, and filthy basements were some of Nick's least favorite places to explore. Nothing good was ever left behind in them, and when they weren't regularly cleaned and used, lots of unpleasant things liked to move in and set up house. Snakes. Spiders. Squatters.

Yet someone had been down here recently enough to tear some of the larger cobwebs out of their way, and leave drag marks and some strange powdery residue on the stairs. It made her wonder if she was about to discover a huge stash of heroin or cocaine, or some drug dealer's secret laboratory.

Or maybe this is another disposal site. She stopped on a stair as she remembered the place she'd found outside Marseilles, where the holy freaks had moved into a factory and converted a huge furnace into a crematorium. It had taken her a full night to trash the equipment enough to make it unusable.

This might be worse.

She hated doing this. She didn't owe anyone anything, especially them. And if he was one of them . . . But she couldn't leave, not until she knew for sure. Fear would have to take a number.

At the base of the stairs was an electrical switch, and absently Nick flipped it on. Two small floodlights illuminated a landing area that opened on one side into a bricked passage.

Electricity. Lights. In an abandoned chapel that was

supposed to collapse at any moment. That no one was allowed to walk through. If nothing else shouted, "Be afraid, be very afraid," that did.

"I'm not afraid," Nick muttered under her breath as she followed the smell of evergreen. "There's nothing to be afraid of."

Nick didn't mind lying to herself. The truth never set anything free.

The woodsy scent seemed to be coming from a large tapestry at the far end of the cellar passageway. As soon as Nick trained her flashlight on it, she set down her bag and stepped back to have a proper look. At first it seemed only a threadbare frame for the rat and moth holes eaten through it, and then she picked out what the weaving had once depicted: a pale-haired woman standing beside a tree. The lady had wrapped her arm around the trunk; the tree's branches curled down around her as if the tree were trying to return the embrace.

The Golden Madonna, perhaps?

Even as hope rose, Nick's memory squashed it. She had walked the circular room devoted to the six famous *Lady and the Unicorn* tapestries at the Cluny in Paris. They had the same bloodred background as this one, and in them the maker had woven the same black banners with three crescent moons. No way could this be one of them; it had to be a reproduction or knockoff. Who would leave a national treasure hanging unguarded in the basement of a crumbling ruin to feed the rat population?

When Nick reached up to feel along the upper edge, her touch made the entire tapestry fall. A cloud of dust, dirt, and rotted wool fragments enveloped her. Coughing, she covered her nose and mouth as she examined the wall behind it. New red brick filled in the space of an old entryway to seal off a room. The mortar used must have been mixed wrong, as the seams between the bricks were riddled with holes, and some of the bricks were loose enough for her to push in with her fingers.

"Hello." Nick crouched down and pulled the pile of tapestry away from the wall. A thick layer of mortar dust obscured the base of the new bricks, caked as if it had been there a while. "Father Claudio, you'll never land a job as a bricklayer."

Come to me.

Falling back onto her ass didn't improve Nick's mood; nor did scraping her palms on the stone floor. She stood and put an ear to the brick before stepping back again. "Is someone in there?"

Silence.

"If you hadn't noticed, this is private property, and I'm trespassing," she told the wall. "The French police aren't very fond of Americans breaking and entering, either." She waited for a response. "If you really want my help, friend, tell me if you're in there."

Silence.

Nick realized something. "Do you speak any English?" She repeated that in her phrase-book French, along with, "Are you stuck in there?" Brilliant question. "Do you want me to get you out?"

Silence, and evergreen.

"We'll call that a yes." Feeling ridiculous, Nick bent down, unzipped her bag, and took out a hammer and chisel. After a glance at the brick, she put them back and removed a small sledgehammer. "If you're near the door, move back. Shit is about to hit the fan."

A hail of mortar dust followed the metal-on-stone slam of the sledgehammer. Bricks shifted, two falling into the space behind them. Grinning, Nick swung the heavy steel head again, and a foot-wide hole appeared.

Seeing that much brick implode made her stop and bend over to peer in the gap. Air rushed around her face as if the pitch-black room on the other side were sucking it in. Invisible branches of evergreen seemed to close around her.

"They didn't even leave you a night-light? Cheapskates." She shoved in a brick, scraping her knuckles, and something dark and wet dripped onto the back of her hand. Blood, and not hers.

Beneath the blood, her scratches disappeared.

"Fuck." She paused long enough to put on her leather gloves before she wrenched at the brick around the edges of the hole, pushing it away and widening the space. A strange urgency hammered inside her head, as if an invisible alarm clock had gone off on the other side of the wall. *I have to get him the hell out of here before they come for both of us.*

The hole was finally large enough for Nick to squeeze through. "Here we go." She poked her head and then her shoulders inside. The evergreen scent on the other side of the wall didn't cover the other, awful smell—as if someone had emptied a couple of trash cans in the hidden room— but she'd smelled worse. She climbed in, groping for a handhold, but her fingers found nothing but floor. More brick collapsed under her weight, and she fell on her face. Something long and hard bruised her thigh.

Flashlight. She pulled it out and switched it on.

The tiny room still held the empty racks where some long-dead aristocrat had kept his best bottles of wine and brandy. From all the tangled, dusty cobwebs hanging from the ceiling, it appeared as if no one had entered the space for years. Nick stood up and swept the flashlight slowly around her. A rickety-looking table and two scarred old chairs waited empty in front of a dead fireplace overflowing with ancient ash.

No sign of life, however. "Where are you?"

Chains rattled behind her.

She turned around and pointed the flashlight toward the sound, and saw him. The light wavered before she controlled her hand. "Bastards."

They'd crucified this one.

Nick saw she was partially wrong—chains had been wrapped around his neck, arms, waist, and legs—but two huge copper bolts had been hammered through his wrists.

He'd worked at one, apparently, and could move it enough to rattle the chains around that arm. A black rag had been tied over his eyes, and a wide band of welded copper covered the lower half of his face. Dark green tattoos mottled his naked body, along with dried blood, open wounds, and filth.

Despite his sad condition, he still looked beautiful, the way they all did. This one resembled a green god, carved from dark jade.

Nailed to a cross.

The holy freaks had done this to him. Nick had never seen one this bad, but the deliberate, mocking crucifixion had the same feel as the others she had found. The question was, why? If they wanted them dead, why not just kill them? Why the torture and humiliation?

The prisoner turned his head slightly and moved his hand, disturbing the chains again.

Nick lowered the flashlight as she walked to him. "Sorry." She didn't know why she was apologizing. None of this was her doing, and if she had an ounce of brains left she'd run out of here before the old man found her screwing with this thing. Lucky for this one she was an idiot. "How do I get you off this without tearing you to shreds?"

The chains rattled a third time as he gestured toward the wall beside him.

Nick reached out through the hole and groped until she grabbed her bag and pulled it inside. Once she had retrieved her bolt cutters, she looked around the crude wooden cross. The chains had been threaded through rusted iron rings driven into the wall around him. She started there, cutting the rings open and tugging the loops of chain away. The weighty copper links felt icy and sticky, and wherever they had touched him, they left dark impressions of their links on his skin.

This close Nick could smell nothing else but the evergreen scent he radiated. How long had he been sealed in this room? Weeks? Months? His matted brown hair shifted and his head moved back, as if he were trying to see under the edge of his blindfold.

"Want to have a look at me?" She stopped cutting long enough to remove the black rag from his eyes. His closed eyelids didn't open, and he sagged a little. "I'm Nick," she told him as she went back to work on the chains. "And you're a mess."

She freed his neck and arms, and examined the copper band gagging him. It had been welded together at the ends, but it was thin, and her tin snips cut through it nicely. The raw skin under it began to heal at once, and she flung the copper to the floor in disgust.

"I've got to pry these bolts out." His mouth matched the perfection of his body; she saw that right away. Were any of these things ever ugly, or even a little plain? "It's going to hurt, maybe as much as when they went in."

Nick heard a jerking, tearing sound.

"Ce n'est pas nécessaire." The voice sounded as dry and shredded as the feel of the trembling hand that pushed her back. "I can do the rest. Leave me, girl."

Like an animal in a trap, he'd ripped his wrists free of the bolts. Maybe that was all they were: gorgeous two-legged animals.

Not very grateful ones, either. "You want me to leave *now*? Before you thank me, and say good-bye, and tell me to have a wonderful life? Tell me, is that what Jesus would do?"

He leaned forward, his eyes still closed. "If you remain, and if I look upon you," he murmured, "I will kill us both."

He sounded like the genie that'd been kept too long in the bottle: enraged and wanting some payback. Of course, he needed blood, and she was the only source present. In his state he'd lose control and try to drain her dry.

"I'm not leaving until I cut through enough of these so that you can get out on your own." She went back to work on the chains.

Bugs found their way into the room and began flying at

her head. Absently she swatted at them until she remembered all the bugs were upstairs in the chapel.

She hadn't left the cellar door open. How had they gotten down—

Father Claudio was right there, his walking stick raised high, and then he clubbed her across the head with it. Nick couldn't avoid the blow, and in the explosion of pain that followed felt her scalp split and the heat of her own blood. She went down like a sack of stones.

The last things she heard and saw before the night took her were chains falling on the floor, and two bare, dirty, beautiful feet walking across the stone.

The last time Alexandra had walked into a private laboratory as expensively outfitted as the one Richard had installed in his dungeon, she had ended up operating on Michael Cyprien. Later, she had also been served up by Éliane as Michael's first postop meal.

Being reminded of what had taken her human life from her and changed her into a blood-dependent mutant made her want to do something slightly more intelligent this time around. Like set fire to the place.

But if she were going to get back home, she had to at least go through the motions.

"I'll need a bigger autoclave," Alex said as she walked down the row of new equipment. "Another clot timer for multiple specimens, and a coagulyzer."

Michael Cyprien. She needed Michael. Now.

She paused for a moment to cover her agitation by tapping some keys on an efficient-looking PC before moving on to the microscope. "Nice computer. Scope's okay for now, but we may have to upgrade to something more powerful."

Michael was powerful. Michael was what she needed.

Alex stopped and glared at a cheap import model of something she really needed. "Who picked out this centrifuge?"

"I did," Éliane said. "It resembled the one you requested while you were in New Orleans."

"That was a great piece of equipment, top of the line. This? This is a piece of junk." She went over and opened up the supply cabinet to inspect the instruments, beakers, and vials inside. "I'm not seeing any syringes, scissors, pipettes, or biopsy needles here."

Or Michael.

The scent of cherry tobacco stung the air. "My *tresora* does not yet trust you with sharp objects." Richard's distinctive footsteps came up behind her. "Nor do I."

"How am I supposed to take blood and tissue samples from you? With my teeth? Don't answer that." Alex closed the cabinet and moved on to the portable X-ray machine, culture racks, and what she thought might be a genetic analyzer of some sort. "This is going to take longer than I thought."

"Why?"

"I'm an American, used to working on American equipment. This stuff is all European. I'll need more operating manuals, especially on the electronics." She pointed to the analyzer console. "I'm not even sure how to turn that on." She also couldn't stop thinking about Cyprien, or the way her dermis seemed to want to divorce her muscle tissue.

Get it together, Alexandra.

"All you need will be provided for you." Richard turned and hobbled toward the door.

Nice work, Alex. Who knows how long it will take for him to get all the manuals? Why the hell do you care how everything works? Not like you're going to use it. You're never going to get out of here.

Alex agreed with her common sense, but there was more to it than helping the monster who had kidnapped her. Richard's changeling blood might reveal something she hadn't yet found in studying other Kyn. Something that might cure the condition and allow her to take back her life.

Fuck life. You need Michael.

"Hold your horses, high lord." She walked over to the exam table. "I can still do a physical."

Richard turned toward her, removing his mask as he did. Out of the corner of her eye, Alex saw Éliane quickly look away, as if the sight of the high lord's distorted features repelled her.

The high lord's face was, Alex had to admit, pretty revolting. Black and silver hair stubble darkened the skin around his bulging eyes, lipless mouth, and over his flattened nose.

As bone structures went, his was a nightmare. His forehead was gone, as were his chin and the lower half of his cheekbones. She probed and discovered that the bone hadn't been removed or crushed; it simply wasn't there anymore. Spiky bunches of white hair sprouted from his eyebrows, which had become a single, three-inch-wide strip of hair rolling across the grossly pronounced brow ridge shading his eyes.

The features would have been bad enough on their own, but hearing Richard's human voice coming out of that mouth, and seeing the intelligence in those alien eyes, gave the impression of a man trapped inside the body of a beast—as if Richard had been swallowed alive.

Alex definitely preferred him when he was the man behind the mask. But after years of repairing some of the worst facial injuries human beings could endure, she'd acquired a lot of tolerance for the unnatural and repulsive, even as extreme as Richard's case was.

"Take off all your clothes and get on the table." She reached for a pair of gloves. When the high lord didn't move, she glanced at him. "What, you can't undress yourself? Want me to ring for your valet?"

"I can disrobe." As he unfastened his cloak, his eyelids dropped, hiding half of his almond-shaped, gold-green eyes with their slitted pupils. "Were you this abrupt and demanding with Cyprien?"

"Much worse. He had to wear earplugs." She circled around him, gesturing for the Frenchwoman. "Can you take down some notes, or will that violate your sacred oath of standing around doing nothing so you can look pressed and pretty?"

"I will assist." Éliane sounded as aloof and uncaring as always, but her hands trembled when she took the chart that Alex handed to her, and her breathing sounded like someone about to have an acute asthma attack.

"Maybe you should send someone else in to help," Alex suggested, and got a nasty look in return. "Screw me. Got it."

Alex took Richard's clothing as he removed it and draped it over the back of a chair. It helped her conceal her own reaction to seeing the high lord's extreme physical mutations.

The changeling condition had distorted his body even more so than his face and skull, curving his spine in three places and reversing the elbow and knee joints. His enlarged hands and feet were no longer recognizably human.

"Are you ready for this?" she asked once he stood naked. After he nodded, she said to Éliane, "All right, Blondie, start writing. Patient is Richard Tremayne, a mutated human male, approximately seven hundred years old. Step over here." She had him climb onto the scale and measured him. "Seventy-two inches tall, one hundred ninety-seven pounds. Is that close to what you were before this happened?"

"Yes."

"No loss of body mass," she said. "All right, hop up on the exam table and lie on your back."

Alex checked Richard's heart rate, temperature, and blood pressure, all of which were far below normal human limits but were slightly elevated for what she knew to be normal Kyn limits. He watched her without blinking.

"Patient presents what appears to be hypertrichosis," she said after having Éliane note the vitals. "With the exception of the palms of the hands and soles of the feet, the entire body is covered with dense black hair. Face has been recently shaved." She took some measurements. "Hair ranges from one-half to eight inches in length on limbs and torso." She glanced down at him. "When did the abnormal hair growth begin?"

Richard looked up at the ceiling. "A long time ago."

"Need a year," Alex said as she picked up a light scope.

"Eighteen forty-nine."

She did the math in her head. "Hypertrichotic condition first manifested one hundred fifty-eight years ago." She moved some of his thick, curly mane to inspect his left ear, which sat high on his elongated skull and had acquired a distinct pointed profile. The human outer whorls and folds had disappeared altogether, and she could not see his eardrum. "What caused the condition?"

"The Brethren."

She remembered what Lucan had told her. *You are what you eat.* "I need more specifics. What did they do to you?"

"I cannot say." His gaze shifted away from her. "My memory of that time has become unreliable."

She didn't believe him, but it didn't really matter how he lied to her.

"Make a note of the memory loss on the chart, Blondie." Alex looked into his eyes with the scope and noted how the pupils did not react to the intense light. "Have there been any consistent symptoms since the hypertrichosis manifested?"

"I cannot feed on humans. My moods are sometimes uncertain." He closed his eyes. "I lose time."

Alex wondered if she could manage to do a brain scan on Richard before she escaped the castle. "Define 'lose time' for me."

He sighed. "I go to sleep without wishing to. When I awake, it is often two or three hours later, and I am in a different place."

She tried to make sense of what he was telling her. "Do you mean you sleepwalk?"

"It does not always happen during the day," he said. "I never know when such spells will come upon me."

"Patient complains of having blackouts. Tell me if you feel any discomfort or pain." Alex palpated Richard's torso and discovered that the changeling condition had also lengthened and narrowed his rib cage. Unlike some of her former male patients, he did not become erect when she inspected his genitals. "Any changes down here? Other than the hair covering things?"

"I am larger than I was." He sounded slightly smug.

"Good for you." Alex found two rows of odd bumps on either side of his shaft and tapped one. "Are these old or new?"

"New."

"How nice. Note some enlarged or infected follicles on the penis. Any problems having sex?"

Richard's upper lip split open as he bared teeth too long and pointed to be human. "None."

Alex glanced at Éliane, who had stopped writing, and whose face had turned almost as white as her blouse.

Terrific. Aside from the danger to the Frenchwoman, now every time Alex saw her or Richard she'd imagine the two of them going at it. But something was wrong here, very wrong, as evidenced by the bloody spot Éliane had gnawed into her bottom lip.

"That's it for the chart," Alex lied. "If you're not busy, Blondie, I'll need those supplies that aren't in the cabinet, and a better centrifuge."

"I will see to it, Doctor." The Frenchwoman all but ran from the lab.

"She is modest," Richard said as he sat up.

More like she was head over heels about him, Alex guessed. But Richard had been a changeling for a hundred fifty years plus; how could Éliane have lost her heart to that face?

You began falling in love with Cyprien when he didn't even have a face.

Out loud Alex said, "I'll need you back to draw some blood as soon as Blondie gets the rest of what I need. I'd also like to review all of your medical records, past lab tests, and any X-rays or scans performed on you."

He began to dress. "I will see what was recovered by my guards. Do you know why your blood did not kill Lucan's woman?"

She kept her expression bland. "Why, no, I don't."

"You are a poor liar. It was a remarkable thing. No Kyn has turned a human since Michael changed you." Awkwardly he buttoned his shirt. "Now you are changing humans just as easily as we once did."

Easily her ass. "I didn't change Samantha Brown; Lucan did. I tried to stop him. I didn't ask to be changed, either. Shouldn't you be talking to Michael about this?"

He pulled his cloak on with the careless movements of a man used to wearing one daily. "When you take my blood, you will have Éliane take yours as well. You may compare your blood to that of any Kyn here that you wish. I want to know how you do it."

"Blondie is not sticking me, and besides, that wasn't part of the deal."

He eyed her. "I made no deal with you."

Shit. "What I meant is, I'm only going to work on helping you. I'm not going to risk poisoning another human on the off chance that it will turn them into Kyn."

"It did not poison the woman in Chicago," he said in a reasonable way.

"Jema Shaw was a baby when she was accidentally exposed to Valentin's blood," Alex said, trying to keep her temper in check. "A crazy man spent thirty years drugging her to keeping her from maturing and changing, and probably from dying."

"Indeed. How do you explain Samantha Brown changing?"

"Detective Brown was dying from a fatal gunshot. Lucan was desperate. I don't . . ." What was she doing?

Discussing this with him? "It doesn't matter. I'm not testing my blood. No one is taking my blood. My blood is officially off-limits."

The dark odor of cherry tobacco became smothering. "You will do as you are told."

Richard's words bored into Alex's head, echoing through her mind. It wasn't the first time he'd used his talent on her, but he'd never thrown this much at her. Her eardrums seemed to press in, and her entire body wanted to go stiff.

Not this time.

Alex barely hid her astonishment as the effects of Richard's talent ebbed out of her, leaving her unmoved and unafraid. It wasn't her ability to resist it; Richard's ability to influence humans and Kyn was changing. "I said, you can't have my blood."

The high lord hobbled over to her and peered into her eyes. "Congratulations, Doctor. You are the first Kyn to fully resist me in seven centuries."

If what Alex suspected was true, she wouldn't be the last. "Immortal life's a bitch."

"There is something I would show you before I have Korvel lock you in your room." Richard sounded almost bored as he went over and switched on a monitor that Alex hadn't spotted. "This is from a security camera I had installed yesterday in the quarters for our newest American guest."

Alex's blood chilled. "Who is it?"

"Come and see."

She thought of Samantha, and Jema, and even Grace Cho, her former office manager. But when she saw who was pacing the floor of the guest room, she swore viciously. "You shit son of a bitch."

John Keller turned his back on the security camera and went to stare out the window.

"Doubtless I am," Richard said softly. "I assure you that no harm will come to your brother. He will be shown every possible courtesy . . . as long as you do not defy me again."

Alex felt her own fingernails cutting into her palms. "If I do?"

"Then, Doctor, I will see to it that John suffers pain that not even he, with all of his tragic experiences in Rome, can imagine." He showed her all of his teeth. "Personally."

Chapter 9

"A girl." The old man's laugh grated against Gabriel's ears. "Benait will soil his pants, he see I caught this little mouse in his trap. You good as stinking cheese, *maledicti.*"

Opening his eyes had decided many things for Gabriel, who had freed himself and now walked up behind the old man. Claudio turned, his shriek dying under Gabriel's fangs.

Piercing the old man's sour flesh disgusted Gabriel, but blood was blood. He fed, taking only enough to partially heal his wounds and render Claudio unconscious. Strength returned Gabriel's control, enabling him to lower Claudio's limp body to the floor instead of tearing it apart. He would need to feed again, and soon, but he had to attend to Nick and take her out of this place.

. . . *this little mouse in his trap.*

Claudio may have meant to kill the girl, but the old man's gloating had effectively caged Gabriel's thirst. They had not brought him to this place to punish him, or kill him, or do anything more to him. All had been done. Benait had merely used him as a lure.

But what did the Brethren want with an American tourist?

Gabriel stripped off Claudio's trousers, pulling them up his own bare legs before he knelt down by the unconscious girl. After checking her pulse, which was faint but steady, he lifted her carefully into his arms. It would not do to drop her in a moment of weakness.

She weighs nothing.

Gabriel carried her over to the hole she had knocked through the brick and climbed through it with her. As a cloud of buzzing drifted toward them, he opened his mind, reaching out to the tiny insects with his talent. They responded by swarming in front of him, a tiny airborne army he thought of as the many. Humans found them annoying, even frightening, and Gabriel had once used his ability to summon and control all insects to help him on the hunt. Since being taken by the Brethren, however, Gabriel had depended on the many for his survival. As he did now by connecting with the group mind of the swarm, and commanding them to guide him up and out of his prison.

Free.

The moment he stepped out of the chapel, his skin came alive. Fresh, deliciously cool air caressed him, the fingers of a shy lover. Being in the world again, unfettered, unguarded, bound only by earth and sky, was almost more than he could bear. He stood, fighting back terrible urges to run and shout and destroy everything in his path, and made himself feel the quiet of the night. Gradually he realized it was the weight of the girl in his arms that kept him from losing the last of his self-control.

Gabriel shifted her so that he could touch his mouth to the top of her head. *"J'apprécie ce que vous avez fait pour moi, mademoiselle."*

She stirred and groaned. "My head."

American, she is American. "Do not be afraid." He spoke excellent English, but it had been so long since he had talked to anyone in that language that the words came slowly. Or perhaps it was the fact that she spoke in the voice from his dreams. "You are safe with me."

Out in the open, the swarm tried to disperse, attracted to the delicious smells of refuse coming from nearby trash bins. Gabriel released them before he turned in the opposite direction, toward the woods.

Walking through the grass made the soles of his feet tingle with delight, but passing through the first of the trees felt like being admitted through the gates of heaven. At last he was in his element, the forest, the one place on earth in which he could virtually disappear.

Nick had come through here, too. He could smell the leaves and spores on her clothing, and if he concentrated enough, he could probably track and retrace her path. She must have hidden her motorcycle in the woods before coming to the chapel on foot; that was why he hadn't heard the engine sound. She had not wanted Claudio to catch her again.

Cunning and cautious. He could hardly believe she came back for him without the constant influence of his scent. *Who is she?*

The sound of a stream drew him like a magnet; water would help revive her to full consciousness and allow him to clean the blood and filth from his body. The second was almost as important to him as the first. The Brethren had never permitted him to bathe; occasionally they had tossed a bucket of cold water on him to revive him or to neutralize some of the odor when his wounds had festered.

Since being sealed in the chapel basement, Gabriel had been only too aware of his body's growing stench. Using *l'attrait* had masked most of it from Nick, but Gabriel couldn't keep her bespelled indefinitely.

It didn't matter how he smelled. *I must question her and then send her far from this place.*

Water rushed in merry abandonment a few feet in front of him, and Gabriel carefully climbed down the gentle slope of the bank until the current rushed over his feet. He crouched, bringing her face close to his as he freed one arm and touched her head, searching for wounds. Nothing marred the smoothness of her skin and the pleasing contours of her features. Soft, full curls sprang from the passage of his palm; he wondered why she kept such wonderfully thick, sleek hair shorn so close to her head.

He traced the edges of her hairline. *She keeps it cut like a boy.* Yet Claudio's words had assured him that she was not.

At last his fingers found a large swollen spot on the back of her skull where the old priest must have struck her. Gently he bathed the spot with a cupped handful of water and felt her rouse again.

"That hurts."

Had Claudio killed her with the blow, it surely would have snapped the last strand of Gabriel's sanity. "I imagine it does." Her voice sounded so young and uncertain that guilt pummeled his chest and gut. "I am sorry."

"Why?" Her voice grew steadier, stronger. "You didn't hit me."

"I should have"—*smelled him*—"known that he would come into the room." The mass of curls above her nape became a sodden tangle. "Do you feel ill?"

"I feel wet. And stupid."

Such head injuries made humans nauseous and dizzy. She might have a concussion. He could not leave her here like this, but how was he to get her to a hospital? In his condition, he could not drive her motorcycle.

"I'm okay." She gave him a weak push and tried to swing her legs out. "You shouldn't be carrying me."

"Wait." Feeling his own strength ebbing, Gabriel carried her to the bank, where he sat down with her on his lap. "What is your name, mademoiselle?"

"I told you. Nick."

Americans had an astonishing disregard for formality, as well as gender-confusing names. "Only Nick?"

"Nicola Jefferson. It's just Nick, okay?"

Nicola, Nicola. Gabriel rolled the syllables through his mind, polishing each one into a bright gem. "You have a lovely name."

"It fills in the dotted line." She touched the back of her head. "If you told me yours, I forgot it."

"I am very grateful." His control of her was uncertain; thus far he had been unable to wholly command her. Perhaps his physical weakness had limited the effect of *l'attrait*. "Why did you not go when I told you to do so?"

"I have this thing about leaving guys nailed to crosses in bricked-up rooms. Seems so rude." Her hand touched her forehead and she groaned. "I think I need to lie down."

Gabriel swept out his hand, finding a patch of lush, soft grass where he lowered her. "I owe you my life, Nicola Jefferson."

"Then call me Nick, and next time tell me to duck."

She didn't say anything for many minutes, and Gabriel sat beside her, using the silence to indulge his senses with her. He already knew the feel of her skin and hair, the honest simplicity of her scent.

Now he listened to her breathe in the dark, and heard the whisper of her garments as her chest rose and fell. Beneath her skin her blood rushed, young and strong, and he imagined tasting her.

Shame and hunger snarled inside him. He had been locked away from humans for too long; everything about her entranced him. *Send her away now.*

"Are there any other holy freaks besides Claudio here?" she asked him.

He had never smelled anyone else since Benait left, but that meant nothing. "I do not know." He hesitated. "Holy freaks?"

"I tried to think up another name, but 'pretend priests,' 'nutcases in cassocks,' and 'nasty pastors' didn't have the same ring." Nick tried to sit up and groaned again. "Jesus, what did he hit me with? A lead brick?"

"Stay where you are." He put his hand to her shoulder when she made another attempt to rise. "You are not yet well enough to walk." He would not be able to let her go, not in such a state. She might lose consciousness while riding her motorcycle, and kill herself on the road. Humans seemed so horribly fragile compared to Kyn.

"I don't think you're in any shape to carry me back to the village," Nick said, reminding him of his own sorry state. "Do I have to call you 'very grateful' every time I want your attention, or will you tell me your name?"

The one question his captors had never asked. The one answer he should not give her.

He wanted to hear her say it before she left him. "I am Gabriel."

"Gabriel. Very angelic. I like it." She shifted on the grass. "So what happens now, Gabriel? Are you going to walk off into the night to bite someone else, or do me like the old man first?"

"Either would be poor recompense for your efforts on my behalf." He heard an odd note in her voice, almost wistful, before what she said registered. Perhaps she was joking; modern humor often escaped him. "I do not bite."

"Sure you do. You're a vampire."

She knows. Gabriel sat silent for a full minute, trying to work his bruised thoughts around this. "How do you . . . Why do you say this?"

"Too late to fake being human; the fangs are a dead giveaway. I've met lots of vampires. You're not exactly like the others. I didn't see these on any of them." Cool fingers glided over one of his scars. "You feel like you're running a fever, too. Are you sick? Is that why they had you in that place?"

"I am only weak." Kyn body temperatures remained low until they fed, and then for a brief time they radiated intense heat. Her questions disturbed him. *Her knowledge is incomplete; why?* A *tresora*, even one in training, would not ask such things. "Do you serve my kind?"

"Uh, no. I'm more the self-serve type."

He needed to understand her. She knew enough about the Kyn to fear him, and yet she had risked her life to release him. Unless she had been compelled . . . "If you do not, why did you come here in search of me?"

"I wasn't looking for you," she said, stunning him anew. "I like to photograph old icons and churches. I keep finding vampires in them, though. I've tried to walk away in the past—you know, not my problem, that kind of thing? When I found out what they were doing to you, though, I just couldn't."

The trap. Claudio had mistaken her for the ring of thieves the Brethren were trying to capture. "How many others like me have you released?"

"I haven't kept count." Grass rustled under her weight. "Ten, fifteen maybe."

The Kyn could not track and find the imprisoned. She had to be exaggerating—or had some connection with the Brethren. "Do you know the men who imprison us? Do you follow them?"

"No. I'm good at finding things." She turned toward him. "Why do they do this stuff to you? Are they some kind of torture cult? Are you criminals? Why doesn't anyone in authority know about this?"

Kyn never trusted humans with knowledge of their existence and their nature. Neither did the Brethren. Yet this girl had somehow stumbled into the middle of their war and released the helpless prisoners of it. He would not repay her with silence.

"Those who imprisoned me are fanatics," he said. "They believe my kind are evil and demonic, and must be destroyed. They torture us for information about others like us."

She drew back. "Are you? An evil demon, I mean?"

"Some think that we were cursed because we are evil creatures, but I believe it was something else. Something in our time that we do not yet understand." Her silence made him add, "We have lived for many centuries. We depend on humans for blood as vampires do, but we do not harm them. We try to live in peace with you."

"So you don't have to kill someone to survive?"

"No."

"I thought so. I mean, none of the others tried to kill me. Not that I exactly waited around for them to have a go." Her voice changed, became softer. "I'm glad."

Gabriel bent his head, breathing in the delicious scent of her skin. He wanted to rub his hot face against her, feel the tender resilience of her flesh caressing him. He also knew he had no right to touch her, and that if he did the long denial of his captivity might very well end with her death and his enthrallment.

Command her before you are no longer able to send her away. "If you are steady enough to ride your motorcycle, Nicola, you must leave me now."

"Leave you? Here?"

The only protection she had against him was his own restraint. Others like him would not care . . . yet she implied that she had quickly left the others that she had released before him. She had not been bespelled; he could smell no trace of his kind on her skin—but any Kyn might have used *l'attrait* to command her to forget them.

"It is best." His questions would have to go unanswered. "I have been locked away and starved for a very long time. I do not trust myself."

"I'm tougher than I look, and I've been tapped before this." Her hand curled over his shoulder, gently guiding him down to her. "Go ahead. Just leave me a pint or two, okay?"

She was offering him blood. Freely, agreeably, as if a gift between friends. It humbled him. That his kind *had* used such generosity outraged him. "Not from you."

She pushed his hair back, tucking it behind his ear. "You know, you're the most polite vampire I've ever set free. Definitely the best-looking." Her thumb whispered across his bottom lip, so fast and light Gabriel thought he imagined it. "But your fangs are still out. You're wobbly. Take the blood."

She would not be so willing unless she was fully succumbing to his scent. "You have given enough." He could
not evade her touch or push it away. He had dreamed of
holding her too many times to resist. "Please move away
from me now."

"I'm not afraid." She inched closer to him, brushing her
body against his. "It doesn't upset me. I know you need
blood to heal." She fit her hand to the back of his neck
while she used the other to outline one of the scars on his
chest. "I can't believe what they did to you. If I could find
the one who did it, I'd kick his ass from here to next Tues-
day."

"There were many. You would break your foot." Now
she was seducing him with the enchantment of her voice,
her presence, her compassion. He could not keep his hands
from her. Was it possible in his current state to become en-
thralled? He needed to focus on something else. "How did
you come to find this place, and me?"

"A painting, local superstition, and a few other things."
She turned on her side to face him. "Do you know anything about the Golden Madonna? Did the holy freaks talk
about her?"

"No. I have never heard of such a thing." She had mentioned her photography. "Is this Madonna an icon?"

"No. Just something that used to belong to my family.
It was stolen, and I'd like to find it again." She sounded a
little disappointed. "How long have they had you down
there?"

"Can you tell me the date?"

She touched the watch on her wrist. "September fourteenth."

That long. Time had escaped him; he had thought it
only July. "Six months."

She drew in a quick breath, swore, and then just as suddenly stopped. "Hey." She sat up. "Why are your eyes
glowing like that?"

Gabriel turned his head. "I am happy to be free."

"Not that kind of glow. Like fire, if it were green. Very spooky. Wait." She hunted in her pocket and pulled out something that she held in front of his face. "Here, look."

He caught her wrist out of reflex. "I believe you, Nicola."

"Can't you see when your eyes light up like this?"

"No matter what they do, I cannot see anything." He closed his useless eyes. "They blinded me."

Nick forgot the pounding at the back of her head that felt as if Father Claudio were still whacking her. She dropped the little square mirror that she always kept in her pocket. She forgot that the man sitting beside her was a starved, scarred vampire. She forgot the world as she got on her knees and turned his face toward her.

The strange green glow radiating from his eyes had disguised the fact that they didn't move, but remained still in a fixed stare.

Gabriel *was* blind.

"The holy freaks did this? Deliberately?" She didn't wait for an answer. "What about the tattoos? Did they do that, too? To mark you or something?"

"These?" He touched the hard places on his skin. "These are places where they burned me."

Burn scars? Up close, the curious marks looked something like fern leaves. "Why are they green? Are they infected? Is that why you're running a fever?"

"No. I am not ill, and I have caused trouble enough for you." He stood. "All that matters is that I am free. I thank you for everything you have done, Nicola."

She didn't have to dump him, Nick thought as she got to her feet. He was more than happy to pat her on the head and send her on her way. It would have been fine with her—she'd left the others to cope on their own—but the others hadn't been blind.

Maybe he didn't want her sympathy, but there was no

way she was ditching him, not blind and lost. The holy freaks would just scoop him up with a butterfly net.

"I want to know more about you and the other vampires." At least that much was true. "You owe me, right? So you can fill me in."

"We are not important." He pulled her close, resting his cheek against the top of her head. His scent, like Christmas morning, comforted her as much as his embrace. "Do not mistake my meaning. You saved my life, and I am grateful. But you must forget about me, and this place, and what you know about my kind. Go back to your home. Avoid us. Forget us. Be happy, Nicola."

"That's a very sweet, brave farewell speech, your lordship, but I'm not going anywhere." How could such a brave man—vampire—be so stupid? "Think about it. You want me to leave you here, in the middle of the forest, where that crazy old man could find you and do worse? Besides, you're hurt and maybe sick."

"I will heal." A muscle in his jaw tightened.

"Not from blindness, you won't." She pulled away, backing out of his arms. "Are you mental? Jesus, I didn't bust you out of there so that you could get caught again."

His scent changed, growing deeper and almost smoky, like an evergreen log tossed in a fireplace. "I am dangerous to you."

"To yourself, maybe. Let me worry about me." She pulled away from him and went to the stream to splash her hot face with water. The moonlight showed her dark stains on one side of her T-shirt. "Is this my blood?" She saw smears on his face and neck and absently touched the side of her throat, but felt no wounds. "Did you bite me somewhere while I was out?"

"No. I only took Claudio." He came to the water and began splashing his face and chest with it, washing away more blood.

Nick felt no sympathy for the old man, but she was responsible for what had happened to him. "Did you kill him? The old guy?"

Gabriel shook his head.

He was shutting her out. She hadn't expected him to talk much—like she'd ever hung around to have a conversation with a vampire—but there was something different about him. He had the same noble, rather snotty manner of speaking, but he didn't scare her the way the others had. Sure, he had a scary stillness about him that made him seem as if he were partly disconnected from what was happening, but the guy had been locked up and tortured. He had a right.

That he wanted to wash muted the last of her doubts. If he had meant to try to drain her dry, he'd have gone after her first and cleaned up later.

"Here." She pulled off her T-shirt, soaked it, and handed it to him. He handled it gingerly. "It's my shirt. I forgot to pack a washcloth."

"Thank you."

She finished washing up as best she could and sat on the bank to watch him. He didn't act prissy but scrubbed at himself slowly and thoroughly. The grime and dirt on his skin washed away, but the moonlight made his burn scars appear almost black. When he tried to reach his back, he staggered a little, but he didn't ask for help.

He wouldn't. She'd bet good money that he'd been alone too long to ask for anything. *Pride is all you can rely on.*

"Let me." She went to him, took the shirt, and nudged him around. The fiery tinge to his scent had vanished, but the cool water didn't seem to affect the heat of his skin. The scars felt cooler, but were hard, almost scaly. Two huge, healed gouges just below his shoulder blades caught her attention. There were others, not as deep, farther down at his waist. "Do you know that you've got some pits in your back the size of my fist?"

"They hung me from hooks for several weeks." He said it with no emotion in his voice. "When they tried to take me down, they found that my flesh healed, so they had to tear them free."

"Assholes." Nick's throat tightened as she gently washed the accumulated grime out of the deep depressions. "You're a lot braver than I am."

"I am . . ." His shoulders tensed. "You need not do this."

She didn't want to do it, not when every wipe revealed more green burns and healed-over gouges. How could he have survived such things?

He's a vampire. They survive anything.

He reached for the cloth, but Nick bumped his hand away. "Nope. You can't see how dirty you are. I can. Soap would be a huge help, but I didn't exactly plan on you and me taking a bath." She stepped around to see his front, and he promptly moved away from her. Pity and compassion made her eyes sting. "Gabriel, if I wanted to hurt you, I'd have done it in the basement."

"Pain comes in many forms."

In that instant Nick knew precisely what he was thinking and feeling. Afraid to be touched, wanting to be touched. Hating hunger as much as the fear. What they'd done had changed him inside, damaged him in places where the scars didn't show. Imagining what he'd gone through plowed into her, a fast, hard fist to the belly.

The moonlight softened, adding new shadows to Gabriel's face, and suddenly Nick knew why he had seemed so familiar. She'd seen him a hundred times. She'd drawn his profile on napkins in cafés and in the sand with a stick of driftwood and in fine, indelible lines of love in the hidden places of her heart.

My Green Man. My dream man.

"I won't hurt you," she said, a little shaken to be standing face-to-face with what had been until ten seconds ago a figment of her imagination. "I swear I'm not like them."

"You are human."

He might be entitled to some bitterness, but she wasn't

taking this snide shit from him. Even if he was her fantasy forest lover. "I'm the human who cut you loose, vampire."

"My name is Gabriel, not *vampire*." He bent to splash his face again before he straightened and turned to her. The water streamed down his chest, winding through the maze of dark green scars. "Each moment that you are with me puts your life at risk. That is what I know. You must leave me here. Now."

He didn't sound angry. All the emotion had vanished from his voice. They were good at that, giving orders, not feeling anything. Nick knew that, and still she didn't care. "Okay, Gabriel. Before I go, would you tell me one thing?"

"If I can."

"Why have I been dreaming about you for months?" She waited for him to answer. When he didn't, her face burned. "Right." Now he thought she was crazy. "Never mind."

He took her arm and turned her around. "What about your dreams?"

The scent of lightning-struck evergreen burned Nick's nose. "Well, for one thing, I keep meeting you in them. You're different in them: all green, like you were a jade statue. You also had pine needles for hair, and you weren't this thin. But it was you. Your face, your hair, everything is the same."

"It is night. You cannot see me properly."

"I can see you fine." She rested a hand on his chest—she couldn't seem to stop touching him—and bumped his right hip with her left. "It sounds stupid; okay, I know that. I've never seen you in real life, and yet here you are, glowing green eyes, green scars, and you smell like a Christmas tree. Dream man come true."

"Coincidence." He gestured around them. "We are in a forest of conifers. I may resemble other men you have met in the past."

Again with the noble act.

"I know about the great smells you guys all have, but I

haven't exactly run into that many green-eyed, green-scarred vampires." She took a step back to check him out from head to toe. "Actually, so far, you're it."

He began to reach for her, and then turned it into a dismissive gesture. "Whatever your dreams have been, they do not make you responsible for me, Nicola."

"Sometimes dreams are just reality turned inside out," she murmured. "I know you can't see me, but did you ever dream about a girl you'd never met? About five-seven, on the thin side, black leather jacket?"

"I do not dream." His scent grew thick. "Go. Now."

"You need to work on lying—you suck at it. And what would you do if I really did leave you here?" She watched him frown. "You don't know anyone. You probably don't even know where you are."

"St. Valereye. A village east of Bordeaux."

"Okay, so you know," she conceded. "But how are you going to get anywhere? You're blind, half-naked, and barefoot. You planning to Braille your way through the forest?"

He lifted his face toward the moon he couldn't see. "The forest is my home."

"What are you, Bambi?" She felt like breaking her promise not to hurt him. "There are no people around here for miles. No one to tap when you get thirsty. Your strength will run out before you get to the next working farm. I know drinking from animals doesn't work."

"You know too much," he told her, his voice toneless. "I can take care of myself."

"Yes, you've been doing a bang-up job of that so far, from what I've seen." So much for her dream man wanting her. This was beyond pathetic. "I might as well take you back and brick you in again; you'd live longer."

"Nicola." At last some anguish came through with the low, lyrical way that he said her name. "Don't regret saving me."

She didn't. He was everything she wished she could be:

brave, noble, honest. What would he think of her when he discovered what she did?

He never has to know.

"I'm not abandoning you," she said, wrapping her hand around his fist. Slowly he opened his fingers and entwined them with hers. She raised their hands until her wrist brushed his mouth. "Go on. Nobody's coming to look for us; we're okay here for a while. Take what you need."

"I cannot. I *will* not."

"You won't kill me. I'm your only way out of here." Although it bruised her heart, she made her voice stern. "You have to do it, Gabriel. I need you stronger. I can't carry you, and I'm not dragging you. Take the blood."

Gabriel hesitated so long that she thought she might have to slash her own wrist and rub it on his mouth, and then he bent his head to whisper a kiss across the thin skin over her veins. "A taste, then."

"Exactly." As his mouth opened and his teeth sank into her skin, pain and something else streaked up through Nick's arm. Something warm and wonderful and utterly wicked.

Oh, shit.

A moment later she stopped shaking and braced herself against his bare torso. He needed her as his food, his medicine, and that was all. That much she did understand about them. But as his mouth tugged and she felt the flow of her blood into his mouth, something changed. The disgust and self-loathing she felt were strangled by a turning, tightening need.

It's why they're so beautiful, she told herself, forcing her heavy eyelids to open, watching his throat move as he swallowed. *You want them so bad that you don't fight it.*

Evergreen made her the lady of the tapestry, enveloping her, holding her there. The night blurred into something dark and green and beautiful. She resisted the urge to wrap herself around him, but only just.

His mouth moved, the sharp ends of his *dents acérées*

grazing the inside of her forearm. He didn't slice her open or break her skin at all, but his lips and tongue moved against her flesh. She waited for the next bite, but it never came.

"Again." Was she begging for him to take more? Hell, she was. "Please."

Gabriel pressed his palm against the punctures in her wrist as his cheek brushed her upper arm. He was murmuring something in French, words too rapid and soft for her to catch.

Nick twisted, restless, wanting but not knowing what she wanted. It didn't happen this way, not to her. Desire came up from some hidden void inside her, dividing into twin, scalding geysers of want and need. "God, is it always like this?"

"Only with you." His free hand landed on her shoulder, lifted, and moved to her waist, then her arm, then her cheek, the jerky, uncertain way someone might touch something they weren't quite sure was solid or real. *The way you'd touch a dream.* "Only now."

Everywhere his hand landed, her skin tingled and warmed. "This is crazy." An odd laugh escaped her. "What are you doing to me?"

"I don't know." Gabriel kept touching her in that strange, wondering fashion, and the warmth became heat, and the tingle deepened to an ache. Her mouth burned and her body shook. "Shout at me. Hit me. Run away from me, Nicola."

Much more of this and *he'd* need to run. *"Gabriel."*

His hands lifted away, and they were shaking. "Forgive me."

"I don't mean . . ." Incoherent now, she grabbed his hand and pressed it between her breasts. The weight and warmth steadied her, brought back a moment of rational thought. "Keep going."

"No." His fingers danced up to trace the hollow in the

base of her throat. "As much as I wish to, we are strangers."

"We don't have to be." Not begging, demanding now, but she had to. Every time his hands left her, it hurt. "Please, Gabriel, I can't stand this. Do something."

"Calmez-vous." He used both hands now, stroking them from her ribs to her hips. "I will take care of you."

"Good. Great." Relief flooded her with new warmth, until he turned her away from him, placing her back to his chest and bracing her hands against the shiny-smooth bark of a beech tree. "Wrong side."

"Easier." He had the front of her jeans open and tugged them down.

Frustrated, Nick tried to turn. "Damn it, let me—"

"No," he breathed against her ear, holding her in place when she tried to let go and turn around toward him. "This way I cannot enrapture you."

Enrapture? She looked down, saw his hand spread over her abdomen, his palm covering her navel. He'd bunched her jeans and panties around her knees; his damp trousers pressed against her bare bottom. She held on to the beech's trunk and lifted one leg and then the other until she worked herself free of the tangle. She should have been embarrassed by the way she spread her legs for him, but she wasn't.

If she wasn't enraptured, she would be in about five seconds.

Gabriel's left hand pulled her wet bra up, freeing her breasts to his touch, while his right hand stroked down to trail his fingertips through the light patch of hair covering her sex. He touched her slowly, reverently. The burn scars on his arms felt like calluses, gently rasping over her softer skin as he cupped her.

The abrasion of his scars roused her out of the sensual haze.

What was she doing? He was right; they were strangers.

He was injured, blind, lost in the dark, probably in pain, and here all she could think about was fucking him.

But his cool, clever fingers were playing between her thighs, parting her and stroking her, and wanting trampled thinking as it threw itself at the rising heat.

"Close your eyes, *chérie*." His breath touched the side of her neck a moment before his mouth did. "Be with me in the dark."

Nick dug her fingernails into the glossy bark under her hands, her head falling back against his shoulder. Gabriel might be blind, but he knew exactly where he was on her, his long, insistent fingers finding every fold, every recess, painting them with the brush of his fingertips and the slick tempera of her desire.

"Like so." He breathed in. "Ah, *chérie*. You feel like a garden in the mist."

She felt more like a waterfall studded with rocks. Her breasts weren't large enough to fill his hand, but they felt heavier and harder under the slow massage of his palm. She regretted that she didn't have more for him to touch, because the way he played with her tight nipples made her want to scream.

Nick jerked her hips in reaction when he penetrated her with two fingers and felt his erection press against the small of her back. The edge of his palm nudged the top of her mound, exposing her clit. The contact made her tighten around his fingers and twist against his palm.

"Feel me touching you," he murmured. "Give me what I want."

She felt him, and let him touch what he wanted, and panted and suffered through it, until the friction against her clit and thrust of his fingers into her body brought her to the very edge.

He knew. His hand left her breasts and his arm lifted her, settling the separation of her ass against the thick rod of his penis. His fingers pushed deep as his mouth grazed the outer curve of her ear. "I have you. Come to me, *ma bien-aimée.*"

That did it. Nick bit down on her lip in time to stop the shriek of pleasure, but her body convulsed, out of control now, and the heat exploded inside her, fire and rain and moonlight; she was caught in his arms, coming beneath his hands.

"Again." His voice became a thick, low purr sifting through her hair as he brought her down and back up, relentless, shoving her into the fire until she thought she might collapse. *"Très bien."*

Unable to take any more, Nick dislodged his hand, thinking she might very well fall on her face and not get up for a week, wrung out and destroyed as she was by what he'd done with only his fingers. But she could still feel him against her, hard and unrelieved, as needy as she had been before he'd blown her mind and given her a personal tour of pleasure hell.

Oh, no, that wouldn't do.

She pushed away from the tree, turning in his arms, her hand slipping between them.

The green glow of his eyes brightened for a moment before he tried to catch her wrist and stop her. *"Non,* you need not, *chérie."*

"Quit being polite. You need this." Good thing Father Claudio's trousers hung so loose on him; she didn't have to fumble with buttons or a zipper. There he was, all that stiff, satiny length, and after the first exploratory stroke she gripped him in her fist. "And you owe me."

As soon as she had him, he shuddered. His hips gave an involuntary jerk, pushing his cock through the center of her grip. His foreskin felt like ribbed velvet. "It is not for you to do this."

"In America, we call it payback." She could feel how close he was; a couple of strokes and he'd go over. She leaned in. "Among other things." Working her hand up and down, she caressed him. The delicious friction and the urgency that racked his frame made her smile. "This is where you took me. Feel it the way I did."

It didn't take him long. His arms came around her and he went still, his penis ramming between her fingers one last time before semen jetted all over her hand. She milked him with her fist until he sagged, and then she went down with him, curling up beside him, still holding him in her hand.

"You did not have to do that," he said when he could speak again.

"I don't have to do anything." Nick stared up at the stars. "I wanted to."

Sex had never felt less complicated, and she wanted more. She wanted him on top of her, in her mouth, riding her ass and squeezing her breasts. He was going to turn her into an animal.

She was thinking about doing it again. She'd just engaged in a mutual jerk-off session with a strange, injured vampire, and she couldn't wait to jump him a second time. What the hell was wrong with her?

"I'm sorry. That was"—what could she even call it?— "rude."

"You must be very rude to me, then. Several times. Every day. My God." He shifted and made a sound. "I had forgotten how it feels."

She'd pleased him. This beautiful man, who was everything she wasn't, who'd endured nothing but pain, had come for her. She'd given him that much. She'd remember it forever.

He groaned, and she thought of his raw wounds. "Did I hurt you?"

"Hurt?" He rolled toward her, covering her hand with his. "No, *chérie,* no. You make me forget what that is."

"Okay." She closed her eyes, helpless to stop the tears, glad that he couldn't see them. "Okay."

Chapter 10

"Will that be all, Mr. Cyprien?" the waiter asked as he finished placing the bottles of French wine in the rack behind the suite's wet bar.

"A moment, *mon ami.*" Michael rested a hand on the man's shoulder, and watched his eyelids droop. "No need to speak of this delivery, or what you saw here. You will discard all records of it as well."

"No need." The man's head bobbed. "No records."

"Merci."

Marcella waited until the waiter silently exited before she came over and removed a sealed container from the refrigeration unit beneath the bar. Her movements, languid and negligent as they were, did not quite mask her restlessness. "When do we leave for Ireland?"

"Tomorrow night." He took the container from her and poured its contents, chilled human blood, into three crystal wineglasses. He diluted the thick fluid by adding a measure of burgundy. "If we are not discovered."

Phillipe joined them. In his hands he held reports faxed from Orlando. "Byrne has sent his trackers throughout the city. They have been unable to locate Alexandra's brother. There is no indication that anyone using his name or matching his description left the city."

John Keller had vanished on the day they had left America. Michael had suspected the former priest of walking out on their pact, until Byrne discovered that all of the security cameras in the parking garage had been disabled minutes before Keller had disappeared. As the Brethren did not know that Knight's Realm was owned and operated by the Darkyn, and Byrne controlled or monitored all transportation points around the city, that left only one possibility. "Richard arranged to have him taken."

"Keller may have chosen to abandon our cause," Marcella suggested. "He has no regard for the Kyn—"

"But he loves his sister, Cella, and he would not abandon her now." Michael handed one of the glasses of the bloodwine mixture to her. "Of that I am convinced. He would not leave except to go after her on his own."

"So Richard has him, and we must rescue both." She sipped from her glass and sighed. "The high lord still blames Keller for exposing your *jardin* in New Orleans, seigneur."

For the sake of his *sygkenis*, Michael had tried to protect the human priest from Richard's wrath by passing along the medical research Alexandra had been conducting on the Kyn. Ironically that research had resulted in her kidnapping.

"Under the present circumstances," Phillipe said, "Father Keller is worth more to the high lord alive than dead."

Marcella drained her glass. "Unless Richard discovers we are in England."

"That will not happen, madam," Phillipe assured her.

Michael and his seneschal had gone to great lengths to conceal their presence from Richard's suzerain and their border sentries. In addition to traveling mostly by day and using multiple false identifications, Michael had erased the memory of their arrival from the minds of every human with whom they came in contact since leaving America.

Usually Michael stayed at his private penthouse suite at the Savoy anytime he came to England, but they belonged to the suzerain of the London *jardin*. Michael had no desire to persuade Geoffrey into betraying his loyalty to the high lord. Instead, he had directed Phillipe to use contacts outside Geoffrey's influence to arrange accommodations, discreet transportation, and the other necessities for their journey.

Now Michael had to discover what he could about what was happening at Dundellan.

"I will question Father Leary now," he told his seneschal. "Make the final preparations for our journey." He glanced at Marcella. "Do you know how to use a computer?"

She arched a dark eyebrow. "I am Kyn, my lord. Not a Mennonite."

"*Bon*. Check the e-mail and see if Valentin has sent copies of the floor plans for Dundellan. If he has not, check the medieval Web sites to see if anyone has drawn or scanned them." He nodded toward the laptop Phillipe had connected at the suite's elegantly appointed workstation, and then went over to Leary.

Since being brought to the suite, the Brethren priest had been sitting and watching a soccer match on television. As Michael approached him, he looked up and smiled. "Yes, my lord?"

"I must speak with you, Orson." Michael sat across from him and took off his jacket. Each day he had been separated from Alexandra had made his scent grow deeper and stronger, and now it filled the room with the fragrance of roses in the sun.

"Can you not read his mind?" Marcella asked as she booted up the laptop.

"No." Michael gazed into the calm, peaceful eyes of the Brethren interrogator, watching as the human's pupils dilated. "That is not part of my talent."

"Then how is it that you make them forget things?" she asked.

"I cannot erase memories; my gift only finds and conceals them," he corrected. "The memories remain masked until I choose to lift the suppression."

Dark eyes shifted to Leary's benign countenance. "And if you do not lift it?"

"The memories are lost to the human forever." He knew Marcella had an aversion to using talent, as hers was particularly powerful. Still, he could not spend the rest of his time in England catering to his second's prejudices. "We each have our gifts, Cella. Perhaps you will allow me to use mine now, so that we may learn what we can before we leave for Ireland."

Leary's expression remained placid as Michael focused on him, and his pupils fully dilated as he succumbed to *l'attrait*. "Roses. Pretty flowers."

"Yes, they are." The human appeared completely under his control now. "Tell me, Orson, what you do for the high lord Richard?"

"Anything he wants." Leary lifted his hands palms up. "Lord Tremayne commands; I obey."

"Do you pass information to him about the Brethren?"

"Once I did." Leary's eyes grew watery. "But no more."

"Why did you stop?"

"Lord Tremayne told me to leave, and then had his black-hearted beast kill my brothers in Dublin." His gaze wandered. "The Lightkeeper exiled me to London, and will tell me nothing now. I am almost useless."

"But you still serve the high lord." Until Lucan came to America, he had served as Richard's chief assassin. It would be all too like the high lord's twisted sense of justice to force a Brethren to serve as Lucan's replacement. "Do you kill for him?"

Leary shook his head.

"He knows nothing that will help us." Marcella came to stand behind the priest. "We should release him."

"If he does not serve as a killer or an informant, he has to be a procurer," Michael told her. He caught Leary's drifting attention. "Do you bring humans to the high lord's castle?"

"Four times a year," Leary said, his voice dreamy. "Twenty fresh ones, every quarter."

Marcella muttered something terse and ugly under her breath.

"Who do you take, Father Leary?" Michael asked.

"Scum of the streets." He smiled. "Runaways and whores and junkies. The ones no one sees, no one cares for, they are best. No one misses them."

Unseen energy rippled through the air. Overhead, plaster cracked, and a fine white dust rained down from the ceiling. At the same time, a swirl of gray silk came around the sofa.

Michael barely had time to catch Marcella's hand as she reached for Leary's throat.

Phillipe ran into the room. "Madam, no."

"Away from me." Marcella whipped her head to one side, and a marble-topped side table flew at the seneschal and exploded against his chest, knocking him to the floor. "This man is mine."

Michael tightened his grip. "No, Marcella."

"You heard him. He preys on the weak, the hyena." Marcella's *dents acérées* flashed, fully extended, and bits of plaster fell like tiny hail, salting her black curls. "Let me take him, my lord." The floor rumbled beneath their feet. "Give him to me!"

Michael slapped her. *"Arrête."*

The rain of plaster dust and rumbling abruptly ceased. Marcella pressed a slim hand to her cheek, her eyes wide.

"Je m'excuse," he told her softly.

"Il n'y a pas de quoi." She straightened and gestured toward the laptop. "Jaus has sent the floor plans. I . . . I must go and pray."

Phillipe got back on his feet and stepped out of Marcella's way as she strode out of the suite.

"You should give her to my master," Leary said, his grin widening. "He likes females, and the ones I bring do not last long. In a week they will be consumed."

Michael knew Richard's changeling condition did not permit him to drink human blood, and no Kyn could consume flesh. "How so?"

"It is the new communion," Leary said, nodding. "To

partake of ruined flesh, turn polluted blood into wine. It is fed to those in rapture so that they might know the power and glory of the lord. Sometimes I am permitted to watch."

"Madam was right," Phillipe said, his disgust plain. "He is a jackal."

Leary gave the seneschal a lofty glance. "You will never serve my master."

"No." The thought that Richard was feeding his humans to one another revolted him. "He will not."

Michael continued interrogating Leary, compelling him to tell him about the number of times he had traveled to Dundellan, where in the castle he had been permitted to go, and what he knew of Richard's guards and household staff.

"The high lord uses the dungeon for special things," Leary told him. "Some of the doctors who check the new ones I bring take them there for tests. All of the passages are guarded."

The thought of Alexandra being kept in Richard's dungeon made Michael's fury rise like a scarlet wave, engulfing him with new rage. He was barely able to finish questioning Leary and allow him to return to watching the soccer match.

Alexandra. Her name beat, an echo of the lifeblood pulse in his head. *I am coming.*

Michael found Phillipe standing on the balcony of the master bedroom. Moonlight painted his broad, scarred features with gaunt, pale strokes.

"We will have to take him with us," Michael said. "Are you injured?"

"I have healed." His seneschal absently rubbed the place on his chest where the table had struck him. "Forgive me, master. I did not expect Madam Evareaux to attack me."

"It is her temper and her talent. Cella can do to worked stone what Lucan does to living things," Michael told him. "Anger made her lose control for a moment. It will not happen again."

"She makes a formidable siege weapon." His seneschal looked over the railing down to the street. "Does she truly go to pray?"

"Yes. She makes a pilgrimage to St. Paul's every time she visits London. She still believes that God will someday reveal His purpose in making us." He looked out into the night, somehow knowing that Alexandra was doing the same. "At least prayer provides comfort to her."

"I have prayed for Alexandra." Phillipe sounded almost ashamed to admit it. "She is truly innocent. Whatever God has done to us, surely He would not turn His face from her."

Michael lit a cigarette and looked out at the revolving lights of the London Eye, the largest observation wheel in the world, built to mark the new millennium. Behind it, Big Ben and the Houses of Parliament seemed like toy models. "Do you remember how pleased my father was when I took my vows?"

His seneschal nodded. "The master thought much of the Templars."

"I did not. After my mother died of plague, I no longer believed in God. I joined the order only to escape his bitterness." Michael released a thin stream of smoke and watched it curl in the air. "For centuries I thought that was why I had been cursed and made Kyn—because I had worn the cross over a faithless, empty heart. In the beginning I believed that Alexandra had been cursed because she also does not believe."

"There is much that I no longer believe in," Phillipe said slowly. "I think it is as Alexandra has said. That we lost our human lives to this thing that she calls a pathogen, and that God has nothing to do with it."

"Whether He exists or not, we are what we are. It does not matter." Nothing did, except taking her back. "Richard will see me dead before he releases her. Should that happen, you will do whatever is necessary to bring her home."

"Of course I will, master—"

Michael faced his seneschal. "When I am gone, when you have her safe, you will make her your *sygkenis*."

Phillipe opened his mouth, closed it, and then shook his head. "You need not ask this of me. She is yours. You will prevail."

"We did not choose Richard as our high lord because he could be easily taken." His head pounded with a maddening, gnawing craving to destroy something. "None of us is indestructible, and if he takes my head, Alexandra will suffer. You are the only one she trusts, the only one who can take her in hand. You do love her."

"I do," Phillipe said slowly, "but as I would love a sister."

"I must know that she will be safe. If I am dead, there are others who will come for her." He forced the words out. "She will need your strength and protection. I must demand this of you, old friend. Swear to me that you will take her."

A door slamming in the next room interrupted Phillipe's reply. Michael crushed out his cigarette. "Leary."

Out in the sitting room, the television still broadcast the soccer match, but Orson Leary had vanished, as had the keys to the van.

"He will go to Richard," Michael said. "Phillipe, arrange for another car at once."

The outer door to the suite swung open and Marcella strode in carrying Leary under her arm. "Your informant, my lord." She dropped the limp body without ceremony in front of Michael and tossed a ring of keys to Phillipe. "I did not kill him."

"Thank you, Cella."

She gazed down at the unconscious priest. "This time."

Riding to the village on the back of Nicola's motorcycle gave Gabriel some time to think, but the thrill of the air rushing over his skin and the little bumps and jolts from the road entranced him as much as sitting astride the bike, his body pressed to hers. He kept his hands on her hips, where she had placed them when she had told him to hold on, but he longed to slip them inside her clothing so he could again feel the delicious coolness of her skin. Wanting her—wanting more of her—made him ache from his fangs to his groin.

She saves me, he thought, *and all I want is to use her for my own pleasures.*

Like most country innkeepers, the couple in the village locked the doors of their inn at night, but Nick produced a key and let them in through the back door.

"Up some stairs." She took his hand and slowly led him to her room. "We'll be okay here for the day. Jean isn't nosy, and Adélie makes up the room in the evening."

Her room smelled of fresh-cut flowers, furniture oil, and clean linens. So accustomed was he to the scents of mold and dust and despair that it was as if he had been whisked away to another world.

Her world, not his.

"It's nothing fancy." She sounded gruff, almost angry. "I can't afford the five-star places. But it's clean and quiet."

It took a moment to register what she meant. She thought he was offended by her room. "I cannot see it, Nicola, but it feels and smells charming."

"There aren't any cockroaches. Here, lie down." She guided him to the small single bed and pulled back the covers. "Whoa, wait. Take off those pants first. They're mud city."

He stripped out of Claudio's damp, dirty trousers. "I must obtain more clothing."

"I can get some tomorrow," she said as she went into an adjoining room. Gabriel gingerly lay back, but it had been so long since he had occupied a real bed that the comfort felt as alien as the smell of the room.

"I have this place in England," Nick said as she came back into the room. From the sounds she made, Gabriel guessed that she was undressing. "It's in the country, nothing special, but it's out of the way and safe. We could go there, lie low for a while. Just until you're stronger."

Gabriel had not considered how utterly destitute he was. "I will need money and papers to travel."

"I can take care of it," she assured him. "Do you want me to call any of your friends for you, tell them you're okay?"

"There is no one to call." He took the too-soft feather pillow out from under his head and pushed it aside. "My home is outside Toulouse, in the hills near the border. That is where I must go."

Clothing fell against something made of wood. "Yeah, but shouldn't you let the others—what did you call them, the Kyn?—know you got away from the holy freaks?"

The bitter fact was that this human girl had done more for him than his own kind. "If my life mattered to them, they would not have left me to rot in the hands of my captors."

She said nothing for a long moment, and then asked, "Don't you have any family?"

Gabriel pushed away thoughts of Angelica. "My *tresora*, Dalente, looks after my estate in Toulouse. He is human, but I have complete faith in his loyalty. He will care for me, and arrange other matters as I need them."

One of her boots hit the floor with a small thump. "You mean you guys really do use human servants? Like in all the vampire movies?"

"Our *tresori* do serve us by guarding us during the daytime and handling our affairs, but they are more like trusted friends." Dalente would know what had happened to the Kyn in the two years since Gabriel's capture. Perhaps he would have him contact Michael Cyprien. If nothing else, Gabriel could persuade Michael to arrange a safe haven for him in America.

"We're not that far from Toulouse," Nick said. "I can take you tomorrow night."

If he spent much more time with her, he would not be able to let her go. "I will make my own way, thank you."

"You don't have any money," she informed him, "and even if I bought you a bus or train ticket, I don't think you want to travel that way. Not with all those green scars showing. People will freak out."

"I have Dalente keep cash and papers for me at the house," he said. "He will wire the money to me."

"Which you'd need identification to collect. Easier if I just take you home." Her voice moved closer. "How did they burn you like that?"

"They draped me with rosaries." Absently he brushed a hand over one of the hardened scars on his chest. During the first year of his captivity, the burning pain and open wounds caused by the copper beads had been a particular torment. Yet in time the pain gradually faded, until he felt little more than a drawing, warm sensation on his un-marked skin, and nothing where he had been previously burned.

"But . . ." Nick's slight weight tugged at the side of the bed as she sat on the edge. "I know crosses don't burn you guys. Why would rosaries do this?"

"They were strung with copper beads soaked in holy water." More knowledge she should not have, but Gabriel found himself abandoning his reservations and explaining the Kyn's sole weakness. "Copper is the only substance that can harm us. It can cut our flesh, poison us, and pro-longed contact with it results in burns like these."

She touched his jaw. "Why didn't that copper gag turn your face green?"

"The metal was impure, copper mixed with tin or pot metal." He turned on his side to face her, and had a sudden startling suspicion that she was as naked as he. "I can cover my scars with clothing, and compel a human to drive me home. You need not worry."

"Hey." Nick caught his hand in hers. "Quit trying to get me so fast. I've got wheels, contacts, and I know what you are and what you need. I'll be your *tresora* until we get to your place."

All of the things he imagined doing to her flashed through his mind, and not one of them fell within the boundaries of *tresoran* service. This need for her would take his control, and Nicola's life. He also despised the thought of making her play the role of his servant. "It would not be appropriate. I can only cause you harm."

"Well, you can *try*." She was not upset; she was laughing at him. "I have other ideas."

"That is not what I mean." Gabriel allowed his fingers to trace the fine tendons in the back of her hand. "Claudio will contact the Brethren as soon as he regains consciousness. He will report that I am gone and give them a description of you. Dalente will protect me, but you must leave France as soon as possible."

"I can handle the holy freaks," she countered, flopping down beside him. "Besides, I can see them coming. You can't."

The brush of her body revealed that she had indeed shed all of her garments, and intense curiosity speared him. Were he not so ashamed of using her as he had in the forest, he would be on top of her now, whispering to her as he eased her thighs apart and slid himself into the flower of wet, soft heat between them.

"Nicola, what happened between us . . ." He didn't know how to tell her that it wasn't enough, that he wanted more of her than she could possibly survive. It would be the same as throwing down a dare. "I should not have put my hands on you."

"Not a problem. You don't have to touch me again." She started to rise. "You'd better get some sleep."

"No." Gabriel put an arm around her waist. "I meant, I should not have taken advantage of your kindness as I did."

"You know what, Gabriel?" She leaned close, until her sweet breath heated his mouth. "I'm not that fucking kind."

"I compelled you—"

"No one"—she rolled on top of him and straddled him, planting her hands on his shoulders— "makes me do anything. No matter how gorgeous and sexy they are, or how great they talk."

She did not understand *l'attrait*, or the depth of his own yearning. "There are ways I can influence you without even meaning to."

"I do what I want, when I want, with whoever I want. Hey." She sat up, tucking the notch of her sex on top of the half-hard ridge of his. "Maybe I'm the one using you. Did you ever think of that?"

"You make a poor choice. I can be of no use to you." Unless she kept wriggling about.

She bent down and kissed the tip of his nose. "You'd be surprised. I expect my vocabulary to improve two hundred percent by the time we get to Toulouse."

As she climbed over him to lie down on his other side, Gabriel tried to fathom what she had said. She seemed a mass of contradictions, with the confidence of a seasoned, experienced woman, the audacity of a rebellious adolescent, and the playfulness of a girl just coming into her womanhood. She did have a rather simplistic way of expressing herself, but he suspected it was due more to a lack of formal education than any defect of mind.

Unless . . .

Gabriel remembered tracing her features but not feeling any age lines or wrinkles, and a sudden, cold dread filled him. "How old are you, Nicola?"

She curled up against him. "I don't celebrate birthdays anymore. No family, so no one brings me any cake or presents."

The remark sounded offhand, but he heard the loneliness beneath it. "If you did, how old would you be?"

"Twenty-six, although I still get carded everywhere I go." The gruff voice again, this time tinged with resentment.

He relaxed. "Good."

"No, it's a pain. So, how about this thing with you?"

He had not celebrated a birthday since rising to walk the night. "I am much older than twenty-six."

"I mean, how did this thing between you vampires and the holy freaks get started?" Her hair brushed his chest just before her cheek touched his shoulder. "Long story?"

He imagined condensing seven hundred years of their secret war into a comprehensive anecdote. "I think, yes, it is."

"You don't have to tell me now." She yawned. "We've got plenty of time."

Putting his arm around her and tucking her closer against his side felt only natural. "What else can I give you for helping me?"

"Some sex would be nice." She lifted her head. "Not now, but you know. After we sleep, before we get to Toulouse." Her voice became uncertain. "It wasn't just from being locked up for so long, was it? You do like me, don't you?"

Like her? He was half in love with her already.

Gabriel dared to lift a hand and bring her head back to its resting place. He had no right to claim her, not as young and trusting as she was. Nor would he reject her request.

"I like you very much." Her hair bubbled through his fingers, effervescent silk. "You must tell me if I ask more of you than you wish to give."

"Let's see: I've given you freedom, blood, and a quick but pretty good orgasm. It didn't kill me." She snuggled close to him. "Go to sleep, Gabriel. We'll figure it out on the way to your place."

Chapter 11

With Richard now holding John hostage, Alex had no choice but to abandon her plans to escape Dundellan. She spent a day analyzing Richard's blood and tissue samples while she tried to think of how to convince the high lord to return her brother to the States. The rats in her brain didn't want to run through that maze, however.

All she could think of was her lover, and where he was, and why the hell he hadn't come to get her.

The separation anxiety had gotten bad. Twice she was tempted to ram her head into an expensive piece of equipment to stop herself from thinking about Michael, wishing she could see Michael, and other symptoms of what she was beginning to see as total Michael Cyprien withdrawal.

When they got back together, she and Michael were going to have a very long talk about what it meant to be a *sygkenis*. He was going to tell her everything about it this time, because she wasn't going cold turkey like this again.

Other distractions helped. Korvel had posted two guards outside the lab, but the captain came and personally checked on her several times during the day. It was near twilight when he made an unusual request.

"Lady Elizabeth wishes to know what progress you are making," the seneschal said as he studied the beaker of fluid she was measuring into tubes. "What are you doing?"

"Mixing up some plastic explosive so I can blow this place to Mars." She gave him a guileless look. "Got any fuse cord you can spare?"

"Be serious, Doctor."

"You know what I'm doing, Captain." Alex queued the first profile pages from the analyzer to print. "Tissue biopsies, standard blood tests, and a little genetic look-see. Right now I'm breaking down your lord and master's blood into separate components. Who's this Lady Elizabeth?"

"She is my lord's wife."

"He's *married*?" Alex instantly thought of Éliane. *Poor Blondie, in love with a two-timing monster.* "Since when?"

"I believe the banns were posted in twelve thirty-four." He hovered behind her, looking down at the neat pile of reports feeding out from the printer. "You can make copies of those?"

"Sure." She tapped a few keys to produce a second set. "Although if you're going to give them to Lady Liz, you'd better call in a consultant. I doubt she'll be able to decipher them."

"My lady has some knowledge of the master's condition," Korvel said, "and is keen to follow what progress you make."

"Assuming I make any. What I found today only tells me that your master should be dead." She printed out duplicate reports and stacked them in a file. "Where is this chick? I'd like to meet someone who's put up with being married to the bastard and his bullshit for seven hundred plus years. She's got to have some very unique coping skills."

"Lady Elizabeth resides in the west wing." Korvel held out his hand. "I shall take them to her."

"Seriously, it really would help if I could speak with her myself." Alex felt the loose twist of hair at the back of her head slipping but kept her poker face on. "Richard claims to have been suffering from regular blackouts ever since he became a changeling. Maybe she can fill in some of the details that he can't remember."

"I shall relay your request to her." He took the file from

her. "You have worked through the night and day. It is time for you to feed and rest."

Alex stretched. "Sounds good to me."

Korvel checked her pockets and jacket before he escorted her from the dungeon to her new room. In this one they had removed all of the furnishings except a bed and a table. There were no security cameras, but copper bars had been welded over the two windows, and the door to the adjoining suite had been fitted with a dead bolt. An open bottle of wine and an empty glass had been placed on the table, and a set of fresh, folded scrubs sat on the end of the bed.

"See you tomorrow," Alex said as the seneschal locked her in the room. She went over and poured herself a glass of bloodwine, grimacing at the taste as she drank it. Somehow all the blood at Dundellan tasted slightly off. "Nothing like a lousy daycap." She released the clip holding the twist of her hair and the slim screwdriver she had concealed under it, and went over to work on the dead bolt.

It took ten minutes to remove the back plate of the dead bolt and release the lock from the inside of the mechanism.

No one occupied the adjoining bedroom, but it had not been stripped, and Alex took a couple of hairpins and a small diamond brooch from an exquisite porcelain jewelry box sitting on the vanity. Knowing Korvel would check her pockets if he found her wandering around, she tucked them inside her bra before moving to the hall door and opening it a crack.

No guards; the corridor was empty.

Alex had not been given a tour of Dundellan, but she had memorized every part of it she had seen during her earlier attempts to escape, and recognized where she was. It took a short, quick walk down the hall and through another to get to the west wing.

She expected to see guards, but evidently Lady Elizabeth liked her privacy. *Now to figure out which of the dozen rooms is hers—*

Sweet, sweet boy.

The cloying scent of lilies flooded Alex's head, along with the image of a young man in a white satin robe. Scarlet stains spotted the lapels, and more blood seeped from a fresh bite wound on his throat. Fear and horror plainly showed in his eyes, open so wide that Alex could see the whites all around the dark brown irises.

They tried to keep you from me, did they not? When I summoned you.

Alex staggered under the force of the laughing, murderous thoughts, bracing herself with a hand against a wall as more images poured into her mind.

An older man with long brown hair appeared beside the boy in the white robe. He knelt, bare chested and sweating, with his hands tied behind his back. A nude woman with short black hair shuffled over and crouched to huddle beside him.

The boy in the white robe didn't twitch a muscle, but tears began dripping down his cheeks.

I will make her bleed for you. Daggerlike nails attached to a dark, monstrous hand whipped across the nude woman's throat, opening the arteries with a violent spray of red.

The boy stood frozen, his eyes riveted on the dying woman, while the bound man lurched forward, his mouth opening on a scream—

Alex groped until she found a doorknob, and stumbled into a room. The scent of lilies closed around her like a cool, perfumed hand.

"Good evening." A woman in a pale lemon gown looked up from the hoop of embroidery in her hands. "You would be Dr. Keller."

"Alex. Hi." She had to blink a few times before her head cleared, and then the dazzling lights reflecting around the room itself made her a little dizzy. It looked as if the whole place had been lined with gold mirrors. "You Lady Elizabeth?"

"I am." Elizabeth placed her needlework in a basket by

her hip. She stood and dipped into an elegant curtsy. "Please come in; join me."

Alex squinted through the glare of the room, most of which seemed to be coming from the twelve-foot mirrored wall panels. Once her dazzled eyes adjusted, she could see that they actually were solid, yellow-orange mirrors that reflected the light coming from the flame-shaped bulbs in dozens of brass candelabra sprouting from the walls. More glassy, polished doodads in every shade of yellow from dark topaz to pale sunshine glittered from pretty little shelves and niches.

The aroma of honey, cognac, lilies, and some sort of oil greeted Alex. The unusual combination seemed to be mostly coming from the gilded walls.

Alex checked out the floor, which had been paved with inlaid rare woods and bits of ivory and more topaz-colored stones to form a very ornate mosaic, before she focused on the other woman. "Where's your husband?"

"I cannot say." Elizabeth smiled like a blond Mona Lisa. "I see you're admiring my chamber. There is nothing like it in the world."

Except the color of urine from a patient in kidney failure. Alex tried to think of something kind to say. "Very, uh, bright and cheerful." If you were into having your retinas fried.

"It is the Янтарная комната."

"Bless you."

Richard's wife chuckled. "That is the proper name, Doctor. In English it means 'the Amber Room.'"

"This is it?" Even Alex had heard of Czar Peter the Great's eighteenth-century jeweled chamber, which had been stolen by the Nazis and vanished during the Second World War. "The real deal."

"Yes. Just before the initiation of World War Two, my husband persuaded the Russians to allow him to remove it and keep it safe from Nazi looters." She moved to an onyx-and-marble mosaic and caressed its ornate edge. "It took the Prussian artisans six tons of solid amber and ten years to create this room."

"That's terrific." Actually, it was a bit creepy, considering that amber often held bugs trapped in the fossilized tree sap, but Alex could be polite. "When are you planning to give it back?"

Elizabeth gave her a pitying look. "My dear, the Russians believe it was destroyed by fire in Königsberg over sixty years ago."

Alex frowned. "So you stole it."

"Amber that is not given proper attention will crumble into dust," Elizabeth said. "I saved the greatest artwork ever to be created in amber."

That was one way of looking at it. "Didn't I read something about some millionaire industrialist re-creating the room from some old pictures and diagrams of the original?"

"A paltry imitation." Elizabeth's face darkened. "Nothing can compare to the true beauty of my Amber Room."

"I guess not." Alex noticed most of the niches were occupied by amber statues of a very familiar female. "You're Catholic, I take it."

"I was." Richard's wife returned to the velvet settee and picked up her embroidery. "Sit down, Doctor. We have much to discuss."

Alex took a seat in one of the tapestry-covered chairs, which was about as comfortable as sitting on a canvas-covered rock. So much for great art. "I assume you know that your husband kidnapped me and brought me here against my will."

"Richard is the high lord." She made a small stitch and pulled the thread through the cloth. "He need not ask anyone for anything."

Alex eyed Elizabeth's needlework, which depicted an angel hovering over a young Virgin Mary. "That's a pretty medieval attitude."

"I was born in medieval times," Elizabeth said. "Tell me about the tests you have accomplished thus far."

Alex related in the simplest terms she could what little information she had culled from the tests. "Richard's blood chemistry is highly abnormal, even for the Darkyn."

Golden eyebrows rose. "In what manner abnormal?"

"Red blood cells in humans don't have some of the internal structures found in other types of cells. They're designed that way because they have to perform specialized functions. But Kyn red blood cells are eukaryotic." Alex saw her blank look and added, "They have a nucleus. Human blood cells don't."

"I do not understand why that matters." The other woman lifted a shoulder. "We are not human."

"We *were* human." Alex gritted her teeth and pushed on. "I found another anomaly while examining Richard's cells. The cell's nucleus contains hereditary material—we get that from our parents—that controls the cell's growth, metabolism, and ability to replicate. Normal humans have twenty-three pairs of chromosomes per cell. For some reason, Kyn have twenty-five. The tests I ran on your husband show that he has another, extra set of paired chromosomes in his blood cells that don't match the original twenty-five. That brings his total up to fifty."

"How delightful."

"Ah, no. Not really." The woman knew absolutely nothing about hematology or cellular biology; that much was obvious. "The extra chromosomes encode more than they should and result in very serious physical and mental defects. If Richard were human, I'd diagnose him with a rare form of polyploidy. But any genetic damage like this causes spontaneous death of the afflicted, usually in utero."

Elizabeth glanced up. "Fortunate, then, that he is Kyn."

"You don't understand. Your husband is in the end stage of a mutation that should have killed him, but it hasn't. He's not human or Kyn anymore. I don't know what he is."

She went over the other unusual aspects that testing had turned up, and then finished by stretching the truth. "That's as much as I'm going to learn about Richard's condition, because I'm a surgeon, not a geneticist. He needs to be treated by specialists in the field."

Elizabeth had put down her hoop and sat silently staring at the faux flames in the mirrored fireplace.

She's his wife; of course she's upset.

"I honestly can't do anything to help him," Alex said. It was true; she had no treatment for the extensive genetic damage Richard had suffered. "I don't care what he does to me, but he also kidnapped my brother, who is still human. He's threatened to hurt John if I don't find a cure for his condition."

Elizabeth nodded.

"You're okay with that?"

"I am wife here, not mistress. What I think or want is irrelevant." She took a small pair of silver scissors out of her sewing basket and used them to clip a thread hanging from the edge of her left sleeve. "Is this why you sought me out? To enlist me as your advocate so that I might plead your case?"

Nailed.

"I don't want you to overstep your bounds, or piss off your husband," Alex said carefully. "But yeah, I need some help. John has already been through torture once, when the Brethren had him in Rome. That, combined with the fact that his sister now has fangs and drinks blood, has probably traumatized him for life. He's not part of this war, Elizabeth. If you have an ounce of decency . . ."

Ghostly images rose behind Alex's eyes.

". . . you'll see that . . ."

Sweet girl. Claws sinking into pale flesh. *So sweet.*

Alex pressed a hand to her temple. "Is your husband hanging around here somewhere?"

"I cannot say. You must be thirsty after all this talk." Elizabeth set aside her needlework and clapped her hands.

Like magic, one of the wall panels opened into the room, and two Kyn males appeared. Both wore old-fashioned gold-and-white garments that reminded Alex of some Merchant Ivory films she'd seen. Between them they held a human male dressed in a dark suit and a full-face black mask. Although Alex couldn't see his face, the human's dark eyes had the same empty, unfocused cast to them as those of the other zombies in the castle.

"You've got your own secret passage?" Alex asked Elizabeth.

"It amuses my husband to move about undetected. He has had them built on nearly every floor." She rose and shook out her skirts. "I find them convenient for discreet deliveries."

The human male seemed weirdly familiar to Alex, but he wasn't the one she'd seen in the white robe during the killing vision she'd had in the hall. "What's with the mask?"

"Another amusement. Would you care to feed first?" Elizabeth asked, as if offering Alex a cup of tea.

"I'm not thirsty, thanks."

Elizabeth dismissed the Kyn males and went to the human. The scent of lilies almost choked Alex, but the zombie-eyed man didn't move from his spot. Richard's wife embraced him, pulling his head down to hers.

"The faithful have such hot blood." Elizabeth sank her fangs into his neck and pushed her hand into the front of his trousers.

Alex saw awareness flicker through the dark eyes. "Hey. He knows what you're doing."

Richard's wife lifted her mouth from her victim. "I want him to feel it." She struck a second time.

The man made a sound, and pain and disgust clouded his eyes.

Oh, no. Alex grabbed the laces at the back of Elizabeth's gown and used them to jerk her away. "Get off him."

"Of course." Richard's wife took a white handkerchief from her sleeve and daintily patted her lips. "It has been some time since you've fed directly from a human, has it not?"

"I don't feed from humans." Alex checked the four puncture wounds, none of which had penetrated any major vessel, and then carefully removed the mask. "Johnny?" She tore away the strip of yellow silk gagging her brother. "John, it's all right."

Her brother stared over her head and said nothing.

Alex turned on Elizabeth. "What did you do to him?"

"It is Stefan's talent, not mine. The dear boy cannot do anything but obey me, but he will feel every sensation." Elizabeth smiled, showing bloody teeth. "We will share him."

"Thanks," Alex said, "but I don't eat family members, and you've had enough."

"We are your family now, Alexandra. Two Kyn feeding at once prevents thrall. We can still enjoy him in other ways." She reached out and ran a finger down between Alex's breasts. "Don't you want to see me riding his cock while you bespell him?"

"Cheat on Richard with someone else." Alex grabbed her wrist and bent it until the joints cracked. "You're not touching my brother again."

"I give the order, and your brother will die." Elizabeth peered at her. "You're not afraid."

"Of you? Sorry, no." She caught another flash of the killing vision. "So this is your thing. Who was the kid in the white robe, Liz? Who were the people you butchered in front of him?"

Elizabeth's gory smile faltered. "You cannot read my thoughts."

"Oddly enough, it's my talent. Reading the minds of killers." Alex turned to John, and saw the alarm in his eyes. "You're going to get my brother out of here."

"I certainly shall not."

Alex knew the Kyn had to feed, and preferred to take blood straight from the source, but this was too perverted for words. "If you don't, I'll go to Richard and tell him everything."

"Be my guest." Elizabeth dropped her soiled handkerchief on the floor. "I've done this hundreds of times, and Richard has never cared. He's even had me torture some of his Brethren prisoners. You see, Doctor, the fear and pain they feel as I feed comes from *my* talent."

Alex drove her fist into Elizabeth's belly, knocking her back against one of the amber panels. She went after her to punch her again, but this time someone caught her from behind.

"Enough." Éliane, with a tranquilizer gun in one hand. "I apologize for the intrusion, my lady. Guard. The mistress is done with the human."

Stefan came in and led John out of the room.

When Alex tried to wrench free, Éliane pressed the muzzle of the gun into her side. "I will see to it that the doctor does not disturb you again."

"Saved by my husband's whore." Elizabeth pushed away from the amber panel and fussed with her skirts.

"You'd better keep your teeth out of my brother," Alex warned. "Or I'll make it my purpose in life to ruin that pretty face of yours."

"Will you." Elizabeth's hand shot out and she caught Alex's face in a bruising grip. She leaned in, almost kissing her mouth before she added in a whisper, "The one thing you had better not do, Doctor, is cure my husband. If you do, I will kill your brother, and make *you* watch."

The dark shifted around Nick, becoming less empty as the shadows swelled. Whatever was happening, she wasn't meant to witness it. Aside from her own body she couldn't see or hear a blessed thing.

Dreaming.

Her other senses told her that grass, cool and crackling,

flattened under her steps, and gardenia and roses bloomed nearby. Her skin lit up with nerves, absorbing textures from all the unseen things she brushed against: the slick gloss of leaves, the bumpy roughness of bark, the silken glide of petals.

Being Helen Keller in the nightlands seemed about as smart as playing Marco Polo with razor blades, so Nick stopped walking. "I'm not moving again until someone turns on the lights."

Someone did.

Nick saw that she was standing on the edge of a small alpine meadow, a pool of grass framed by endless acres of pine and ringed by towering mountains. Millions of dandelions studded the clearing's green carpet and filled the air with the wish fluff of their seeds.

Despite the peace and serenity around her, she felt something coming, and braced herself.

Nothing touched her but cool breeze and floating dandelion seed. She was about to sit down in the grass and wait for what had better show up, and soon, when the Green Man stepped into sight, twenty feet away from her on the other side of the meadow. He wore Father Claudio's bloodstained trousers, and his blind eyes glittered with metallic green light.

Nick watched him. He seemed to return the inspection. "Gabriel?"

Gabriel is lost.

He began walking toward her, and with every step the dandelions within two feet of him began to droop and wither. The air within the dream grew frosty.

"I found you, remember?" Nick could see her breath puffing out as she spoke. "We got away from them."

Gabriel will never be free. Gabriel died in that cellar.

The words, not the cold, made her shiver. "Who are you, then?"

He halted just out of reach. *The remnant of what he was. A shred of soul. I belong to the many now.*

"The many what?"

They are all around you, wherever you go. The Green Man moved then, too sudden and speedy for Nick to avoid, and knocked her flat on her back. He lay full-length on top of her. *Yet you never see them.*

"You're the one who's blind." She wanted to go back to the forest, where he had done nicer things to her. Why couldn't she have a nightmare about having sex with Gabriel while he subjected her to the horrors of continuous orgasms?

I see everything. He pinned her wrists to the grass, his hands slipping a little on her wet flesh.

Suddenly they were both completely, comprehensively soaked: their clothes, their skin, even their hair—his dripped beads of sweat or water all around her face. It came from what appeared to be a stream running across the sky and pouring over the entire meadow simultaneously.

"You're hurting me," she told him, resisting a terrible urge to dig her fingernails into his wrists. Instead she blinked the water out of her eyes, trying not to fight. Even like this, she didn't want to hurt him. He needed love—her love—and here she could give him what she couldn't in the waking world.

I do not wish that. He looked around, puzzled now, as if he wasn't sure where they were. *Where are the mourning hens?*

Now he was worried about depressed chickens. "I don't know."

The rain stopped, and the air around them turned frigid. The glittery green glow of his irises expanded, making his pupils shrink to mere slits. The rain on his skin turned in tiny scrolls of frost, elongated bindi bejeweling the solid-emerald flesh. His body felt too big, too hard on top of hers, but Nick refused to struggle.

Do you not want me now? he murmured, watching her face.

The cold didn't seem to affect Nick; she felt as if on

fire, so hot that her own skin and clothes went from saturated to flash-dried.

"Everyone always wants the coolest guy around, don't they?" She watched a veil of ice crystals form over his hair while wisps of steam rose from around her own head. "I guess that would be you."

He bent his head, making tiny chips of ice like confetti pelt her. *Open your mouth.*

"What f—"

His thinner, harder lips used hers like cushions, sinking into them, pushing them apart. Despite the frost coating his skin, his kiss felt warm instead of cold, masculine, demanding. Hard-mouthed men had always turned Nick on. If that weren't bad enough, the slow, slick trespass of his tongue about made her come right there. Then they were tasting and sucking and biting, lost in it, as explosive as ice to fire, and everything she'd felt in the forest paled like a maiden aunt, packed its overnight bag and went home whimpering.

He lifted his lips from hers. *Do you love me, or him?*

"I'm not in love with anyone." Jesus Christ, yes, she was, but until this moment it had been mixed up with wanting and sex and disbelief and being afraid for him. Why did they have to meet like this, in this unreal place, to talk about their feelings? Was he even the same guy who was sleeping next to her? "Why do you care?"

He would love you if I could, Nicola.

"We'll work with what we've got." Something moved under her, biting into her ass. Literally—she could feel tiny teeth piercing her jeans.

I'll never have enough. Neither will you.

"Optimist. Damn it." She rolled over, forcing him onto his back, and reached between her legs to pry something small, green, and snapping from the seat of her pants. She held it up between them and frowned. "A dandelion? With thorns?" She yelped as it wriggled, bending over to bite the side of her hand and draw blood. "Ouch." Disgusted, she flung it away.

Two green hands grabbed her hips. *Stay where you are.*

She turned her head and saw that the dandelions near her face were uprooting themselves, their fluffy heads parting and flashing pointy little fangs.

So, this was bad news. "I'd better call this a night."

You cannot leave without finishing this.

"I don't want to leave you, but the weeds look hungry." Nick tried, but for once she couldn't force herself awake. "Shit." She redoubled her focus, ordering her body to rouse, but remained locked in the nightmare. "Listen, we're in trouble. You're sleeping beside me. See if you can wake up."

Gabriel sleeps beside you. He turned his head slowly, assessing the area around them. *I exist only here, with you.*

"I can't catch a break, can I?" She noted that every single dandelion in the meadow had come to life and was going feral. One dandelion bite on the ass wasn't fun. One hundred thousand of them . . . "Give me another option."

I have none to give. You control these nightlands. You have to burn them.

"*I* have to burn them." And here she'd forgotten to pack a flamethrower. "With what?"

The Green Man's pine-needle hair whisked across her cheek. *It has no name.* As Nick stared at him, he seized her hand in his. *What you feel when we touch.*

Oh, *that* heat. The fanged dandelions were starting to break free of the earth, and they were all turning toward them. "How?"

Feel it, hold it, use it. He pushed her hands flat against the ground. He held her wrists so she couldn't lift her hands away. *Quickly.*

Nick didn't like the feeling of the grass under her palms, or the faint squirming sensation that she suspected came from the dandelions squashed under her.

The Green Man's grip tightened past painful, grinding the bones under it. *Burn them now or the nightlands will rip us apart.*

Understanding precisely what he wanted her to do never happened. Something instead bit Nick's forearm. She dug her fingers into the dirt and felt something rise inside her. It spread, a bad fever, an outrageous climax, both and neither. Whatever it was, it slammed through her arms and shot out of her hands.

Black fire erupted all around, a sweeping dark flash of a circle that blasted outward, reducing every feral dandelion in its path to a little pile of dark ash. The circle of fire kept expanding until the entire clearing had turned into smoldering soot, and then it seemed to blow itself out at the tree line.

As soon as the Green Man released Nick's sore wrists, she rolled away, curled over, and got to her feet.

"What's going to happen to Gabriel?" she asked the Green Man.

He didn't stand as much as he floated to his feet. *Gabriel is dead.*

"He's sleeping beside me at the inn," Nick argued. "I can feel him breathing. You're part of him. If you could get back together—be one man instead of two . . ."

The Green Man shook his head. *The body lives. The soul dies.*

More dream riddles. "Could you for once talk in a way that I can actually understand?"

Ask Gabriel what he dreams. The Green Man turned transparent. *Ask what he feeds the many. It is what keeps us apart.*

Nick came awake with a gasp and a lunge, and got out of bed. As in the dream, she was soaked from head to toe, although with a clammy sweat instead of sky-bound stream water. She looked back and saw Gabriel's scarred torso, and the tangle of his hair on the pillow. He had turned away from a shaft of light that had filtered through a gap in the window curtains.

Nick decided against waking him, and quietly dressed before getting on her laptop. Using her Midi-Pyrenees maps, she planned out her route to Gabriel's estate in Toulouse. Even with the pit stop, if they left just before sunset and took some shortcuts, she'd get him home by midnight.

Leaving him there with his servant seemed a little cold, but she didn't have to be a stranger. If his place was secure enough, she might ask him to let her drop in now and then. She didn't have many safe places to stay in France. It was probably a very cool house. A lot of wealthy people with extensive properties lived in or near Toulouse.

She'd take him there, say good-bye, and hit the road. Under the circumstances it was the smartest thing to do. She didn't need him in her life right now, and he certainly didn't need her.

Maybe, after she found the Madonna, she really would come back and see him again. See if the feelings were still there.

That's not it. You don't want to let him go.

Blood was going to be a problem; Nick knew that she couldn't keep feeding him hers. She'd stop in Nîmes and see if she could make a clandestine withdrawal from one of the city's hospitals or blood banks.

Nick looked over at the man sleeping in her bed. There was something about him that echoed inside her, as if they were back in her dream. But why did the Green Man insist he wasn't Gabriel? Why did he talk about Gabriel as if he were dead? Did the dream have any meaning? She figured the dandelions represented all the new doubts and old fears gnawing at her; only she could rid herself of them.

She would, too, as soon as she found the Golden Madonna. She'd never be free to love anyone until she did.

Chapter 12

Gabriel woke soon after Nick finished packing, and carefully got to his feet. "Has the sun set?"

"Almost." She picked up the towels Adélie had provided and tucked her scissors into her back pocket before she handed one of the towels to him. "Wrap this around your waist; we're going to take a shower."

He didn't move. "I will be seen."

"As long as you're quiet, no one will come looking." Nick tugged on a long, snarled piece of his hair. "This needs washing and trimming. Unless you're into the homeless-hippie look."

Gabriel allowed her to lead him to the bathroom, but caught her hands when she tugged at the towel at his waist. "I am not completely helpless," he told her. "I can bathe myself."

"We had this argument last night. You lost. Besides, if we share, the innkeeper won't get suspicious about how much water I'm using." Nick removed the towel and started the shower. "You're okay with being naked with me, aren't you?"

"*Oui.*" He reached and with startling accuracy ran the tip of his finger down the hollow of her throat. "I only wish that I could see you."

"I'm nothing special. But you . . ." Nick admired the width of his shoulders, and the hard, lean muscle under the mottled skin of his chest. The green burn scars didn't disguise how beautifully he was made. "You're very hot, even for a vampire."

"You're kind." He sounded as if he didn't believe her.

"Rarely." She quickly stripped down to the skin before stepping into the small cubicle. "Here we go—step over the edge, like that—there you go. Hair first." Once she had him inside, she reached up and pushed his head back to wet the tangled mane.

"It feels good." He turned his face into the lukewarm spray.

Nick worked her hand through his hair to make sure it had gotten saturated before she tapped his shoulder. "I can't reach you all the way up there. Bend down."

Gabriel put his hands on her waist and knelt in front of her, his mouth level with her chin. "Is this better?"

If only she were six inches taller. "That's fine." Nick concentrated on the shampoo, and getting it out of the bottle and onto her palm. "Close your eyes."

"Soap will not harm me."

This close, Nick felt as if she could dive into his eyes. "They're distracting."

She worked the shampoo through the matted length of his hair and used her fingernails to gently scrub his scalp. Mud-colored foam and water ran down his back, and it took two more scrubs and rinses before Nick got the last of the dirt out.

"You've got a major rat's nest going here," she said as she massaged a handful of shampoo into the clean but knotted length. "I might have to cut it pretty short if I can't comb them out."

"I do not care."

Nick lathered a washcloth with the bar soap and went to work on his body. The dip in the river had gotten off most of the blood and surface grime, but what she had thought was an uneven tan turned out to be another layer of dirt. Beneath it his skin was golden brown where he wasn't burned and dark green-brown where he was.

His hands moved up as his head bent. "Let me have the soap."

Nick placed the bar and cloth into his hands. He dropped the cloth and rubbed the bar between his palms. "Let me look at your back again," she said.

"I want to wash you now." His soapy hands encircled her neck, sliding down and over her collarbone before sweeping up to lather her shoulders. "Lift your arms."

Nick reached for the ceiling, shuddering as Gabriel stood and followed the length of her arms with his hands, first up to her wrists, then down the insides. His thumbs explored the soft crescent spaces under her arms—two places on her body that Nick had never considered erotic until that moment—before chasing the line of her ribs.

The foam on his hands, she saw, had been washed away. "You need more soap." And she needed to step out of here before she wound herself around him like a starving octopus.

"You need to eat more," he murmured, moving his hands under her breasts to cradle her waist. "You feel so thin."

"I've got a weird metabolism. I told you I wasn't much to look at," she tried to joke. She glanced down to see what he was doing and saw his erect cock, the slick, engorged head pushing out from his foreskin, bobbing between them.

His palms grazed over her breasts, dragging at the tightly puckered nipples. "Are you cold?"

"Not exactly." She swallowed against a suddenly dry throat. "I see a spot I missed."

Now Nick went on her knees, steadying herself with one hand on his thigh. Soap still clung to her breasts, and she cupped them, catching his penis between the inner curves and massaging him from the purple-red tip down to the broad base.

Gabriel's hand slapped the tile wall as he braced himself. "What are you doing, *ma mie*?"

"Guess." She tilted her head, allowing the shower spray to rinse off the foam before bending her head and kissing the glans.

His hand threaded through the wet curls at the back of her head. *"Faites comme vous voulez."*

Nick nipped the inside of his arm. "Oh, I intend to do *exactly* as I please."

She moved up and then down, sliding his shaft between her breasts. She gave the straining head of his cock a quick, light suck when it came up far enough to touch her lips, and then freed it to squeeze it between her aching breasts.

Nick knew that, much as she wanted to, she couldn't spend the afternoon playing with him in the shower. As soon as she felt his shaft swell and tighten, she released her breasts and took him in her mouth. Breathing in and pushing down until her lips met his body, she held him and caressed him with her tongue, sucking as he muttered her name, as his hand pulled at her hair, as his hips jerked. His semen burst from his cock in one long, delicious gush, as cool and thick as cream.

Nick loved how good it felt to give him the pleasure he had been denied for so long. She let him slide from her lips with slow, greedy reluctance. "All nice and clean now."

Gabriel lifted her up to meet his mouth, and kissed her so deeply and passionately she almost came right there. But the water had turned cold, and if they stayed any longer someone would be coming upstairs to see what was going on.

"We gotta get out of here." She reached behind him and shut off the spray.

"You owe *me* the payback now," Gabriel told her, pulling her closer. "And I very much want to collect."

She chuckled. "It'll have to wait until we get to your place." She nuzzled his chest. "We seem to have this thing going with water. Have you got a good, hot shower?"

"Five of them, and a sunken bath, and a whirlpool." He kissed the wet top of her head. "We will make love in all of them."

Nick dried off with Gabriel, dressed, and left him in the room while she went downstairs to pack the bike and settle her bill. After she had thanked Jean for a pleasant stay and made one final arrangement, she made a detour to Adélie's washroom and swiped some of Jean's freshly laundered clothing from a basket, and brought it up to the room.

"I will be seen wearing this when we leave," Gabriel said as he dressed.

"No, you won't. The innkeeper and his wife went out for dinner." Nick tried not to watch him, but her eyes kept straying to his body and the way he moved. Being this close to him, smelling him, remembering how his cock felt gliding in and out of her mouth only made her want more. Nick was beginning to feel like a socket without a plug. If she didn't get her libido under control, being around Gabriel was going to turn her into a sex maniac.

Annoyed with herself, she finished checking the room to make sure she hadn't left anything behind before she handed her jacket and helmet to Gabriel. "Put this on."

"You should wear them."

"Claudio only saw me once," she said as she put on her darkest sunglasses and tied a red bandanna around her hair. "You need to keep your face covered until we put some miles between us and the holy freaks."

"I meant that you should wear them for your own safety," he told her. "A fall from your motorcycle will not harm me. It could kill you."

After all Gabriel had been through, he was worried about her. The man was too sweet for his own good.

"I don't fall off my bike." She took the helmet and fit it over his head before adjusting the chinstrap. "Keep the visor down; your eyes are shining like little traffic lights."

In back of the inn, Nick secured the panniers and checked her fuel tank before climbing onto the seat and holding the bike steady while Gabriel did the same. Carrying the additional weight would make the engine use more petrol, so she made a mental adjustment on where and when she would stop for refueling.

"Ready?" she asked before she hit the ignition.

His hands gripped her hips. *"Oui."*

To avoid attention, Nick took the back alleyways out of the village and detoured around the road that led to the château. From there it was a straight run through the farmlands to La Garonne, which she followed to Toulouse, the capital of the Midi-Pyrenees region, nestled at the foot of the mountains that had long served as a natural boundary between Spain and France.

Nick loved riding through this part of France during the day. The roads were long, uncluttered by traffic, and wound through villages that looked like they'd avoided the ravages of time for the last four or five hundred years. People planted flowers everywhere, and where they couldn't they hung garlands and wreaths and swags of dried corn, wildflowers, and berries. The air sometimes smelled of oranges, sometimes of grapes, and sometimes of fresh laundry still flapping in the breeze. Nick was sure there were ugly villages somewhere in France, just not here.

Unfortunately she couldn't take Gabriel out during the day. Even if she did, he couldn't see France as she did. He'd never see anything again, thanks to the holy freak show.

Nick didn't consider old people fair game, but she still wished she could go back to the château and beat Father Claudio to a wrinkly pulp.

She stopped in a meadow about a mile from the city to let her passenger stretch his legs while she checked the bike. She took out her portable lantern and looked around to see if there were any dandelions in the general vicinity before she propped it on the seat.

Crickets chirped in one loud, creaking chorus around them as Gabriel removed the helmet and hung it by the strap from the back of the seat.

His hand brushed the lantern. "A light?"

"It's pretty dark out here," she said as she knelt by the front tire. "I need it to check the bike. And the local weeds."

"Weeds?"

"From a nightmare I had about vampire weeds. Dandelions with fangs." She shuddered. "I am never making another wish on them as long as I live."

"Nor will I," he said. "But, Nicola, is it not dangerous for you to be driving this machine at night?"

"Not at all. The bike has a good headlight, and I'm used to it." He sounded weak again. She hadn't been to any hospitals specifically in Toulouse, but she knew how to get in and out of one quickly. "You need more blood, don't you?"

"Not for some time. I am accustomed to going without feeding for weeks, even months." He cocked his head. "That is an interesting sound. Tell me what you are doing."

"Loosening up." She had taken her baseball bat from the back of the bike and swung it a few times. "It would help if you could pitch me some balls."

"May I?" He held out his hand.

She placed her most precious possession in his grasp. "It's a homemade baseball bat. My stepdad made it for me when I got homesick for America. All the kids in the village were into soccer and cricket and English stuff, so he used to pitch balls to me after dinner every night." She grabbed the lantern from the seat of the bike. "I really love baseball."

He ran his hands over the smooth wood. "You came to England when you were young?"

"Thirteen. My real dad died when I was a baby, and my mom and I were alone until then. She met Malcolm through this Internet site for widows and stuff. I had a fit when she told me we were moving to England, but Mal had this great place, and he didn't push me to call him Dad or anything, and . . ." She pressed her fingers against her eyes. "Anyway, it worked out."

He handed her the bat but didn't release it, using it instead to lure her over to an old olive tree. "Come and sit with me."

Nick carried the lantern over and sat down beside him, bracing her back against the tree. The long bike ride had

another, less convenient side effect—all that vibration between her legs had kept her damp and edgy. She would not
think about climbing onto Gabriel's lap and kissing him
and rubbing up against him. However much she wanted to.
"You said you'd tell me more about this thing between the
holy freaks and the Kyn."

"The Darkyn," he corrected, tapping her leg with the
end of the baseball bat. "That is what we have been called
since we first changed into *vrykolakas.*"

A soft, fluttering sensation made her flinch, until she
saw it came from a small green moth that had landed on
her arm. *Drawn by the light.* She didn't try to brush it
away. "*Vrykola*-what?"

He repeated the word slowly, drawing out the syllables.
"That is what people once called souls damned by their
sins. Cursed to wander through eternity and feed only on
the blood of the innocent."

"It means all that?" She eyed the moth, which wandered
down to her elbow. Another, larger brown moth joined it,
and they circled each other, dancing on her skin. "No wonder it's a mouthful." The comical movements of the moths
made her chuckle.

"Does something amuse you?"

"I have two moths crawling on my arm." She laughed
as a third, black moth joined them. "Make that three."

He smiled. "They are attracted to your warmth."

"Or my sweat." She propped her arm against her thigh.
"Who came up with the name 'Darkyn,' anyway? Sounds
like something you'd title a bad B movie."

"You have to understand that we were born in a dark
age, surrounded by superstitious, fearful people," he said,
and from there told her about the terrible plague that had
turned infected humans into the "dark Kyn."

Nick absorbed every word. Some of it made sense with
what she knew about the vampires, but the rest sounded
like something out of a historical-religious thriller.

"So you're a priest." And she'd had sex with him twice

now. More crimes to add to the long list she was hauling around. The moths flew from her arm as she opened and took a drink from the plastic canteen she'd filled with water at the inn. "Don't you think you should have mentioned this a little earlier?"

"I was forced to leave the church when I became Kyn," he told her. "I have not been a priest for many years."

"Good. I mean, I'm sorry you quit or got fired or whatever happened." High time to find out more details. "Are you married?"

"We do not marry. Sometimes we take a *sygkenis*, a life companion, but very few females rose to walk the night. Once I thought that I might . . ." He shrugged. "But there was never anyone who came into my heart."

That odd hesitation made Nick think that there might have been someone special in Gabriel's past. He had been alive for so long; how could he have spent all those years alone? But at least now she knew she wasn't poaching on someone else's territory. "What was it like? Being a Templar?"

"Bernard of Clairvaux called us warriors who were 'gentler than lambs and fiercer than lions, wedding the mildness of the monk with the valor of the knight,'" Gabriel said. "But even he did not understand what we were. We took back the Temple of Solomon, but we adorned it with weapons instead of jewels. We went into battle not for fame, but for victory. We were taught to be silent, never to waste speech or action, never to laugh or gossip, never to embrace vanity or idleness. We protected the weak, the faithful, and those who could fight for themselves. We tried to take back all that was holy to us. Clairvaux said that we were many, but we lived in one house, according to one rule, with one soul and heart. Sometimes we were."

"That's really pretty," she said, somewhat taken aback by the description of his former human calling, "but I just can't picture you reading from the Bible and handing out communion wafers." Maybe because she'd gone down on him in the shower, and had been fantasizing about all the other things she wanted to do to him as soon as they got to his place. *Do you go to hell for giving an ex-priest vampire an orgasm?*

He smiled sadly. "I am sorry to say that I did not do much of that during my human life."

She passed the canteen to him. "Can you still drink water?"

"In small amounts." Gabriel took a sip before handing it back. "I spent most of my priesthood fighting alongside my Templar brothers in the Holy Land. We engaged in countless battles against the Saracens, but they proved too many for us."

Too many. Nick remembered what the Green Man had said, and raised the canteen to her lips. "Do you dream when you sleep?"

"Kyn do not sleep, precisely. We rest our bodies. Our minds, our dreams . . ." He stopped and thought for a moment. "I cannot describe it adequately. I call them the nightlands."

Hearing her own word come out of his mouth made Nick almost choke on the water.

"My friend Thierry, he can share the dreams of sleeping humans," Gabriel continued. "Even alter them."

Had her dreams been fiddled with? Had he manipulated her into falling in love with him? "Can all of you do that?"

"No, only Thierry."

That made her feel a little better. "I know he's your friend and all, but that's kind of creepy."

He made a negligent gesture. "That is being Kyn."

"There's one other thing I don't get," Nick said, watching the moths march down her forearm in single file. "You said that your sister and some of your friend's relatives also changed into Kyn. But your sister and the others, they didn't go on the Crusades, right?" When he nodded, she added, "If this Darkyn thing really was a curse from God for what you did in the Holy Land, then they shouldn't have gotten it."

"That has long been my own belief." Gabriel turned toward her. "Have you found any female Kyn during your travels? My younger sister, she looks like me—"

"No. No women. Only guys." Nick stood up, sending the trio of moths fluttering away. "We'd better get back on the road."

Being abrupt with him made her feel like hell, but Nick had been on the verge of blurting out everything she knew about the Golden Madonna. Thank God Gabriel had reminded her why she had to keep her mouth shut. However nice and understanding he seemed, and however hot she got for his body, she had excellent reasons not to trust him. She couldn't let him get in her way, not when it came to the Madonna. If she told him everything, he might try to stop her. His own sister . . .

No, she told herself as she climbed on the bike. *Don't go there.*

"We're right outside the city," she told him. "So tell me how to get to your place from here."

Gabriel gave her simple directions on how to reach his home, and added, "Dalente will have the grounds secured. The code for the front gate is six-one-four-seven."

Rather than ride through Toulouse and risk drawing any unwanted attention, Nick took a narrow, winding utility road into the hills, past the pretty houses and shaded gardens of the Côte Pavée and into a more affluent, exclusive area where the homes were more of the mansion variety and the properties extended for dozens of acres.

When she found the turnoff for the dirt road Gabriel had described, she saw two old statues of lions carved from some dark marble at the other end flanking an open, rusting gate.

So much for the secured grounds.

She slowed to a stop in front of the gate and looked

down a trail of weeds sprouting from the rose brick-paved drive. The house stood dark, with no lights inside or out.

It looked like utter shit, too.

"Gabriel?" Maybe she had the wrong place. "Is there, like, a huge forest behind your place?"

"Yes. Also two lions by the front gate."

That clinched it. "Uh, how long has it been since you've seen your house?"

"I was taken in Marseilles, while I was spending the winter with my friends. Almost three years now." He took a deep breath. "Do you smell that? Rosemary and thyme. Dalente still tends to his herb gardens."

Nick glanced down at the fragrant herbs, which were growing wild and woody in a drainage ditch. "Uh-huh."

She drove down the drive and parked in front of the house, which looked as if it had been completely abandoned. Most of the windows on the first floor had been broken or left open. She'd seen nicer crack houses in Paris.

Without saying anything to Gabriel, she took out her crowbar and stuck it in her back pocket along with her lock kit. "This servant of yours, does he live in town?"

"*Non.* He lives here." He started toward the door and stumbled over a loosened paving stone. "Will you lend me your arm, Nicola? I do not wish to fall on my face before I step foot in the house."

"Sure." She grabbed her flashlight and switched it on before putting his hand on her forearm and guiding him up the stairs. "Hang on." She pulled one of the lock picks she carried on her belt and used it to open the entry door.

"You have only to ring the bell," Gabriel told her. "My *tresora* will hear it in his room."

"It's almost midnight. Let's not give the guy a heart attack." She swept the empty front foyer with her flashlight. Mud and dirty footprints soiled the light tile floor, and spray-painted graffiti of various colors decorated the peeling wallpaper. The faint, ugly smell of garbage and human waste colored the air.

"Dalente imported all of the antiques from Italy," he said as they walked inside. "As you can see, I have a particular fondness for marble statues."

Nick aimed the flashlight's beam all over the interior, but didn't see so much as a kid's bag of marbles.

"That one." Gabriel pointed to an empty space beside a wall scrawled with obscenities. "That is the Aphrodite I commissioned Rodin to sculpt for me. Not what the classic Greeks imagined her to look like, I know, but she is my favorite marble. Is she not lovely?"

"I've never seen anything like it." Nick had to get him out of here. "Listen, I don't think this Dalente guy is here. Maybe we should stay in the city tonight, and deal with this tomorrow."

"Paolo must have moved to town so he would not be so lonely. I cannot blame him; I have been absent too long. But come." He tugged on her arm. "Let me show my home to you."

In the receiving room, Nick ducked to avoid a snare of cobwebs floating down from a smashed chandelier and nearly tripped over a pile of crumpled bags and empty soda cans.

"The family rooms are upstairs, but most of my personal art collection is kept on display in the room to the right of the stairs." He gestured in that direction. "I have a small arrangement of Pissarros and Renoirs over the fireplace, but with all the statuary my *tresora* insists on calling it 'the marble room.'"

She stopped him at the threshold and looked down at the crumple of tinfoil and an empty, broken syringe glittering next to her right foot. The room, like the foyer, had been stripped.

She trained her flashlight on the walls and saw some piles of rags and an old crate topped with candle stubs. Along the walls were rows of light, square-shaped patches where paintings had once hung. A splash-shaped stain and a lingering odor indicated someone who had recently occupied the room had been violently sick. Another person had answered an urgent call of nature in the corner, several times.

Thank God he's blind. "Gabriel, I'm a little wiped out from the ride, and you need blood," Nick said, trying to turn him around. "Let's head into Toulouse. We'll come back tomorrow after sunset." That would give her a day to think of what to do next. He couldn't stay here. "Come on."

He wasn't paying attention to her. "This is odd, but I don't remember the house smelling like this. Dalente must be keeping all the windows locked. He needs to take out the garbage, too." Nick tensed, and his grip tightened on her arm. "What is wrong?"

Everything.

"Nothing." How could she tell him his place had been gutted and turned into a flophouse for junkies? "You said you had some money and papers stashed here. We should get those first." That way she wouldn't have to bring him back. "Where are they?"

"In the library." He pointed toward the opposite hall. "The third door on the left."

Nick had a hell of a time guiding him around the accumulated refuse left behind by the squatters, but she managed to get him to the library without a stumble or a mishap. She couldn't do anything about the smell of garbage, but the cold air coming in from the broken windows brought with it the scent of wild herbs and flowers, which helped to mask it.

"Here." He switched on the light switch, but the room remained dark. "I know, it must look like a university library to you, but I like to read."

The shelves were empty, the books and furniture gone. Cigarette burns had rendered the lovely old Persian carpets scattered on the oak floor worthless. All that was left were some old tapestry curtains that had been stuffed into a missing windowpane to keep the cold wind out.

"You stay right there and tell me where it is," she said, her heart breaking for him, "and I'll get it."

"I must telephone my *tresora*." Gabriel released her and, before she could stop him, crossed the room, his arms out. "Dalente always loved to rearrange things." He stopped. "Where has he put the desk?"

Nick scrubbed her hands over her face. "Gabriel, there is no desk in here. There's no furniture in here."

"Of course there is. Dalente wouldn't put the furniture in storage; he—" Gabriel bumped into a bookcase and steadied himself before moving his hand across the empty shelf. "My books . . ." He groped his way to another shelf and felt it, and did the same to a third. His tone changed from puzzled to bewildered. "Nicola, where are my books?"

"They're gone." She should never have brought him in. This was going to kill him. "All of them are gone."

He turned around slowly. *"C'est une blague ou quoi?"*

"No, Gabriel." She swallowed against a tight throat. "I wouldn't joke about something like that."

"What else has been taken?"

"I don't—"

"Tell me."

"It's all gone. The books, the furniture, the statues, all of it. They cleaned you out. From the dust and the cobwebs, I'd say it happened a while ago." She didn't have to tell him about the signs of drug users and squatters. "Let's get out of here, okay? I'll spring for a nice hotel in town, check into what happened up here. Maybe your guy put everything in storage."

"No." He went from shelf to shelf, stirring up dust and feeling for the books that weren't there. "They must have discovered that this was my home."

"You mean the holy freaks." Nick kicked one of the ruined carpets aside, and saw that one of the oak floor panels under it didn't match the others. "Wait a minute." She used her crowbar to pry up the wood and found that a space had been chiseled out of the cement foundation under it. "There's a long metal box here. It's not locked, but it has a red cross on the top of it."

"Open it."

Inside the box Nick found a bundle of papers, a thick padded envelope, and a long, dark-colored sword. The envelope contained several thousand dollars in cash, five passports, two velvet pouches, and a typed letter.

Nick poured the contents of one of the pouches into her palm, and found herself holding a handful of diamonds. Temptation made her fingers close over them for a moment. He couldn't see; he'd never know. But she couldn't steal from a blind man, especially not one who had lost everything that mattered to him.

She was a thief, but she wasn't a fucking thief.

She tipped the diamonds back into the pouch as she described the rest of what she had found in the box, reading the names off the IDs and out of the passports.

"There's a handwritten note here, too. It's in English, and it's dated about a year ago."

"Dalente preferred to write to me in English; none of the household staff understood it." He came over and crouched beside her. "Would you please read it to me?"

She opened it, trained her flashlight on the loose scrawl, and began to read out loud:

> *My lord Gabriel,*
> *Forgive my brevity; I believe that I do not have much time left. Lord Tremayne has sent word that you were executed by the Brethren, but I do not believe it. Our bond is such that I am convinced that I would have felt you passing from this world to the next.*
> *This morning your enemies came to the estate to question me. They speak of you as if you are dead and this house now belongs to them. They demanded that I turn over the contents and the property to them and vacate the premises.*

*I pretended ignorance, and showed them the deeds,
as always, but despite this I expect they will return and
try to take possession by force. They know I cannot
risk summoning the authorities without betraying you
and the Kyn. I am old, but I vow that I will not
surrender without a fight.*

*I also know that it is unlikely that I shall survive
this skirmish. That is why I must write of the
disturbing news I have learned from our friends across
the Atlantic. Angelica betrayed you—as well as
Thierry, Jamys, and the Durand family—to your
enemies. I fear that she has been in league with your
enemies from the beginning.*

*I will place this cache where your enemies cannot
easily find it. Angelica's betrayal means that there is
no place in France where you will be safe. I beg you
go to Ireland and take sanctuary with the high lord.*

*I am grateful for the long and happy life I spent in
your service, and the many pleasures I have known in
our long friendship. I remain, as always, your loyal
servant, Paolo Dalente.*

Nick folded the letter and placed it back in the envelope. "He sounds like a nice man."

"He was." Gabriel rose and moved to the center of the
room. "He is dead."

He sounded as if he didn't care, but Nick understood.
What you couldn't handle, you had to disconnect from.
"You don't know. Maybe he got away. Maybe—"

"If he lived, he would still be here, as would my pos-
sessions." He turned around slowly. "The property—
everything I own—was in his name, not mine."

The holy freaks had killed the old man to take the stuff
from the house. While they had been burning and hurting
Gabriel. Was there anything they wouldn't do to hurt the
Kyn? "I'm so sorry."

"*Maudit.*" His voice went low. "He deserved better than

to die at their hands, Nicola. I should have known. I should have taken measures to better protect him in my absence."

Nick moved the flashlight toward him and saw the way he stood, a fighter left in an empty ring. "How could you have known? You were grabbed and locked up, remember? This wasn't your fault. It was them."

"Dalente wasn't Kyn. He posed no threat to them. He was seventy-three years old and growing frail. He spent most of his days planting and weeding in his garden. He should have lived out his life doing the same." He turned his head, and a faint, scratching sound came from outside the room. "They killed him for the things I had, things that he cared for in my absence. He died for serving me."

Nick didn't need her flashlight to see his face. The light from his blank eyes illuminated his features with an eerie green glow. "We should get out of here, you know? We could . . ." She wasn't sure what to do.

"No. I will see it all. *All of it.*"

Something clicked and scratched all around her, and when Nick angled the flashlight down, it showed her hundreds of huge black beetles erupting from the space in the floor.

"Shit. This place is infested." She scrambled backward and to her feet, just in time to see what was left of the library windows implode. "Gabriel, look out."

Clouds of wasps flew in swarms through the shattered windows, streaming across the room and slamming into Nick. She covered her head with one arm and backed up to the wall, only to see something slithering. Jerking the flashlight, she illuminated countless worms that had bored their way out of the panels and were oozing down the walls.

"Gabriel," she shouted again, but he and the wasps were gone. Something deadlier than a wasp whizzed from the window past her face to bury itself in the wall. She flicked the flashlight up and saw termites pouring out of a brand-new hole. "God, this place is coming apart."

Something in the distance cracked, and what was happening finally registered when plaster exploded by her face, showering and cutting her as a second hole appeared in the wall.

Someone outside was firing a gun into the house.

Gabriel strode out of the library, drawing the many around him and forcing them to show him the destruction of his home. What had been his only retreat from the worlds of man and Kyn had been reduced to a haven for addicts and wanderers, scarred by their indifference and painted with their contempt. Filthy epitaphs, piles of desiccated shit, the sour stink of despair. The art of desperation and disgust. They had filled his house with it.

And for this, Dalente had died.

What the Brethren had inflicted on Gabriel he had accepted as the price of his immortality. But his beloved *tresora* had been made yet another martyr in the war, as innocent and blameless as all the others who had given their human lives to serve the Darkyn.

The many flew into the marble room, showing him the stripped walls and drug paraphernalia left behind by the addicts who had used the house. They found scatterings of marble chips and dust that hinted of the fate of Gabriel's statues.

Had the Brethren destroyed every one of them?

Through the buzzing of the many and the roaring in his head, Gabriel heard gunfire and a woman's scream. Into cold outrage poured hot fury. The swarm undulated around him, held by his will but undirected. He lifted a hand and parted them, sending half out of the room. Through their tiny eyes he saw men in black garments using the stocks of rifles to clear broken glass from the windowpanes before they climbed over them. All three wore night-vision goggles, and one of them crossed himself before he lifted his weapon and began a sweep of the room.

Brethren. Killing Gabriel's *tresora* had not been enough for them. Now they meant to murder the woman he loved.

"*Sors de là*," Gabriel whispered.

The many dispersed, reforming into a near-solid horizontal column as they poured out of the room.

"*Fils de chienne*," one of the intruders shouted, swatting at the stray wasps circling around his head. As the column drove him into the room, he turned and screamed.

The many swallowed the man and his fear, and brought him forward into Gabriel's hands. He bit deep into the man's neck, taking in the hot gush of blood and drinking deeply.

A man ran over the threshold and stopped, training his weapon on Gabriel. "*Mais qui diable êtes-vous?*"

"*Ange de la mort*," Gabriel told him, letting the unconscious intruder drop to the floor. Around them, piles of garbage began to rustle. "Have you confessed your sins to your God?"

"*Maledicti.*" The man began firing at him.

Gabriel pulled the many from the floor up in front of him, their black, hard bodies forming a moving but solid shield. He thrust his hand against the writhing mass of beetles and roaches. "*Baise-toi.*"

The wall grew taller, stretching to the ceiling. On the other side the man stopped firing and looked up just as the wall fell on him.

Gabriel left the second man clawing his way out from under the mound of hungry beetles and walked back to the library. The many, excited by the blood they had tasted and wanting more, massed behind him, an angry comet's thrashing tail. They showed him Dalente's cache and Gabriel's battle sword, still lying on the floor where Nicola had dropped them. Nicola had vanished—and then he heard the buzz of her motorcycle, heading into the forest behind the house.

Nicola.

A bullet struck Gabriel's arm but did not penetrate. Instead, it seemed to bounce off. A second whizzed past his face as he bent to pick up his sword. He did not have to check the slugs to know that the bullets were copper-clad.

"*Allez à l'enfer,*" the third Brethren shouted hoarsely, shifting his rifle and aiming for Gabriel's head.

Go to hell. But he was already there.

"*Tais-toi.*" With a sweep of his arm Gabriel threw the sword.

The blade deflected the shot meant for Gabriel's face and neatly decapitated the man. His body pitched forward as his head dropped and rolled out into the hall. The many descended in a blanket to drape the remains and to feast on them.

The many showed him one man carrying the other out of the house and to a waiting van. He could have sent them to batter the vehicle and devour the pair, but he could hear Benait's voice ringing in his memory.

Unlike you, I am no monster.

Now all you will know is darkness.

Then Nicola's voice, sharp and disapproving: *Is that what Jesus would do?*

He was no monster. He was lost, alone, and afraid. He no longer knew who he was or what he would do. Killing these men would not change that, or make him feel repaid for his suffering. It would only further horrify Nicola, who had shown him nothing but kindness and pleasure, who had risked her life twice now to save his.

Gabriel reined in the swarms and watched through them as the remaining Brethren escaped. As he did, the blood he had taken from the human hummed through him, healing the last of his wounds and investing him with new power.

He retrieved his sword and gripped the hilt in a hot fist as he searched the room. Moths fluttering around the flashlight Nicola had dropped, eagerly seeking the warmth promised by the light, came to him. He needed to find her at once and explain.

Take me to her.

Chapter 13

Gabriel followed the moths through the tangled, over-grown ruin of his *tresora*'s gardens and into the woods where he had spent so many peaceful hours over the last century. More moths came out of the trees, joining the ones he had taken from the house and adding their individual ommatidial vision until he could clearly see all around him.

He found Nicola's motorcycle by the smell of the exhaust and the bright orange glow of the still-warm engine. She had propped it between two trees and covered it with leafy branches stripped from young trees. Yet there was no sign of her anywhere near the bike.

Through the many's oval, compound eyes, Gabriel followed a trail of the very faintest reddish orange, some small, residual trail on the forest floor that Nicola's passage had left in its wake. It wound in an erratic trail around the trees, through brush with broken branches and over fallen logs.

Gabriel tracked her for several minutes before the moths at last homed in on the dark shape of a woman. Nicola sat curled up against the black, gnarled trunk of a massive oak. She should have been dark red, the color moths saw human forms, but her color was lighter and thinner, as pink and delicate as a blush.

"Nicola." He stopped a few feet away from her, and breathed in. "Dear God. You are hurt."

"I didn't . . . I'm not . . ." The shapes of her hands

moved from her face to the ground, and her color darkened from pink to rose. "I'm fine."

"I smell blood." Remembering the reddish orange trail, he went to her, ignoring her cringing and using the moths to see the shallow gash on her neck. "The men who broke in, they shot you."

"No. I got cut by a piece of plaster from a ricochet." She covered the wound with her hand. "Did you do that? That thing with the bugs? Make them come out of the ground and the walls and everything?"

"Yes, I did. It is my talent." He knelt before her. Shame for what he had done seemed a distant, untouchable thing, but he regretted terrifying her. "I was angry and I lost control of it. I am sorry that I frightened you."

"I thought you were pissed at me, that you . . ." She turned away and her voice thickened. "You need to find someone else to be your *tresora*, Gabriel. I'm not the right person. I can't do it anymore."

"I understand." The last remnant of his heart died in his chest, and he went down on his knees. "Will you be so kind as to perform one last service for me?"

"I'll take you wherever you want to go."

"I have only one destination in mind." He extended the sword to her. "It is very sharp. If you swing it in the same way you do your baseball bat, it should go through my neck in one pass."

She took in a quick breath. "Are you asking me to cut off your head with this sword?"

"I am."

"Really." Her voice sharpened. "And how do you feel about me shoving it up your ass?"

"Vlad the Impaler may have thought otherwise, but that will not end my life," he told her. "I killed one of the humans who came into the house. Think of it as an even exchange."

"I'm not cutting off your fucking head, Gabriel." She stood up. "Stupid. This is so stupid, all of it; it's so pointless. Don't add to it."

"I agree." He would have to persuade her. "My life has been destroyed by murderers and thieves and liars. My own sister among them, feeding them information, betraying our kind. My friends are dead or indifferent to me. You wish to leave me, and you should. I have intruded on your life long enough. I have no wish to continue living in such a world."

"I'm not listening to this." She walked around him, heading back toward her motorcycle.

Gabriel followed and caught up with her, stopping her. "I don't have the strength to do it myself, or I would." He held out the sword again. "Please do this one last thing for me. I beg you."

"No."

He gestured toward the ruin of his house. "You may take the money and the diamonds—"

"No." She knocked the sword out of his hands. "I don't want your money, or your diamonds, or your sob story. Your life has sucked; okay, I get that. But you can't put this on me. I'm not cutting off your head. Go to Iraq. They love doing it over there. Just stand in the street and yell out that you're an American oil company executive. Or Jewish."

"I understand. I forget that you are human, that such things are abhorrent to you." He reached for the blade. "I will find another—"

"I don't *think* so." She threw his sword into the brush.

He felt his blood run cold. If she would not release him, then the torment would never end. "Have I not suffered enough? Is my humiliation not complete?"

"Run the part about your humiliation by me again."

She did not care for him, could not love him. He understood her reasons: The Brethren had reduced him to a blind, unfeeling ruin, and he had badly frightened her. He had pushed her too far. But he would not make her feel responsible. She would never carry the burden of guilt over him.

"You read the letter Dalente wrote," he said. "Angelica, my own sister, was the one who betrayed us. She put me and her husband and her own son into the hands of our enemies. She knew about this place, and sent them here to kill Dalente. How can I live with what she has done?"

"You didn't do it; she did. She has to answer for what she's done." She stepped closer to him and jabbed her finger into his chest. "Maybe you should quit whining and go find her. Stop her from hurting other people."

"I'm too tired." His shoulders sagged under the weight of his sorrow. "Tired unto death of this ugliness, this horror. It never ends. How much more pain and humiliation must I endure before I have earned my rest?" And how many lonely centuries more would he live without her?

This time her hand connected with his face, her palm shockingly hard as it struck his cheek.

"You shut up," she snarled. "Pain and humiliation, my ass. You keep talking like this and I'll clean your clock so hard you'll wish that you were *back* in the torture chamber."

"Nicola." Gabriel felt appalled by her threats.

"I mean it," she insisted. "I didn't save you to listen to your bitching and moaning and watch you kill yourself. I did it because . . . because if I can keep going, then so can you."

She did care for him. "Tell me how."

"Well, for one thing you can try trying to be so goddamn noble about everything," she snapped. "The Renaissance days or whatever it was like when you were human? They're over. If you want to survive in *this* day and age, then you *have* to toughen up and be smart. You deal with the murderers, thieves, and liars. Yes, it's awful, but that's the way it is. The world's full of them. You have to think the way they do. For all you know, I could be one of them."

"I do not think I am strong enough." Gabriel could taste her tears, hear the swallowed sobs beneath her sharp words. That seemed far worse than the blow she had given him. "They didn't break my body, Nicola. They broke my heart."

"You're breaking mine now." Her voice trembled. "Don't you know that? I know you're blind, but can't you feel it, what's happening between us?"

Gabriel kept his hands at his sides. "What I feel is wrong."

"Giving up, that's wrong. I lost everything that mattered to me ten years ago, along with everyone I loved, and I haven't thrown in the towel yet. I've still got a heart, don't I? It works, most of the time. Jesus, I hit you. You're making me nuts. Come here." She put her arms around him and pulled him down so that their foreheads touched. "I'm not giving up on you. There's a reason we found each other. Let's find out what it is."

Hopelessness dragged at him. "I did not intend to make you angry."

"Guys never do." She slowly rolled her brow against his. "Look, we can be strong together, right? We're survivors, you and me."

"Survivors."

"Exactly. So the world fucked us over; who cares? It doesn't have to be all about that. We're free." She grabbed a handful of his shirt. "Once I find the Madonna and take care of that, we can go wherever we want. We can get away from the holy freaks and the Kyn. We can *live.* We're good together, aren't we?"

He was infecting her with his despair. She was healing him with her dignity. Which one of them would succeed?

"I think," he said, very slowly, "that of the two of us, you are the noble one."

"You're crazy." She brushed her mouth over his in one of her quick, startling kisses. "And you're shaking." She turned her head and drew his down to the wound in her neck. "Take it."

Her blood wet his lips, sweeter than any honey, more tempting than any wine. "I fed on one of the shooters."

"So don't take much." She pressed her slim body against his. "I like it. It felt good when you did it in the forest. I want to feel that way again."

Her embrace and her softness proved stronger than his self-disgust. He drank from the bleeding wound, tasting her, savoring her as he felt the violent coldness inside him retreat. Madness and sorrow evaporated, replaced by a grinding, demanding need for more of her flesh. That hunger became so intense that his cock swelled between them and pressed into her flat belly.

He put her at arm's length. "If you despise me as much as I do myself, you should go now."

"Not going to happen. We need each other." Her hands slipped under the edge of his shirt, and she rubbed herself subtly against the ridge of his penis. "Every time I'm near you, I don't know whether I should kiss you or jump on you. I couldn't help myself in the shower. You feel it too, don't you?"

He gave his heart to her in that moment. Loved her, a human woman, as he would never love another. And as he stooped to pick her up in his arms, he found that he didn't care.

"Hello. Blind man." Her arms went around his neck. "You're going to walk into a tree."

"I know where I am going." He carried her back to the oak where he had found her, and lowered her onto the bed of moss there.

Gabriel wanted to rip her clothing apart and feast on her body, and feared he might do just that if he fell back into the darkness. He reached out with his talent, dismissing the moths and summoning the quietest creatures in the forest, the patient watchers who formed and wove their hungry threads into silken traps.

"Do spiders frighten you?" he asked as he stretched out beside her.

"No, I . . ." She went still. "Uh, Gabriel?"

He followed the bridge of her nose with his finger, gliding over the curves of her lips and chin and sliding down the slope of her throat.

"Did you ask me that because there are about two hundred spiders hanging over us?"

He nuzzled her hair. "I want to see you," he murmured against her ear. "Through their eyes, I can." He sent for a very specific forest dweller, calling them from their burrows in the ground and under the tree bark.

"Does this seeing-through-them thing involve their crawling on me?"

"No." He took her hands and stretched them out over her head as he rolled on top of her. "I'm going to do that."

The spiders showed him the long lines of beetles marching up the trunk of the oak tree, flashing green bioluminescent light from their abdomens until there was enough to illuminate Nicola's face and body.

"Your eyes shoot laser beams, too?" she asked, looking up.

"Fireflies," he told her, fascinated to see that she had a sprinkling of freckles across the bridge of her nose. What other parts of her were dusted with these little gold specks? She shifted under him and tried to pull her hands free, but he held her tight. "Be still."

"I can't." She lifted her hips, driving them into his. "I've been wanting you all day. All my life. I don't want to wait another second. Hurry up."

"Shhhh." He put his mouth on hers, opening her lips with his tongue and tasting her with slow, deep strokes. He lifted his head and breathed in her gasp. "You will have me."

Gabriel stripped off her T-shirt, taking her bra with it, jerking open his own shirt so that he could feel her breasts against his skin. He peeled her jeans down and off her legs, inserting his hands between her knees to coax her thighs apart. The pants she had borrowed from Jean Laguerre were loose enough for him to shake off, but he couldn't wait now, not smelling the delicious dampness of her exposed sex. He reached down to push them out of the way, taking his cock and guiding it to her.

She felt plump and hot and meltingly sweet against the dry, tight bulb of his penis head, sending a surge of answering wetness through his shaft. It had been so long—too long—since he had put himself in a woman's body that Gabriel feared he would spill his seed before he fully penetrated her.

"Oh, my man."

Through the many he saw that she was looking down at their bodies, her eyes narrow and her bottom lip caught between her teeth. He watched her face as he worked in the head of his cock, finding the angle of her sheath and pushing in past muscles tight with nerves. Her arousal eased the way, but the rest of her body was as tightly wound as his.

"Take me as you did with your breasts, your mouth," he said, kissing her brow.

"No soap," she whispered. "No water."

He moved his hand to cup her sex. "Feel how wet you are?" His fingers made a vee around his cock, massaging her with her own moisture. "So soft and smooth."

Gabriel exposed her clit and tucked two fingers on either side of it, pressing and stroking the insides of her labia but not touching it. At the same time he sank deeper into her, making her take more of him, feeling her lower labia stretch around the thickest part of his shaft.

Nicola had caught her breath; now she seemed to forget how to release it. Her eyelids lowered and opened, and she stretched under him, arching and tightening until he impaled her fully, and then she uttered a moan that nearly sent him over the edge.

Not yet, not yet.

He recoiled, pulling out of her until only his head remained embedded in her, and then thrust back inside her with one long, smooth stroke, angling higher, catching the tiny bulge of her clit and dragging at it. Their body hair tangled and her hips rolled as she shuddered under him, not there yet but speeding toward it.

Gabriel wanted to tell her how lovely she was, how good she felt on him, but the words would not come. His balls had tightened as much as his throat. So he showed her with his fingers and mouth and penis, working her as sweetly and slowly as she clasped him, putting his mouth to her breasts and his teeth to her nipples, licking the drop of blood from her lip before giving her his tongue and kissing her as deeply as he was fucking her.

Nicola thrashed under him, trying to force him to thrust faster, but he held her down and buried himself inside, feeling the head of his cock nudging the mouth of her womb. It was agony not to move, but he brought his hand to her breast and cradled it, holding it up for his mouth. He held her like that until she trembled and whimpered, and then he put his *dents acérées* to her breast, grazing her skin with them before he sucked hard, and then drew back and drove his cock into her as deeply as he could, once, twice, three times.

Pleasure so sharp it might have been pain surged out of him and gushed inside her, mingling their fluids and wrenching cries from both of them. Then Gabriel pulled out and up, working the beating pulse of her clit against the base of his shaft until she came again, the contractions dragging his cock back inside her body and milking the last drops of semen from him.

Gabriel slipped from her and eased to her side, his hand still cradling her breast, his softening cock caught between her thighs.

An eternity later, Nicola's eyes slowly opened. "Damn. I could have had that."

He ran his hand through her curls. "You just did."

"I could have had that this *morning*." She tapped his shoulder with a limp-fisted mock punch. "You held out on me in the shower." She touched her breast where his fangs had grazed but not pierced her skin. "You can also bite me while you're having sex with me anytime you like. It was . . . I thought I was going to . . . Well." She sighed. "Damn."

A distant rumble of thunder made him send the spiders to do other work, and he used the fireflies to see Nicola. "What color is your hair?"

"Mud brown."

He kissed the part in her hair above her left brow. The hair close to her scalp was much lighter than the rest of it. "I meant, under the mud brown dye."

"White. I'm really a little old lady of sixty who's had two hundred face-lifts." She laughed.

Even her laughter made him hard. "You should pay your plastic surgeon triple his fee. His work is flawless."

"It won't help us much with the holy freaks." She sat up. "We should get out of here before those two come back with reinforcements."

"You brought your bike here; they will think we left the house. My watchers will alert us if anyone comes into the forest. I want to be with you." He pulled her back to him and lifted her left leg to ease inside her. "You make me feel alive again. Feel so much, so many things."

"You've been locked up for a couple of years." She curled her leg over his hip, stiffening for a moment and then relaxing into the rhythm of his movements. "I think we can do better than 'damn.'"

Gabriel buried himself in Nicola's eager young body, taking her as many ways as she could manage. She never turned him away. Each touch inched him away from thoughts of oblivion, until he could not imagine not being a part of her, moving in her, kissing her and holding her as she found her pleasure and brought him to his.

He kept her unaware of the thousands of spiders above them, some serving as his eyes, the rest weaving a tent of protective silk around them. When he drifted off into the nightlands, he felt a contentment he had never before experienced.

In the nightlands Gabriel found Nicola standing over him, naked, a stiletto in her hand. It did not alarm him. Nothing about her could. Still content, he watched her use the knife to cut her way out of the tent of webs.

Where was she going? Afraid of alarming her, he sent his watchers after her.

The spiders skittered through the forest, catching up with Nicola in Dalente's neglected garden, where she was drawing water from the old well.

"Okay." She flicked out the stiletto and stared at it.

"He's gorgeous and sweet and sets my body on fire. I let him fuck my brains out because we both needed it. He needs someone to take care of him. Just because I'm falling for him doesn't mean I get the job."

She used the blade to cut up a shirt, and then soaked the pieces in the bucket of water before pouring a bottle of dark, watery fluid over them. Gabriel directed his spiders to climb up the sides of the well so that he could better see her face.

"I don't need a blind boyfriend. He doesn't need my shit. I'll just take him to the others and get him safe and forget about him." She sniffed and rubbed the back of her hand against her nose. "It's the only way."

Nicola was talking herself out of caring for him, something that after the events of the night he could well understand. Still, that she would abandon him so ruthlessly tore at him, until the many moved to where they could look upon her countenance.

The wet marks on her face ran from eyes to chin. She was weeping.

Unaware that she was being watched, Nicola put the soaked strips of fabric on the edge of the well, turned the bucket over to dump out the water, and then propped her leg on the bottom of it.

"If you love something, you have to let it go." The blade flashed as she brought it down, stabbing herself in the back of the leg. "So let him go, Nick; let him be free or you'll fuck up his life too."

Nicola. He almost sent the many to her, to wrench the stiletto out of her hand.

"It'll be for the best. He'll be happy. I'll get over it." She worked the knife from side to side. "Maybe in a couple hundred years."

A dark, deformed slug dropped with a bloody *splat* into a patch of chickweed, and she grabbed the soaked fabric, pressing a wad of it to the back of her leg—

"Nicola."

Gabriel woke with a lurch, turning at once to grope with his hands. He found her curled up beside him, her head pillowed on her hand, and ran his fingers over her. No gunshot wounds marred her bare legs, although he checked over every centimeter of her skin twice.

It had been his imagination, a fantasy that had played out in his head. But if it had been only that, then why had he been blind? In all of his dreams, he could see perfectly.

His hand strayed up to her face and felt the cool, damp remnants of tears.

Sometimes dreams are just reality turned inside out.

Gabriel lay back, pulling her to him and holding her against his pounding heart.

Although Michael Cyprien had been to Dublin countless times over the centuries, the lack of skyscrapers and two- and three-story buildings in the city allowed him to recall the place as it had been before the age of steel and concrete. Dublin was still something of a squat, overgrown village divided in half by the river Liffey, with its back against the pewter sea.

There were changes, radical and subtle. Perhaps the most lasting was the Irish resentment of British colonialism. Dublin displayed it very subtly, as with the street signs written in English and Gaelic, as if to remind visitors that the inhabitants had had their own language, even if no one spoke it anymore. Yet the Irish wanted respectability, and tried to project it with the many buildings prefixed with tall, white Grecian columns.

As Richard's people monitored all of the best hotels in the city, Michael had directed Phillipe to book them in a small, somewhat dismal bed-and-breakfast on Dublin's working-class northside. The proprietor, a widow whose wardrobe seemed to consist only of long-skirted black crepe de chine dresses, warned them that she had gone along with the city's ban on smoking in pubs and restaurants, and would eject them the minute she smelled to-

bacco or caught anyone lighting up in their rooms. To
Michael's displeasure, the innkeeper proved to be one of
the rare humans who had a natural resistance to *l'attrait*. It
had been a relief to leave the place and take Leary down to
the local pub for a meal.

"So you've just come up from London, then?" the dark,
wiry bartender asked Cyprien as he handed him a glass of
wine.

"Yesterday." Michael looked over at Phillipe and Marcella, who had taken a table in the corner of the pub and
were watching the doors. Between them, Leary sat slowly
masticating his way through a plate of corned beef and
cabbage.

"Lovely cities the Brits have, don't they? Five or six
thousand pubs in London alone. Can't build a proper beer
in any of them, but you're in Ireland now, lad." The bartender patted his arm. "You're safe."

Michael remembered the last time he had tasted Irish
beer. In that era it had been dark, rough, and almost chew-
able—not very different from this brew. "Thank you."

A couple of men dressed in overalls and smelling of fish
came in, drawing the bartender down to the other end of
the bar and giving Cyprien a moment to think.

On the journey to Ireland, Marcella had told him that
sending Phillipe and Leary into Dundellan was too dangerous. She didn't believe his seneschal could make a convinc-
ing pretense of being yet another drug addict Leary had
brought from the streets, or that Leary could be trusted at all.
She disdained what she called old siege tactics and wanted to
use more modern methods to gain entry to Dundellan.

Cyprien had disagreed. The guards would recognize all
of the Kyn, if not by sight then by smell, and the only way
to penetrate the castle's defenses was with humans.

Michael was not worried about getting caught—he had
every intention of confronting Richard—but like Marcella,
he worried about Leary. The man had sat in the very back
of the passenger van, his hands and ankles bound to pre-

vent him from making another attempt to escape, but leaving London had not disturbed him. When told they were going to Ireland, Leary had smiled and even giggled.

"Seigneur."

Michael turned to look into haunted dark eyes. "What is it?"

"I am leaving for the village now," Marcella told him. "I would speak to you privately before I go."

He glanced over at Phillipe, who nodded before speaking in a low voice to Leary. Cyprien paid for their drinks before he followed Marcella out of the pub.

"This plan is not sound," she told him as they walked down the street of old brick buildings and brightly colored doors. "Richard holds the advantage. Leary cannot be trusted. We are only three. If you mean to besiege Dundellan, let us return to America and raise a proper army."

"This is not the fourteenth century," he reminded her. "I cannot invade England."

"Very well. There is one thing more I would say to you." She led him around a corner and onto a street of furniture stores. "I did not speak of this when I agreed to serve as your second because it was not my place. Phillipe will not tell you because he is your man."

He lifted his brows. "No one wishes to talk to me?"

"Not in your present mood, my lord." Her mouth twisted. "We are all very fond of our heads."

"I vow not to touch a hair on your head. There." He spread his hands. "Say what you will."

"The bond a Kyn lord shares with his *sygkenis* is for life, but yours and Alexandra's is particularly strong," she said carefully. "Testing such a bond results in serious consequences, as I well know."

Michael frowned. "You have never belonged to a Kyn lord."

"My brother Arnaud lost his *sygkenis* during the Revolution," Cella said, her voice falling to a whisper. "Madness and sorrow nearly destroyed his life. It is why we came to America. To escape all of the things that reminded him of his loss."

Michael remembered how Thierry Durand had also lost his mind after believing that his wife had been tortured to death. "You think I will go insane?"

She shook her head. "I fear that you will be made the victim of your feelings for Alexandra."

Michael fought back a surge of anger. "The separation will soon be ended."

"The strain of being apart from Alexandra is affecting your ability to make rational decisions now. You are becoming more and more reckless. Such as your decision to bring Leary with us." She halted in front of a mattress and bedding shop that promised, NO MORE BACK PAIN OR YOUR MONEY BACK! on the advertisement posters plastered in the windows. "There is something very wrong with this man. Have you not heard him muttering to himself?"

"I have heard him muttering." It was all the man seemed to do. "His prayers appear to comfort him."

"He is not praying," Cella said sharply. "He whispers filth under his breath. He is obsessed with some woman, and plans to do great harm to her. What if he means to harm your *sygkenis*?"

"I have taken away his fear of the Kyn," Michael said. "He has no reason to hurt Alexandra, but if he tries, Phillipe will be there to protect her."

"I hope you are correct." She flagged down a taxi. "I will be waiting in the village. God be with you, seigneur."

Cyprien kissed her cheeks and helped her into the cab, standing and watching as the taxi headed out toward the northbound beltway. His temper had become quicker to flare since leaving the States, but they were all on edge.

A hand touched his arm. "Master."

"Take Leary to gather his quota," Michael told Phillipe. "As soon as he collects them, we leave for Dundellan."

Chapter 14

The captain of Tremayne's guard, Korvel, had just finished cleaning the wounds on John's neck when Alexandra and another guard came into the castle infirmary. Or, rather, John's sister strode in with the guard chasing after her.

"Doctor, you are not permitted in this part of the castle," the guard said in a strange, pleading tone. "If you would—"

Alexandra turned and punched the man in the face, knocking him across the room. He hit the floor and sat there rubbing his jaw and looking more like a crushed schoolboy than a wounded man.

"Hey, John," his sister said as she came to him. "Korvel, take Stefan and get out of here."

John knew that tone. "I'm all right, Alex. She didn't take enough to hurt me. It just left me with a headache."

"I'm the goddamn doctor; I'll decide what condition you're in." She pulled up the edge of the taped dressing. "That bitch. Another centimeter over and she'd have punctured your carotid." She eyed the captain. "Do I have to belt you, too?"

"You lied to me," Korvel said with matching chilly courtesy. "You broke out of your chamber and intruded on Lady Elizabeth's privacy."

"Oh, yeah?" Alex's expression darkened. "Lady Elizabeth was *feeding* on my brother. In *front* of me. I'm not thinking privacy's a big priority in her life."

The captain's brows lowered. "I will not trust you out of my sight again."

"Like you did before. Did you irrigate these wounds with antiseptic?" When Korvel nodded, she taped the dressing back into place and spoke to John. "I didn't know it was you under the mask at first."

"That guard over there"—John nodded at Stefan, who was finally getting to his feet—"he did something that made me unable to move."

"Stefan's talent is to paralyze humans," Korvel said.

Alexandra took out a penlight and checked his eyes. "When did the headache start?"

"I don't know. That woman—Elizabeth—hypnotized me to make me frightened, I think. It gave me some kind of vertigo, too. I was afraid that I'd throw up with the gag on." John squinted. "The light's not helping, Alex."

"Nauseated, photosensitive, and generally disoriented. Headache bad?" When he nodded, she glared at Korvel before adding, "I wouldn't have let her do that to you."

"You live on blood, don't you?" he couldn't help asking. "If it comes from me or another human, what difference does it make?"

"She didn't need your blood. She was doing it to mess with my head. I don't bite people, either." She pressed her hand to his cheek for a moment. "You're still my brother, John. Jesus."

"Doctor, you must leave here now," Korvel demanded, "before the high lord discovers your presence."

Alexandra gave John an expected hug, and murmured, "They've got you on candid camera, bro." When she straightened, she nodded toward the mirror across from his bed.

"Wait." John rose and took his sister's hand. "Have they been treating you well?"

"Not counting the threats and scaring me, yeah, they have." She stared up at him. "The castle isn't so bad. It's just like the mansion in my favorite Nancy Drew book."

The Hidden Staircase. John remembered the novel because Alex had demanded he read it to her over and over. In the story, the girl detective investigated a mansion haunted not by ghosts, but by a fugitive using secret passageways to try to scare off the elderly owner. Alex had spent months tapping the Kellers' walls in hopes of finding a secret passage. "Is it."

"We will go now." Korvel took her by the arm and escorted her out, locking the door behind him.

Orson Leary watched the scarred-faced man, Phillipe, as he drove the van from the pub into the city. Now that he was back in Ireland, he felt happier than ever. His savior had destroyed all the old fears, and now he could attend to the women properly.

He felt impatient with his escort, however. The man plodded along as if he and Orson had all the time in the world. "Do we go to see the high lord? His castle is in the country."

"We will collect the humans first," Phillipe said.

"Where do you take them?"

"A special place," Leary said, feeling more cheerful. Once he collected his quota, they would go to the demon king, and he would be able to complete the work. "Turn left there."

Leary directed Phillipe to Meath Street, and from there to a darkened laneway where cars cruised slowly.

All along the street, clusters of two and three young men moved from the shadows of the shops and businesses to make quick exchanges with the drivers of the cars. Other thin and hungry-looking youths wove their way down the walks, going from cluster to cluster. As people came together on the street, they spoke briefly and traded small twists of cellophane and tinfoil for rolls of money.

Leary had once despised coming here—frightened of the disease and despair, always fearing he would be caught in the act—but no more. These weaklings, for whom he had sometimes felt pity, were nothing to him now. He didn't fear infection or contamination. He feared nothing. *This last time, and then I will be free of them as well as her.*

A shriek drew Leary's gaze to a thickset man who backhanded a young girl away from him. She tumbled into the street, where she got up on her knees and promptly vomited all over herself. The sight gladdened him, for if he was taken in this battle, surely others would carry on his good works.

Phillipe parked the van on a side street. "What is this place?"

"Needle Paradise," he said, watching the girl collapse on top of her own puke. "It's where they sell most of the heroin and crack in the city."

"You are to collect humans, not drugs."

"I always come here to make up my quota," Leary told him. "No one cares what happens to the addicts. They're easily persuaded."

Phillipe shut off the engine. "Make this quick, Father."

Leary climbed out of the van and walked out of the alley. A lone skeletal figure standing by the corner darted a look at him. From the way the young man was shivering, he was in need. Leary gestured with a folded fifty between his fingers. When the junkie stepped into the light to reach for it, Leary saw open sores on his arms and the yellow mark of jaundice on his face. He snatched the bill back just as the dirty fingers snatched at it.

"Wot d'ya want, then?"

"A quick one." Leary swept a hand toward Phillipe and the parked van.

"Both of ya?"

Leary shook his head. "Just me."

The junkie hunched his shoulders and trudged down the alley to the back of the van.

Leary opened the doors and gave the young man a nudge. "Inside."

"Wot's tha' smell?"

Honeysuckle sweetness wafted out of the back of the van. "Come, *mon ami*," Phillipe said, reaching out to touch the addict's neck. "You look in need of a rest."

Leary caught the junkie as he crumpled. "What's wrong with him?" Usually he had to drug or beat the humans he collected.

"I put him to sleep." Phillipe took the young man and put him on the floor of the van. "Bring the rest of them here, to me. I will do the same to them."

The Brethren interrogator found four more young men who were willing to sell themselves, and a lone dealer interested in making a buy, and led them all into the alley to Phillipe, who sent each one into a deep, sound slumber. Leary felt very happy with the arrangement, until he saw her at the end of the block.

"This is enough," Phillipe said. "We will leave this place."

"I've got to take a piss," Leary told the vampire. "Then we'll go."

The fair-haired girl stood with her hips against the back of a rusted-out MINI. She looked older than the other addicts, her skin as pale as milk. Grease spots and food stains spattered the front of the polyester uniform she wore, and as Leary drew closer, he smelled oily potatoes and fried fish.

It was a clever disguise, of course. The bitch would not lower herself to serve others.

Leary didn't want to speak to her—she didn't deserve such kind attention—but this was too public a place to do what was needed.

"Evening, miss," he said as he stopped a few feet from the MINI. Pretending to be fooled by her ruse would keep her from suspecting that he'd recognized her. "All by yourself, then?"

The girl stabbed the air with her middle finger. "Piss off."

"I don't mean to bother you," Leary protested with a phony, genial heartiness. "I'm looking for someone to share what I've got."

"I'm waiting for me boyfriend," she said, checking her cheap wristwatch. "He sees you here, he'll rip off your arm and crack your skull with it."

She sounded so real, but then, she always did.

"Getting a bit late." Leary glanced around. "Maybe he's not coming. You have something if he doesn't show up?"

"He wouldn't . . . Ah, fuck it." She wrapped her arms around her middle. "How much then?"

"No charge but the pleasure of your company." And that soft, flabby throat between his hands.

"You sods all want something," the girl said bitterly. "What is it then? A knobber in the backseat once I'm cranked, is that it? Or you take me back to your crib so your mates can have turns?"

Leary shook his head. "I like to see a bird get off, but I don't have to. You watch my back; I watch yours." He showed her two twists of heroin that he'd taken off the dealer. "A snort's better than a needle; you know that. Dirty needles'll kill you."

"Yeah. Got me friend Jamie just last winter." The sight of the drugs made her eyes shine. "Yeah, yeah, okay. But me first."

She was going through with it to the end. She probably thought to take him once he'd snorted the heroin. The stupid bitch.

"I'm a gentleman," he told her, gesturing toward the MINI. "We'll do it right here."

She took out a set of keys, and then stopped abruptly. "You're like that Percy in *Silence of the Lambs*, aren't you?" She started to back away. "You're not cutting me up like clothes—"

"Shut up." Leary caught her by the hair in midstep, ramming her face into the side of the MINI, breaking her nose and stunning her. "You think I don't know who you are?" When she sagged, he dragged her around the car and down into the shadows of the alley.

Rats squealed and disappeared into the nearest cranny. Leary hoisted the girl under his arm, clamping her to his side as he looked for anyone sleeping rough in the alley. He needed a dark place where the shadows ran deep, where no one walked and no one looked—

"By doze," she said, spitting blood out and twisting in the circle of his arm. "By doze, hugh broke it."

"Quiet." Leary pulled his elbow in tight and stepped into a narrow space behind a row of rubbish cans. "You talk too much." He dropped her onto the ground, pinning her wrists under his shoes. "You always talked too much." Blood roared in his ears as he checked the front and back of the alley for anyone she might command to stop him. "No one can hear you now."

Leary had to kneel in filth as he straddled her, but it seemed only fitting. The alley sullied his trouser legs as much as her neck contaminated his hands.

"This won't kill you," he told the girl as he cut off her air, and ignored her fingers clawing at his sleeves. Her pretense didn't fool him. "I know it won't. There are too many of you. But you'll not use this body for your evil anymore."

He had almost choked the life out of her when honeysuckle filled the alley, and a hand snatched him up and held him over the coughing, thrashing girl.

"What have you done to her?" Phillipe demanded.

Paralyzed, Leary could only look down at his dangling feet and the one he should have killed. He had not been cautious enough. He had failed. If he had been able to move, he would have torn Phillipe's heart from his chest with his bare hand.

Now was not the time to attack. He had to be more cunning. "I don't know," he blubbered through forced tears. "She wanted money. She threatened to kill me."

Phillipe put him down, although Leary still could not

move. The vampire reached for the girl, but she crawled backward, shaking her head and covering her bruised throat with one hand. She didn't seem to be able to speak.

"You cannot attack people like this," Phillipe told him. "Do you understand?"

You must fear me.

You must not fear the Kyn.

Take them.

You will not harm them.

Kill the women.

You cannot attack.

Something tore inside Leary's head. "The master said to take them and I obeyed."

Phillipe grabbed him by the throat, and for a moment Leary thought the young vampire might snap his neck. "We are done here."

Leary thought he would go into the dark place where it was safe, and never come back, but then all the voices came together into one. He feared, but he did not have to fear. He took, but he did not have to be taken. He killed, but he was not to be killed.

The one voice kindly explained everything to Leary as his body began walking on its own toward the front of the alley.

There was so much to do, but for tonight his work was done.

A soft blue-and-rose glow lured Gabriel from his rest, filling his eyes with the hazy colors of a sunset sky. He reached for Nicola, but found only soft moss and leaves under his hand.

It wasn't until he automatically blinked and experienced a momentary return of the blackness that he realized that the colors he saw in his mind were not coming through the shared vision of the many, but from his own eyes.

It cannot be. Benait blinded me months ago.

Gabriel stood, turning and seeing the blue-and-rose blur

turn to brown and green. He could not make out shapes, but the colors of the forest were there, just as he remembered them. He brought up his hand in front of his face, added the mottled green paleness of his own flesh to his vision.

Unconvinced, he covered his eyes with one hand, shadowing them. The light dimmed, and the blurred colors appeared only through the separations of his fingers. As he stared, the blurring sharpened a single degree.

His ruined eyes were healing.

"Nicola." Aware that the Brethren may have returned to the house, he didn't shout. "Nicola, where are you?" He had to tell her. He had to see, even in a blur, her face.

The only answer he received was the calls of songbirds.

Gabriel stepped out of the cobwebbed tent and halted just outside, shocked anew. In his dream Nicola had used a stiletto to cut her way out, and he had just stepped through that opening.

He nearly panicked, until he remembered waking near dawn and checking her legs. She had not been injured. She was not hurt, and he was healing. No more would he have to rely on the many to be his eyes. He could be free of them and look upon the world once more, a whole man.

I could go to Ireland and watch the look on the high lord's face when I present myself to him. I can see if Richard knew that I was left to rot in the hands of the Brethren.

Gabriel couldn't summon the cold anger he had felt for so long toward the Kyn. Benait had lied to him; that much was obvious from Dalente's letters. Had Richard believed him dead, he would have had no reason to continue searching for him. He would never know what had happened until he spoke to the high lord himself.

He had to know the extent of Angelica's betrayal, too. If his sister had to be brought to justice, he would be the one to do it.

Restless now, Gabriel turned and breathed in deeply.

Making love to Nicola had drenched him with her scent; he could track her in his sleep. He bent down and found her trail leading away from the tent and toward the house.

Why did she go up there?

Using his blurred vision and his memories of the forest allowed him to follow her scent path, but it veered away toward the back of the house rather than the front. Weeds had nearly overgrown the irregular sheets of slate Dalente had placed as a walkway through the garden, but Gabriel remembered the way it curled through the flower beds. Nicola had followed it, too, up to the old well by his *tresora*'s toolshed.

Gabriel smelled blood, and saw a pile of white and red left by the base of the well stones. He reached down and picked up a handful of torn, damp T-shirt fabric. He pressed his face against it to be sure, but he knew from his dream the blood on it was Nicola's.

A dream that had not been a dream at all.

He found her leather jacket left draped on the edge of the well by the bucket pulley. He ran his hands over it, feeling again the bulges in the lining. Yesterday he had not disturbed them, but now he found the folded seams that opened them and slowly went through the contents of each.

Nicola carried several rolls of euros, rail passes or tickets of some sort, and a folded book of traveler's checks, but no coins or wallet. One small, hard plastic case contained a dozen slim, bent metal instruments Gabriel guessed were lock picks. He also found a canister of spray lubricant, a pair of folding binoculars, and a long, flat piece of metal that he had seen on television as something car thieves employed. From the last pocket he pulled a bundle of identification cards, passports, and work visas.

Nowhere did Gabriel find the film, lenses, or any other camera accessories he had expected.

It was not photography or random accident that had brought her to the château. Nicola carried too many specific tools for him to believe that anymore. It seemed that she was the human thief that his interrogators in Paris had spoken of—the thief whom the Brethren had been trying to trap by using him as bait.

Why did she deceive me?

Gabriel carefully returned the items he had examined precisely where he had found them, and put the jacket and the bloodied fabric back where Nicola had left them. He turned and silently followed his own path to the spider-silk tent.

What else has she stolen?

Now that he knew this about her, some things made more sense. Why she dyed her hair: to alter her appearance; she likely did it regularly. Why she traveled by motorcycle: to have the means to get away quickly; a motorcycle could weave in and out of traffic and go places off-road where cars could not.

But what did she steal? Did she take relics and antiques from these churches and chapels she had claimed to be photographing?

Why had she kept this from him?

I would not tell a stranger that I was a thief, he admitted to himself. *But after yesterday and last night, are we still strangers?*

The enormity of his discovery would have bothered him more if she had been lying to him for a long period of time, but in truth they had known each other for only three days. Enough time to become lovers, but not to establish trust. Perhaps she was ashamed of what she did, and sought to conceal it from him for that reason.

Or she is up at the house this minute, taking the money and the diamonds that Dalente left hidden for me.

Gabriel found that he didn't care if she did take them for herself. Nicola had saved his life, but more important, she had salvaged his soul. She could have anything she wished for that.

In her own way, she had tried to warn him. *You deal*

with the murderers, thieves, and liars. . . . The world's full
of them. . . . You have to think the way they do. . . . For all
you know, I could be one of them.

Something touched his neck. "If I were a holy freak,
you'd be a dead vampire."

"Fortunately for me you are not." He caught Nicola's
hand and brought it to his lips. "I missed you."

"Well, I had to do some recon and get some supplies."
She placed a cold, thick plastic bag in his hands. "Some
breakfast."

"Blood?" He could see that it was from the dark red
smear of color, but decided to keep silent about his returning vision. If she could keep secrets, then so could he—at
least until he had some better idea of what she stole, and
why.

"Blood and more blood," she said, placing a small, box-
shaped object next to him. "This is a cooler with six more
units. It's fresh from the blood bank at the city hospital."

"How did you get it?" Had she stolen this as well? "A
hospital would not sell bagged blood to you."

"I sort of borrowed it," she said. "It's okay; it's type O,
and I made sure they had plenty in stock. They won't
miss it."

Was that how she thought of what she did? As borrow-
ing? How did so generous and kind a woman become a
thief? None of it made sense to Gabriel.

"I picked up some extra bungee cords so I can strap the
cooler to the bike." She sorted through a bag. "Got jeans,
T-shirts, and some decent shoes. You're about a size nine,
right?" She moved closer. "Aren't you hungry?"

"I am." Hungry, and puzzled, and not sure of what to
do. "Where did you get the clothes?"

"From a men's sportswear shop in town; where else? I
picked out some long-sleeved tracksuits. They'll cover
everything, but they're cotton, so you won't sweat to
death." She brought his hand to a shirt. "See? Nice and
soft. I got them in solid colors: dark green, blue, and

black." Her voice went uncertain. "I didn't know what to do about underwear."

The Brethren had denied him the dignity of clothing. That she would care about such a small detail touched him deeply. "It doesn't matter. I am not accustomed to wearing it anymore."

"Well, I got three pairs of cotton boxers in case, you know, you decide you want to. I couldn't picture you in briefs." She tapped the bag in his lap. "Go on; drink up. We have to catch a train."

"A train."

"First-class sleeper compartment," she added. "I picked up some rail passes. They run the *Occitan* to the coast now."

She couldn't have stolen train tickets—could she? "I thought we would take your motorcycle."

"Well, I'm not leaving it behind." The blur of her face appeared in front of him, and he had to remember to keep his gaze fixed. "I remove the front wheel and crate it at the station as cargo. The train's good for staying out of sight while we travel during the day, and I think we need to get out of France."

That much he agreed with. "Where are we going?"

"The train takes us all the way to Calais," she said. "I'll put the bike back together there, and then it's twenty minutes through the Eurotunnel to Dover. From Dover, it's a couple of hours to my place."

She had done this before, obviously. "You are taking me home with you?"

"Unless you'd rather go somewhere else, yeah." She bent forward and kissed him. "That okay?"

"Very much so." Gabriel set aside the bag of blood and pulled her into his arms. "There is someone I should see in London first, to find out what has happened since my imprisonment. Will you take me to him before we go to your home?"

"Sure." She linked her hands around his neck. "Is

everything okay? You seem kind of out of it this morning." Her voice softened. "I guess you've had nothing but one rude shock after another."

"I will, as you say, handle it." Gabriel held her close. He would be lost without her now. "Only stay with me, Nicola."

Chapter 15

The door to the lab opened and closed again. A certain tall, blond Kyn cleared his throat.

Alex didn't stop working, and sent a wish to the medical research fairy to open a bottomless pit inside the lab door.

"The high lord wishes to know what progress you have made," Korvel said from behind Alex.

If the captain of Richard's guards interrupted her one more time, Alex decided, she was going to beat him to death with her coagulyzer. A girl just couldn't rely on the medical research fairy anymore.

"I'm four more blood tests and one partial extrapolated blood absorption simulation ahead of where I was yesterday," she told him. "Half of one comparative screen farther than I was an hour ago. No farther along than ten minutes ago." She paused and stared at her watch. "Why, look, I'm still not any farther along."

"I meant, have you any reports prepared?"

"Not a one. I hate reports, and I really hate typing. How's my brother?"

"I have posted new guards, and instructed them to alert me if Lady Elizabeth sends for John," Korvel said. "Your brother tells me that his migraine has improved, but he would like aspirin."

"Aspirin promotes bleeding, and his neck injury hasn't healed yet. He stays on the Tylenol. Just don't let him drink any wine." She didn't look up from the scope. "What else?"

"The high lord wishes a progress report," he reminded her.

Of course he did. "Tell the royal pain in my ass that I'm not going to get anything done if he keeps sending you in here every five minutes."

"I have not bothered you every five minutes."

She sighed and jotted down her counts. "You want me to start clocking you, Captain?" She swiveled her chair around and saw his expression. "Look, this is a process. Processes take time. Testing can't be rushed, because it screws up the tests. And I'm working on stuff I haven't done since I was an intern and read about it in the textbooks. When I have something more definite than the number of weird blood cells currently running around in Richard's veins, you'll be the first to know."

"His condition grows worse." His voice rasped on the words.

"It's not going to get better on its own." Alex felt as tired as Korvel sounded, and focused on his pale, drawn features. "You look like you could use a transfusion or three. Has Elizabeth been tapping you?"

"No." That surprised him. "The lady only uses humans. I am well."

"My ass." She went over and checked his pulse. His skin felt cold and stiff to the touch, a sure sign of Kyn dehydration. His fresh-baked-pound-cake scent had also grown noticeably weaker. "Just out of curiosity, how long has it been since you've fed?"

"I do not know. Some days now." He frowned as if he couldn't remember. "My duties have occupied me."

Alex noticed a slash mark on his neck, a recent injury that had healed on the surface but that she'd bet good money was still knitting beneath the dermis.

"I can't give you a Tylenol for this, Korvel. If you don't feed, you don't heal. Wine by itself doesn't count. The pathogen needs a blood chaser, and it will take it out on you if you don't give it . . ." She stepped back. "Holy shit."

Korvel's eyebrows rose. "I cannot eat shit, Doctor. Blessed or otherwise."

"No, that's not what I mean. It's something Lucan said to me in Florida. You are what you eat. You are . . . Tylenol . . . and the wine mixed in . . . holy shit." She went to the computer and pulled up the profile on Richard's blood count. She heard Korvel retreating. "Hold it, Captain. I need a sample of your blood. Grab a stool and roll up your right sleeve."

Alex grabbed a copper-tipped syringe from the supply cabinet and brought it over to Richard's seneschal, who had bared his arm. She tied a strip of rubber above his elbow and tightened it.

"How will my blood aid you? I am not a changeling."

"You're normal, for Kyn, and you're as old as Richard, and you've hung with him for seven centuries, and he infected you. This is going to sting." She plunged the needle into one of the raised veins under his skin and drew a sample. As soon as she withdrew the needle, the hole stopped bleeding but did not immediately close. "You really haven't fed in a while."

He averted his gaze. "I have had no desire to feed."

That definitely wasn't normal. And why was the captain suddenly acting like a shy kid? "Anyway, depressed as it presently is, the pathogen in your blood should be identical to the one Richard had before he contaminated his."

"Contaminated?"

"You are what you eat, Korvel. Richard hasn't been eating humans." She transferred a few drops of Korvel's blood onto a test strip and fed it into the analyzer, running a second profile. "Hold on to your helm, big guy. Last time I did this, I found out a human with diabetes was actually a repressed vampire."

The efficient equipment conducted the tests and created a blood profile for Korvel, which Alex transferred to the computer and put up next to Richard's aberrant profile.

"Same cell counts, different DNA. Now watch; this is cool." She ran the absorption simulation she had been working on with Richard's blood. "Richard's DNA mutated, creating an extra, distinct set of chromosomes that should have dusted him the minute it happened, but didn't. Since our chromosomes determine what we look like, I blamed the extra set for his physical changes and altered physiology. Thing I couldn't figure out was why the DNA mutated. As far as I can tell, Richard wasn't exposed to any toxin, radioactive material, or other substance responsible for the mutation."

The captain peered at the computer screen. "What has that to do with my blood?"

"Human blood cells die almost immediately after they're removed from the body. Kyn's remain alive and active for three weeks. Now watch this." She ran the simulation of introducing human red blood cells into Richard's blood sample. "See how the pathogenic cells try to absorb these red blood cells, and then spit them out? It's almost the same type of toxic reaction that happens in the human liver when someone ingests wine with Tylenol. Richard can't digest whole human blood anymore."

"We know this, lady," Korvel said gently.

"Wait, there's more." She changed the simulation parameters. "I'm going to feed a little rodent blood into your sample. Watch what happens."

The same violent reaction occurred as Korvel's pathogen rejected the animal blood cells.

"I cannot feed on rats any more than I can eat shit," the captain said. "I also know this."

"But wait; there's more." Alex mentally crossed her fingers as she mixed equal portions of rat and human blood cells, and fed them first to Korvel's blood sample, and then to Richard's. A few of the cells in each sample were rejected, but the majority were absorbed. "I knew it, I knew it, I knew it. This is a fifty-fifty mix; half human blood, half rat. See? It's not discriminating as much this time."

He shrugged. "All Kyn can tolerate small amounts of animal blood."

"Yes, but this test proves that you could handle more if you drank it mixed in with human blood," she told him, running the simulation a second time. "The same way you can drink wine as long as it's mixed with human blood. Korvel, the pathogen needs blood. It lives on it. It's willing to tolerate—even absorb—foreign cells and substances as long as it gets its fix. If it doesn't, it's forced to adapt. Ergo, extra set of chromosomes and unpleasant physical mutation."

Korvel seemed dazed now. "I do not understand."

"I thought it was about physical changes. I'm an idiot. This all starts at the cellular level." She tried to think of how to put it in layman's terms. "Richard was forced to live on animal blood for years. To survive, the pathogen created a new set of DNA to process the foreign cells and attract the new blood supply. It changed Richard so that he would attract it. Like any evolving organism, it's simply been adapting itself according to its environment. If it adapts once, it'll definitely adapt again."

Korvel looked stunned. "You mean, this can be reversed?"

Alex remembered Elizabeth's threat. She'd have to cure Richard on the condition that he have John returned to the States first. Then Elizabeth couldn't do anything to him.

"We deny the new DNA what it wants, absolutely." Alex realized that a cure was also her ticket out of Dundellan, and felt like kissing the computer, the captain, and every rat in the castle. "It shouldn't take that long, either—Richard still has Kyn DNA lying dormant in his cells."

"Do I indeed."

Alex stopped feeling so great and stooped to pick up the plump tabby that had strolled in with Richard. "Hey, kitty," she said, stroking the affectionate feline. "Look what you dragged in here."

"Korvel, leave us."

"Yes, my lord." The captain walked to the door, turned back, gave Alex what she could classify only as a dire warning look, and left.

"My wife tells me that you called on her in her apartments," Richard said as he went to the lab door and locked it. "I do not recall giving you permission to do so."

"I don't recall asking permission." Alex shut down the simulation. She could tell Richard that his wife had threatened to kill John if Alex made any progress, but she doubted he would believe her. Elizabeth was his wife, the home team; Alex was the unwilling, uncooperative captive. "What can I do for you?"

"According to my captain, I killed the last of the humans we keep as blood suppliers. I cannot recall doing so, but I have lost most of the last two days." He removed his mask, revealing his distorted face and the thick layer of hair and long, bunched whiskers that had grown in.

With the hair in place, Alex finally understood what Richard had been feeding on. She looked down at the tabby, and ran her thumb through the fur around its neck, feeling a number of puncture wounds. "It's the cats. You're feeding on the cats."

Alex recalled all of the cats running around the castle. There were dozens, and half of the females were pregnant. He probably encouraged them to breed to provide him with a steady supply. And she was going to puke if she kept thinking about it.

"When the Brethren held me prisoner in Rome," Richard said, "they refused to let me feed. I endured the deprivation as long as possible, but in time it became apparent that I had to feed on something or wither away. My choices were limited to the rats that infested the catacombs, or the stray cats I assumed had wandered in from the city streets to feed on them."

"I'd have picked the cats," she admitted.

"Their bodies contained a greater quantity of blood, so I had to feed less often." He bared his pointed, feline teeth in a grotesque smile. "It wasn't until after some years of feeding on them that I discovered the Brethren had deliberately put both types of animals into the Kyn cell block."

"Jesus. Why?"

"They wished to see how feeding on animal blood would affect us." His pupils expanded to black diamonds as he limped toward her. "I expect there was some hope of soul saving or reformation involved initially. Then it seemed to become some form of entertainment for them."

"And hell for you." Despite everything she felt about the high lord, Alex experienced a small twinge of sympathy. "Nothing but cat blood ever since, right?"

"Not entirely," Richard told her. "I have never told anyone this, but I have managed to control my condition by also drinking a little human blood each day."

That supported her theory, and may have explained why Richard's Kyn DNA had remained dormant instead of being replaced by the feline-adapted DNA. "How little?"

"A teaspoon in every feeding, or a single swallow from a human. Any more than that makes me violently ill."

"Who do you get the blood from? Éliane," Alex guessed, remembering the *tresora*'s penchant for high-necked blouses.

"Providing me with sex and blood are part of her duties." He made it sound like secretarial work.

That clinched it. "You know, you're a total jerk with women, but we'll save that chat for another time. I have an idea, if you want to hear it."

He leaned against her dissection table. "Tell me."

Alex explained why she believed the blood of stray cats Richard was forced to live on had caused the Kyn pathogen to alter his DNA, the reason behind his physical mutations. "I think I can reverse it, too. You'll have to stop feeding on feline blood."

"Do you propose to starve me, as they did?"

"No." Alex checked the refrigeration unit, but saw her human blood supply bin was empty. She couldn't remember using the last unit, but she had been wrapped up in her research. "I want to inject you with a serum. It'll be human blood mixed with a small amount of feline blood. If that works, I'll add some Kyn tranquilizer to the next batch."

"Why must you tranquilize me?"

"I'm pretty sure this is going to make you feel sick, so the tranquilizer will slow down your body processes and help keep your reaction to a minimum. The presence of the feline blood should force the pathogen to digest the human blood cells. We'll have to take it slow, but by decreasing the amount of feline blood with each dose, I think we'll wake up your Kyn DNA and put the changeling process in remission."

He looked at her for a long, silent moment. "By doing this, you will save me."

She didn't want his gratitude, or the credit for what she was about to do. "You saved yourself, Richard. If you hadn't ingested human blood daily, you would never have held on to your humanity, such as it is, for as long as you have." She hit the intercom. "Korvel, I need a unit of human blood, please."

One of Richard's servants delivered the bag of blood and, after giving the high lord a frightened look, hurried out of the lab.

"How many humans did you slaughter this time?" Alex asked as she prepared the serum.

"I cannot say." He bared his arm for her and watched as she injected him. "What does it matter?"

"Humans are our friends. We like humans. And if we kill all the humans, we don't have any dinner." She withdrew the syringe and sighed. "I hate being a vampire. It's really freaking out my brother. Have I mentioned that?"

Richard got up quickly from the stool and turned his back on her. "I can feel it moving in my veins."

"It might make you puke." She looked around for an empty container. "Just relax and let it happen."

"Let it happen." His voice dropped to a low growl. "I am done with letting it happen. It should not have happened. Not to me. I am king."

The anger startled Alex. "Richard? Look at me."

He looked. His pupils had shrunk down to slivers, and his fangs shot out of his mouth, three times longer than Alex had ever seen them.

"Right, this is not working." She grabbed the bag of blood, but it was marked as human, type A. She took a sip from it and immediately spit it out. "Goddamn it, this isn't human blood. What the *hell* is going on?"

"You think to poison me." Richard whipped out his arm, sending a row of beakers and a microscope crashing to the floor. "I am king. I will never die."

"Then let's go for calming down the king," Alex said softly, not moving. "Someone gave me the wrong bag, Richard. That's what's making you nuts. Hang on, and I'll—"

"Bitch." He picked up the edge of a table and turned it over. Her computer exploded in a fountain of sparks, and the cracked console of the analyzer began spitting out sample strips. The high lord tore out of his cloak and dropped onto all fours, where his twisted body assumed a new, powerful configuration.

Alex backed away, turning to run.

From behind Richard leaped at her, latching onto her back with his curved claws and dragging her to the floor. His hot breath burned the back of her neck as he held her head down with one paw and began ripping at the back of her lab coat with the other.

"Richard." Alex could feel his erect cock jabbing at the seat of her trousers. Something sticking out from the side of his shaft penetrated her clothing like sharp thorns, and she remembered an article she had read about male cats having barbed organs.

She'd tear out her own throat before she let him put that inside her.

Alex screamed, throwing her head back and smashing it into Richard's teeth. He roared, digging his claws deep into her shoulder and ripping at her flesh. She tried to throw him off, but he had her pinned too well.

"My lord," a cool voice said. "Forgive me."

Alex felt Richard stiffen and fall over, and scrambled out from under his weight. A pressure dart planted in the center of his back wiggled back and forth.

"Doctor." Éliane put aside the tranquilizer gun and helped Alex to her feet. "You are badly injured."

"No shit. I think I owe you a huge apology." She looked over the *tresora*'s shoulder to see Korvel and Stefan rush in. "I think someone gave me pure feline blood instead of human. It made him do this."

"Who?" Éliane demanded.

"Lady Elizabeth," Alex said. "She wishes him dead."

"You have no proof," the captain said.

"She told me that she'd kill my brother if I found a cure for Richard," Alex said, groaning as she tried to feel how badly the high lord had ripped up her back. "Does that work for you?"

"Why did you not tell me?" Korvel demanded.

"Like you'd have believed me." She was dripping blood all over Richard, and saw his lacerated lips heal under the crimson splashes. "Wait a minute." She dropped down and wiped her blood from his face with her sleeve. All the hair around his mouth came with it, and the split in his upper lip disappeared. "Pick up that microscope and see if it's still working." Through the shrinking tunnel of her vision, she groped for a box of slides Richard had knocked to the floor.

"You are hurt." Korvel reached for her.

"I'll heal. Take him out of here . . . and get me some human blood. . . ." She saw Éliane's hands appear in front of her, and sighed as she fainted into them.

*　　　*　　　*

Nick led Gabriel past the curious eyes of the travelers in the crowded, six-berth couchette compartments and through the back of the car. "I think it's up here."

Few tourists bought tickets for the *Occitan*'s expensive first class, preferring the cheaper reclining seats in second class. The younger travelers gravitated toward the partying, college-dorm atmosphere of the shared couchettes. But Nick didn't mind paying double the fare plus the extra supplement charge so that they could have one of the lower, two-berth rooms. Gabriel needed privacy as much as she did, and that always came with a price tag.

She found their compartment nestled in the back of the very first car, which, aside from two well-dressed businessmen, seemed deserted. "Here we go." She steered Gabriel in through the narrow door.

He stood still. "I confess, I have never slept on a train."

"You need to get around more." She took his hands and used them to show him the room by touch. "There's a sofa here, and two bunk beds up top, near the ceiling. The bedding isn't the greatest, and you'll probably have to curl up, but they're pretty comfy. Soap, towels, washbasin. The bathroom is at the other end of the car."

"Is there a place you can dine?" he asked. "You've not had anything to eat."

"I grabbed something while you were sleeping back at the inn," she told him. "I can get something from the attendant when he comes around later." She checked the compartment locks before stowing their bags in the tiny corner cabinet. "This door has a security latch on it that can't be opened from the outside, even by the train attendants. We'll keep that locked." She went to the window and looked out at the station platform. She hadn't seen anyone suspicious, but she wouldn't relax until she got Gabriel out of France. "I don't think anyone was on the lookout for us."

He came up behind her, reached out, and with uncanny

precision pulled down the window shade. "I think we are safe here. All we have to do is occupy ourselves until the train reaches Calais."

Nick leaned back against him, letting the heat of his body melt the tension out of her muscles. "What have you got in mind?"

He guided her over to the small sofa and pulled her down next to him. "We should talk."

"About what?" She tugged down the zipper on the front of his jacket and slipped her hand inside.

He promptly took it out and raised it to his lips, brushing a kiss across her knuckles. "You."

"Not much to tell." Nick shifted closer.

"I want to know more about you," Gabriel said as he put an arm around her. "You said that you've been alone for ten years. You lost your family when you were only sixteen?"

"Yeah." Nick needed to change the subject. "I don't like talking about that, okay?"

He nodded. "Then tell me about the Golden Madonna. I have some knowledge of art; perhaps I know of it."

Nick started to get up, but he held her in place. "Gabriel, you couldn't possibly . . . It's all tied up with bad stuff that happened a long time ago. I just need to find it. That's all."

"But what is it, Nicola? A painting? A triptych?"

"No." She sighed. "The Madonna was this statue that my stepdad found buried under our house. The original owners built it on top of a bunch of old ruins. After this bad rain, Malcolm—my stepdad—found the edge of a wall in the garden. It ran under the house, so he started digging in the cellar to see how far it went. I think my mom was worried about the stability of the foundation or something."

"What did he find?"

"Well, a lot of old Norman stuff from when they came over and kicked Saxon butt. They built an outpost on top of a Saxon keep they burned down. The Saxons made that from parts of this really old Roman fortress. It was all in layers and stuff. Malcolm took pictures of everything he found and then covered it back up."

Gabriel frowned. "Why?"

"He didn't like messing with things. He was afraid of archeologists finding out about the site, too. He thought they were glorified looters." How silly that seemed now, considering what had happened. "The only thing Mal ever brought up from the cellar was the Madonna." She blinked back hot tears. "I don't know why, but it fascinated him. He tried to find out where it came from and who made it."

He rubbed his hand up and down her arm. "What did it look like, this Madonna?"

"I only saw it once; Malcolm kept it locked up." She described the statue, and added, "It didn't do any good."

"Someone stole this statue from your home?"

"Yes, and I want it back. I've been searching for it ever since." She bolted off the sofa. "I think I am hungry. I'll go get something to eat and be back in a few minutes."

Gabriel came after her, putting his hand over hers and making her close the door. "Did the thief kill your parents, Nicola?"

"I told you—"

He whirled her around. "Does the murderer have the Madonna?"

"Yes. So the Madonna could be returned to her shrine. Only I don't know where her shrine is." Was that her voice, so thin and cold? "So I'm looking through all of them. Any chapel, church, or holy place I can get into, I search. I'll find her someday." She shoved at him. "Satisfied? Or do you want to hear how they were tortured before they were killed?"

"Your parents were tortured?"

"My stepdad wouldn't give up the Madonna. Not until he . . ." She refused to sob. "Hey, we could compare notes, see if it was worse than what the holy freaks did to you."

"That is why you've been releasing the Kyn." The compartment filled with the scent of evergreen as Gabriel moved toward her. "What is done to us is the same thing that happened to your parents."

Revulsion filled her. "No. It's not the same. They weren't . . . You don't understand." She covered her face with her hands. "Please, Gabriel, I can't talk about them anymore. Please stop asking me questions."

"Forgive me." He bent down and kissed the tears from her face. "I only want to understand better what has happened to you." His breath warmed her cold lips. "You can trust me, Nicola. I swear it."

If only he knew. "I trust you as much as I can, Gabriel." Nick burrowed against him, needing his warmth as much as she needed air to breathe. "Come to bed with me."

Gabriel held her at arm's length. "But I have upset you, and made you weep."

She brought his hand to her heart. "Start kissing here, where it hurts."

A short time later Nick was breathless, half-undressed, and wedged between Gabriel and the sofa. She watched him expertly tug her jeans and panties down the length of her legs. "There are two perfectly good beds in here, you know."

He tossed her clothes out of his way. "Both of us will not fit on one berth. So unless you wish to gaze at me from afar—"

"Floor's good." Nick took the cushions from the sofa and pushed them together into a makeshift mattress. "I kind of miss the spiders, though."

He sat up, went still for a minute, and then grinned. "There are several dozen living in this car. Shall I summon them?"

"Don't you dare." Laughing, she tackled him. "I love you, but the bug thing is really . . . not so . . . great." Had she just blurted that out? She had. No wonder he looked as if he'd turned to stone, and acted as if she'd sucker punched him. "It's the dreams. You know how women are. We get emotional about stuff like that."

"Not you, *ma mie*." He pulled her down until only a whisper separated their lips. "Tell me again."

"It's not—"

"Tell me again." Gabriel rolled over, tucking her under him. "Tell me when I'm inside you."

"Gabriel." She wound her legs around his hips, offering herself to him. He pushed into her, hard and fast, almost knocking the breath out of her. "I love you."

Alexandra woke up naked and lying facedown on an uncomfortable pallet. Someone with very gentle hands was washing the wounds on her back, but whatever they were using didn't irritate or sting but soothed. For a few minutes she simply enjoyed the relief.

"I'd like the recipe for whatever you're putting on me," she said at last.

"Water boiled with willow bark and valerian," Korvel told her, "left to cool."

"Sounds herbal. You sure you boiled it?" Alex craned her neck to see the captain in only a pair of trousers, sitting on a three-legged wooden stool by the bed. Barely healed claw marks slashed across his chest in four places. "Did you lock him up?"

"My master is sleeping."

"That's not what I asked you, Korvel."

"Dr. Keller, I cannot *lock up* the high lord of the Darkyn." He rose, picked up the stool, and moved it closer to her upper body. "Be still. I am not finished."

Alex laid her cheek on her folded hands and studied Korvel's face. In the firelight, like now, he seemed more ordinary than movie-star handsome, but there was something compelling about him. "What's your talent?"

He didn't answer, but squeezed out a soaked cloth over her back, letting the warm liquid pour over her wounds.

"I can read the minds of killers," she offered. "Is yours worse than mine?"

"Kyn do not trade tales about talent." He pulled up the

sheet covering her legs and hips and tucked it around her. "It is undignified."

"So it's worse than mine."

He almost smiled. "Does anything discourage you?"

"The Bush administration, our foreign policy, and Alison getting kicked off *Project Runway*," she told him. "So on a scale from one to ten, how bad is your talent?"

"It has never failed me." Korvel got to his feet. "Even when I wish that it would."

Under the grim all-business, fight-to-the-death warrior facade was, Alex suspected, a very nice man. Why else would he be playing her nurse?

"I'd help you, but intelligent design screwed up our arm-to-back motor skills." She tested her shoulders, moving them and wincing. "He really did a number on me, huh?"

He nodded. "You do not heal like us."

"When I'm not being held hostage, I actually heal pretty fast. Being here has slowed me down on a couple of levels." She frowned as a clear image of herself being beaten with a copper pipe passed through her mind. "Quit thinking about killing me."

"I do not wish to *kill* you."

She didn't like the way he said it, at least until she breathed in. "You know, when you get pissed off or upset, you smell like vanilla pound cake."

"Larkspur," he said, coming over and looking down at her face. "When I go to wash at dawn, I can sometimes smell lavender on my clothes. From you."

"That's nice. Makes me feel all warm and fuzzy." Too warm, too fuzzy. "And a bit like a skunk."

"You do not smell like one."

Alex was staring at his mouth, but she didn't know quite why. Then she did, all in a rush, as soon as her breasts tightened and something very neglected and sulky stirred between her legs.

Which brought home some facts: She was naked, alone

with Korvel, and in his bed. In a very small room with no real ventilation. "I have to get out of here."

"Yes." Korvel didn't move. "Unfortunately, so do I. It is not your doing, Doctor."

Pornography popped into her head, starring the captain of the guard and herself. "You know what I'm thinking?"

"My talent put the thoughts in your mind." He flashed his fangs as he spoke. "No human woman can resist me. Neither, I fear, can you."

"You can make any woman want to . . . *fuck*." She pushed herself up with her arms. "Give me my clothes." She remembered Richard had torn them from her. "Give me *some* clothes. And turn off your talent. This minute."

He brought a light robe to her and went to stand by the fireplace, averting his gaze. "I apologize. I have always controlled myself before this."

Alex wanted his hands on her breasts. His tongue in her mouth. His cock in her pussy. "Try harder."

"I am not seducing you," he pointed out. "However much I wish to at this moment."

Alex felt herself go wet. "Yeah. No. Christ, I am out of here." She went to the door, startled by how sore she was and how slowly she was moving, and stopped there. "Thank you for patching me up, Captain."

"I am at your service, my lady."

"God, don't ever say that to me again." She opened the door and hobbled out.

Chapter 16

Although some Brits returning from the Continent grumbled incessantly about it, Nick never minded riding at the back of the Eurotunnel shuttle. The shuttle company put bikers in the back for safety reasons, but all Nick cared about was that they let her book and pay for her ticket online, and the thirty-five-minute trip from Calais to Folkstone meant that she and Gabriel didn't even have to get off the bike. Besides, the most interesting passengers on the trip were always the bikers.

Making the channel crossing today were mostly weekend solo bikers, but one German couple on a wicked black-and-silver Triumph Tiger outfitted for transcon touring parked next to her and exchanged admiring looks. Knowing Gabriel couldn't see it, Nick described the couple's bike to him.

"You sound as another woman would when she describes a diamond necklace," he teased.

"I can't ride a necklace," she told him. "That bike I could take around the world. In a heartbeat."

"BMW GS?" the German man asked her.

Nick seesawed her hand, making the man's wife giggle. Her German was nonexistent, so she pointed to the different parts of the bike she'd rebuilt and named the make of the new parts. She then pointed to the reinforced molded luggage containers fastened to the custom rack at the back of the Triumph, and fluttered her hand over her heart.

Gabriel unexpectedly said something in very precise,

rapid German to the couple, who responded enthusiastically. When he had finished, he said to Nick, "I told them that you admired their motorcycle. They are envious of your ingenuity with your engine refittings."

"*Danke,*" she said to the couple. At least she could say that much. She glanced back at Gabriel. "I should take you with me every time I cross over. You could be my interpreter."

"I have never traveled through the Channel Tunnel," Gabriel said. "I suppose it was the thought of being under so much water."

"We're forty-five meters down. We could swim, but it takes a whole day and my bike would rust to pieces." She leaned back against him and enjoyed the way his arms came up around her waist to pull her closer. "I was really bummed to hear that the company that built this had to file for bankruptcy over the summer. I'd hate it if they have to shut it down; it's the fastest way to get from France to England and back again."

He kissed the side of her neck. "You are impatient about everything."

"You didn't think so on the train from Toulouse," she reminded him.

Nick wasn't quite sure how to classify what Gabriel did to her. He had sex with her, of course. That was the clinical way of looking at it. Over the last couple of days they had gone at it like bunnies. But he also made love to her, the way the heroes did in chick movies. And then he took her, too, as dominantly and erotically as some of the Emma Holly novels she'd read.

"That trip should have taken much longer," Gabriel insisted. "They drove the train too fast, and then you rushed us through the station."

Nick thought about the Interpol bulletin she'd seen when they'd passed through the station at Calais. Whoever had given them the description of her had told the artist that she was a boy, but despite that it was a fairly accurate sketch of her face on it. The list of properties she'd burglarized didn't include the ones where she'd found Kyn and released them, so the holy freaks were definitely involved.

She couldn't tell Gabriel she was being chased by Interpol any more than she could explain about her parents; he'd want to know all the details. She also wondered if the same bulletins were being posted around London, and how she would feel if he found out she was a thief—and a liar.

He won't find out. He can't see me or them.

Nick knew she might be able to keep the truth from Gabriel because he was blind, but that wouldn't keep the authorities away. They could see her just fine, and with Father Claudio and the men from the house in Toulouse helping them, they'd soon change the description on the bulletin from a boy to a girl.

As the shuttle stopped at Folkstone station and the vehicles were driven off, Nick's nerves got the better of her. She wasn't sure she could even do this. "How long do you think this meeting with your friend in the city is going to take?"

"Only an hour at the most."

Not much time for her. "Can he get you in touch with your friends? I mean, the ones who are Kyn?"

"Croft serves the suzerain of London. He can put me in contact with any Kyn in the world." Gabriel tugged at a piece of her hair. "Why do you ask?"

"Just curious." She saw a customs officer and two police constables approaching the rear of the shuttle, led by an elderly man walking with a familiar-looking cane. "Gabriel, we might not make that meeting."

His arms tightened around her. "What is it?"

"Father Claudio is here. They're checking each shuttle deck." She saw Claudio pointing at her and Gabriel, and the two constables picked up their pace. "Fuck me; he just made us." She turned, checking the clearance in front and behind the bike before kicking up the center stand. "Strap on the helmet and hold on to me."

The German couple on the beautiful Triumph both looked back as Nick started her engine, and the husband glanced from Nick to the approaching constables and frowned. His wife whispered something in his ear, and he winked at Nick before he rolled his bike forward. The Triumph's bulk blocked the side entry and gave Nick enough clearance to go around him.

No matter what country they came from, in an emergency bikers were always happy to give you a hand.

"Whatever you do," Nick shouted over the sound of her revving engine to Gabriel, "don't let go of me."

As she released the parking brake and shot forward, a fluttering cloud filled the deck, causing the passengers to shriek. Nick drove through the swarm of moths, nosing the bike around the vehicles in front of her and speeding up and out of the tunnel station.

Gabriel's moths provided enough of a distraction to get them safely out of Folkstone, but Nick didn't stop until they were miles away. She pulled off the road to shake off some moths still clinging to her shirt, and make sure Gabriel wasn't too freaked out by what she had done.

"We're good," she told him as she helped him remove the helmet. The sunlight irritated his eyes, so she handed him her spare pair of shades. "You all right?"

"I am wishing I had killed that old man," he muttered, stroking one hand over her head. "It would have saved us much grief."

"We got away. What's a little grief, huh?" She hugged him, which turned into a kiss, which threatened to end up with the two of them rolling around the grass in the ditch. "Whoa. Save that for later, and tell me how to get to this guy Croft's shop."

Nick followed Gabriel's directions into the business district of London, and ended up in front of an old rare bookshop.

" 'Mr. Pickard's Emporium of Literature'?" she read

from the ornate sign painted in white across the spotless window. "Sounds like the captain from that second *Star Trek* series."

"My name is not Jean-Luc, young woman," a crisp, cultured voice informed her. It belonged to the man stepping out of the shop. "I am, regrettably, equally as bald and stuffy. I say, is that vampire on the back of your motorbike bothering you?"

Nick grinned. "Not really."

"Count yourself fortunate." He made an elegant sweep of his hand toward the sun. "Daylight does not make them turn to ash, but they become bloody damn infants, whinging on about irritated eyes and sluggish limbs and so forth."

Gabriel climbed off the motorcycle and embraced the short, thin bald man.

"Croft, it has been too long since I've listened to your insults." Gabriel kissed both of his cheeks before turning toward Nick. "This is Nicola Jefferson. Nicola, although he would have you think otherwise, this is my very good friend Croft Pickard."

Pickard clasped Nick's hand between his before urging them into the shop. "Come inside before some religious zealot has at you with a pike or something."

Nick knew from the moment she stepped under the glass door's tinkling bell that she had entered someplace special. The aroma of old paper and aged leather tickled her nose, but so did another scent; something like mint and chocolate.

Croft's shop, she decided, had the perfect name. Elegantly carved, freestanding bookcases held shelf after shelf of antique books. Most were bound in leather and still showed their titles stamped in faded gilt on the spines. Some were displayed open under round glass domes, like cakes, while others were bound in sets of three and four with cream and gold silk ribbons.

Precious, beautiful things had to be kept safe. This more than anything decided things for Nick.

One sparkling crystal dish offered wrapped Swiss chocolates for the customers, and a live mint plant sprouted in one corner of the desk from a brass urn. Nick bent over to breathe in its fragrance. Mint and chocolate, two things she had genuinely missed.

"I hate to say it, but of all the Kyn I have expected to walk through that door," Croft said as he closed the blinds and locked the front door, "you never made the list."

"The Kyn believe I'm dead."

"They sent the word out on you more than a year ago. We had a very nice memorial service over at the club." Croft switched on an electric teakettle. "I know you can't stomach the stuff, but your charming escort appears in very great need of a cup of tea."

That was her cue.

"I can't stay." Nick stuffed her hands in her jacket pockets and forced a smile. "I have some things to do. Gabriel, I'll be back in an hour to pick you up."

Croft stopped spooning tea leaves into the ceramic pot in his hand. "You don't have to leave, surely."

"You guys need some time to chat. By the way, they blinded him," she said, nodding toward Gabriel, "so don't let him wander out into traffic, okay?"

"Heavens, no." The bookshop owner looked horrified. "Completely blind?"

"Yeah." Nick kissed Gabriel on the cheek, keeping it casual. "See you."

She left the shop before he could say another word or she could change her mind. Because she wasn't coming back in an hour, and would never see him again, she didn't look back.

Gabriel was a gentleman. She was a thief. They had no future together.

If Nick stayed with him, she would risk leading the holy freaks to him. She'd rather never see him again than know she had helped put him back in some bricked-up room to die.

She didn't owe Gabriel anything, either. On the contrary.

Nick felt a little better as she climbed onto the bike. She'd done right by him; no one could say that she hadn't. She'd taken care of him, gotten him to his friend, and now she could take off and know he'd be all right. Being blind, he couldn't help her find the Golden Madonna. He'd only slow her down. He belonged with better people, people like Croft. All she'd do was get him arrested. The holy freaks knew how to use the cops to get what they wanted; they were experts at it.

Gabriel deserved better. He'd get back together with the Kyn, and she could go on with her life. She'd pack up her stuff at the farm and move north. She liked Scotland; maybe she'd try spending the winter in the Highlands. Once the cops lost interest she'd make some other changes and start fresh on her search for the Madonna in the spring.

She got as far as Hyde Park before she had to pull into a parking space and jump off the bike. Her chest heaved with the pain of breathing in cold, damp English air. This was going to kill her, leaving him like this, without knowing, without a word. Would he ever forgive her?

The Kyn had abandoned him, his sister had betrayed him, and now she was dumping him. He'd been lost for so long, just like her. How would he feel when he realized she wasn't coming back for him?

He'll hate you forever.

Oh, God. What was she doing?

"I'll go back." She checked her watch and saw she still had ten minutes before he would expect her to return. "I'll ride by one time and look in the window and make sure he's okay. But after that I have to head out of town and forget about him."

Well, she'd head out of town, anyway.

Nick turned around and drove back toward Croft's shop. She couldn't ride by, she realized; Gabriel would hear the bike. She'd have to find a spot by the corner and take a look from there.

One look and that's all. Nick knew that if she did any more than look, she'd never be able to leave him.

The south corner of the intersection nearest Croft's shop had a phone box that gave her some cover while allowing her to see the front of the shop. Croft had rolled up the blinds in the big front window, probably so he could watch for her.

But she wasn't going back.

Nick eyed the telephone. Maybe she would call and tell Croft she was taking off and leaving Gabriel with him. Just so he knew and didn't wait there for her for hours or think something had happened to her. Croft wouldn't hate her for it. Not if she told him how much she loved Gabriel, and how dangerous she was to him.

This is why you don't get involved with anyone, she told herself viciously. *Because you don't know how to walk away.*

A book hit the inside of the shop window and slid down it to knock over Croft's artful front display. Nick frowned and reached into her jacket, taking out her binoculars. Through them she clearly saw three strange men standing inside the front of the shop. Two of them were holding Croft by the arms. The third had Gabriel by the front of his shirt.

The Kyn couldn't have gotten there that fast.

As she watched, the man holding Gabriel punched him in the face.

Rage exploded inside her. "Oh, *fuck* this."

Nick pulled down her visor, grabbed her bat from the back of the bike, and rounded the corner, cutting off a Jag and darting between a delivery van and a cab. She jumped the curb, scattering shoppers as she sped toward the front of the bookshop. At the last moment she locked up the brakes and let the bike skid sideways, slamming the rear tire into the display window.

Glass smashed and rained down on her as she put the bike in park and jumped off, using the bat to knock out the last jagged section of glass before climbing into the shop.

"Hey, asshole."

The man who had punched Gabriel stared at her in shock. He had a gun tucked in his belt.

"Yeah, you." She swung the bat at his head, and knocked him back into a collection of Victorian poetry. "Home run."

The other two rushed at her, guns in their hands, but she shoved the bat into the belly of one and clipped the other in the jaw with the grip. Both tottered backward, but not far enough to miss her second and third swings.

She saw that Croft was braced against his desk but unhurt. "Sorry about the window."

"My dear girl," he breathed. "Do not apologize." He hurried over and collected the guns the two men had dropped and the one still tucked in the belt of the third. "Guns are illegal in this country," he told the groaning men. "So is pummeling innocent vampires."

Nick went to Gabriel. "Let's get out of here." She took his arm and dragged him through the window.

A small group of startled Londoners had begun gathering, but they backed away as she helped Gabriel onto the bike and swung onto the seat.

"We'll get you, Seran," a man shouted, and Nick saw that one of the men inside the shop had gotten to his feet. "Every Brethren in England is hunting you and your thief bitch now. You can't hide forever—"

Croft stepped up behind him and slammed a large volume on the back of his head. The man collapsed in a heap.

"My apologies, dear boy," he called out to them. "It seems I've been compromised. If you need to reach me, you'll have to contact Geoff. So sorry you couldn't stay for tea, my dear."

"Next time." Nick looked down to see Gabriel's hands on her waist, and took off.

Michael left Phillipe and Leary with the van and took a horse from a nearby stable to ride along the boundaries of Dundellan.

Riding around Richard's stronghold should have calmed Michael, for it had been months since he had indulged his love of horseback riding and solitude. But Marcella's predictions had come true. Over the last days his temper had worn down his will, and not an hour passed that he did not feel as if his skin would crawl off his body. Often now he thought if he spent another day without her, he would go mad. In his head Michael understood it was the bond he shared with Alexandra, and the price of it, but in his heart all that mattered was to be with her again.

We are here. I will take back what is mine.

Michael led the horse out of the shadows, risking being spotted by the castle guard, but unable to resist looking up at the light shining from one of the narrow windows in the east stone tower. He had no way to know if Alexandra was being kept in that room or, as Leary suggested, had been locked away deep in the bowels of Dundellan.

A measure of calmness came to him as he focused his thoughts on her, the memory of her face, the smell of her skin. *Soon,* mon amour. *I will be with you again, very soon.*

Once Michael finished scouting the property, he put together the signs that all was not well at Dundellan. Richard had twice the usual amount of men patrolling, but they kept to the castle itself and did not stray out onto the surrounding acres. The neglected condition of the land indicated his household staff had possibly been locked in, dismissed, or perhaps killed. He suspected that as the high lord's mind deteriorated, his Kyn guards might begin quietly abandoning him. Perhaps, hearing of Lucan's attempt to assassinate him, they already had.

Michael met Phillipe back at the van. Inside, Leary sat watching the castle while the addicts they had taken from Dublin, made docile by Phillipe's compulsion over them, looked at nothing at all.

"The patrols are riding no more than two hundred yards out from the castle," he told his seneschal. "Six Kyn guard the delivery entrances at the west and north sides. The windows have been secured but the fences are falling apart. Nothing stands in our way."

"I called Marcella from the mobile," Phillipe said. "She has been monitoring the patrols, and says that Richard's men are carrying standard weapons as well as copper."

Armed to kill both humans and Kyn. "He's expecting someone other than us."

Phillipe brought a small case out of the back, which he placed on the hood of the van. He opened it and produced what appeared to be a Young Fine Gael campaign button and put it on his lapel.

"This is a radio transceiver," he told Cyprien. "It will pick up and transmit my voice and any others within twenty feet of me."

Cyprien fitted the earpiece. "When you are inside, find Alexandra and help her out through one of the second-floor windows, there," Michael told him, pointing to the least guarded area of the castle. "Whatever happens, do not engage Richard."

His seneschal nodded. "You will wait here for us."

"No." Michael stripped off his jacket, revealing the body armor and weapons beneath it. "I am challenging Richard."

"As a diversion?" Phillipe touched his arm. "Master, there is surely another way."

Michael shook his head. "To defeat him, I must kill him and take his throne."

Leary rolled down the passenger window. "It's time to go in now," he said, looking anxious. "They're waiting for us."

Nick rode through the night, stopping only for petrol as she headed north. She spoke little and seemed distant. Gabriel didn't disturb her, sensing that she had withdrawn into herself again. He was only grateful that she had returned to Croft's shop when she had. The Brethren who had cornered him there had fully intended to take him back to France and Benait.

He also didn't know how to tell her that he was no longer blind. Seeing her disable three men with nothing more than a baseball bat had left him speechless as well. She had moved like a trained warrior, with no hesitation and utter ruthlessness.

Whatever she was hiding from him, it had a great deal to do with the way she fought.

After several hours, Nick turned off the main roadway and took a series of country roads toward a farming community. Gabriel's vision, always better in the dark, expanded to take in the hedgerows and slumbering sheep herds. She went down a long drive and came to a stop in what appeared to be an old farmhouse.

She tugged off her helmet and tucked it under her arm as she climbed off the bike. "This is my place."

From the stones and portions of ancient walls scattered to the right and left of the farmhouse, her place appeared to be built within the ruins of a far older structure.

"Come on." She took his arm, reminding Gabriel that she still thought he was blind. "Don't worry. My house is in better shape than yours."

Nicola guided him to the door, which she pushed open with her hand.

"You do not secure your property?" he asked.

"I don't live in the house." She led him through an empty kitchen and to a padlocked door, for which she took a key from the heel of her boot. "I live under it."

Gabriel put his hand on Nick's shoulder and climbed down a long incline of stone steps through a cellar and into a sublevel basement that was equally bare.

"I wish you could see this. Stay here." She went to one of the bare walls, tapped it in three places, and pushed. The entire wall made a low scraping sound as it swung out, revolving on hidden bearings. "My stepdad meant to fill in this part with dirt, but he died before he could get to it." She came back and took his hand in hers. "It's okay. It's perfectly safe."

She thought he was afraid of her secret underground dwelling, when he was nearly shaking with anger. "Why do you live down here? Why not live in the house?"

"I have to travel a lot," she said. "I rent out the pastures to neighbors and they watch the house, but they think I live in America and visit only once or twice a year. If I lived upstairs, they'd expect me to go to church and hang out at the horse club and be part of the community. It's more private for me this way."

She wanted him to admire this hole in the ground; to her it was a home. "Then please show me the way."

Nicola tucked her arm through his and steered him through the opening in the revolving wall.

"My stepdad thought this might be where the commander of the fortress hid his wife and kids when they were attacked," she said as they walked down a narrow corridor. "A lot of the Brits didn't like the Romans coming here and taking over, while the Romans brought their families and tried to live normal lives, so I guess this was their version of a bomb shelter. Evidently the Saxons never found it."

She walked him through a room so dazzling that he stumbled, and she stopped. "Hey, you okay?"

"A brief dizziness. Give me a moment." He needed a week, a month, a year, for he could not believe his eyes.

The room was filled with Templar gold. Gabriel recognized the crosses and chalices, for he had pressed his lips to them and drunk the blood of Christ from them during his human life. A stack of ivory tablets, sculptured with figures and animals from the Scriptures that had been gilded with fine gold leaf, sat neatly atop an eagle lectern of bronze; boxes in which the Templars had kept the gold and silver coins of pilgrims visiting the Holy Land had been stacked like milk crates.

It was Aladdin's cave, come to life.

In the corner Gabriel glimpsed one of the few traveling altars his brothers had brought back intact from the Holy

Land stand, its polished ash-and-black marble still gleaming, the embellishments showing the martyrdom of Saint Paul, and the image of the Trinity in silver gilt. It had vanished in Paris on Black Friday, when the pope had ordered all of the Templars to be arrested, and it had been rumored to have been destroyed in the flames of a temple burned by its own retreating warrior-priests. And yet here it was, almost as it had been seven hundred years before, when he had knelt and prayed before it.

"Your head clear yet?"

He had to leave the room. "Yes." Blinded now by the sight of the treasures the Kyn had thought plundered and looted and lost forever, Gabriel took her hand and let her take him into the next room.

He expected to see more grandeur, but she brought him into what appeared to be a simple, whitewashed root cellar that had been converted to basic living quarters. A modest dresser and bed were the only furnishings; a plain wooden cross hung on the wall over the bed.

"Where are we now?" he asked her.

"This is where I live and keep my stuff stashed," she said, "until I can sell it."

"Sell it?"

"I steal things, Gabriel. Old things from churches and chapels, like the one where I found you. Sometimes I've taken them off the bodies of the dead people I find hidden away, like you were." She sat down on the bed and folded her hands in her lap.

"I don't understand."

"I started doing it in England ten years ago, when I began looking for the Madonna. I went through every chapel, church, and shrine in the country looking for her. I found other things and took them to sell. I moved on to Scotland and Ireland, and now I'm working in France. It's how I make a living."

"So you never took photographs."

"No. I lied to you. I'm a thief." She said each word

flatly, without emotion. "I'm a very good thief. In fact, I'm one of the best in Europe. Maybe the world."

What she was telling him and the treasures in the next room did not match. "Do you ever keep anything for yourself?"

"Are you kidding?" She laughed. "I can't afford to be a collector. Everything I make off the stuff I take goes to cover my expenses."

Living in a hole in the ground, traveling by motorcycle, what expenses could she have? "What about the Golden Madonna? Do you intend to sell her after you find her?"

"No." Her face darkened. "I'll bury her with her owner."

He went over to the bed and sat down beside her. "You sound tired. Lie with me."

Nick stared at him. "I just told you I'm a thief, Gabriel. I'm wanted by every cop and Interpol agent in Europe. I've committed hundreds of crimes."

"We have spent more time making love than sleeping these past few days," he said. "Even the greatest thief in Europe must occasionally rest."

Her curls bounced as she shook her head. "Sometimes I think you are crazy."

He pulled her down to the mattress and turned her, tucking her back against him. "For now, I would like to sleep with you in my arms."

Gabriel held Nick and listened to her breathing even out as she fell asleep. Only when he was sure she would not wake did he rise and slip back out to the treasure room to inspect its contents. It took an hour of opening boxes and inspecting relics, but by his calculations, Nick had somehow amassed a collection of artifacts to rival that of any world museum.

She had not been exaggerating when she had claimed to be one of the best thieves in Europe. There were a dozen kings' ransoms here if one only counted the value of the gold. Add to it the irreplaceable historical value of the objects and Gabriel suspected the woman who had saved him might be worth millions.

What was very odd was that all of the artifacts, precious icons, and symbols, as well as the pilgrim coins, appeared to belong to the Templars before they became Kyn.

Why hadn't she sold them off? A single box of coins alone would fetch an inordinate amount of money at auction. Why would she lie about keeping them? Did it have something to do with the man who had killed her parents and stolen the Golden Madonna?

Gabriel found the cross his father had given to the Temple master when Gabriel had taken his vows, a simple piece with only a few emeralds; almost paltry compared to some of the other families' contributions. He had been so proud the day his father had given so much.

Gabriel pressed the cross between his hands, and for the first time in years offered a prayer: *God in heaven, help us.*

Chapter 17

"So this is the best you could do?" the Kyn guard demanded of Leary as he looked over Phillipe and the addicts from Dublin. "The high lord expected a dozen or more. He will be very displeased."

Leary's mouth drooped. "I did my best, as I always do."

"Tell that to him with the mood he's in, and he'll tear you to ribbons." The guard seemed agitated. "Still, not my head. Come on, this way."

Phillipe had taken position at the very back of the group. When the guard led them around a corner, the seneschal stepped back and waited until their footsteps faded down the hall. After he listened and heard no sounds, he walked quickly in the opposite direction toward the door Leary had said would take him down to the dungeons.

A human guard stopped him at that door. Phillipe remembered to keep a vacant-eyed look as the guard asked, "They send you for the leech, lad?"

He nodded slowly.

"Go on with you, then." The guard stepped aside.

He climbed down the stairs and passed a number of archaic-looking chambers before coming to a closed door with a glass window. Through it he saw Alexandra and Éliane Selvais working at a table. He tried the door, which was unlocked, and slipped inside.

"Not yet, Korvel," Alexandra said, adding a measure of dark liquid to a beaker of blood.

Phillipe felt such relief at seeing her whole and well that

he could only lean back against the door. "I am not Korvel."

The beaker dropped out of Alexandra's hand, and she whirled around. "Phil? Oh, my God. What are you doing here? How . . . ?" She flew across the room and flung herself into his arms. As soon as he embraced her, she stiffened and hissed. "Ow. Careful. I still have some claw marks back there."

"Claw marks." He tried to look down her collar but saw only the edge of a bandage. "What did you get into a fight with this time?"

Her spiral curls bounced around her face. "I'll tell you all about it on the way home." She hugged him again. "How on earth did you get inside the castle?"

"Carefully." Phillipe held on to her but looked at Éliane. She didn't seem surprised to see him. "Are you ready to come home?"

"Is the pope an ex-Nazi? Phil, it's so good to see you. I can't tell you how scared I've been." Alex stepped back. "But I can't go yet."

"Master, I have found her," Phillipe said over the transmitter. "She is well." He put his hands on her shoulders. "We must leave, Alexandra. At once."

"You don't understand. I have to finish preparing this serum." She nodded toward a row of vials. "It could be a cure for Richard Tremayne's condition."

Confusion made him grope for the correct words in English. "You mean to cure Tremayne?"

She lifted her shoulders and gave him a rueful smile. "I took an oath that says I can't kill him."

Phillipe heard Cyprien's voice over his earpiece say, "Let me speak to her."

"This is a transmitter. The master can hear anything you say." He removed the earpiece and gently placed it in her ear.

"It took you long enough," she said to the button, and cupped her hand over her ear. "No, don't start telling me how much you love me; you'll make Phil jealous again. Listen up, seigneur, because we have serious problems in here."

Phillipe kept an eye on Éliane as Alexandra related to Michael what had happened since Richard had brought her to Dundellan. To that she added, "You have to get John out of here first. He's the one in danger; I have Phil running interference for me, and I'm immortal." She listened for a moment to whatever Cyprien was saying to her. "Right. I don't care. Get John out of here."

The Frenchwoman came over, but stopped when Phillipe moved to block the door. "I have no intention of sounding an alarm."

"I have no intention of killing you," he told her. "Let us not litter the road to hell with either."

"There's something else," Alexandra was saying. "You know how I tune in on killers. . . . Well, Lady Elizabeth has been broadcasting all day. She's found out that I have a treatment, maybe a cure, and she's planning to force Richard to complete his change before I can give it to him. Éliane and I are going to take care of her as soon as I get this serum made. We'll keep the guards busy, too, so Phil can get John out to you. I love you, too, babe. I have missed you so much. I hope you've been taking your vitamins. Yeah." She glanced at Phillipe. "We're embarrassing your seneschal. Quit it. And get going." She removed the earpiece and handed it to Phillipe. "Here's the new plan."

"Father Orson Leary, my lord," the servant announced him.

Leary went into the library, for once eager to see Richard Tremayne. The Darkyn King sat behind his desk, as always, although he had not covered his face, which now appeared as beastly as any hell-spawned demon's. For the first time Leary looked, unflinching and unafraid, directly into his satanic eyes. He could even feel pity for him now.

Being freed of all fear was a wondrous thing.

"They forced me to come here, my lord," Leary said. "The Frenchman and his scarred servant."

"Cyprien," Richard muttered.

"Yes, lord." He bowed his head. "They kidnapped me and forced me to do terrible things. They made me disguise the scarred man and bring him into your stronghold. Cyprien is outside, waiting for a signal to attack. I fear you are in great danger."

"You will stay here." Richard slowly rose and limped to the door.

Leary went over to the wall, where Richard kept a collection of bladed weapons. He found the two-handed sword quite tempting, but was not sure if he could even lift such a blade, much less wield it against the vile one. He helped himself instead to a number of daggers, tucking them inside his clothes, where they would not be seen. Then, after listening at the door, he walked out and crossed to the opposite wing.

It was time to find her.

"I know the rooms where Keller is being kept," he heard a woman say. "We can bring him out this way."

Leary knew the time for his true work had come at last. There would be no more pain, no more Legion. She would never torment him another night.

And there she was, walking with another, her radiance muted by the ugly clothes she wore. She had disguised herself again, as she had in the alley.

He drew one of the daggers he had stolen from the high lord's library and kept his footsteps silent as he came up behind them. It wouldn't do to fail now, not when he was so close.

So close.

So very close.

Close enough.

"Thy name is Legion!" Leary shouted as he buried the dagger in her back. "To hell with you!"

She turned, showing him the face of innocence, the face that made him scream in terror and stagger back, waving his arms to make it stop, make the vision leave him, now, before the worms came, and Leary wheeled around, knocking aside the small dark woman who caught the bitch goddess in her arms and shouted for help and called the demon Éliane.

That was not her name. Her name was Legion. She had told him so.

Leary ran and ran, but none of the doors would open for him, and he was caught, trapped, driven into the dark place where there was only one door that swung open, and the frozen flames of hell glittered all around.

"Father in heaven."

He fell forward, caught by soft, tender hands, shushed by a sweet voice. And when he dared open his eyes, he looked into those of the one he had been sent to kill, the one of whom all the others were but pale copies.

"Orson," she said, her little pink tongue peeping out from between sharp, white teeth. "I have been waiting for you."

Nick had never walked around inside a really good antique shop. Like jewelry stores and chick boutiques, they were not comfort zones for her. Also, the people who worked in them viewed girls in leather jackets with the same enthusiasm they usually afforded SpongeBob SquarePants.

Shame, because this place was nice. A real showcase location, with wide, asymmetrical aisles swirling around little islands of furniture and display cases of jewelry and old silver. Framed paintings of different sizes hung in neat rows across the golden oak walls, and a truckload of crystal and stained-glass chandeliers dangled from the high paneled ceilings.

Nick might have to live underground, like a garden mole, but she could still appreciate the finer things most people could never afford.

Gabriel probably had stuff like this at his place before the holy freaks stole it. She bent over to inspect a five-strand pearl choker that had been strung about the same time the *Titanic* sank. *It's what he's used to.*

Nick felt odd, and straightened to look around the shop. She'd had the forest dream so often that she'd come to expect it, not something like this. She didn't care about old, pricey junk. She had plenty of it stashed in her place, but it had never done anything for her. She'd tried to sell it a dozen times, but every time, almost at the last minute before she packed it up and took it to her fence, something stopped her. The special things, the treasures she kept in the room next to hers, they weren't hers, but she had to keep them. Watch over them.

Sometimes Nick wondered if she had lost her marbles ten years ago and just never realized it.

She saw an old book sitting on a table. It had a silver symbol on the blue fabric cover, a shape that resembled a fat 69. *Yin and yang?* In dreams, a person wasn't supposed to be able to read; the letters got all jumbled. She eased the cover open, and flipped, but the gilt-edged pages were all blank.

No story. She closed the book. *What kind of book has no story in it?* Maybe it was a photo album of some kind. *Or am I supposed to write the story?* She chuckled. She was no writer.

Nick moved on to the next display, a traditional ornate tea service, and checked her reflection in the polished tray. The solid silver informed her that her dye had worn off again and her hair was back to two shades of blond darker than white. She really needed a shampoo and cut. Maybe she'd go black this time. She was tired of mud brown.

I like you this way.

She looked toward the voice and saw the Green Man sitting behind a waist-high cherry-wood keyhole desk where he was using a soft cloth to wipe dust from some fussy statuette.

"What do you know?" she asked. "You have pine needles for hair."

True. He shook out the cloth, draping it over the piece. *Do you truly love him, Nicola?*

He was talking about Gabriel. "I do. But I can't. I'm not good enough for him."

You were good enough to find him, and save him, and to tell him the truth. He came around the counter and walked toward her. Mottled green burn scars covered his body, and as her gaze shifted up she saw blond-streaked brown hair instead of pine needles, and Gabriel's green eyes fixed on her. *It's time. You know what you have to do now.*

"I can't."

The shadows around the truth are what keep you apart. Tell him. One of his/Gabriel's hands lifted toward a chandelier that was a hanging waterfall of prismatic crystal. *Show him. Trust in my love.*

Dimensions changed. The high ceilings began to drop, and the aisles narrowed. Either Nick had begun a very belated growth spurt, or Antique World was starting to shrink.

At least now she knew it was a dream, and she could wake up. And she tried to, but the nightlands wouldn't let her go.

I cannot live in the dark anymore. He spoke so low that she could barely hear him now. *Bring me into the light. Be with me in it. Let me see you as you are.*

"You're—he's—blind. I can't." Nick swiveled, looking for an exit. There wasn't any. A porcelain pitcher and basin bumped into her hip, fell over, and smashed. If she stayed here, she was going to end up a sardine. "How do I get out of here?"

You know the way.

Nick ducked to keep her skull from ramming into the roof, and then something cracked the shop in half and split it open like an eggshell. The whole place fell away from her as she sat up, alone in bed.

"Gabriel?"

Nick rolled out of bed and crossed the room, stopping in the doorway. Gabriel was sitting on the floor with her lantern, holding one of the old books in his hands.

He glanced up at her, and she saw that the strange green glow had vanished from his eyes. As she shifted her weight, his eyes followed her movements.

Blind eyes didn't move like that.

"You can see." He nodded, and a crushing, unseen weight she hadn't known she'd been carrying fell away. It was replaced almost at once by one twice as heavy. "When did this happen?"

"My eyes began healing the night we first made love." He closed the book and reverently set it aside before standing and looking down at her. "Your hair is white."

"I told you it was." She touched it before she ducked her head. "I'm sorry."

"Why did you lie to me about keeping all these things?" He gestured around him. "Did you fear that I would steal them from you?"

"No. I just . . . couldn't. It's hard to explain." She tried to think of reasonable excuses, but her brain wasn't working anymore. "I'm sorry."

"I want to know the truth about you." He started walking toward her.

That was what the Green Man hadn't understood in the dream, what he had been trying to warn her of. But she couldn't tell him, couldn't tell anyone. With a sob she ran around him, dodging his hands and rushing out through the opening in the wall.

Nick didn't know where she was running to, but her feet did. They took her up through the house and out into her mother's rose garden. There she found herself standing over two patches of ground, carefully tended pools of delicate green grass. As the tears spilled down her face, hundreds of butterflies swirled up out of the surrounding flowers and hedges. Nick stood still, unwilling to hurt them with a careless touch. They began landing on her hands and arms, fairy creatures of every color in the rainbow, covering her with their wings.

The butterflies flew off as Gabriel came to stand beside her. "Don't be afraid of me, Nicola. I love you."

"I'm not afraid." She stared down at the ground. "I'm a thief and I'm a liar, the things you hate the most, but I'm not a coward."

"I'm not blind anymore," Gabriel murmured, turning her toward him. "I can see your face now. I can look into your eyes. I know what you feel, because I feel the same for you. There's no need to keep hiding behind more lies."

She wiped the tears from her face with the back of her hand. "I don't know how to be any other way."

"Tell me the rest of it."

"There's not much more to tell." She turned around, hugging herself with her arms. "My parents were murdered here ten years ago. I buried the bodies and went away for a while. When I came back, I made everyone think that they had moved to America." She wandered away from the blank space in the garden.

Gabriel came with her and put his arm around her. "You found the Templar treasures while you were looking for the Madonna."

She nodded. "I'm good at finding things. Everything but her."

He brushed the hair back from her brow. "These objects that you have collected, they all belonged to Templars who rose to become Darkyn."

"I didn't know that. They just . . . felt different. Like things that needed to be guarded. I only wanted the Madonna. If I don't find her, my parents will never be at peace." She sagged against him, exhausted, drained of everything but sorrow.

Gabriel lifted her into his arms. "You have more courage and honor in your heart than any woman I have known. I will help you find the Madonna; I promise."

Nick looked up at him. "What about you and the Kyn?"

"Croft told me many things," he said. "I must go to Ireland and speak with the high lord. I must settle matters regarding my sister."

"I was thinking of moving to Scotland for the winter," Nick said. "Maybe we could go see this lord guy on the way, tell him about all the stuff I have here. I really don't want it. What do you think?"

"Tomorrow." Gabriel turned and carried her back to the house.

Chapter 18

"The doctor injected you with this new serum she has created," Korvel told Richard. "It has counteracted what the feline blood did. I am told that Lady Elizabeth made the switch."

"I will deal with my wife later." Richard noticed the weapons missing from his collection. "You must go and find Orson Leary. Quickly."

Korvel hesitated. "I do not wish to leave you to face Cyprien alone."

"If he can get in, I will remind him that I have what he wants. Michael will not jeopardize her safety to take personal revenge." Richard gestured impatiently. "Go. I will collect our hostages."

Richard did not find Alexandra in the lab, but nearly ran into her as their paths collided at the entrance to the dungeons. She was carrying an unconscious Éliane over her shoulder. Richard saw the dagger left in his *tresora*'s back—his dagger—and his claws extended.

"Who did this?"

"Some crazy-looking man." Alex carried her burden downstairs to the lab.

Richard received a second shock when he saw Phillipe waiting at the lab entrance.

"Has someone killed *all* of my guards?" he asked no one in particular.

"I don't have time for one of your tantrums, Richard.

Shut up or get out." Alex kicked open the door to the lab.
"I'll need help with Éliane, Phillipe."

"Do you mean to leave me?" Richard asked.

"I mean to stop this woman from bleeding to death."
Alex put the unconscious Frenchwoman on the exam table,
facedown, and used a scalpel to cut through the back of her
jacket and blouse. "He missed the spinal cord. Thank you,
Jesus, thank you. Phillipe, get me a suture kit out of the
supply cabinet."

"What does it look like?" the seneschal asked as he
walked over to the cabinet.

"A plastic package that says 'suture kit' on the front."
One slim hand reached up to train the overhead light on the
dagger hilt protruding from Éliane's left upper back.
"Blondie, you are so freaking lucky, I can't believe this."
She grabbed some gauze pads and piled them around the
wound before jerking out the dagger. Crimson blood
spilled out from under the gauze. "Hurry up, Phil."

As Richard watched the emergency surgery, Alex began
to talk. "Your wife is the crazy one around here. She
switched feline blood for the human blood I needed. It was
as if she knew it would make you lose control."

"I regret what happened," he told her. "I cannot remember it."

"Like you can't remember killing half your servants,
and all the zombies the other day." Alex put on a face mask
and gloves and began to work on Éliane's back. "It's aw-
fully convenient how your blackouts coincide with killings
that you can't remember committing, don't you think?"

"What are you trying to say, Doctor?"

"I think your wife killed them and made it look as if you
did it. The blackouts she could have controlled by making
sure you got some Kyn tranquilizer mixed in with pure feline blood right before they happened." She discarded a
bloodied instrument. "She might even be using her talent
on humans that you've already bespelled. Korvel told me

she always sees every human before they are presented to you. Stefan is her favorite guard, too."

"How would that affect the humans?"

"One talent is enough for any human. Being subjected to the pressure of two or more, on the other hand, might just be enough to turn them catatonic."

Richard brooded over what she had said until Alex finished dressing the newly sutured wound and pulled down her mask. "That's it. She's out of danger."

Korvel came down to the lab to report that Leary was nowhere to be found, and Richard ordered him to send guards out of the castle bearing the white flag to invite Michael inside.

"Before you negotiate things with my love," Alex said, coming over with a syringe, "take another hit of the serum."

Richard studied the needle, the contents of which looked like blood but might be anything. "Do you not trust me to control myself?"

"No, I don't," she said, uncapping the needle. "Sleeve up. Now."

The injection did not kill Richard, but made him feel calmer and more collected than he had in months. He left Korvel to guard the women and returned to his library to prepare to receive Cyprien. Perhaps it meant nothing, but for the first time in nearly a century he felt some hope.

Éliane had left several handwritten messages on his desk, which he would have ignored had he not spotted the name. Gabriel Seran, one of the best men Richard had ever known, who had died under Brethren torture and interrogation.

Richard felt the loss of Gabriel most keenly. He had been a superb hunter, an intelligent soldier, and possibly the best tracker among the Kyn. Seran had also been one of the gentlest of the immortal souls in Richard's charge. He had sent Lucan to Dublin specifically to free Gabriel Seran, but by that time the Brethren had killed him. They sent several sickening photographs of Gabriel's severed head and mutilated body.

He picked up the message and read it. The paper drifted out of his distorted hand and rocked through the air until it landed noiselessly beside the desk.

"My lord," Stefan said as he escorted Michael in. His protégé stood dressed in full black body armor and carried two sheathed swords. "Seigneur Cyprien."

Richard rose and inclined his head. Michael did not bow in return. "Leave us, Stefan."

As soon as the guard departed, Michael drew both swords and held them crossed in front of him with the blades down. "I challenge you."

"I refuse. I abdicate to you." Richard sat back down.

Michael said nothing for a full minute. "You think to jest with me, my lord?"

"I think to hand my people over to the one man I know who can rule them." The injection Alexandra had given him had begun to make him feel sluggish, and the news about Gabriel—that he lived—drove twin spikes of amazement and dread through his chest. "I am in the end throes of this thing. Your *sygkenis*, who is a remarkable woman, has done her best. It has not worked, and I believe that I am too far gone to be retrieved. Your last task as my seigneur will be to take my head."

"I did not come here to execute you."

"Now who is jesting?" Richard covered a cough. "You have always been my only choice for my successor. I doubt you will have an easy time of it, but your head was always cooler than mine, even before—"

"I came here for my woman."

"So you shall have her." Another spate of coughing nearly stole his voice. "And the kingship as well."

"I don't want it."

"Neither did I," Richard assured him in a hoarse whisper. "To lead the Kyn, you must serve the Kyn. Remember that."

"What is wrong with you? You have never surrendered. Not even when they dragged you naked through the streets of London."

"I received a message from one of Geoffrey's men in London. He called to say that Gabriel Seran is free, that the Brethren are pursuing him, and that Gabriel and his female companion, a young human, left London this morning on a flight to Dublin."

"The man is mistaken. Gabriel is dead. You yourself have the photographs."

"I believe, as Alexandra would put it, someone has been jerking me off for the last two years." He wanted to rub his face, but his talons made that impossible now. "I know this human, Pickard. He is completely reliable. If he says that he saw Gabriel, then he did. I imagine that Gabriel is coming here to find out why we abandoned him."

"We thought he was dead."

"They knew he was special to me. For two years they tortured him." Richard slammed his fist onto the desk, making everything on it jump six inches into the air. "May their souls rot within sight of the gates of heaven."

Something that had nothing to do with his lungs made him double over and shake uncontrollably. He would have said good-bye to his successor, but Richard could no longer move, or speak, or breathe.

Michael sheathed his swords and went to the door. "Guard! The high lord is ill; get help."

He went over to where Richard had fallen and rolled him onto his side. The convulsions slowed to a stop, but he could not rouse the high lord back to consciousness. When heavy footsteps marched in, he looked up impatiently. "Come; he is very ill."

A petite figure swept in around the guards. Lady Elizabeth, dressed in her favorite shade of peach, looked down at Cyprien and Richard and tapped her cheek with one finger.

"Is he dead yet?"

Cyprien rose. "He will be, if you don't summon help."

"I think not." Elizabeth turned to the guards. "Take this murderer and his leech and confine them to a dungeon cell."

Cyprien came around the desk but didn't draw his swords or fight the guards. "Is this how you repay Richard for keeping you as wife all these years?"

Elizabeth tilted her head. "Wife? To that?" She laughed. "I will miss your notions of romantic love. Frenchmen were always so much better at it." She snapped her fan. "Take him, and drag that body out to the compost heap."

Stefan came forward and looked over the desk, then next to it, and then under it.

"Well?"

"My lady, he is not here."

"Of course he is, you idiot," Elizabeth said as she came around the desk. "He's right over . . . Where is he?"

Michael saw that Richard's body had indeed vanished, and began to laugh as the guards marched him out of the room.

Gabriel and Nick took a flight to Dublin, but once in the city rented a motorbike to take them the rest of the way to the village of Bardow.

"I should have ridden my bike up here," Nick pronounced once she had checked it over. "The rear drive on this one is total crap, and the driveshaft and the valves are almost shot. We'll be lucky if we don't end up walking to see the king."

"Then we will walk." Gabriel lifted her up and put her on the bike. "We can spend a few nights in the woods."

She grinned. "Oh, so you never want to get there."

Much to Nick's disappointment, the rented bike ran fine and got them to Bardow just before sunset.

"Pretty place," Nick said, admiring the quaint cottages and thatched rooftops. Her gaze was drawn to a priest nailing crosses to the front door of a Catholic church. "Very, ah, religious."

The priest turned and began shouting at people passing down the street. "Lock your doors and windows! The beautiful ones are here, the harbingers of evil, the vampires, and they crave your blood!"

"They can have me son," one farmer called back. "For free. I'll even deliver."

As the priest continued ranting, more villagers stopped to listen. Most laughed, and one man offered to buy the priest a pint. A pair of older women crossed themselves and hurried on their way.

"Our Brethren will come to save us," the priest called out. "But you must be on your guard. Keep your children home and stay out of the pubs. The vampires are hunting you like sheep straying from the fold."

No Irishman gave up his after-work pint at the pub, so the few who had been listening to the old man shook their heads and strolled away.

"Sounds like the holy freaks have been spreading the bad word," Nick muttered.

Gabriel scanned the surrounding homes and shops. "We should perhaps keep out of sight until dark."

Nick eyed the priest, who had taken out another cross and was nailing it in place. "Amen."

As they walked away from the village's main street, a tall, dark woman came out of a doorway and stood in front of them.

Nick smelled flowers and stepped up to her. "Call the priest; I think I found one."

"Qui êtes-vous?" She peered. "Gabriel Seran? *C'est toi?"*

"Marcella Evareaux. *Oui, c'est moi."* He caught the gorgeous woman as she flung herself at him and embraced her with the joy of a long-lost lover reunited.

An outrageously large spike of jealousy kept Nick nailed to the sidelines, quietly watching. The two chatted in a strange dialect of French she'd never heard before, so she made out only bits and pieces of the conversation. Her resentment built and then ebbed as she saw tears in the female vampire's eyes. She seemed completely rattled yet genuinely delighted to see Gabriel.

"This is my companion, Nicola Jefferson." Gabriel was introducing her to Marcella. "She brought me out of France, and again rescued me in London."

"Mademoiselle." The woman actually curtsied to Nick. "You have done us a great service by saving Gabriel. The Kyn are deeply in your debt." Marcella turned to Gabriel. "You have come at a difficult time. I assume that Croft told you that Lucan liberated the Durands, and that your sister was killed in America?"

It was time for Nick to get lost.

"I'm going to take a ride around the farms," she told Gabriel. Over both their protests, she added, "I can't follow your French when you talk that fast, and I'd like to get the lay of the land. You and Marcella can catch up while I'm gone." She could also follow this feeling in her gut, which had been growing bigger and stronger ever since they'd come to the village.

"We can speak in English." Gabriel looked torn. "You will come back?"

Nick nodded; no way was she going through trying to dump him again. But while Gabriel was occupied, she could track whatever was setting off her internal radar. "Try not to get detained, captured, questioned, or crucified while I'm gone."

Phillipe and John dragged Richard's body through the hidden passage and into the now-deserted part of the castle where Richard had been keeping John Keller locked up. "You found these passages on your own?"

"Alexandra hinted at them." John checked Richard's neck. "I can't feel a pulse."

"It does not mean he is dead. When Kyn suffer serious injuries, our hearts stop beating for a time." Phillipe lifted

Richard into a wide armoire and nestled him in behind the hanging gowns, arranging the long skirts over him so that he wouldn't be seen. "You should stay here."

John shook his head. "I overheard the guards talking in the corridor. Lady Elizabeth had Alexandra and Cyprien thrown into the dungeon."

"She will be busy taking control of the humans," Phillipe said. "That will give us time to do the same with the guards."

"Won't they be loyal to her?"

The seneschal offered a grim smile. "Not after I tell them she has been slowly poisoning their king."

Alexandra hit the stone floor, rolled, and landed in a pile of moldy, rotting straw. Most of the dim light from the torches outside disappeared as the heavy door slammed shut and someone bolted it from the outside.

"Welcome to the dungeon." She spit out a piece of straw and struggled to her feet, rubbing her hip. It didn't feel broken, which only made her more pissed off. "I swear, Phil had better bust me out of here soon or I'll . . ." She stopped as she sniffed the air.

"Do you wish to leave me so soon?"

That was it. She'd finally lost her mind. Or . . . "Who's there?"

A soft blanket of roses rolled around her, weaving with the bright lavender that answered it. Alex didn't know whether to laugh or cry. She started to do a little of both.

"I imagined this so many times," Michael Cyprien said as he knelt down before her. "Every hour, every minute at times. Never once did I think it would happen in such a place." He took her grimy hand and pressed it to his lips. "I have missed you, my lady."

"Michael." She couldn't get past his name. "Michael."

He started to stand at the same moment her knees gave out. They came together, two souls filling the broken, empty spaces forced between them.

"Oh, God." Alex kissed every inch of his beloved face, drinking in the taste and smell and feel of him until she thought she really would go mad. She began babbling like a lunatic. "I missed you. I love you. Why did you take so long to get here? I missed you."

A face blocked out the small shaft of light coming from the cell window, and a man laughed.

"Save it for the mistress," the guard shouted. "She likes a good show."

Alex stiffened. "An audience. Terrific."

Michael held her close as he gave the door a murderous look before his expression softened. "Elizabeth has taken control of the castle. Richard has vanished, but he may be dead or dying."

Business as usual. "We're up to our ears, then."

He nodded and stroked his hand over her curls. "It is my fault. I might have planned this rescue somewhat better than I did."

"We'll find a way out. We always do." She couldn't get close enough to him. She wanted to rip off the stupid clothes keeping her skin from touching his. "My head's not exactly on straight yet. I know what I'd like to do to you, but not with that guard or Lady Liz watching. Still, I need to . . ." She didn't know what she needed.

He yanked at the collar of his shirt, baring his throat.

"That?" Even with her fangs fully extended and aching for him, to feed directly from his body seemed as intimate as fucking him. Then there was her need. "What if I drink too much?"

"You won't." He cradled the back of her head with his hand and urged her forward. "Take me, Alexandra."

She kissed the smooth skin first, choosing the place where his blood pulsed strongest. Her mouth opened as his fingers entwined with hers. Her fangs slid into him, deep and sure, as if she had taken him like this a thousand times, and then his lifeblood flowed into her, hot and sweet and silky. The world became a river of warm, honeyed rose petals.

Michael's voice reached through the pleasure, adding to it, changing it. "Come back to me, *mon amour.*"

Somehow Alex wrenched her mouth from him, panting, shuddering as she ripped open the front of her shirt. She didn't have to urge him to her; his mouth found the inside of her breast, one of his favorite spots to kiss and nuzzle when they made love. When she felt his teeth, she arched up against his mouth, making him penetrate her as deeply as she had taken him. He sucked at her with a soft, dreamy sigh, and then lifted his head and looked into her wet eyes.

"I love you, Alexandra."

Chapter 19

K orvel intercepted a human female coming toward Dundellan on a rather noisy motorcycle. She stopped when he held up one hand and shut off the bike.

"You are trespassing." He walked up to her and nearly stumbled when he picked up the scent of evergreen from her skin.

"Watch your step." She took off the black helmet she was wearing, revealing a very young face and a headful of blond curls. "You're a vampire, right?"

"No." Korvel reached out to touch her, but she glided out of range.

"No, I don't think so." She glanced at the castle. "I need to talk to the vampire who lives in there. Is that you?" When he said nothing, she sighed. "Okay, can you get me in to see him?"

"There are no such things as vampires." He took another swipe at her, trying to make the skin contact he needed to use his talent. Once he had her panting after him, he'd find out how she had gotten Gabriel Seran's scent all over her.

"Forget it; I'll just go up and knock." She pushed the bike off the road and left it under a tree.

Frustrated by his inability to touch her, Korvel caught up with her and blocked her path. "I won't hurt you, miss." He looked into her eyes and shed more scent, but it seemed to have no effect on her.

"You're very cute, but I don't screw complete strangers.

Most of the time." She sidestepped him. "So you can turn off the charm."

"You cannot go inside the castle," he told her.

"Trouble in Camelot?" She heard his men shouting and tilted her head. "Thanks for the heads-up. Now can I go in and talk to the high lord?"

She had to be a *tresora*. "I am sorry; I do not mean to frighten you." He breathed in the deep, faintly sweet scent clinging to her. "Who do you serve?"

The girl lifted her chin. "I don't serve anyone, but if it counts, I'm sleeping with Gabriel Seran."

Korvel could hardly think straight. "He truly is alive?"

"He truly is." She smiled. "Do you know him?"

"He was—is—a great friend to my master."

"Gabriel's down in the village, talking to some supermodel vampire." She sounded oddly resigned. "Now can I go in there? There's something in this place I really need to find."

Nick thought the big blond vampire was about to have a nervous breakdown, he was so agitated. The scent rolling off him made her feel as if she were locked in a French bakery.

"What's your name?" she asked as she looked up over the edge of the ditch and watched for men on horseback.

"Korvel."

"I'm Nick."

The patrol of four huge-looking armed soldiers passed, and as soon as they had ridden out of sight, the vampire grabbed her hand. "They'll be back in two minutes. We must hurry."

Nick ran with him across to the side entry, pausing here and there to take refuge behind a tree trunk. Korvel opened the door with an impressive show of one-armed Kyn strength, almost wrenching it off its three bolts as they ducked inside.

The interior of this castle, Nick discovered, was particularly cold. It was also as silent as a church. She imagined the place where they were standing had once been a kitchen.

Korvel lifted a finger to his lips and pointed toward an open passage on the other side of the room. "We go through there," he told her in a barely audible whisper, "and down into the dungeons."

"Is that where the king is?"

"It's where my friends are. We have to free them." He picked up a couple of dark-colored swords from where they had been left on the counter. "Can you use one of these?"

Nick nodded. It was slightly bigger than her stiletto. It worked on the same principal.

The vampire led Nick through the corridor, where they met another vampire, this one with a scar running down his face.

"Who are you?" he asked, sniffing her.

"Nick. You?"

"Phillipe," he answered. "You smell like Gabriel Seran."

"Not now," Korvel said, and gestured for them to move down a set of stone steps.

Nick went first, and stepped into what looked to her like a set from one of Vincent Price's old movies. Flaming torches blazed from sconces on the brick walls, while dull copper chains and various nasty-looking apparatuses hung from huge iron rings and suspension bars.

"New guests?"

Nick froze in midstep. A group of dazed-looking humans seemed to appear out of nowhere, and formed a circle around her, Korvel, and Phillipe. They said nothing, but began hitting and scratching at them and kicking their legs and knees. The thin faces were blank, but the eyes were filled with terror.

"Ah, you're here for the tour." Behind them, a fair-haired woman in a bright silk gown appeared. "Welcome to our stronghold."

Nick stopped thinking, shoving three zombie-eyed humans out of her way as she brought her sword up and used it to stab the smiling woman in the shoulder. The blond woman didn't scream, but looked very annoyed.

"Ungrateful little girl." She clasped her shoulder and glared at the humans, who converged and pulled the sword from Nick's hand. "I invite you into my home, and this is how you repay my hospitality?"

Nick saw Korvel attack two of the guards, while Phillipe seemed to be trying to touch as many of the zombies as he could. With each touch the human minions stopped clawing and kicking, and turned toward the woman. Nick struggled wildly against the four that had her by the arms now.

"Elizabeth."

The zombies' eyes suddenly cleared, and their voices rose with very normal-sounding terror and panic as they tried to find a way out of the dungeon's center. It was during the confusion that someone grabbed Nick from behind, clamping a hand over her mouth and dragging her out of the room.

When Nicola did not return within the promised hour, Gabriel questioned a few of the villagers coming in from the fields and discovered from their sightings that she had ridden out to Dundellan.

"You don't have to track her on foot." Marcella brought him to the town stable and removed two white mares from their stalls. "I will ride with you."

Gabriel was more concerned about Nicola, especially when they arrived at the castle and saw it sitting open and unguarded.

"Richard must be dead," he said, "for he would never allow his stronghold to be found so vulnerable."

They tethered the horses to a tree and without invitation walked through the front entry of Dundellan. Gabriel picked up Nick's scent almost immediately. He followed it to the basement access door. "They are all down there."

Marcella nodded. "I smell them, too."

The first person Gabriel saw as he walked down into Richard Tremayne's dungeons was the high lord himself.

"Gabriel." The man was Richard, and a much more human-looking Richard than Gabriel remembered in the past. "You *are* alive."

"My lord." He made his bow. "My traveling companion came here. I have come to collect her."

"She has disappeared, as have my wife and a Brethren interrogator." Richard raised his voice over the cries of the newly awakened addicts. "Calm yourselves."

Phillipe handed Marcella a bunch of keys. "The seigneur and his *sygkenis* are locked in one of these cells."

"I do not need keys," she told him, and placed a hand on the steel locking mechanism on one cell's barred door. Something inside the lock rattled, and Marcella pulled the door open. At the same time, two muffled voices called out. "I hear them. Down here." She led Phillipe down the row of cells.

Gabriel heard his name being called frantically but from some distance away. "Nicola?" He projected his talent, summoning every insect in the castle and sharing their knowledge of the place. The beetles led him back upstairs and into the west wing of the castle. The termites led him to the locked door of a secured, sealed chamber. Behind it, he could hear Nick screaming.

Come to me.

Gabriel's command thundered through the halls of Dundellan, drawing every insect within its cold stone walls. He reached farther, out into the fields for the ants and bees and spiders, and into the woods for the crickets and moths and wasps. He brought together the many that were one mind, one house, one soul, and one spirit, and they poured in through every window in the castle, the winged ones carrying those that could not fly, streaming through the castle in a single column, past the cringing humans and Darkyn and into the west wing, becoming a living battering ram against the door that separated Gabriel from Nicola.

The door exploded inward.

Gabriel stepped into the stream of the many, moving with them into the glittering room made of amber. Richard's wife huddled in one corner, her arms over her head. Leary was jerking his arm up and down, up and down over another woman. Gabriel saw the bloodied knife in his hand and with a guttural roar brought the column of the many down on Leary's arm, severing it cleanly from his body at the shoulder.

Nicola dropped to the floor, her body covered in blood.

The priest tottered around, his left hand grasping the empty socket of his right arm, and smiled at Gabriel. "Their name is Legion," he choked out. "And you are many."

The column descended on Leary and dragged him, writhing within their suffocating mass, out of the room.

Chapter 20

Gabriel carefully slid one arm beneath Nick's lax shoulders and lifted her into his arms. Blood pulsed from dozens of stab wounds in her chest, stomach, and arms. The mad priest had slashed her face, and there were matching wounds on her hands. Bruised eyelids covered her eyes, blood staining the fine lashes. Her blond curls spilled over his arm.

"Nicola." She had saved him, protected him, and now when she had needed him most . . . "No."

She did not stir, and as her breathing faltered the bleeding of her wounds slowed.

Gabriel carried her to a velvet settee as Alexandra and the others slowly came into the amber room. Nicola could not survive such damage to her human body; he knew that. Yet she was young, and strong, and there was still time.

There had to be time.

"Is there a doctor here?" He dropped down with her in his lap, unable to release her, and held her like a child.

"Yeah, me. I'm Alexandra," the woman said, coming to his side.

A breath escaped Nicola's lips but did not return.

"Alexandra." He looked up, desperate. "She is not breathing. Please. Show me what to do."

Cyprien's *sygkenis* pressed her fingertips to Nick's wrist, and then carefully lowered her hand.

"Gabriel," she said very gently, "there's nothing you can do for her now. She's gone. I'm so sorry."

He looked down at Nicola's lacerated face. "You cannot

leave me again. I waited for you. I lived for you. I have only just found you."

Someone—Cyprien, perhaps—touched his shoulder. He ignored it, unable to move, unwilling to release her fragile mortal form. There was no reason to do so. He had nothing left, nothing for which to live.

The touch changed, and Gabriel finally looked up. The blazing colors of the glorious room around him faded from his senses. It seemed right that everything had dulled to a meaningless blur of dull, ugly gray. She had gone and taken his last hope of happiness with her.

He would not allow her to go into the darkness without him. Wherever she was, that was where he had to go. "Kill me."

Michael shook his head.

"Give me a blade, then."

Alexandra made a strange sound, and Michael's gaze shifted to her.

"Not yet, my friend." Cyprien nodded toward Nick.

Gabriel looked down at his beloved's ruined face. The wounds slashed across it were shrinking, the edges pulling together, the raw exposed tissues vanishing.

"So," Alex murmured, fascinated. "That diagnosis sucked."

Watching her heal, Gabriel blanked his mind, until he saw his hand carefully pull aside her jacket, exposing the torn front of her T-shirt. The stab wounds in her chest had also closed and were disappearing.

"She's Kyn." He stared across at Alexandra. "How can this be?"

She shook her head. "Wasn't anything I did this time." She rolled up her sleeve. "But I think I can help her now." She bit her wrist and pressed the wound to Nick's lips.

The younger woman opened her mouth as soon as Alex's blood touched it. She drank and swallowed, and a rosy flush tinted her pale skin under the drying blood on her face.

"That should about do it," Alex said, taking her bloody wrist away.

Nick opened her eyes and pushed out of Gabriel's arms. She staggered as she got to her feet, then found her balance and moved away from him, Alex, and the other Kyn. As soon as she tasted blood on her lips, she rubbed the back of her hand across them.

"She is Darkyn," Marcella said, and breathed in. "But she smells human."

Nick pulled down the shreds of her T-shirt, and then noticed that she was the center of attention. "Stop doing that. Stop looking at me." She pressed a hand to her face, as if to cover what was happening to it.

"Kind of hard to do that," Alex said, "after the show you just gave us. Honey, exactly how long have you been Kyn?"

"I'm not Kyn. I'm not like you. Any of you." Her voice rose to a shout. "I'm human. Do you hear me? *I'm still human.*"

"Okay, you're still human," Alex said reasonably as she got to her feet. "We'll just pretend we never saw you heal from fatal stab wounds and major blood loss in ten seconds flat."

Gabriel tried to go to Nicola, but she backed away from him, and he went still with shock a second time.

"Why didn't you tell me?" he asked.

"Tell you what? I drink blood, I heal fast, and I can't die. There, I told you." She bent down and picked up Leary's gore-smeared knife. "Now get out of my way."

Nick didn't wait for him to move, but went around him. She went past Richard and Michael, past Korvel and Phillipe, and halted in front of one of the niches, taking the small statue of the Virgin Mary from it before moving on to stand in front of Elizabeth. Richard's wife drew back, turning her head away, but Marcella grabbed her and made her face Nick.

"You remember me," Nick said softly. She held up the statue. "And this. Don't you?"

Elizabeth looked down her nose at her. "The statue is mine, but alas, I fear that we have never met."

"Alas, you're a fucking liar." Nick tucked the knife under Elizabeth's chin, pressing it into the soft flesh of her throat. "It was in Hartfordshire, ten years ago. Little dairy farm outside Grandale. You remember. You came to visit my parents one night in June. You came to ask my stepdad about the Golden Madonna. You said it belonged to you."

Elizabeth's expression turned to boredom. "I do not trifle with dairy farmers, and I know nothing about any Madonna. That statue is of the Virgin Mary, and it has been in my possession for over sixty years. Now, would you remove the knife from my neck? I—" She gasped as the sharp blade cut deeper. "Richard, she is deranged. Stop her. Kill her."

"You already did, you bitch." Nick leaned in. "You killed me after you butchered my parents. For this." She shoved the statue in Elizabeth's face.

Gabriel came to stand beside her. "Elizabeth attacked you and your family?"

"She tortured my parents and murdered them. She made me watch while she did it. She made me dig the grave in my mother's rose garden and drag the bodies out to it." Nick smiled. "Only she took too much blood from them, and got a little drunk on it."

Gabriel felt her cold rage building into something worse, but waited, determined to know everything that had resulted in this miracle.

"What else happened, Nick?" Alex asked.

"I got away from her and grabbed my stepdad's shovel," Nick said. "I tried to take her head off with it. It hurt her, but it didn't stop her. Nothing did. She tore open my throat and took a shower in my blood. Then she threw me in the grave. Right on top of my mother's body."

Elizabeth chuckled. "Now I know you are deranged. I would never do such a barbaric thing."

Nick snapped out her arm, and the statue of the Golden

Madonna went flying across the room. It shattered against one of the amber panels and rained in small pieces all over the floor.

Elizabeth's eyes bulged. "How dare you!"

Nick glanced over at Richard. "She your wife?" When he nodded, she said, "She has a scar on her ass. It's dark pink and shaped like a triangle. On the left cheek. Am I right?"

"Yes." Richard regarded Elizabeth. "How does the girl know this?"

Elizabeth shrugged. "Someone told her."

"She doesn't like getting blood on her fancy clothes," Nick told Richard. "She strips down before she does people."

"If I had killed you," Elizabeth said with exaggerated patience, "then why do you still live? My dear, if you wish to deceive us into believing that you are human, not Kyn, then you must invent a better story than this."

"I don't think it's a story, Liz," Alex said. "Nick, when she attacked you, was she wounded?"

"I hit her in the face with a goddamned shovel," Nick said. "What do you think?"

Alex nodded. "I think that, unlike your parents, she nearly drained you dry. You didn't die, Nick, because while she was doing that, she bled on you. She infected you."

"Whatever." Nick didn't seem interested in how she had become Kyn.

"But you don't have *dents acérées*," Gabriel said. "I would have felt them when I kissed you. You cannot possess *l'attrait*, or I would know you by scent. We all would."

"Oh, I have the goods." Nick glanced at him, and the sharp-sweet scent of juniper suddenly colored the air. It was so much like Gabriel's own scent that it stunned him. She smiled, baring fangs that quickly retracted. "I just don't flaunt them. And I can make them go away whenever I want." The echoing scent abruptly vanished.

"She protects herself and lures humans by passing as one of them," Cyprien said. "An interesting talent."

"I'm not one of you," Nick insisted. "I can walk around in daylight. I don't bite people when I can get bagged blood from hospitals. I sure as hell don't butcher them."

"We do not harm humans," Gabriel said.

"Really." She stared into Elizabeth's face. "Then what do you call what she does?"

"If what you say is true, and you have simply mistaken me for the Kyn who took you, you should be grateful," Elizabeth said. "The woman who attacked you compensated you with the gift of immortal life."

"Vampire King?" Nick said softly as she shifted her grip on the blade. "Say good-bye to the wife."

"Wait." Gabriel put his hand over hers so that they both held the knife.

Nick shook her head. "I'm doing it. I've been looking for this sick cunt for ten years. It'll be easier than how my parents died, but she deserves it."

"If this is what you must do," Gabriel said, "then she will die by my hand as well."

Nick didn't say anything, and the blade didn't move deeper into Elizabeth's neck.

"Miss Jefferson, before you cut off my wife's head," Richard said quietly, "I would ask a favor of you. Permit me to punish my wife for her crimes against you and your family."

"So she can live and do it again? Make more like me? Let me think." Nick looked at him. *"No."*

"I will see to it that Elizabeth never has contact with another human for as long as she lives. We live quite a long time, even when we can no longer feed." The high lord's voice remained low and level. "I swear this to you."

"Don't be a fool, Richard," his wife snapped. "She cannot prove any part of her ridiculous story. I've done nothing wrong. She's been sent here by your enemies; can't you see that? I would not be surprised if Cyprien had a hand in this. He turned that leech; he must have the ability to create new Kyn. Kill her and put an end to this."

Nick saw the fear in Elizabeth's wide eyes, and heard it in her sharp voice. "You can really keep her away from humans forever?"

"He can," Gabriel confirmed.

"My husband would never harm me," Elizabeth said, smiling. "He'll do nothing, and you'll be cheated of your revenge."

"You'd rather have me cut off your head than let him deal with you?" Nick didn't wait for an answer, but pulled the knife away. "She's all yours, Your Kingship." She dropped the blade and turned to Gabriel.

He wanted to take her into his arms. He was afraid to touch her. "All this time, and I never guessed."

"I'm just as good at hiding things as I am at finding them." Her eyes scanned the faces around them. "I can't be a part of this, Gabriel. I love you, but . . . I'm sorry." She strode out of the Amber Room.

Gabriel took a moment to disperse the last of the many before he spoke to Michael. "I must go with her."

Cyprien nodded. "Will we see you again?"

"I cannot say." Gabriel could think only of her.

Richard came to him. His eyes, once so alien, were becoming human. "They sent photographs of your body, decapitated, and your head thrust on the spikes of a church gate in Rome. Had I known you still lived, I would never have called off the search."

Doctored photographs. That was all it had taken to convince the high lord of his death.

"There is this computer program called Photoshop, my lord," Gabriel said softly. "You should become acquainted with it. Now I must take my leave of you."

"I will not compel you to live under Kyn rule, not after what has happened to you both," the high lord said. "But know that in this place, you will always have an ally." He performed a bow of deep respect.

Gabriel put his hand on Richard's shoulder for a moment, and then hurried out into the corridor.

Nick was adjusting something on the back wheel of the rental bike and cursing under her breath when Gabriel reached her. "Piece of cheap, run-down Dublin trash."

"We should have brought your bike," he said, stopping a few feet away.

She didn't look at him and said nothing.

"You are not leaving here without me," he continued. "I would have no way to get back to the farm."

"I told you, I can't be a part of this." Nicola stood and wiped her hands on a piece of her shirt. "I'm not like them. I don't want to be like them. You . . . you're like them. You need them. They have mansions and libraries and Mozart. I have a bike and a farm and Nickelback."

"Is Nickelback an American band?"

"Canadian." She stuck her wrench back in her tool kit. "Gabriel, don't try. You know? I'm a peasant. I'm okay with that. You're a nobleman. You need someone like that French chick in the village. I mean, she was hot."

"Marcella is like a sister to me."

She brought up her hands and let them fall. "Okay, so, there are other vampire ladies out there."

"I don't want them. I don't love them." He stepped up to her. "I love you." He took her hands in his. "You went through the change alone. That's never happened to a Kyn before you." As she opened her mouth, he touched her cheek. "It's just a word. But when you came to me, you were seeking something, weren't you?"

"Dreams. I fell in love with a guy from my dreams. It turned out to be you."

"You were looking for me."

"I was *looking* for that fucking bitch in there who killed my parents." Her expression softened. "Yeah, and you. But you're not all green, and you don't have pine needles for hair, and you smell like Christmas."

"I am free of the Kyn." He frowned. "I am homeless and almost penniless as well." He caressed her shoulder. "Perhaps I only want you for your money."

"Gabriel."

"Or I could want you for your body. And your mouth." He kissed it. "And your eyes. And your hair. And your smile." He rested his hand over her left breast. "And your heart."

Their eyes met. Gabriel saw hers warm slowly, timidly, as if she wanted to give him time to change his mind and leave her.

"I will never leave you."

"Fine." She stepped back and handed him the helmet. "Get on. I want to dump this bike as soon as we get to Dublin. You think the vampire king is good for a new Triumph Tiger?"

He waited for her to climb on in front of him, and wrapped his arms around her waist as she kicked up the center stand and took off down the road.

"I think eventually Gabriel and Nicola will come back to the Kyn," Michael Cyprien said. "They need time to be together, and to bond."

"From what I saw in front of the castle yesterday, they need a hotel room." Alexandra lifted her hair off the back of her neck. "Speaking of which . . ."

"I will not detain you." Richard looked down at his hand, which appeared half-human, half-feline. "Dr. Keller—"

"You're covered. I made up the next round of treatments and showed Korvel how to prepare more serum. If you can't trust him, you can't trust anyone." With a decided thump, she placed a small vial case on his desk. "I thought you might like to lock this batch up yourself."

That she had anticipated his request did not surprise him, but that she would grant it did. She had no allegiance to him.

"Will you ever forgive me?" he asked her.

"No." She met his gaze. "But I'm still your doctor. Call me if your symptoms change, you marry another psychotic bitch, or something else goes wrong."

She did care what happened to him. Richard thought of using that, then saw Cyprien's expression and decided against it. "Your generosity humbles me."

"Enjoy the novelty of the experience." She glanced at Michael. "I'll go wait in the car now." She left without looking back.

"That mouth." Richard breathed in a trace of lavender. "I will miss it."

"I will have her call you weekly, if you like. She loves to bend a sympathetic ear." Michael looked at the portrait on the wall behind Richard's desk. "What will you do with Elizabeth?"

"I will keep my promise to Nicola."

His surrogate son gave him a long, measuring look. "I will leave you to it." He executed a respectful bow. "*Adieu, my lord.*"

"*Adieu, seigneur.*"

After Michael departed, Richard took Alexandra's advice and carefully placed the alteration treatments in his safe. She had warned him that the rate of transformation could be slow, and consequently that his change back to human form might take months, even years, but he had all the time in the world.

Time had always been Richard's enemy. Now it would serve as his wife's executioner.

Richard left his study and walked over to the west wing. There he found Stefan hard at work with one of the recovering addicts now employed by Richard, filling in the spaces. He waited until there remained but one stone to mortar into place, and then called a halt to the work.

"Go," he told them. "I will do the rest."

Stefan nodded and took the new man's arm. The junkie gave the high lord a quick, uncertain look before leaving with his guard.

Richard inspected the mortar work to assure it was sound and made of the special mixture he had obtained from an old Dublin masonry yard that guaranteed it to last for five centuries or more.

He looked in through the last gap in the stone. The glorious Amber Room remained perfectly intact, except for the addition of some copper manacles welded around a large wooden cross, to which Elizabeth had been attached. She had first been dressed in her finest gown, her hair brushed so that it fell around her face in a cascade of gleaming curls.

Since she was facing eternity imprisoned in the Amber Room, Richard had felt his wife should look her best.

Elizabeth turned her head and saw his eyes looking in at her, and twisted against the copper chains binding her limbs to the wooden cross. The copper band that had been welded over the lower half of her face allowed her to make only outraged sounds in her throat.

In the center of the world's most beautiful room, Orson Leary's remains had been carefully arranged on Elizabeth's velvet settee directly in front of the cross. Beside him was a small pile of broken amber.

Satisfied that his orders had been carried out to the letter, and that his wife would spend whatever remained of her life facing her final victim and watching him rot more quickly than she did, Richard picked up the last stone, applied a generous amount of mortar, and slid it into place.

Please read on for

an excerpt from Lynn Viehl's

EVERMORE
A Novel of the Darkyn

Coming soon from Signet Eclipse

Jayr watched the couples dancing the branle, but only heard the ensemble's music as if she sat somewhere far removed from the ball. The events of the evening seemed to please the guests of the realm, something that should have gratified her. It was her duty to attend to them and the thousand unseen details that ensured their pleasure. Yet here she sat, doing nothing at all. This unwelcome awareness had made her as useless as a moonstruck girl caught between the two cruelest of heart torments, doubt and hope.

It mattered not. Soon, Jayr knew, her wits would return and drag her back to her senses. Soon she would shrug off this appalling paralysis and get on with seeing to her master's guests. Soon—

Byrne's hand came to rest on her shoulder, half on the velvet yoke of her tunic, half on the bare curve of her throat. He leaned over to murmur, "Rob fancies himself a danseur this night."

Locksley might have been performing a string of triple *tours en l'air* and Jayr would have missed them, so absorbed was she by the weight and feel of her master's touch. His soft breath set fire to her cheek; the warmth of his nearness reduced her to ashes. The world dwindled to nothing but Byrne. She felt the length of his arm pressing across her back, and could it be . . . yes, there, the absent stroke of his thumb against her neck. He was petting her.

An idle caress. It means nothing.

Jayr smelled tansy entwined with heather and swallowed against the ache at the back of her throat. Locksley. Byrne had said something about his dancing. "The suzerain has much skill on the floor," she said.

"How can you tell?" He shifted his palm, causing his calluses to delicately chafe the edge of her collarbone. "Have you danced with him?"

"No, my lord. I have not had that privilege." Thank Christ, the ensemble had nearly finished the set. As the branle came to its elegant end, Jayr forced herself from her seat. "I should check on the bloodwine."

Byrne stood, catching her around the waist and turning her toward the politely applauding couples. She expected him to point out some flaw, some error to be corrected, but his hand urged her forward, through the spiral of tables and to the very edge of the dance floor.

Jayr heard muttered Arabic and low snickering, and felt Nottingham's Saracens staring at her. Ridicule's whip straightened her shoulders, and kept panic at bay, even when her master drew her toward him. He stepped back, and then something happened that froze her in place again.

Aedan mac Byrne made a brief but perfect révérence to her.

It had to be a mistake. The suzerain of the realm never showed such regard to his seneschal, his third blade, the eyes at his back. Such a man made révérence only to his lady, whose silk and lace swathed her soft limbs, and whose long, perfumed curls framed her delicate features.

Jayr could not be seen as a lady. She was not even wearing a gown.

"My lord?" Perhaps he made a clever jest. A moment of mockery to amuse the assembly. That had to be it. No wonder the heathens were entertained.

A lord paramount never bowed to his lowly servant.

Byrne said nothing, only taking up her hands in his. He arranged her arms in counterpoint to his before nodding to the leader of the ensemble. They began to play one of

Strauss's pieces, one Jayr should have been able to name, had her voice and her brains still functioned. Her master turned her again as he guided her out among the whirling couples and into what had long ago been a vigorous and rather silly provincial dance.

He was dancing with her—waltzing, with her.

Jayr could not ask her master if he had gone mad. Moving her feet in the whirling patterns of the dance demanded much of her concentration, and the rest seemed fixed on the lacing at the neck of his shirt. She also suspected that if anyone might lose their wits on this night, it would be her.

"My lord," she finally forced out, "I am honored, but perhaps you could exchange me for a more appropriate partner. Lord de Troyes seems rather ill-matched with his lady, and I would—"

"Jayr?" He spun her down the length of his arm and back to his body.

She braced herself against his chest to keep a respectful space between them. "My lord?"

Byrne seized one of her errant hands and worked his fingers through hers, locking them together. His arm pulled her in until their bodies brushed. "Shut up and dance with me."

"Yes, my lord."

Jayr found no comfort in silence or the waltz. She busied herself with counting steps and avoiding eyes. It seemed as if every lord and lady on the floor was gaping at them. And why should they not? The suzerain of the Realm held his seneschal in his arms. Among the Kyn, such a thing had never happened.

Jayr cursed herself for not listening to Alexandra and donning more feminine attire. She might have looked less the skinny boy in a gown, and the skirts would have enforced a respectable boundary between their bodies. As it was, his person met hers in the most unseemly places: the flat of her belly, the small of her back, the front of her thighs. Little wonder that the waltz had often been condemned in the past as insidious and improper. The intimacy of it, of the constant press of his body to hers, quickly became unbearably erotic.

Behind the torture, a very small part of Jayr hoped that the waltz would never end.

As the music swelled to a giddy madness, Jayr glanced up to see her master's face darken, and followed his gaze. Alexandra, resplendent in an ivory lace gown, laughed as Cyprien lifted her off her feet and kissed her while they still twirled among the other couples.

What would it be like, Jayr thought, to have such love that you did not care who saw you express it? "The seigneur seems blessed in his choice of women," she said before she remembered that she was supposed to be holding her tongue.

Byrne changed direction, leading her through a tangle of couples and into the shadowy end of the floor, far from the sharp ears of those watching from the tables. When a burst of laughter drew the attention of the assembly, Jayr found herself being marched from the floor and around the corner to the empty corridor that led outside to the gardens and herbarium.

"I thank you for the dance, my lord." Jayr stepped out of his hold and straightened her sleeves. "It was most pleasant."

Byrne's broad back blocked out the moonlight streaming through the long, narrow panes of pale blue glass. His scent changed, growing heated and dark. When he put his hand to her throat, Jayr flinched.

"Pleasant, you say?" he asked, his voice dangerously soft.

"I meant enjoyable," she quickly added, feeling his fingers tighten. "Quite enjoyable. You are most accomplished, my lord."

"Pleasant." He walked her backward. "Enjoyable."

She felt cold stone against her shoulders. "I regret that I am not more adept myself. I rarely dance." He had her pinned now, body to body. She averted her face. "My lord, I should return and see to your guests."

"And Rob?" Byrne thrust his hand into her hair, his fingers curling against her scalp. "You will see to him? You will dance with him?"

She glanced up, confused. "Of course. I am happy to see to Suzerain Locksley's desires."

"He makes you happy. Unlike me."

Byrne's scent had fogged her thoughts; surely she had not heard him correctly. "My lord, it is not for you to make me happy."

"Is it not?" He lifted her in the same way Cyprien had Alexandra, sliding her up the stone wall until their eyes were level. "Did I not make you, Jayr?" His gaze moved from her eyes to her mouth. "Did you not swear your oath to me? Do you not belong to me, body and blood?"

Jayr felt drunk on his scent and touch, so much that she lost the last shred of her composure and shuddered uncontrollably against him as she told him the truth. "I am yours, my lord. Do with me what you will."

Byrne bent his head to hers, his long garnet hair spilling against her cheek as his lips touched hers. The contact made her jerk with shock, but he held her in place, his mouth slanting over hers as he deepened the kiss with his teeth and tongue.

Jayr had dreamed of this moment and what she might feel, but those paltry fantasies had not prepared her for how Byrne would take her mouth. He took and bit and thrust, reveling in the claiming, allowing her no retreat. The heat and scent of his passion smashed over her, reducing her to a clinging, moaning wreck writhing between his arms. In desperation she seized his shoulders, clutching at them as she fought her body's shameful response. His body became an oak, as still and unmovable, to which she had been chained. And there, pressing hard between her thighs—thrusting against her crotch—the heavy, stunning weight of his erection.

The ferocious hunger of his mouth eased away.
"Mother of God." Byrne sounded as astounded as she felt.
"What am I doing to you?" He carefully lowered her until
she stood on her own again.

"You kissed me." She saw the pain and regret in his
eyes, and cold, clammy horror crawled along her spine.
She made her bruised mouth form a smile. "Needs are like
cherished guests, my lord. At times they may be inconve-
nient, but one should never allow them to go unattended
for too long."

"You are right." He looked disgusted now. "Jayr—"

"Your guests are waiting. Excuse me, my lord." She
made her bow and ran.